HEROES IN TRAINING

No. 3

GRAPHIC NOVEL

TRAINING

HADES AND THE HELM OF DARKNESS

created by
JOAN HOLUB &
SUZANNE WILLIAMS
adapted by **David Campiti**
illustrated by **Dave Santana**
at Glass House Graphics

Aladdin
New York London Toronto Sydney New Delhi

ALADDIN
An imprint of Simon & Schuster Children's Publishing Division
1230 Avenue of the Americas, New York, New York 10020
First Aladdin edition August 2022
Text copyright © 2022 by Joan Holub and Suzanne Williams
Illustrations copyright © 2022 by Glass House Graphics
Art by Dave Santana. Inks by Flávio Soares with João Zod and
Juan Araujo. Colors by Felipe Felix and João Zod. Lettering by
Marcos Inoue. Art services by Glass House Graphics.
All rights reserved, including the right of
reproduction in whole or in part in any form.
ALADDIN and related logo are registered
trademarks of Simon & Schuster, Inc.
For information about special discounts for bulk purchases,
please contact Simon & Schuster Special Sales
at 1-866-506-1949 or business@simonandschuster.com.
The Simon & Schuster Speakers Bureau can bring authors to
your live event. For more information or to book an event contact
the Simon & Schuster Speakers Bureau at 1-866-248-3049
or visit our website at www.simonspeakers.com.
Designed by Nicholas Sciacca
The text of this book was set in CCMonologus.
Manufactured in China 0522 SCP
10 9 8 7 6 5 4 3 2 1
Library of Congress Control Number 2021945037
ISBN 9781534481213 (hc)
ISBN 9781534481206 (pbk)
ISBN 9781534481220 (ebook)

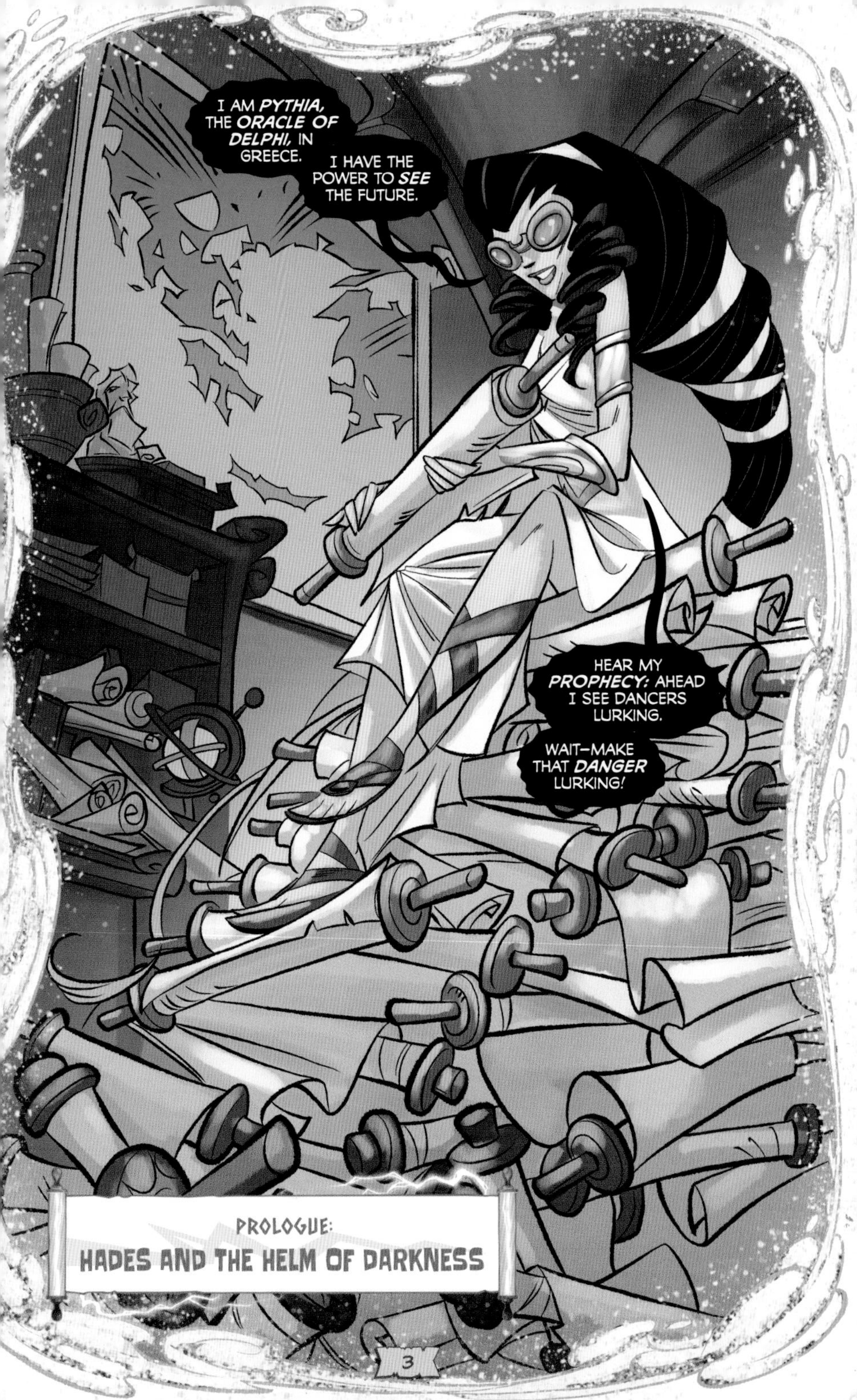
I AM PYTHIA, THE ORACLE OF DELPHI, IN GREECE.
I HAVE THE POWER TO SEE THE FUTURE.
HEAR MY PROPHECY: AHEAD I SEE DANCERS LURKING.
WAIT—MAKE THAT DANGER LURKING!
PROLOGUE:
HADES AND THE HELM OF DARKNESS

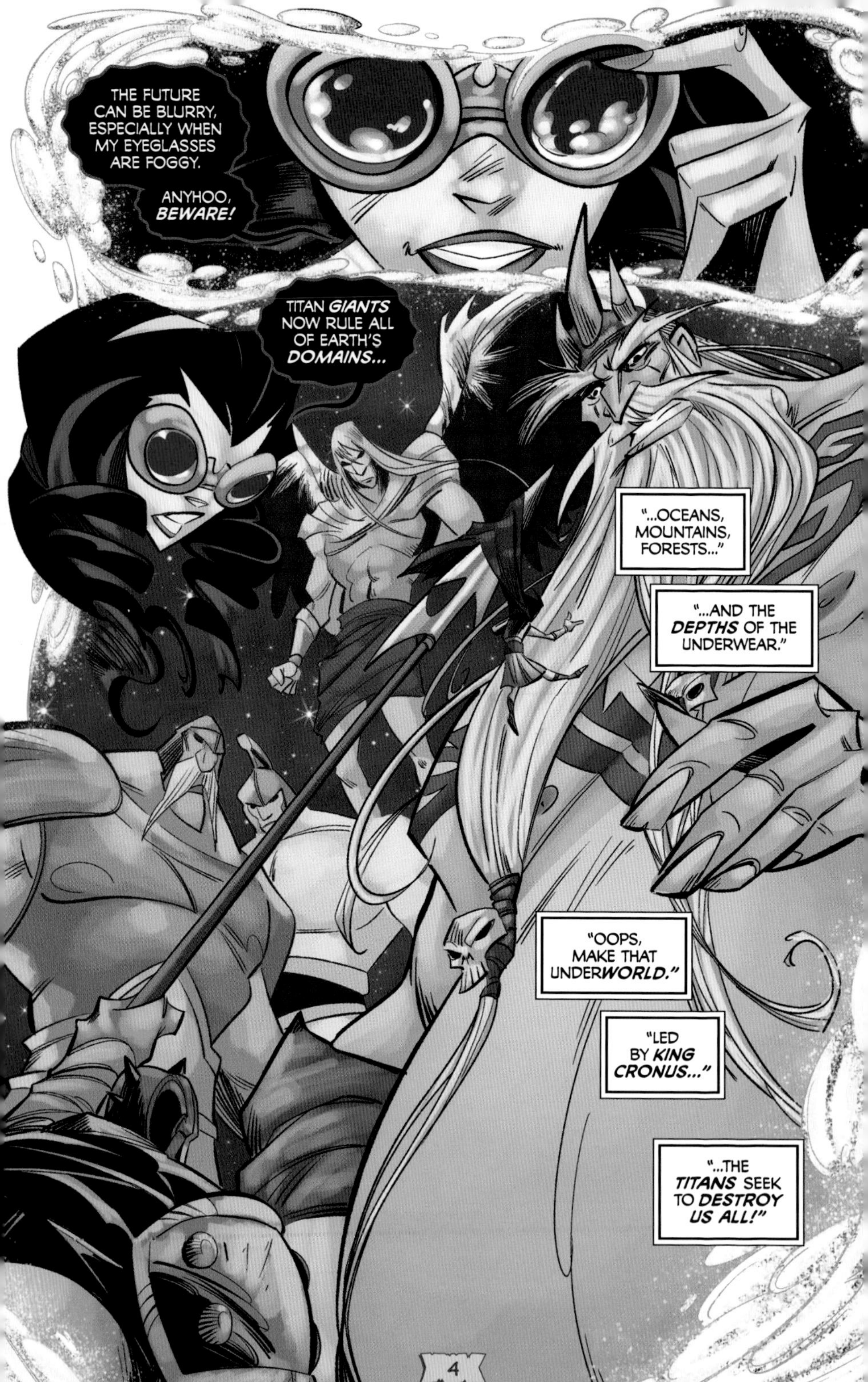
THE FUTURE CAN BE BLURRY, ESPECIALLY WHEN MY EYEGLASSES ARE FOGGY.
ANYHOO, *BEWARE!*
TITAN *GIANTS* NOW RULE ALL OF EARTH'S *DOMAINS...*
"...OCEANS, MOUNTAINS, FORESTS..."
"...AND THE *DEPTHS* OF THE UNDERWEAR."
"OOPS, MAKE THAT UNDER*WORLD.*"
"LED BY *KING CRONUS...*"
"...THE *TITANS* SEEK TO *DESTROY US ALL!*"

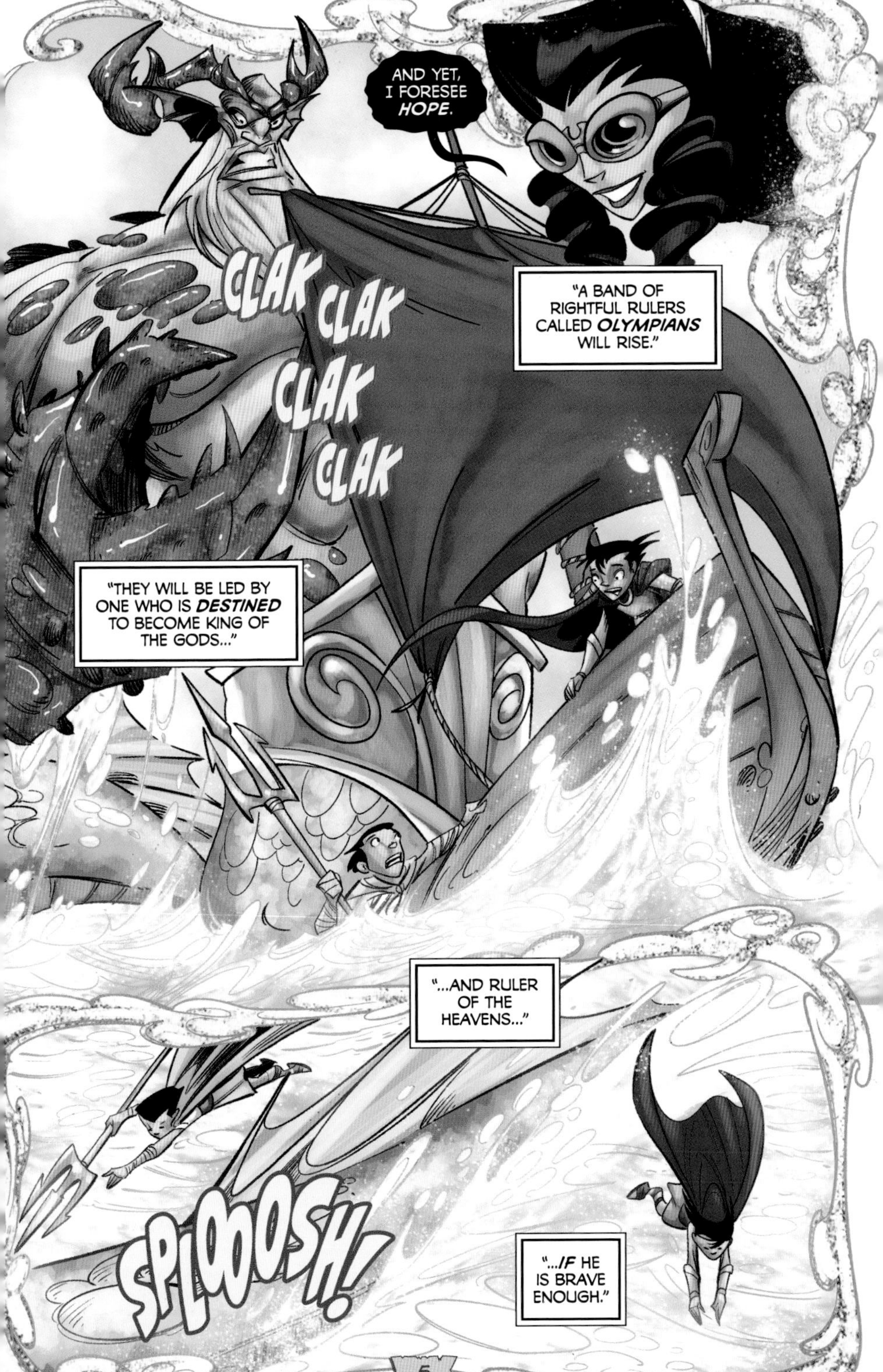
AND YET, I FORESEE HOPE.
"A BAND OF RIGHTFUL RULERS CALLED OLYMPIANS WILL RISE."
CLAK CLAK CLAK CLAK
"THEY WILL BE LED BY ONE WHO IS DESTINED TO BECOME KING OF THE GODS..."
"...AND RULER OF THE HEAVENS..."
SPLOOOSH!
"...IF HE IS BRAVE ENOUGH."

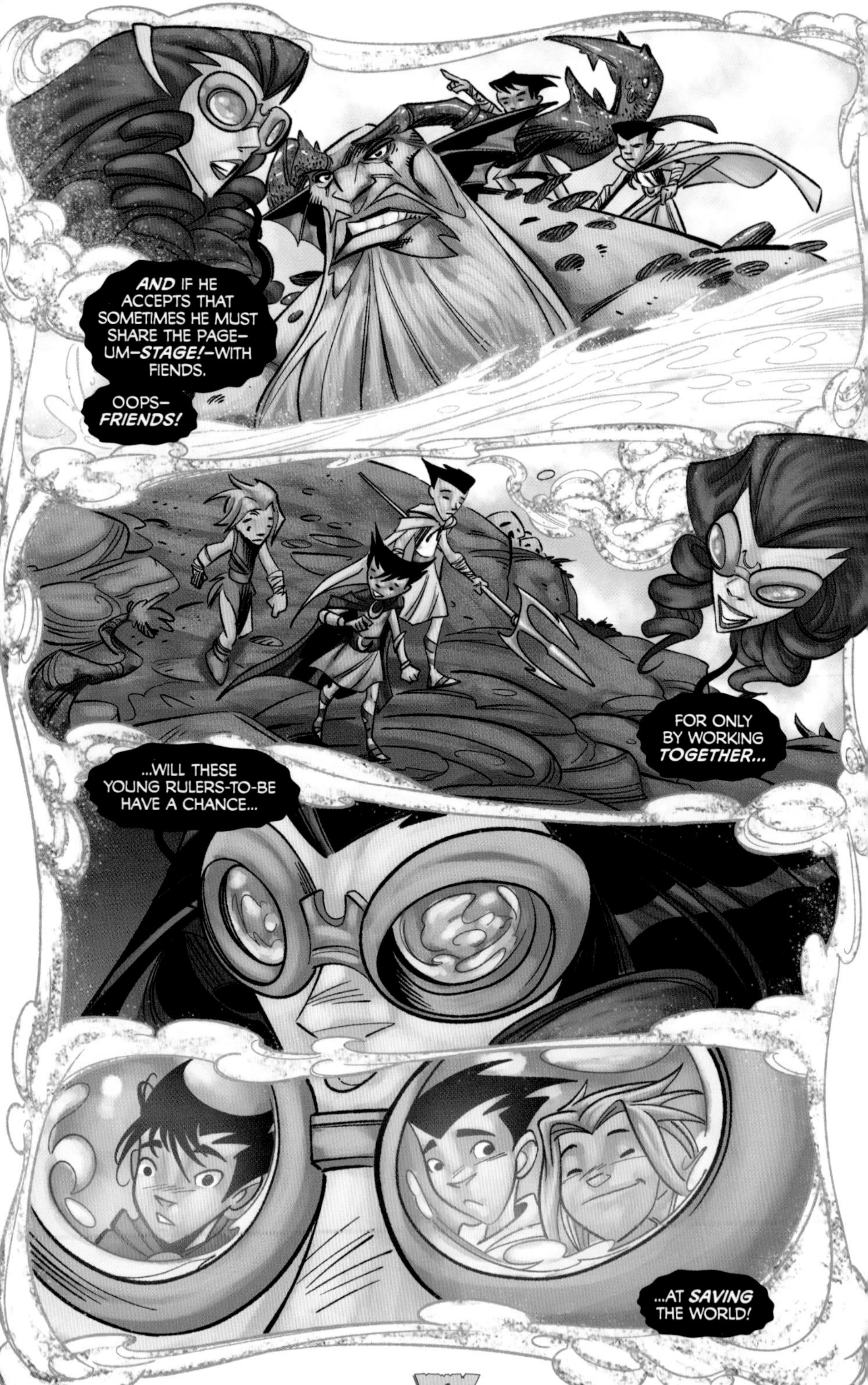
AND IF HE ACCEPTS THAT SOMETIMES HE MUST SHARE THE PAGE—UM—STAGE!—WITH FIENDS.
OOPS—FRIENDS!
FOR ONLY BY WORKING TOGETHER...
...WILL THESE YOUNG RULERS-TO-BE HAVE A CHANCE...
...AT SAVING THE WORLD!

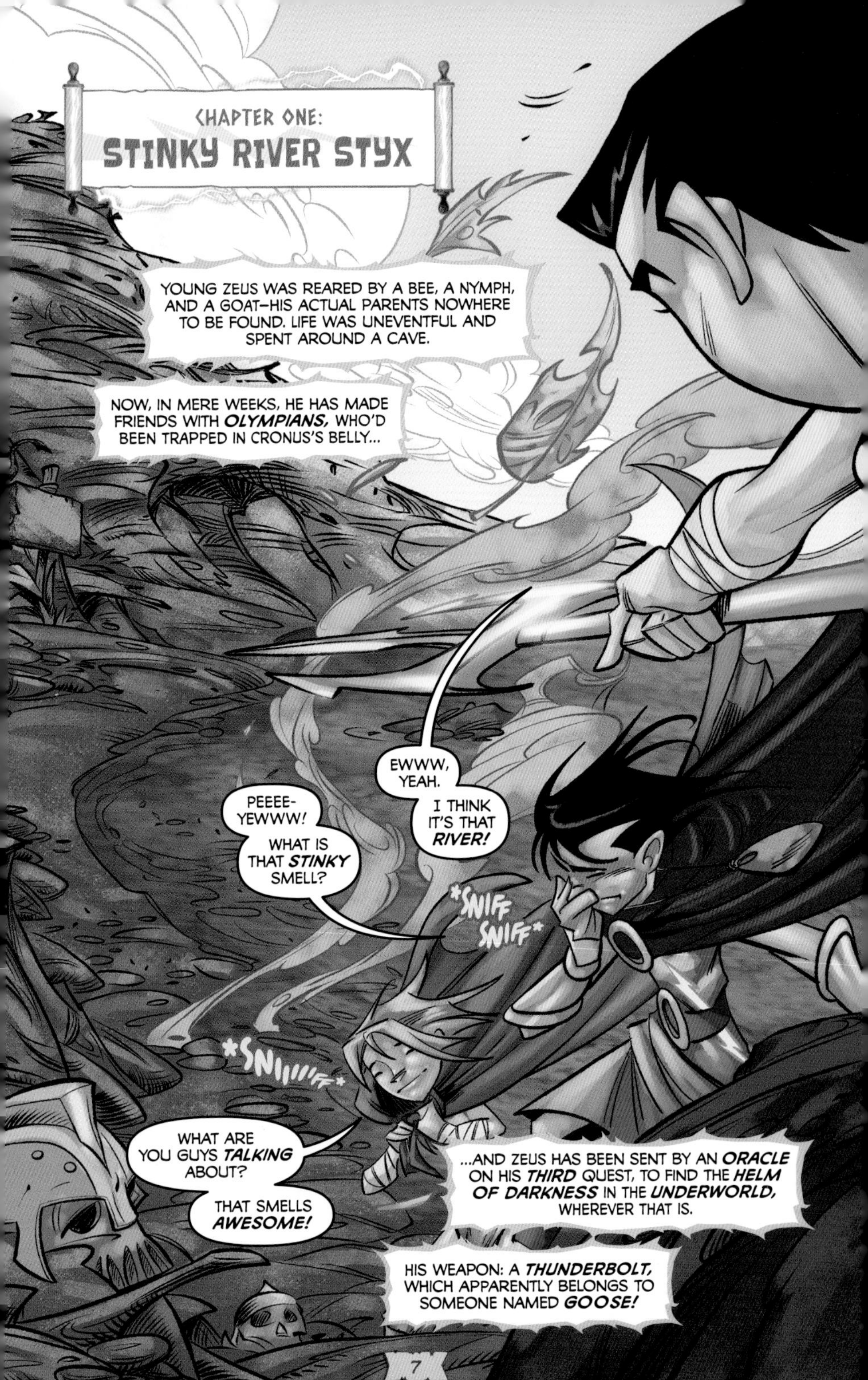
CHAPTER ONE:
STINKY RIVER STYX
YOUNG ZEUS WAS REARED BY A BEE, A NYMPH, AND A GOAT—HIS ACTUAL PARENTS NOWHERE TO BE FOUND. LIFE WAS UNEVENTFUL AND SPENT AROUND A CAVE.
NOW, IN MERE WEEKS, HE HAS MADE FRIENDS WITH *OLYMPIANS,* WHO'D BEEN TRAPPED IN CRONUS'S BELLY...
PEEEE-YEWWW! WHAT IS THAT *STINKY* SMELL?
EWWW, YEAH.
I THINK IT'S THAT *RIVER!*
SNIFF SNIFF
SNIIIIIFF
WHAT ARE YOU GUYS *TALKING* ABOUT?
THAT SMELLS *AWESOME!*
...AND ZEUS HAS BEEN SENT BY AN *ORACLE* ON HIS *THIRD* QUEST, TO FIND THE *HELM OF DARKNESS* IN THE *UNDERWORLD,* WHEREVER THAT IS.
HIS WEAPON: A *THUNDERBOLT,* WHICH APPARENTLY BELONGS TO SOMEONE NAMED *GOOSE!*

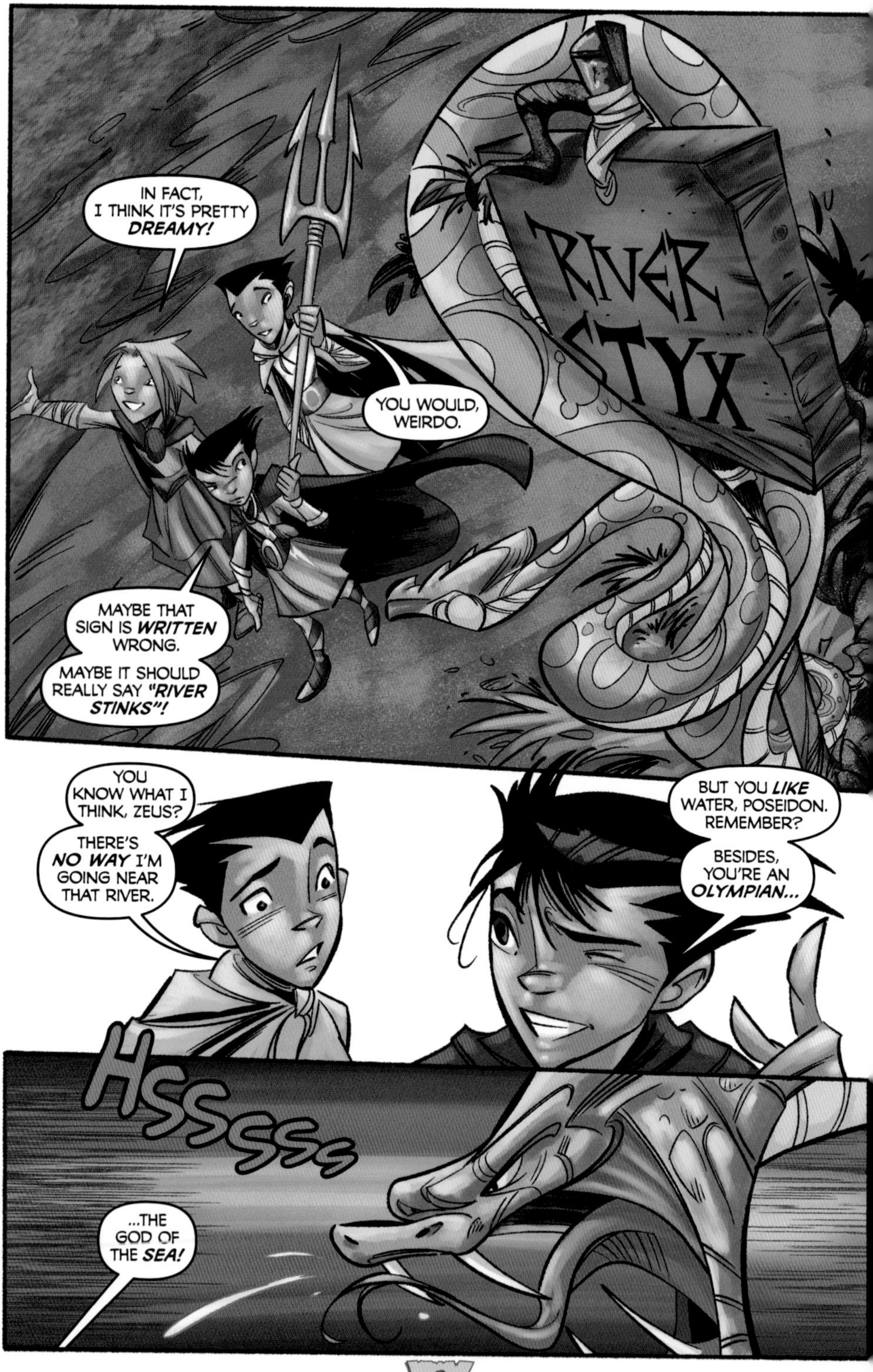
IN FACT, I THINK IT'S PRETTY DREAMY!
RIVER STYX
YOU WOULD, WEIRDO.
MAYBE THAT SIGN IS WRITTEN WRONG.
MAYBE IT SHOULD REALLY SAY "RIVER STINKS"!
YOU KNOW WHAT I THINK, ZEUS?
THERE'S NO WAY I'M GOING NEAR THAT RIVER.
BUT YOU LIKE WATER, POSEIDON. REMEMBER?
BESIDES, YOU'RE AN OLYMPIAN...
HSSSSS
...THE GOD OF THE SEA!

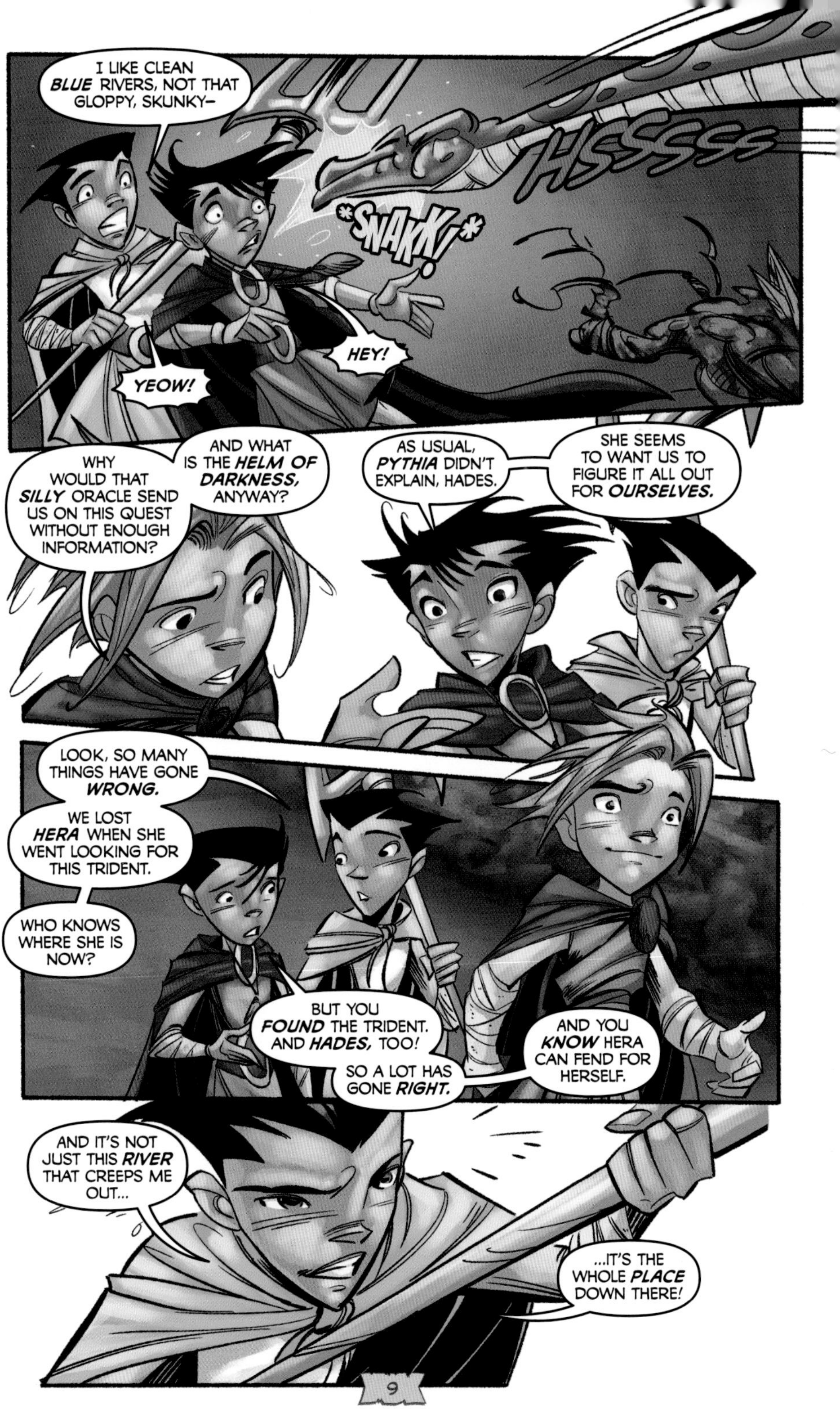
I LIKE CLEAN *BLUE* RIVERS, NOT THAT GLOPPY, SKUNKY–
HSSSSS
SNAKK!
YEOW!
HEY!
WHY WOULD THAT *SILLY* ORACLE SEND US ON THIS QUEST WITHOUT ENOUGH INFORMATION?
AND WHAT IS THE *HELM OF DARKNESS,* ANYWAY?
AS USUAL, *PYTHIA* DIDN'T EXPLAIN, HADES.
SHE SEEMS TO WANT US TO FIGURE IT ALL OUT FOR *OURSELVES.*
LOOK, SO MANY THINGS HAVE GONE *WRONG.*
WE LOST *HERA* WHEN SHE WENT LOOKING FOR THIS TRIDENT.
WHO KNOWS WHERE SHE IS NOW?
BUT YOU *FOUND* THE TRIDENT. AND *HADES,* TOO!
SO A LOT HAS GONE *RIGHT.*
AND YOU *KNOW* HERA CAN FEND FOR HERSELF.
AND IT'S NOT JUST THIS *RIVER* THAT CREEPS ME OUT...
...IT'S THE WHOLE *PLACE* DOWN THERE!

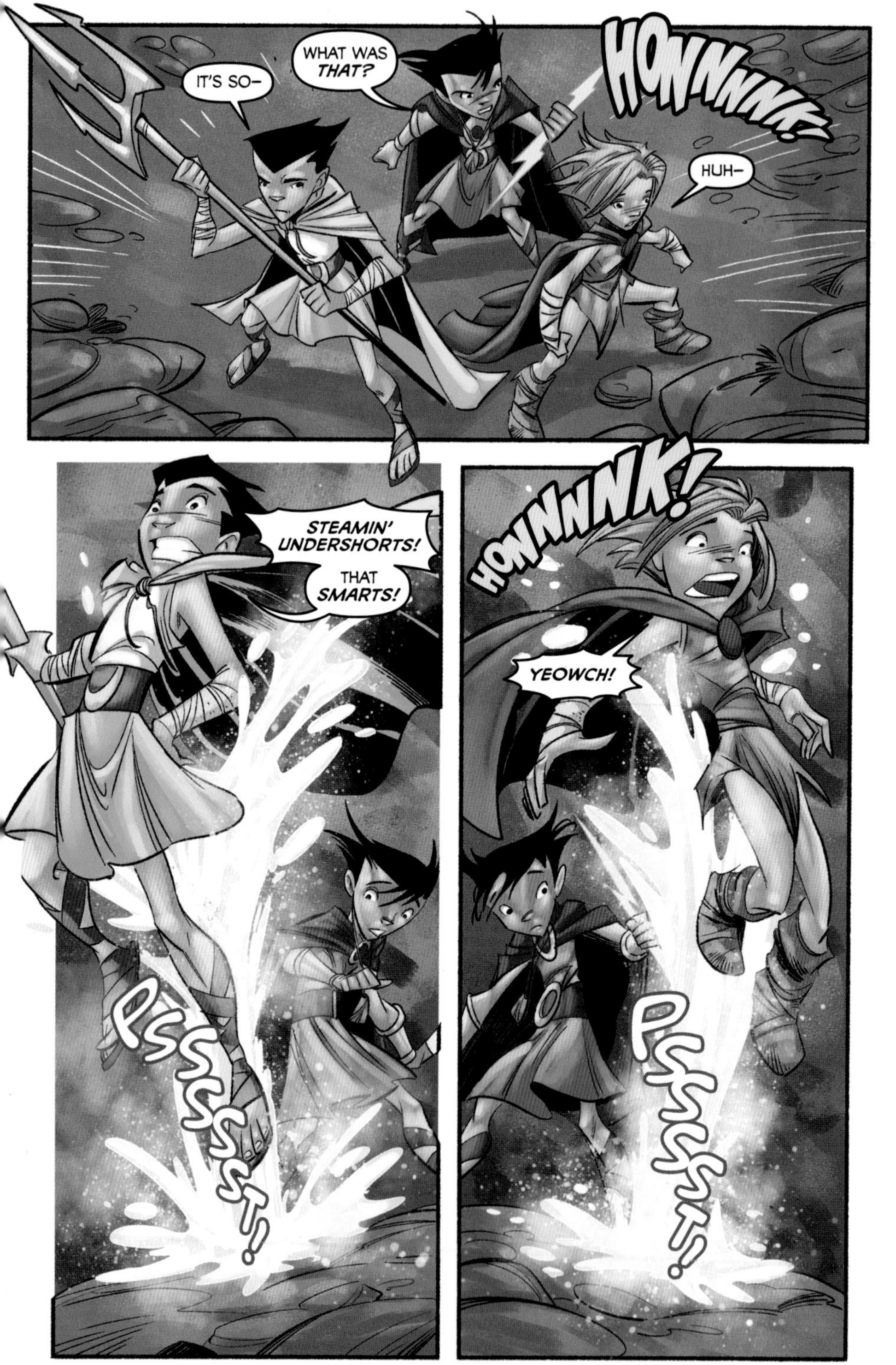

IT'S SO–
WHAT WAS *THAT?*
HONNNNK!
HUH–
STEAMIN' UNDERSHORTS!
THAT *SMARTS!*
PSSSST!
HONNNNK!
YEOWCH!
PSSSST!

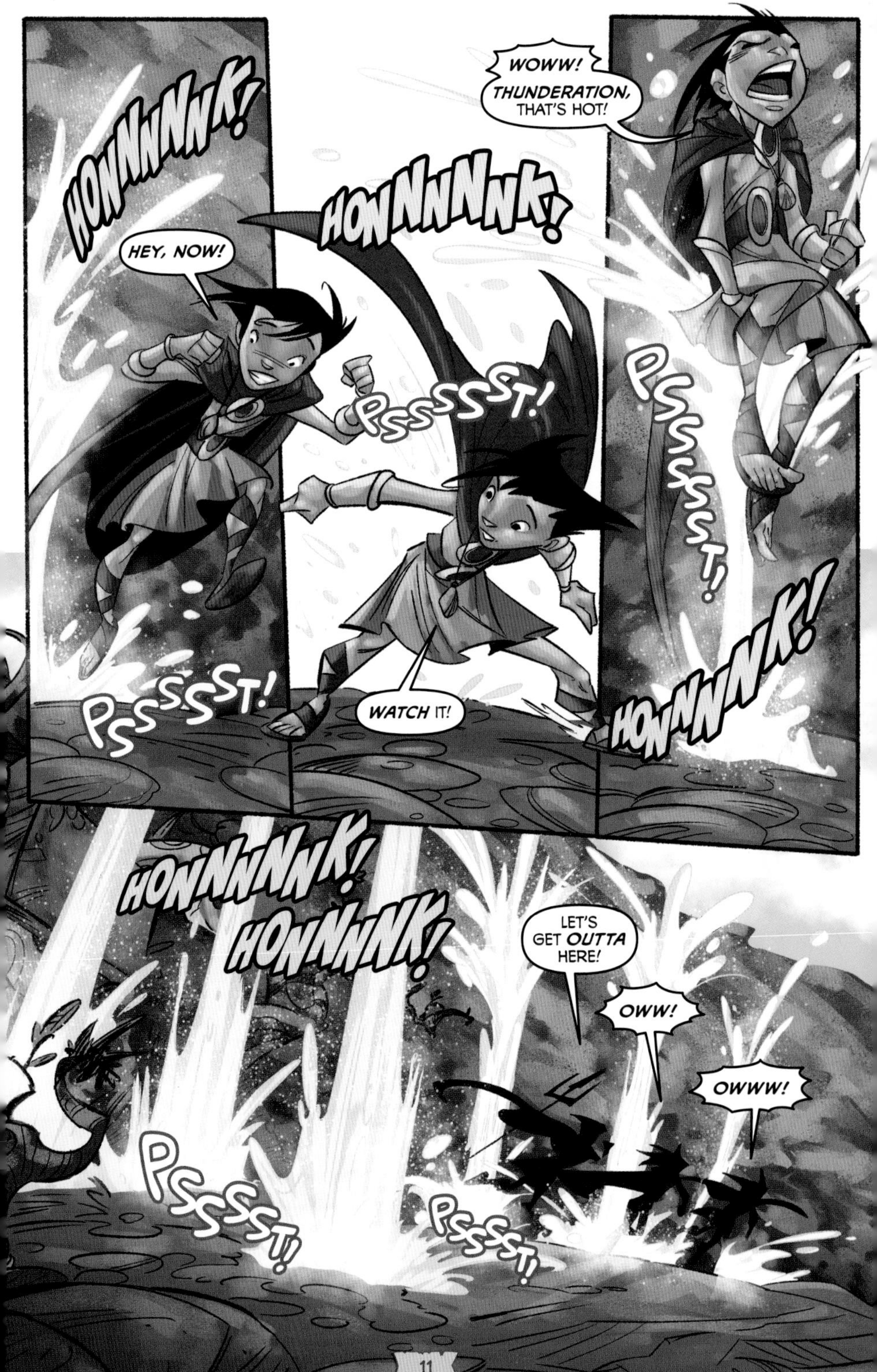
HONNNNNK!
HEY, NOW!
HONNNNNK!
PSSSSST!
WOWW! THUNDERATION, THAT'S HOT!
PSSSSST!
PSSSSST!
WATCH IT!
HONNNNK!
PSSSSST!
HONNNNNK!
HONNNNK!
LET'S GET OUTTA HERE!
OWW!
OWWW!
PSSSST!
PSSSST!

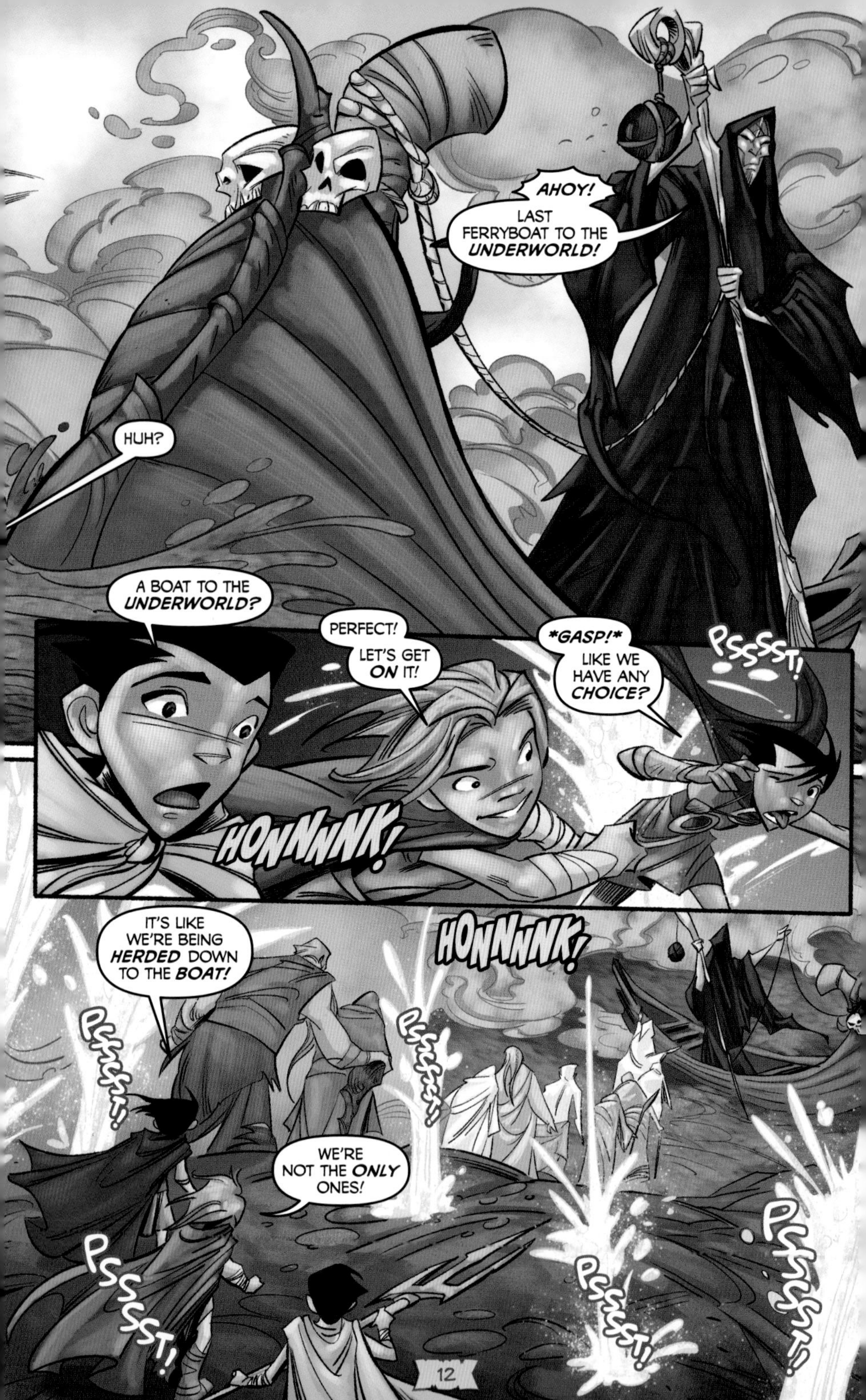
AHOY!
LAST FERRYBOAT TO THE UNDERWORLD!
HUH?
A BOAT TO THE UNDERWORLD?
PERFECT!
LET'S GET ON IT!
GASP!
LIKE WE HAVE ANY CHOICE?
PSSSST!
HONNNNK!
IT'S LIKE WE'RE BEING HERDED DOWN TO THE BOAT!
HONNNNK!
PSSSST!
PSSSST!
WE'RE NOT THE ONLY ONES!
PSSSST!
PSSSST!
PSSSST!

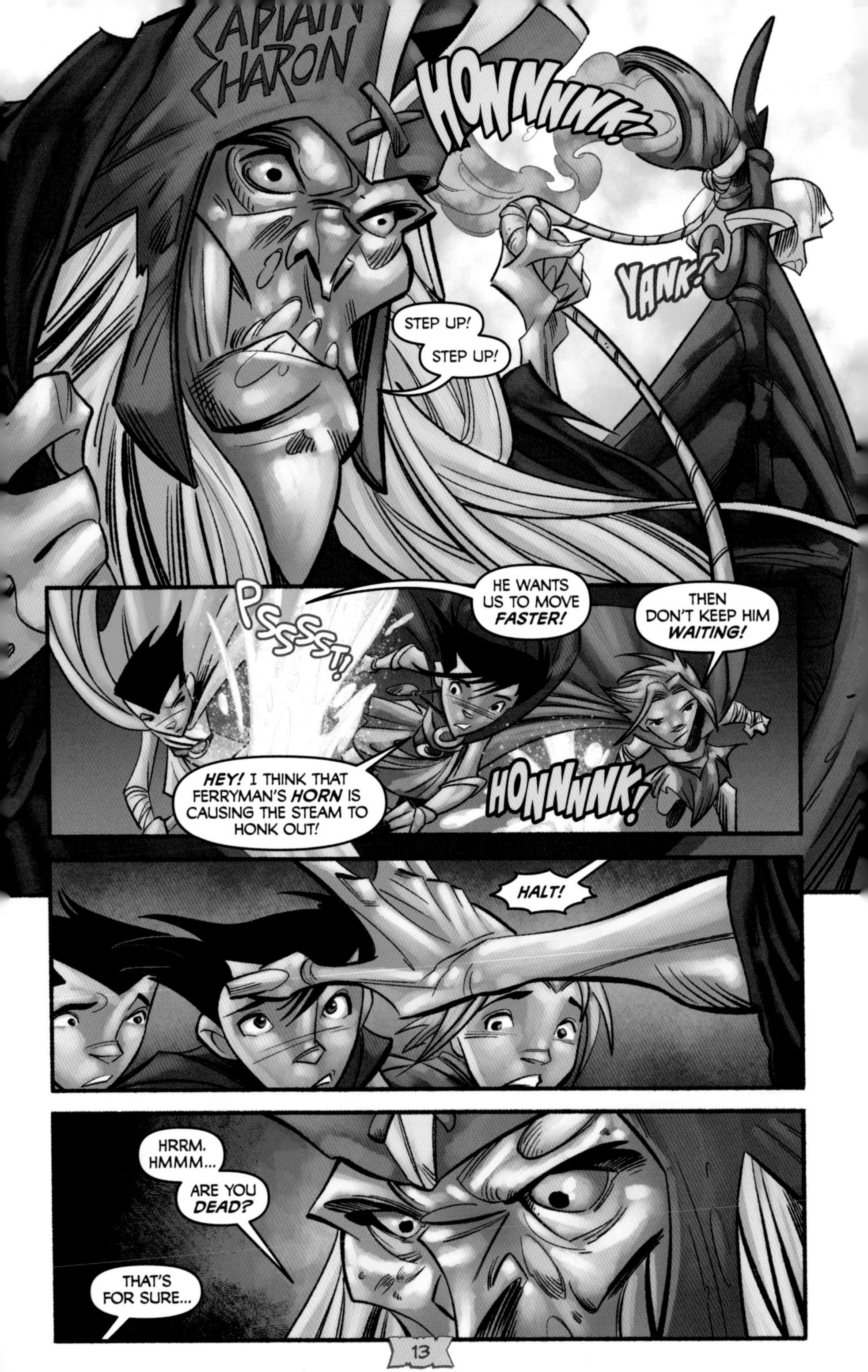
CAPTAIN CHARON
HONNNNK!
YANK!
STEP UP!
STEP UP!
PSSSST!!
HE WANTS US TO MOVE FASTER!
THEN DON'T KEEP HIM WAITING!
HEY! I THINK THAT FERRYMAN'S HORN IS CAUSING THE STEAM TO HONK OUT!
HONNNNK!
HALT!
HRRM. HMMM...
ARE YOU DEAD?
THAT'S FOR SURE...

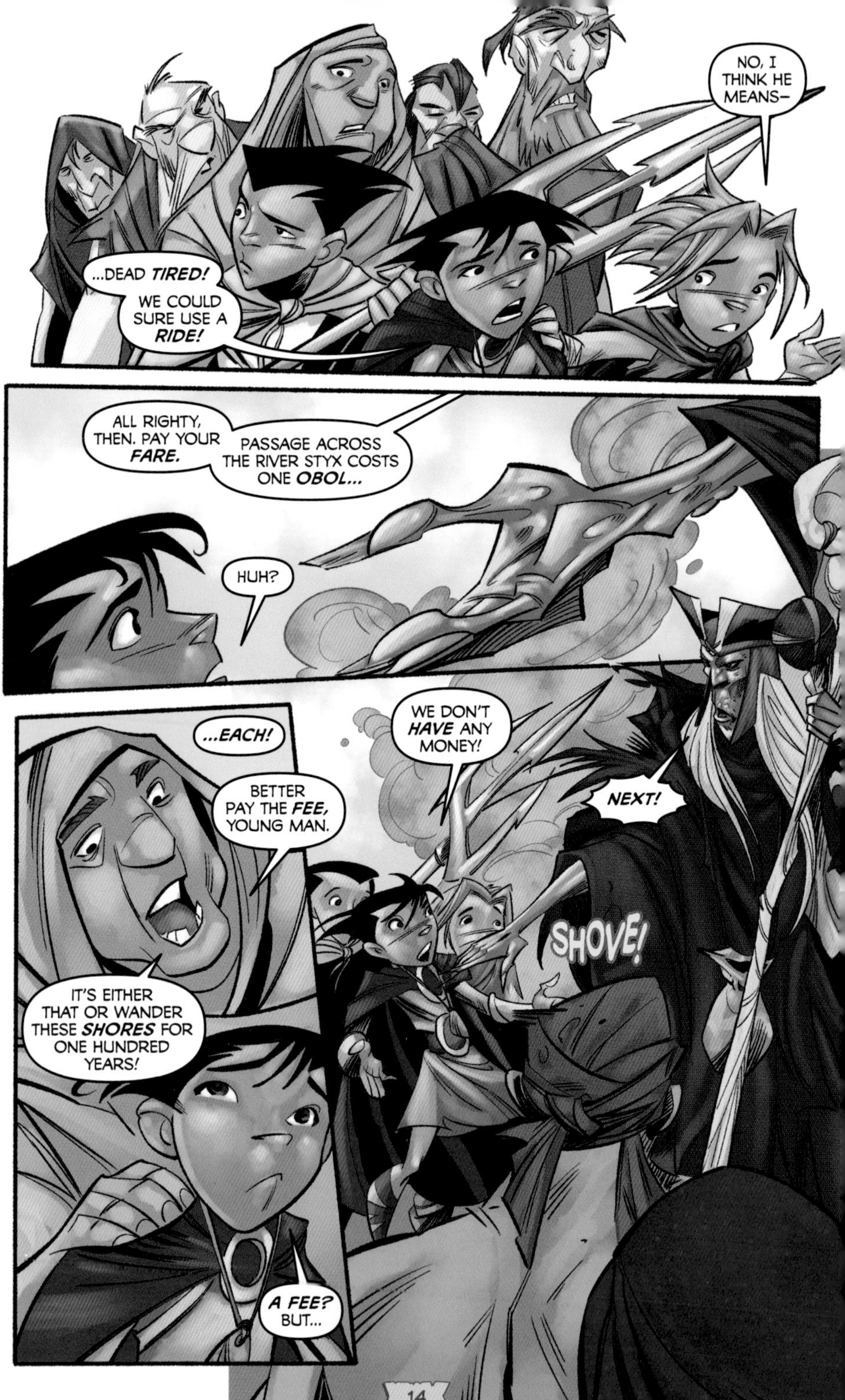
...DEAD TIRED!
WE COULD SURE USE A RIDE!
NO, I THINK HE MEANS—
ALL RIGHTY, THEN. PAY YOUR FARE.
PASSAGE ACROSS THE RIVER STYX COSTS ONE OBOL...
HUH?
...EACH!
BETTER PAY THE FEE, YOUNG MAN.
IT'S EITHER THAT OR WANDER THESE SHORES FOR ONE HUNDRED YEARS!
A FEE? BUT...
WE DON'T HAVE ANY MONEY!
NEXT!
SHOVE!

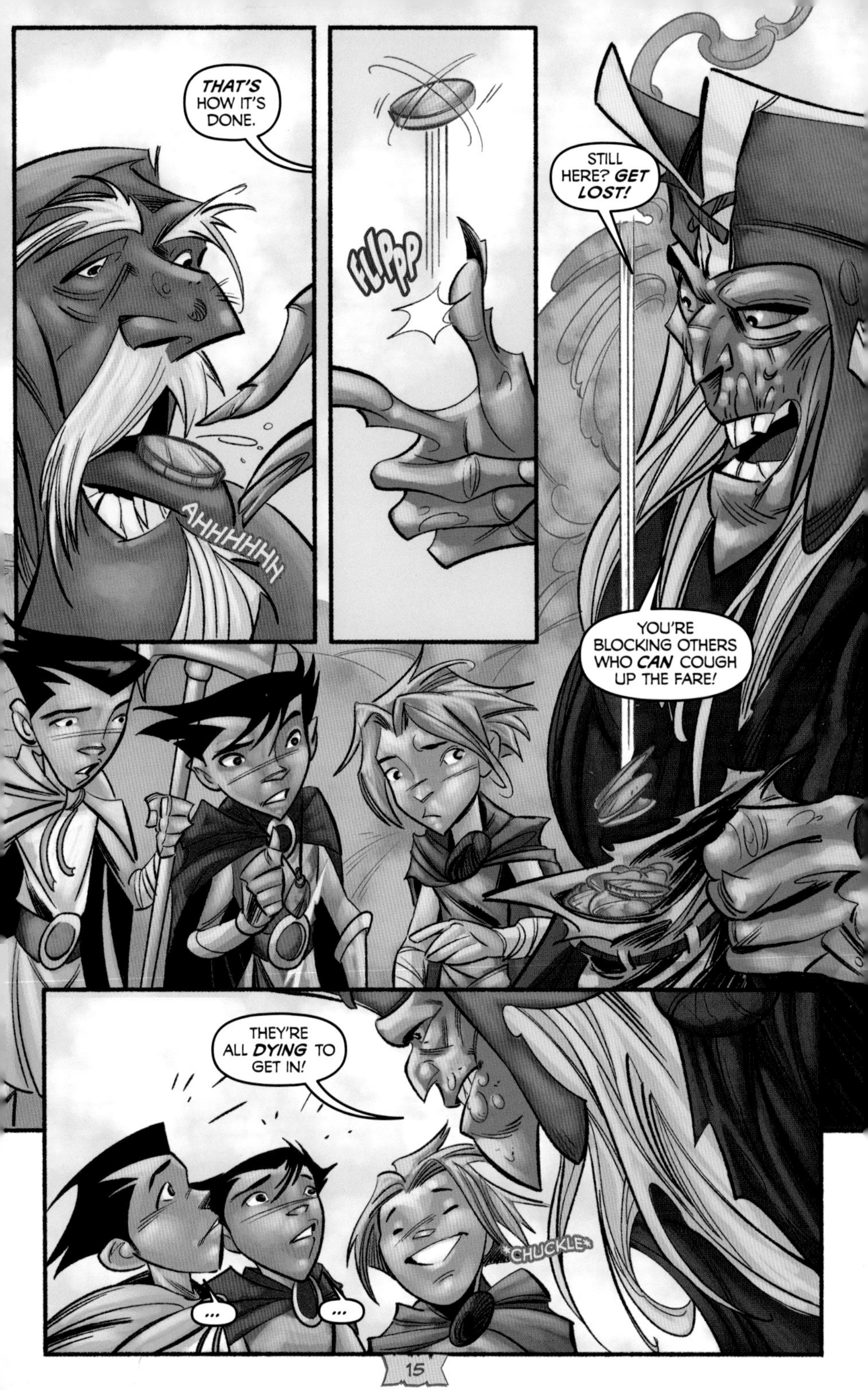
THAT'S HOW IT'S DONE.
AHHHHHH
FLIPPP
STILL HERE? GET LOST!
YOU'RE BLOCKING OTHERS WHO CAN COUGH UP THE FARE!
THEY'RE ALL DYING TO GET IN!
CHUCKLE
...
...

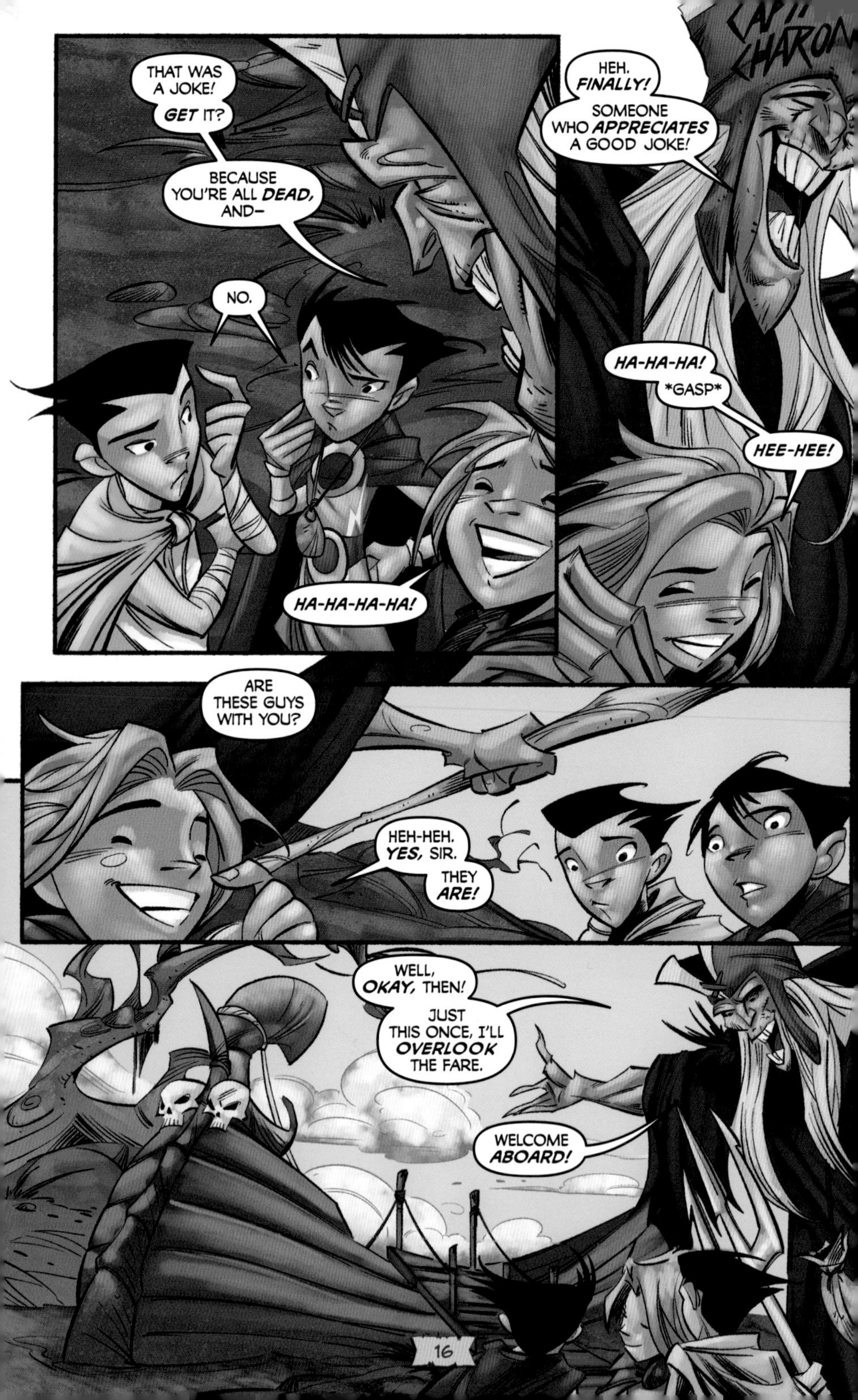
THAT WAS A JOKE! GET IT?
BECAUSE YOU'RE ALL DEAD, AND–
NO.
HA-HA-HA-HA!
CAPT. CHARON
HEH. FINALLY!
SOMEONE WHO APPRECIATES A GOOD JOKE!
HA-HA-HA! *GASP*
HEE-HEE!
ARE THESE GUYS WITH YOU?
HEH-HEH. YES, SIR.
THEY ARE!
WELL, OKAY, THEN!
JUST THIS ONCE, I'LL OVERLOOK THE FARE.
WELCOME ABOARD!

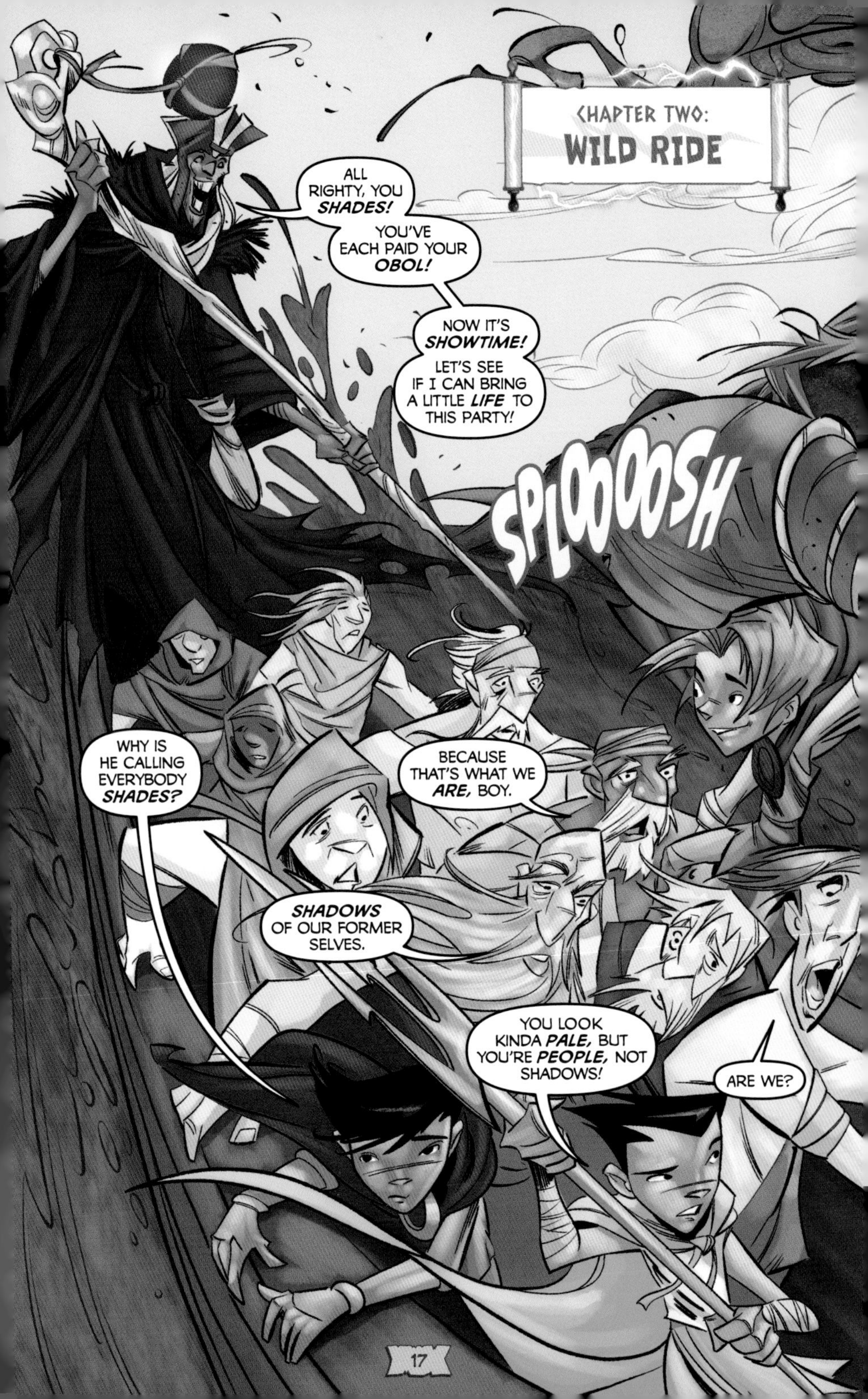
CHAPTER TWO:
WILD RIDE
ALL RIGHTY, YOU *SHADES!*
YOU'VE EACH PAID YOUR *OBOL!*
NOW IT'S *SHOWTIME!*
LET'S SEE IF I CAN BRING A LITTLE *LIFE* TO THIS PARTY!
SPLOOOOSH
WHY IS HE CALLING EVERYBODY *SHADES?*
BECAUSE THAT'S WHAT WE *ARE,* BOY.
SHADOWS OF OUR FORMER SELVES.
YOU LOOK KINDA *PALE,* BUT YOU'RE *PEOPLE,* NOT SHADOWS!
ARE WE?

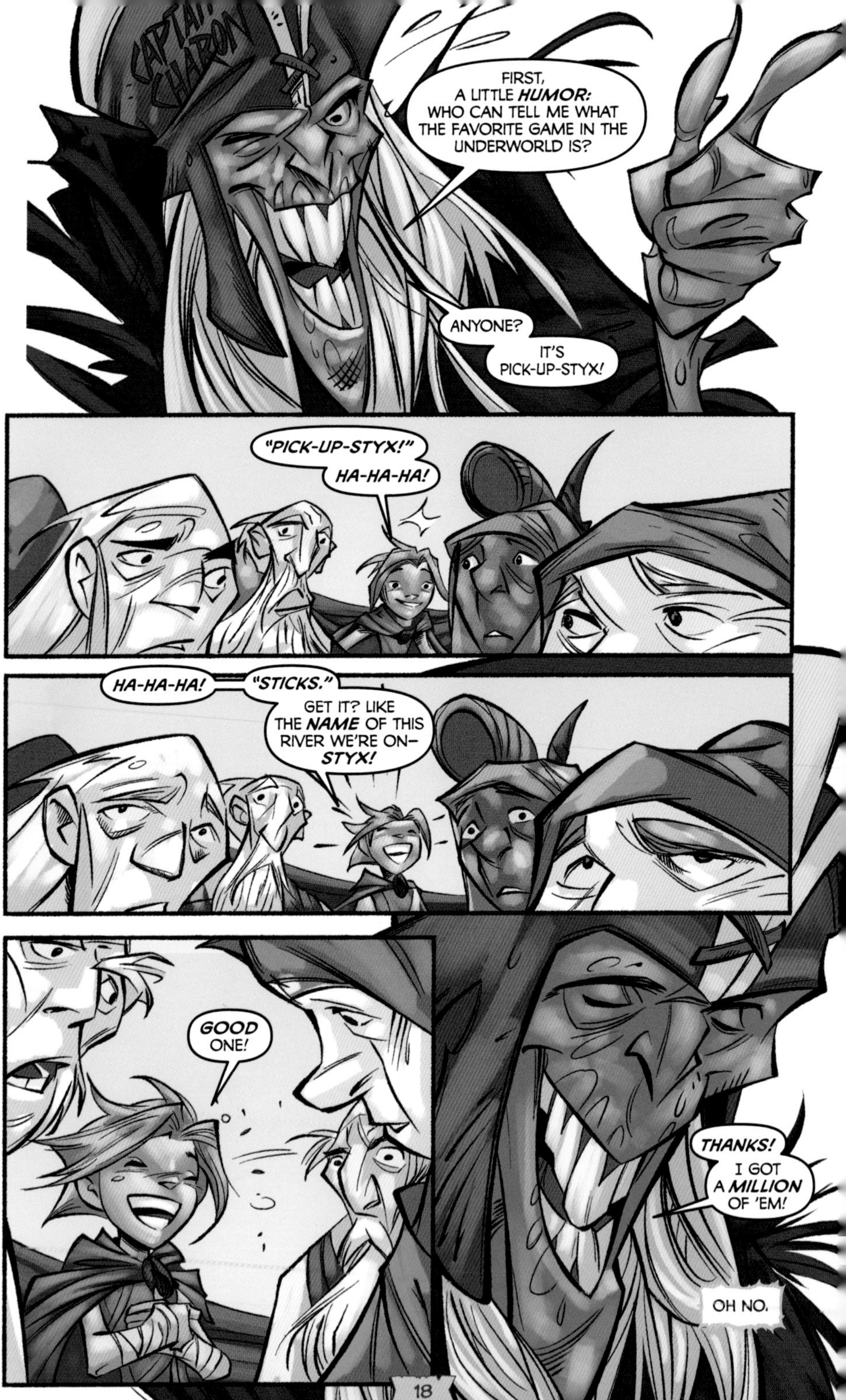
CAPTAIN CHARON
FIRST, A LITTLE HUMOR: WHO CAN TELL ME WHAT THE FAVORITE GAME IN THE UNDERWORLD IS?
ANYONE?
IT'S PICK-UP-STYX!
"PICK-UP-STYX!"
HA-HA-HA!
HA-HA-HA!
"STICKS."
GET IT? LIKE THE NAME OF THIS RIVER WE'RE ON— STYX!
GOOD ONE!
THANKS!
I GOT A MILLION OF 'EM!
OH NO.

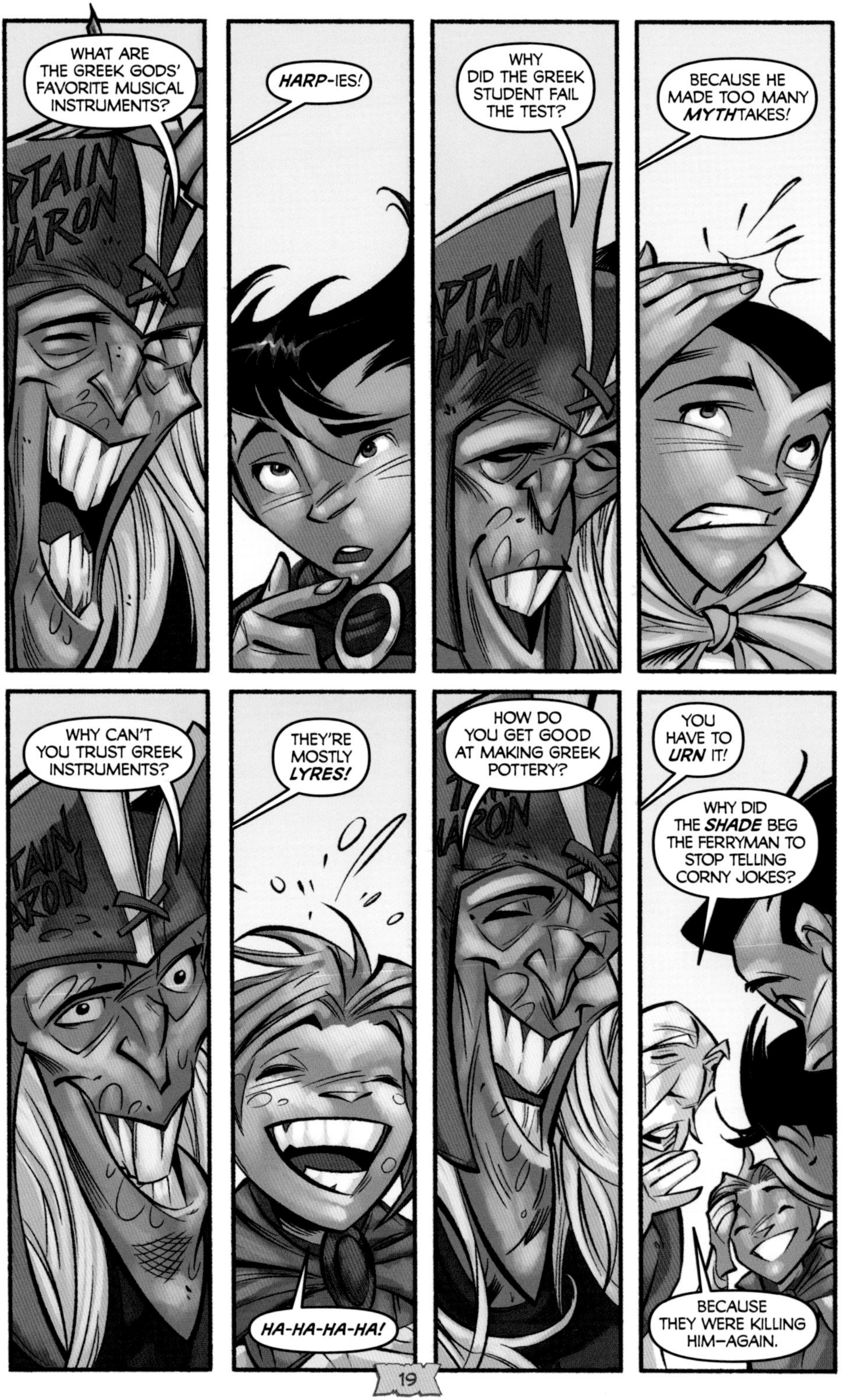
WHAT ARE THE GREEK GODS' FAVORITE MUSICAL INSTRUMENTS?
HARP-IES!
WHY DID THE GREEK STUDENT FAIL THE TEST?
BECAUSE HE MADE TOO MANY MYTHTAKES!
CAPTAIN CHARON
WHY CAN'T YOU TRUST GREEK INSTRUMENTS?
THEY'RE MOSTLY LYRES!
HA-HA-HA-HA!
HOW DO YOU GET GOOD AT MAKING GREEK POTTERY?
YOU HAVE TO URN IT!
WHY DID THE SHADE BEG THE FERRYMAN TO STOP TELLING CORNY JOKES?
BECAUSE THEY WERE KILLING HIM—AGAIN.

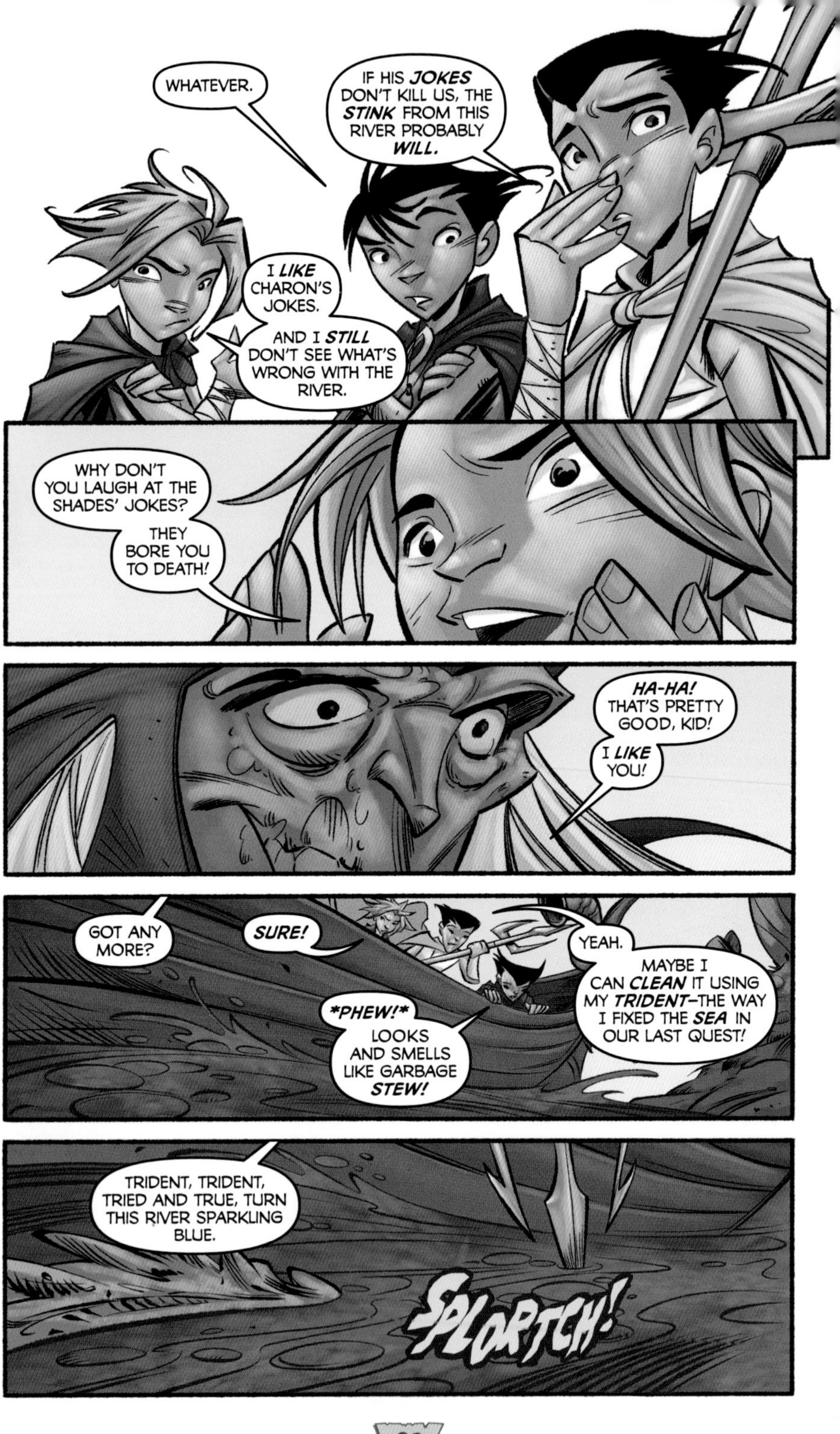
WHATEVER.
IF HIS JOKES DON'T KILL US, THE STINK FROM THIS RIVER PROBABLY WILL.
I LIKE CHARON'S JOKES.
AND I STILL DON'T SEE WHAT'S WRONG WITH THE RIVER.
WHY DON'T YOU LAUGH AT THE SHADES' JOKES?
THEY BORE YOU TO DEATH!
HA-HA! THAT'S PRETTY GOOD, KID!
I LIKE YOU!
GOT ANY MORE?
SURE!
PHEW! LOOKS AND SMELLS LIKE GARBAGE STEW!
YEAH.
MAYBE I CAN CLEAN IT USING MY TRIDENT—THE WAY I FIXED THE SEA IN OUR LAST QUEST!
TRIDENT, TRIDENT, TRIED AND TRUE, TURN THIS RIVER SPARKLING BLUE.
SPLORTCH!

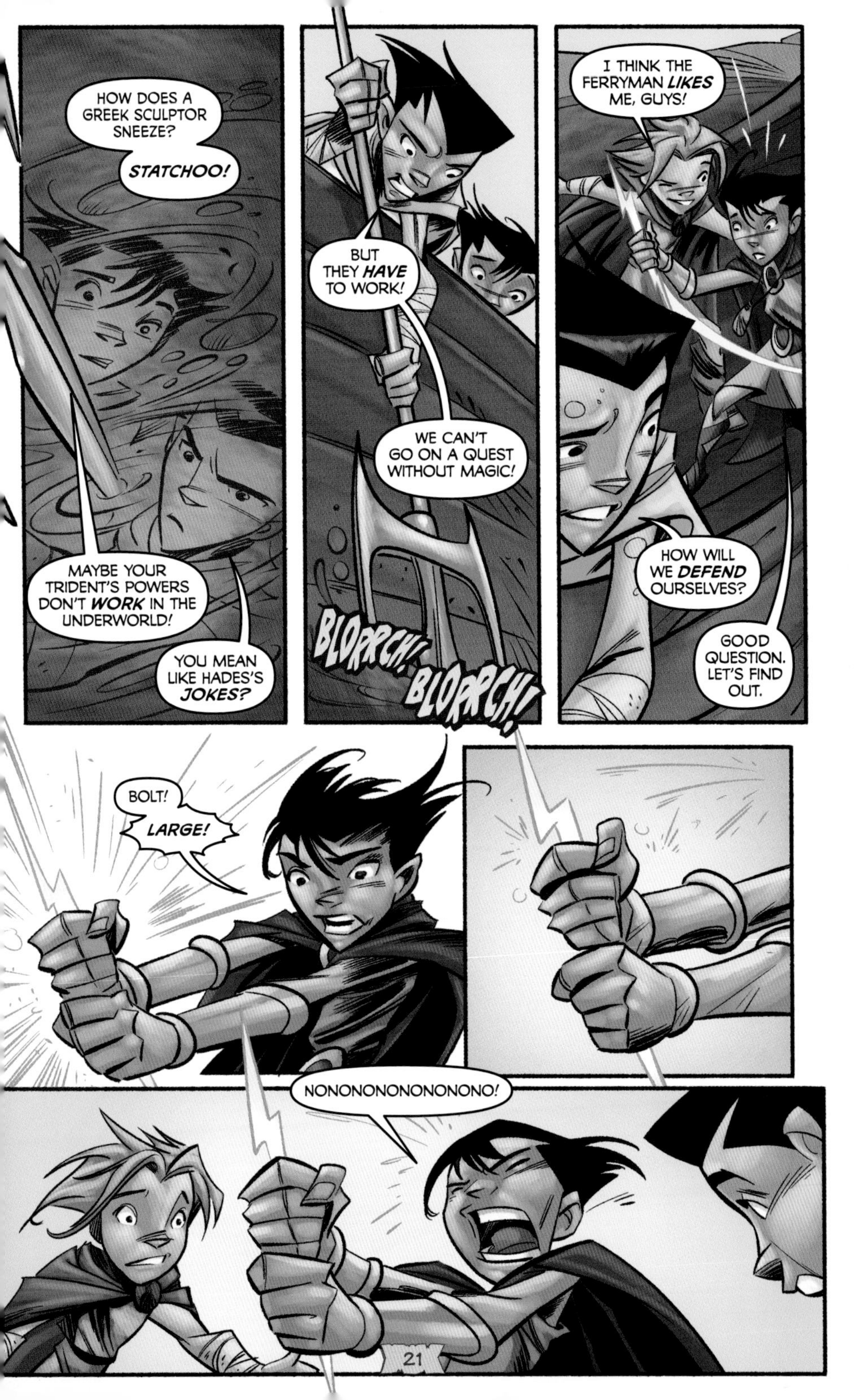
HOW DOES A GREEK SCULPTOR SNEEZE?
STATCHOO!
MAYBE YOUR TRIDENT'S POWERS DON'T WORK IN THE UNDERWORLD!
YOU MEAN LIKE HADES'S JOKES?
BUT THEY HAVE TO WORK!
WE CAN'T GO ON A QUEST WITHOUT MAGIC!
BLORRCH! BLORRCH!
I THINK THE FERRYMAN LIKES ME, GUYS!
HOW WILL WE DEFEND OURSELVES?
GOOD QUESTION. LET'S FIND OUT.
BOLT!
LARGE!
NONONONONONONONO!

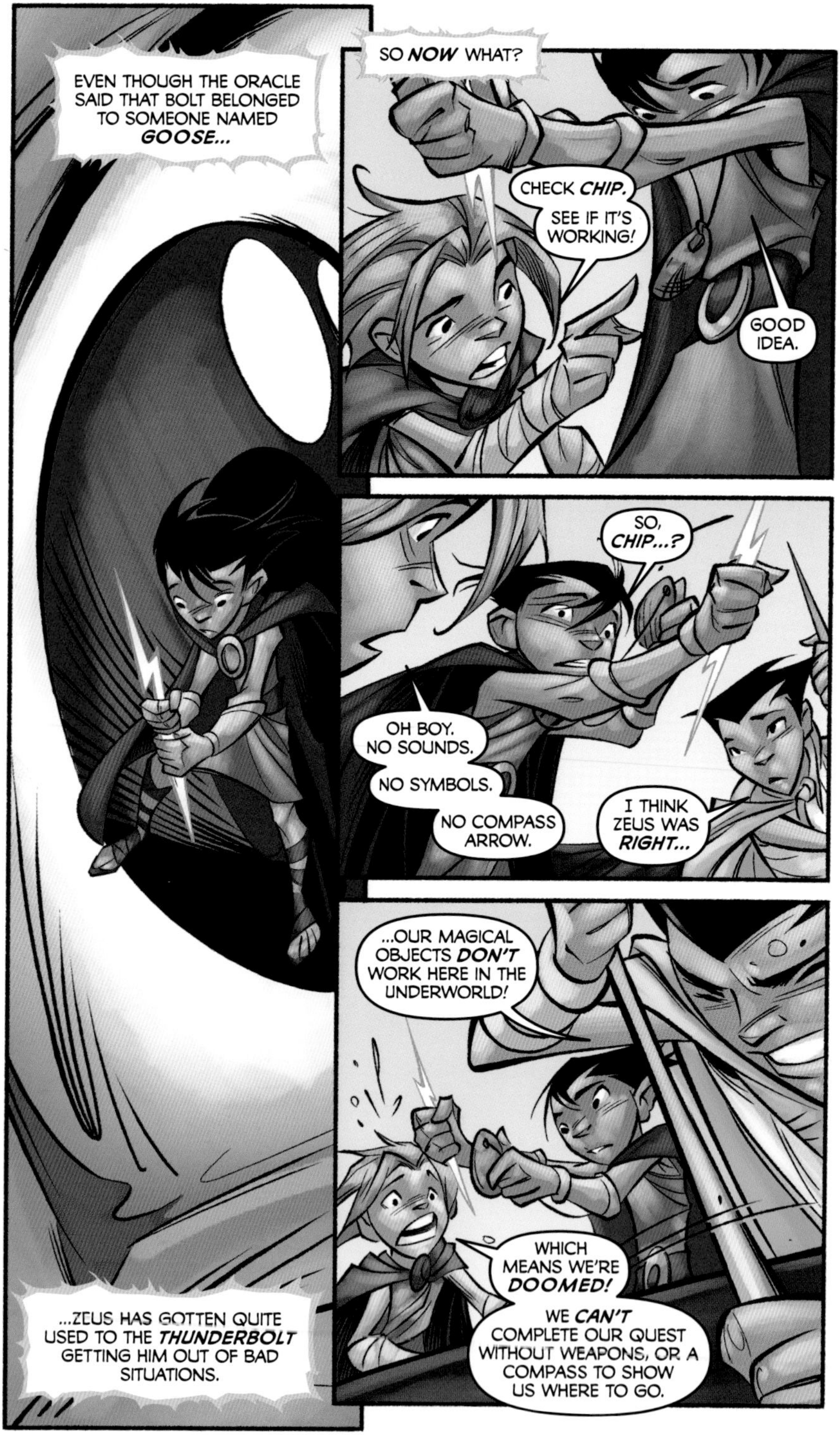
EVEN THOUGH THE ORACLE SAID THAT BOLT BELONGED TO SOMEONE NAMED GOOSE...
...ZEUS HAS GOTTEN QUITE USED TO THE THUNDERBOLT GETTING HIM OUT OF BAD SITUATIONS.
SO NOW WHAT?
CHECK CHIP.
SEE IF IT'S WORKING!
GOOD IDEA.
SO, CHIP...?
OH BOY. NO SOUNDS.
NO SYMBOLS.
NO COMPASS ARROW.
I THINK ZEUS WAS RIGHT...
...OUR MAGICAL OBJECTS DON'T WORK HERE IN THE UNDERWORLD!
WHICH MEANS WE'RE DOOMED!
WE CAN'T COMPLETE OUR QUEST WITHOUT WEAPONS, OR A COMPASS TO SHOW US WHERE TO GO.

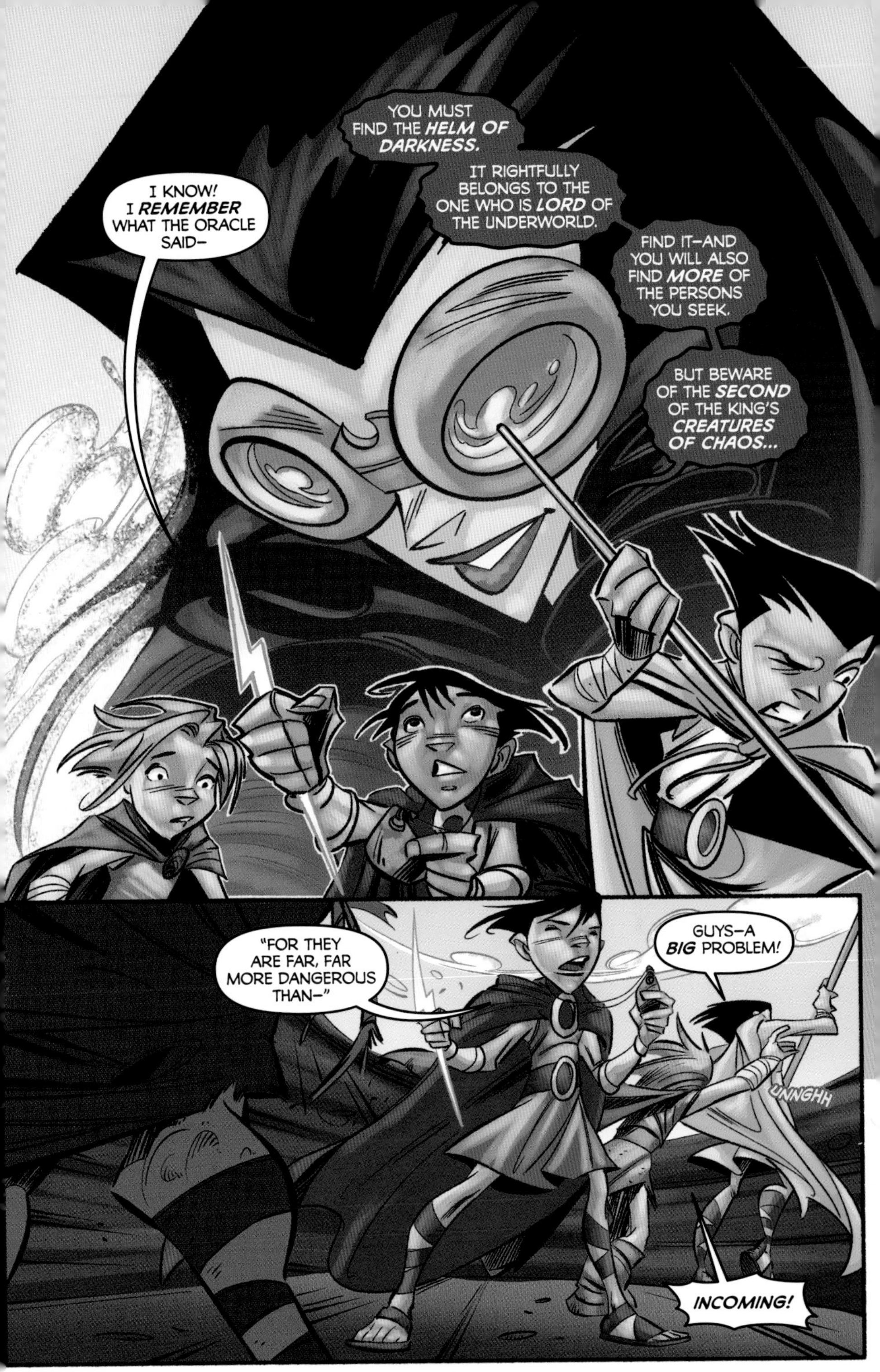
YOU MUST FIND THE *HELM OF DARKNESS.*
I KNOW! I *REMEMBER* WHAT THE ORACLE SAID–
IT RIGHTFULLY BELONGS TO THE ONE WHO IS *LORD* OF THE UNDERWORLD.
FIND IT–AND YOU WILL ALSO FIND *MORE* OF THE PERSONS YOU SEEK.
BUT BEWARE OF THE *SECOND* OF THE KING'S *CREATURES OF CHAOS...*
"FOR THEY ARE FAR, FAR MORE DANGEROUS THAN–"
GUYS–A *BIG* PROBLEM!
UNNGHH
INCOMING!

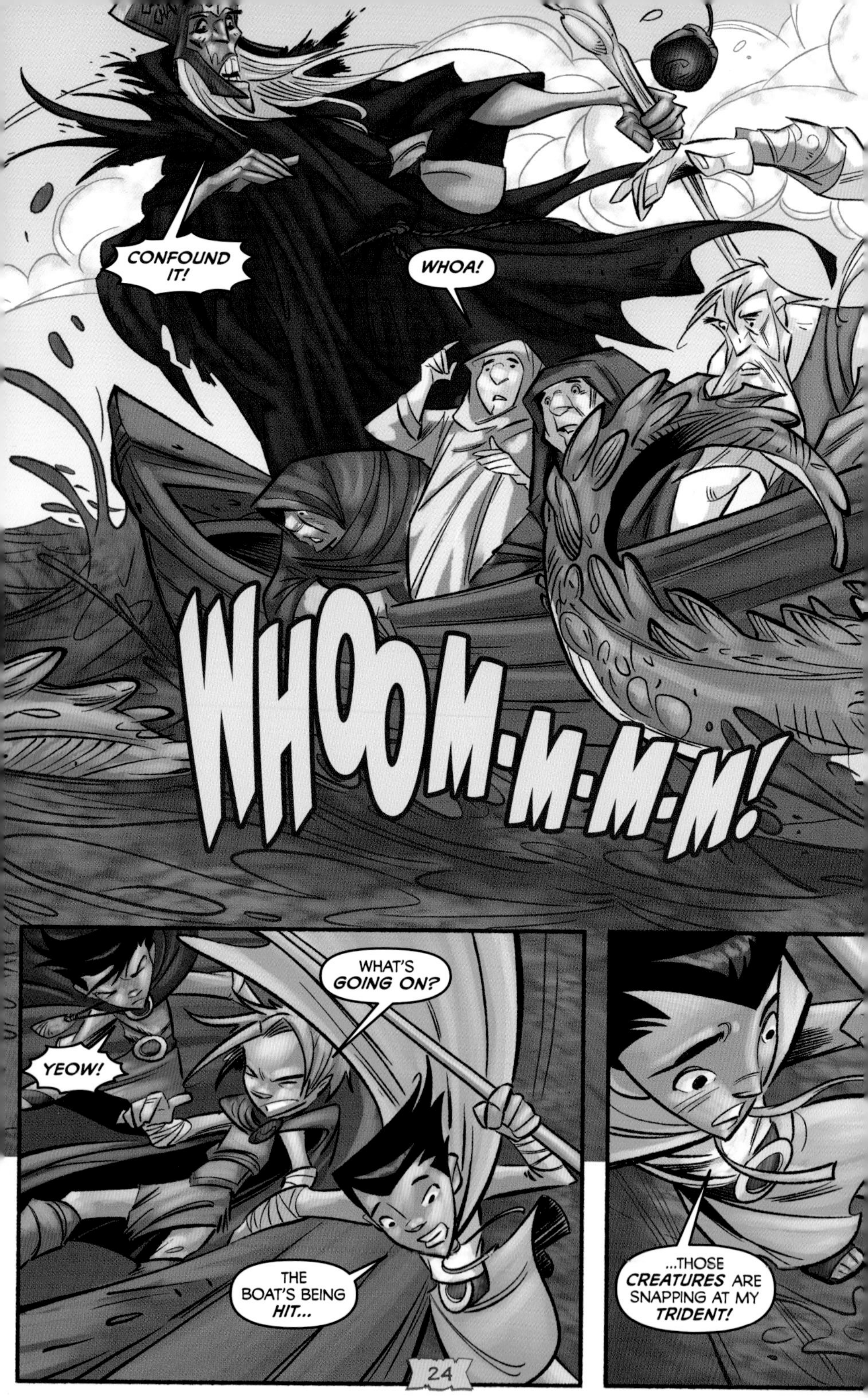
CONFOUND IT!
WHOA!
WHOOM-M-M-M!
WHAT'S GOING ON?
YEOW!
THE BOAT'S BEING HIT...
...THOSE CREATURES ARE SNAPPING AT MY TRIDENT!

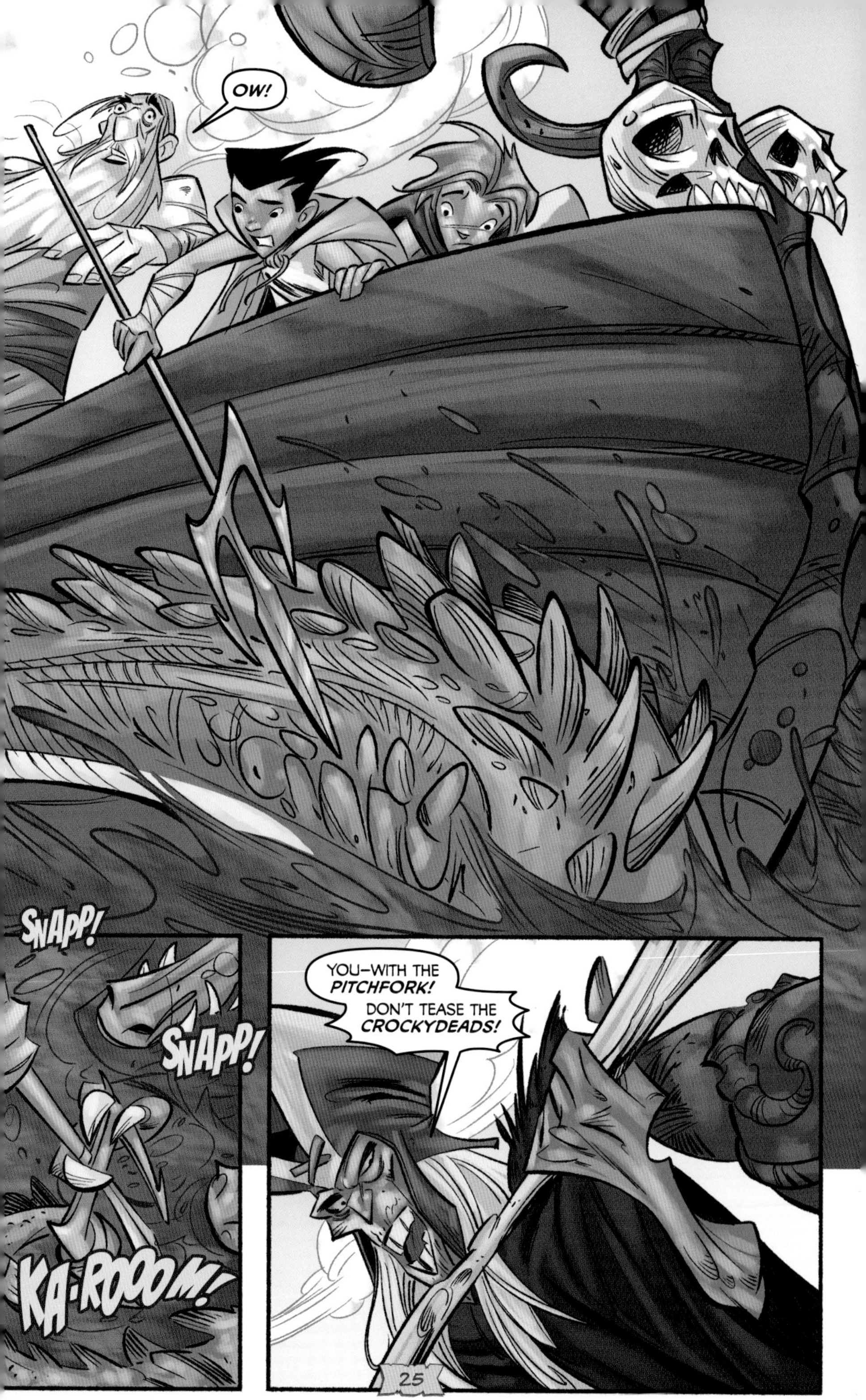
OW!
SNAPP!
SNAPP!
KA-ROOOM!
YOU–WITH THE PITCHFORK!
DON'T TEASE THE CROCKYDEADS!

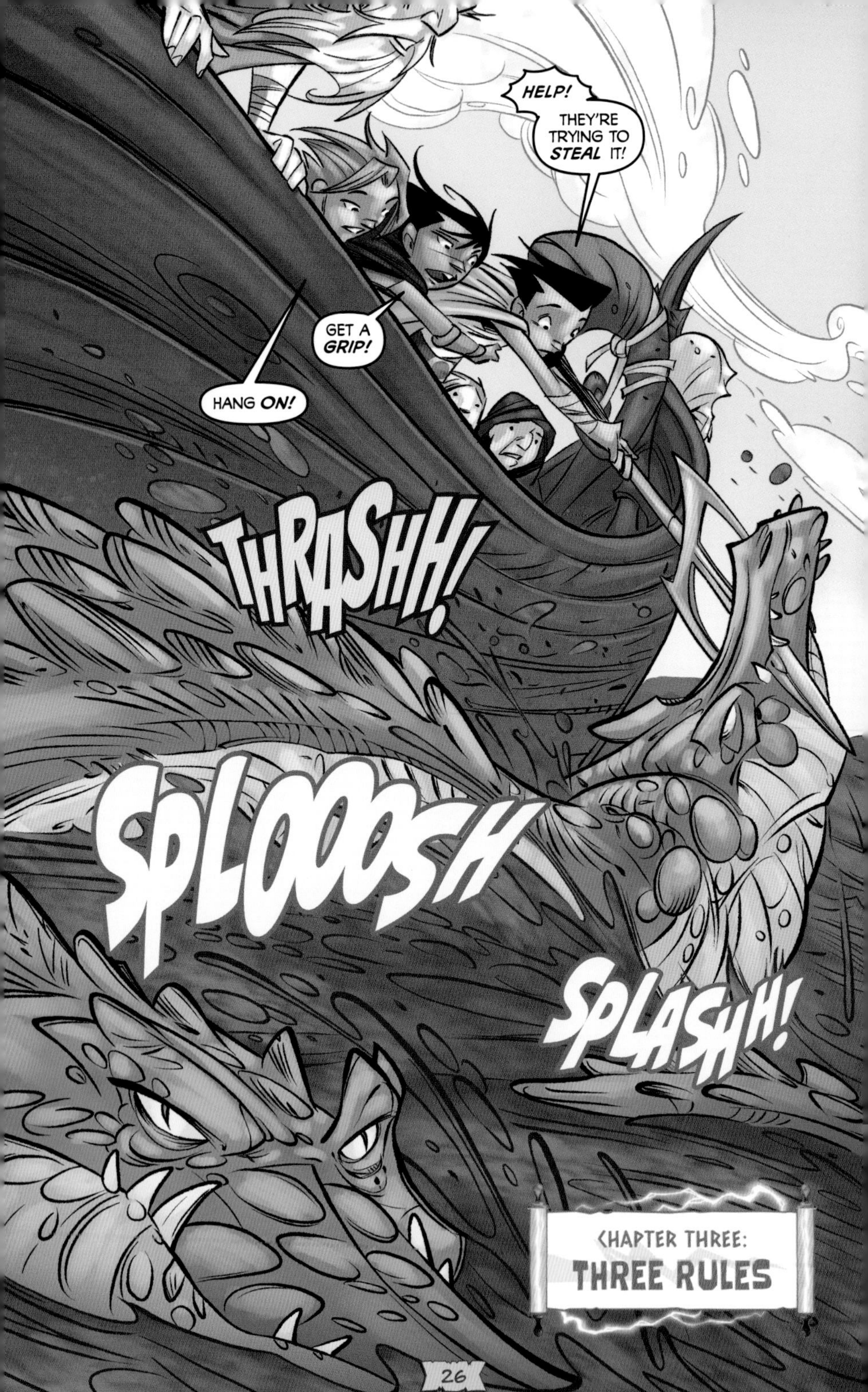
HELP!
THEY'RE TRYING TO STEAL IT!
GET A GRIP!
HANG ON!
THRASHH!
SPLOOOSH
SPLASHH!
CHAPTER THREE:
THREE RULES

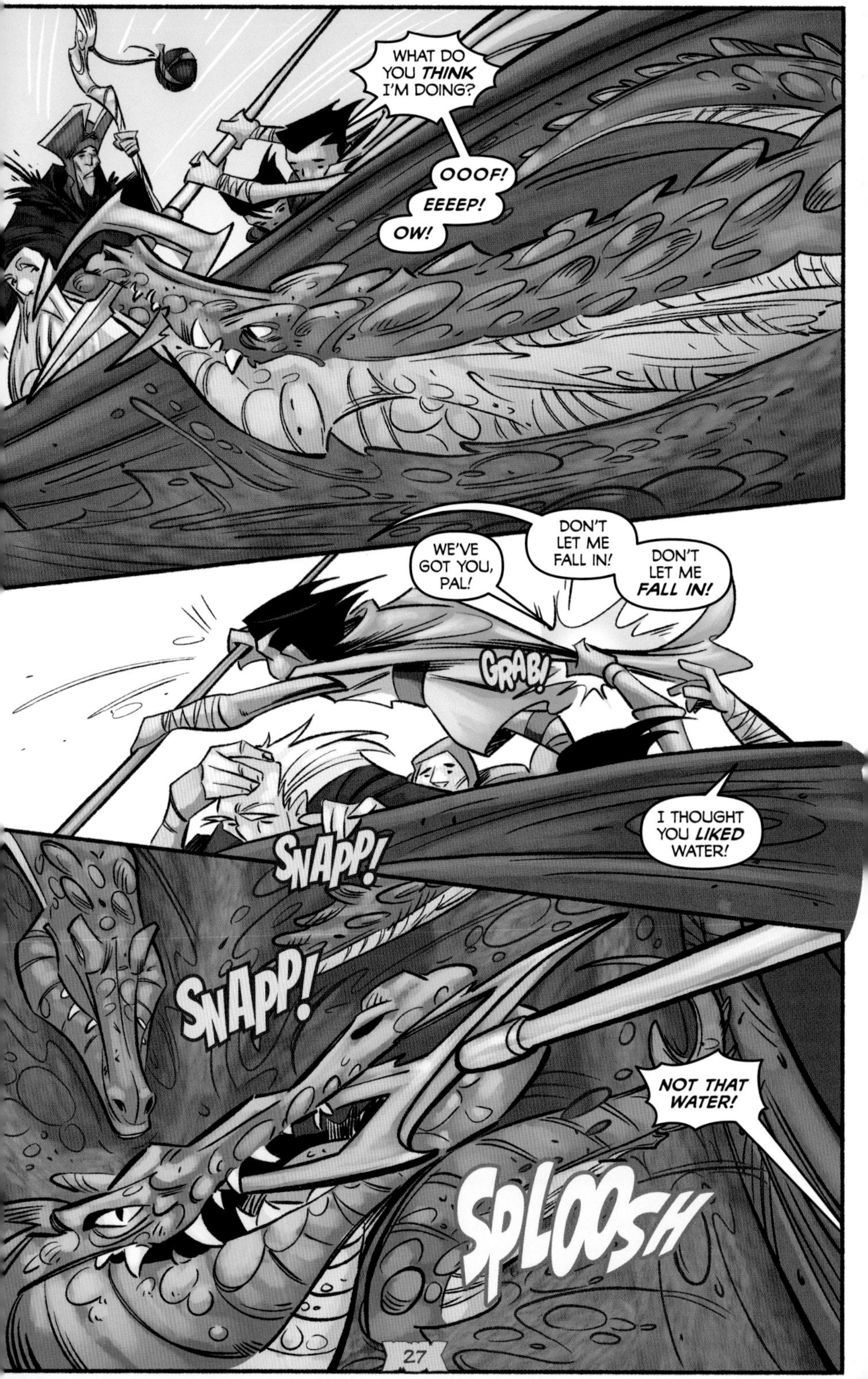
WHAT DO YOU THINK I'M DOING?
OOOF!
EEEEP!
OW!
WE'VE GOT YOU, PAL!
DON'T LET ME FALL IN!
DON'T LET ME FALL IN!
GRAB!
I THOUGHT YOU LIKED WATER!
SNAPP!
SNAPP!
NOT THAT WATER!
SPLOOSH

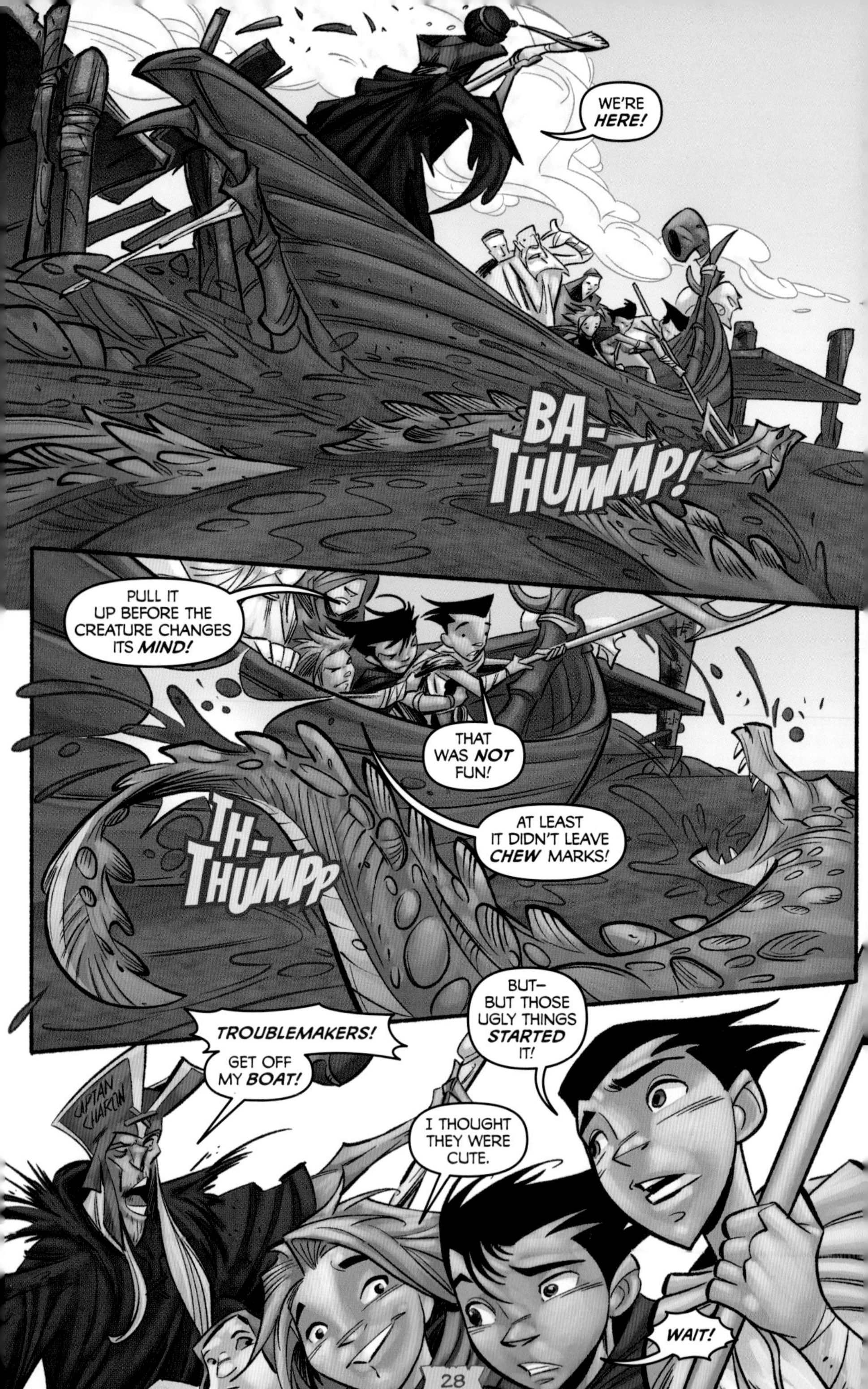

WE'RE HERE!
BA-THUMMP!
PULL IT UP BEFORE THE CREATURE CHANGES ITS MIND!
THAT WAS NOT FUN!
TH-THUMPP
AT LEAST IT DIDN'T LEAVE CHEW MARKS!
TROUBLEMAKERS!
GET OFF MY BOAT!
CAPTAIN CHARON
BUT– BUT THOSE UGLY THINGS STARTED IT!
I THOUGHT THEY WERE CUTE.
WAIT!

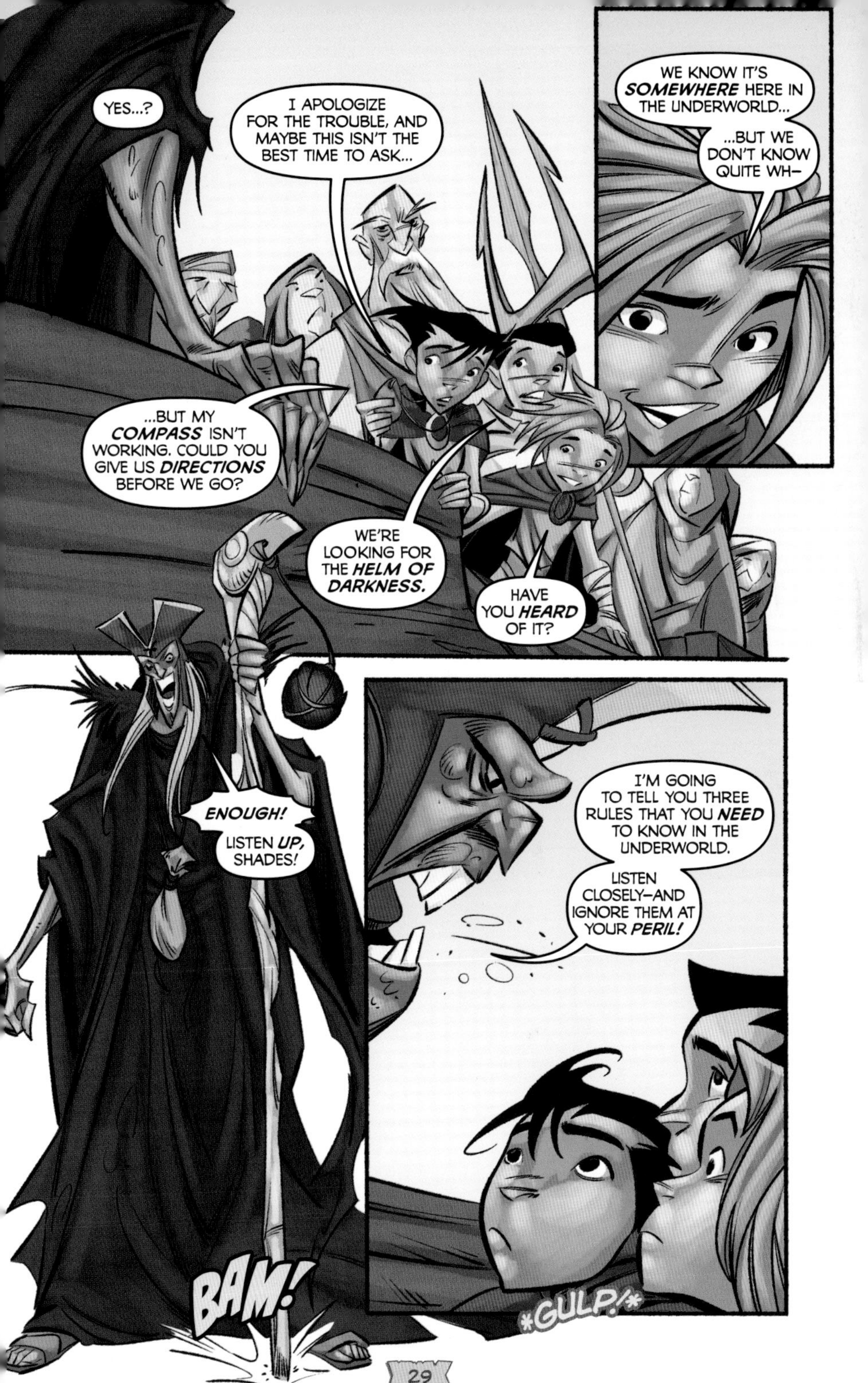
YES...?
I APOLOGIZE FOR THE TROUBLE, AND MAYBE THIS ISN'T THE BEST TIME TO ASK...
WE KNOW IT'S SOMEWHERE HERE IN THE UNDERWORLD...
...BUT WE DON'T KNOW QUITE WH—
...BUT MY COMPASS ISN'T WORKING. COULD YOU GIVE US DIRECTIONS BEFORE WE GO?
WE'RE LOOKING FOR THE HELM OF DARKNESS.
HAVE YOU HEARD OF IT?
ENOUGH!
LISTEN UP, SHADES!
BAM!
I'M GOING TO TELL YOU THREE RULES THAT YOU NEED TO KNOW IN THE UNDERWORLD.
LISTEN CLOSELY—AND IGNORE THEM AT YOUR PERIL!
GULP!

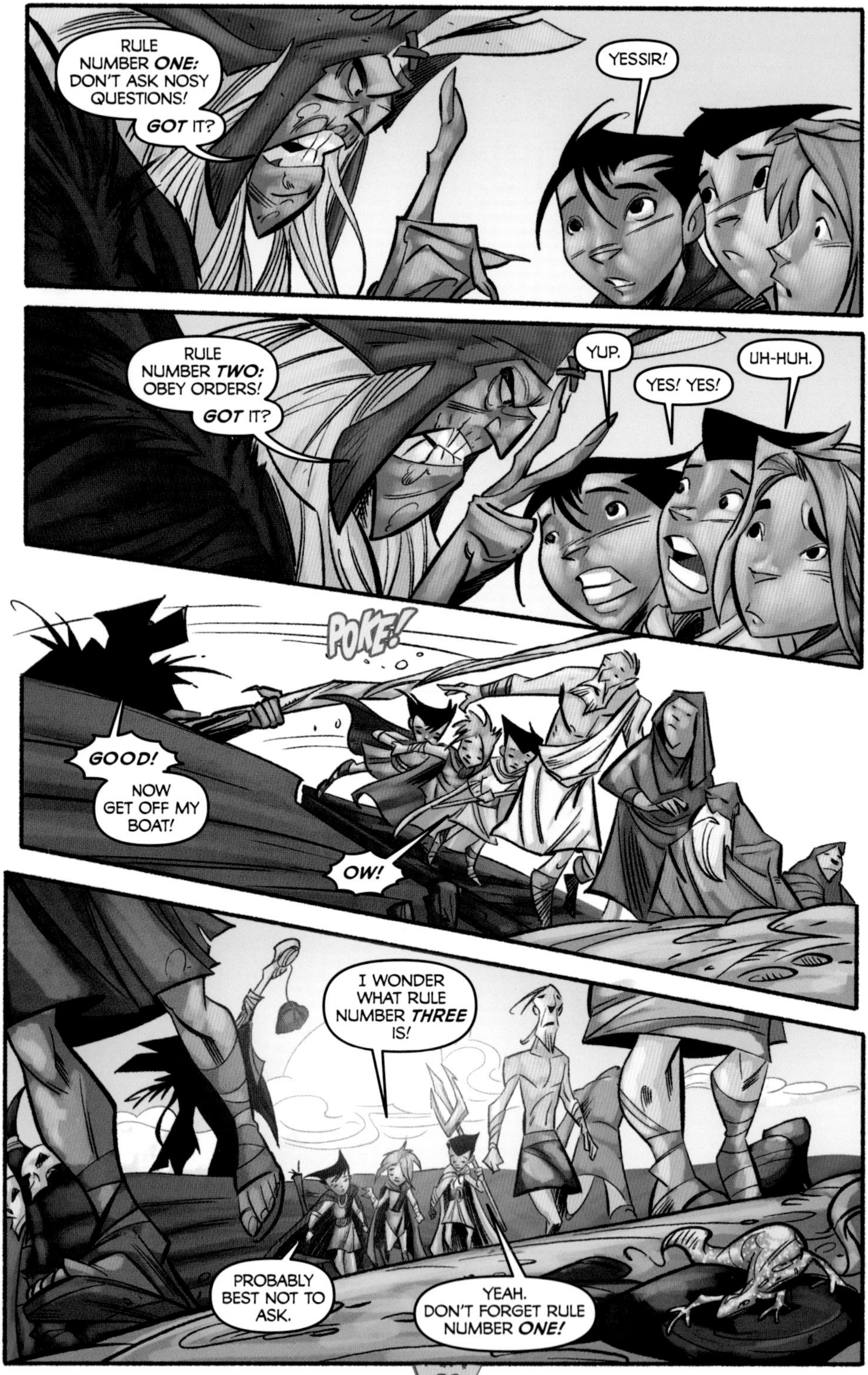
RULE NUMBER ONE: DON'T ASK NOSY QUESTIONS!
GOT IT?
YESSIR!
RULE NUMBER TWO: OBEY ORDERS!
GOT IT?
YUP.
YES! YES!
UH-HUH.
POKE!
GOOD!
NOW GET OFF MY BOAT!
OW!
I WONDER WHAT RULE NUMBER THREE IS!
PROBABLY BEST NOT TO ASK.
YEAH. DON'T FORGET RULE NUMBER ONE!

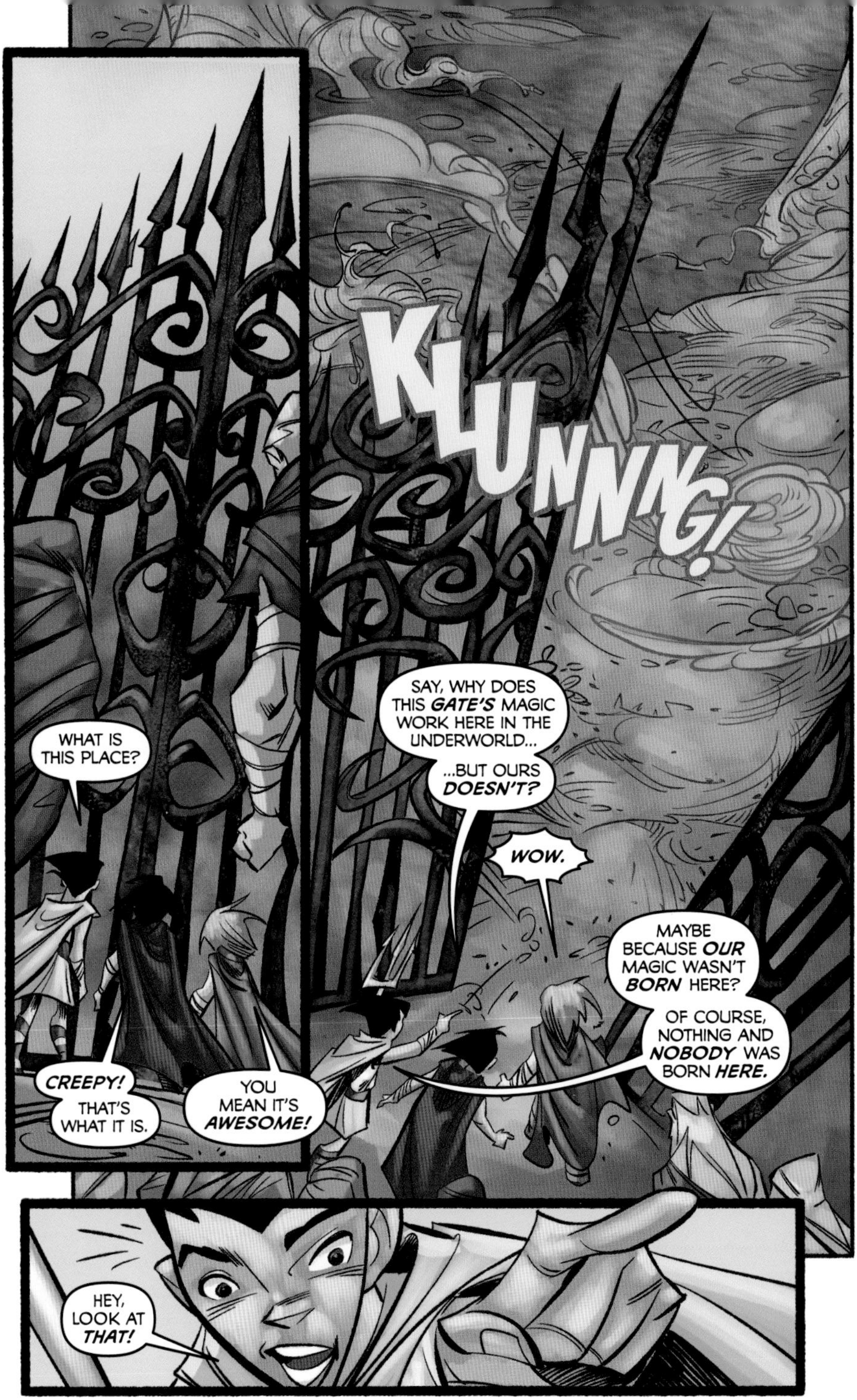
KLUNNNG!
WHAT IS THIS PLACE?
CREEPY! THAT'S WHAT IT IS.
YOU MEAN IT'S AWESOME!
SAY, WHY DOES THIS GATE'S MAGIC WORK HERE IN THE UNDERWORLD...
...BUT OURS DOESN'T?
WOW.
MAYBE BECAUSE OUR MAGIC WASN'T BORN HERE?
OF COURSE, NOTHING AND NOBODY WAS BORN HERE.
HEY, LOOK AT THAT!

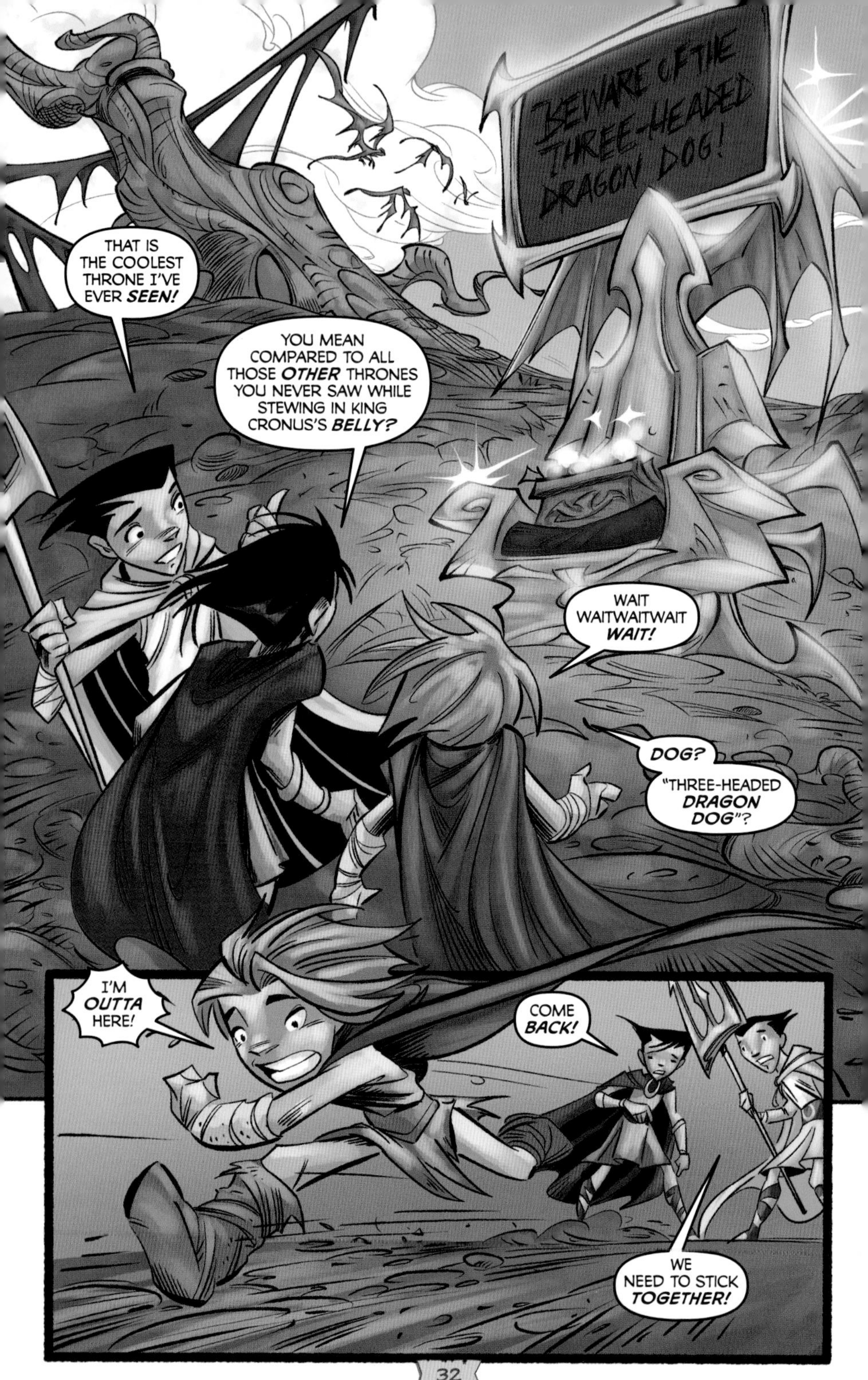
BEWARE OF THE THREE-HEADED DRAGON DOG!
THAT IS THE COOLEST THRONE I'VE EVER *SEEN!*
YOU MEAN COMPARED TO ALL THOSE *OTHER* THRONES YOU NEVER SAW WHILE STEWING IN KING CRONUS'S *BELLY?*
WAIT WAITWAITWAIT *WAIT!*
DOG?
"THREE-HEADED *DRAGON DOG*"?
I'M *OUTTA* HERE!
COME *BACK!*
WE NEED TO STICK *TOGETHER!*

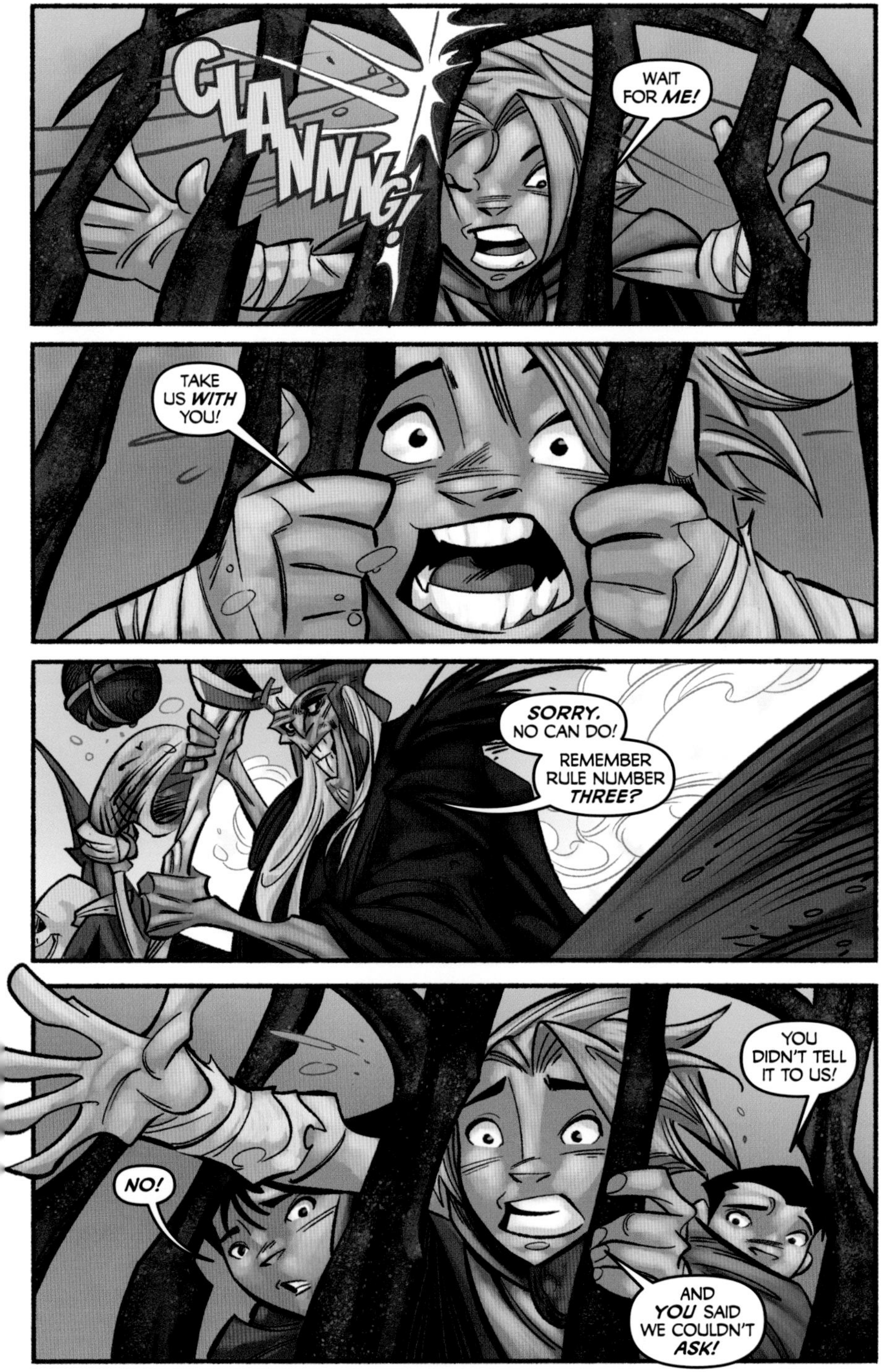
CLANNNG!
WAIT FOR ME!
TAKE US WITH YOU!
SORRY. NO CAN DO!
REMEMBER RULE NUMBER THREE?
YOU DIDN'T TELL IT TO US!
NO!
AND YOU SAID WE COULDN'T ASK!

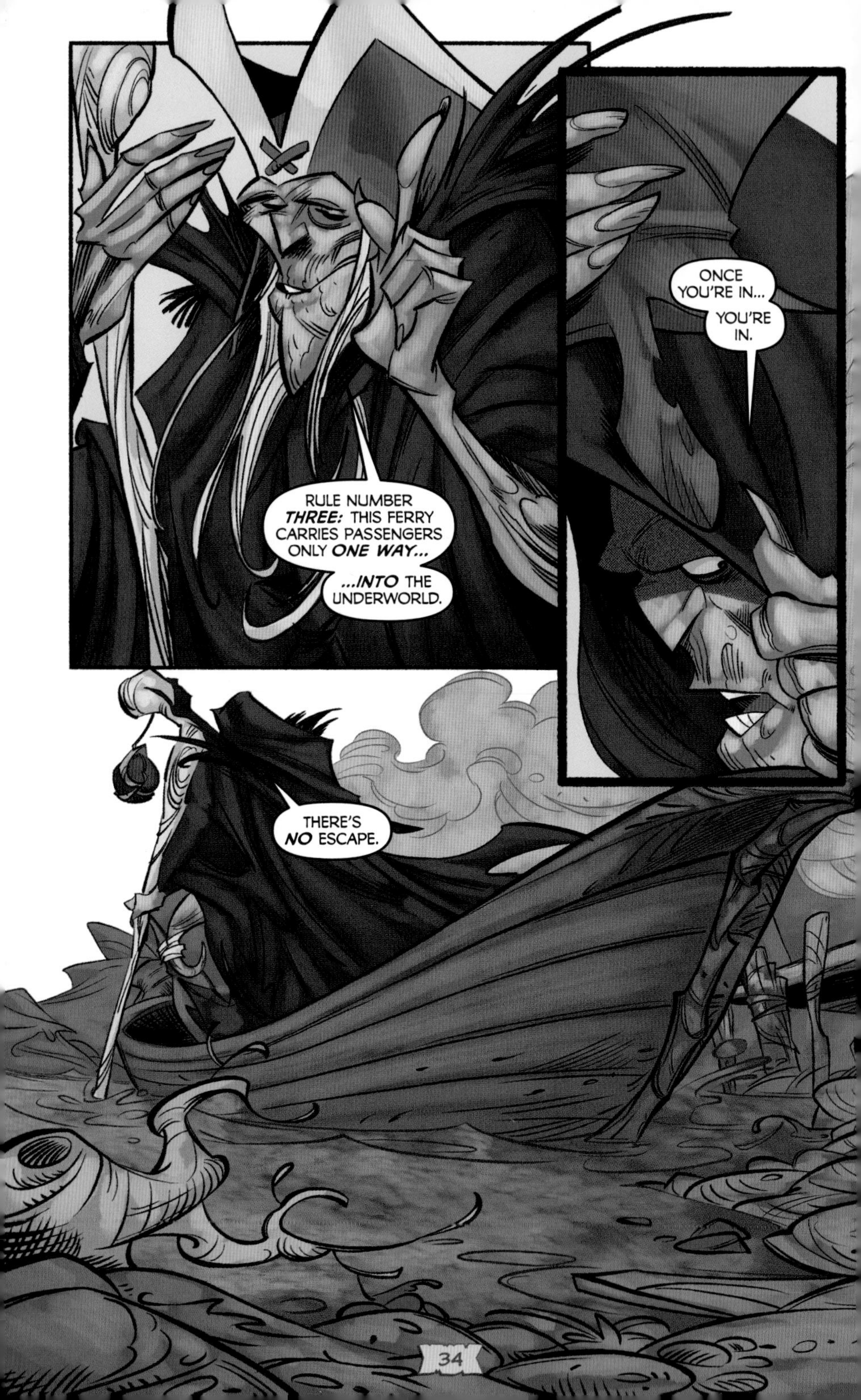

RULE NUMBER *THREE:* THIS FERRY CARRIES PASSENGERS ONLY *ONE WAY...*
...INTO THE UNDERWORLD.
ONCE YOU'RE IN...
YOU'RE IN.
THERE'S *NO* ESCAPE.

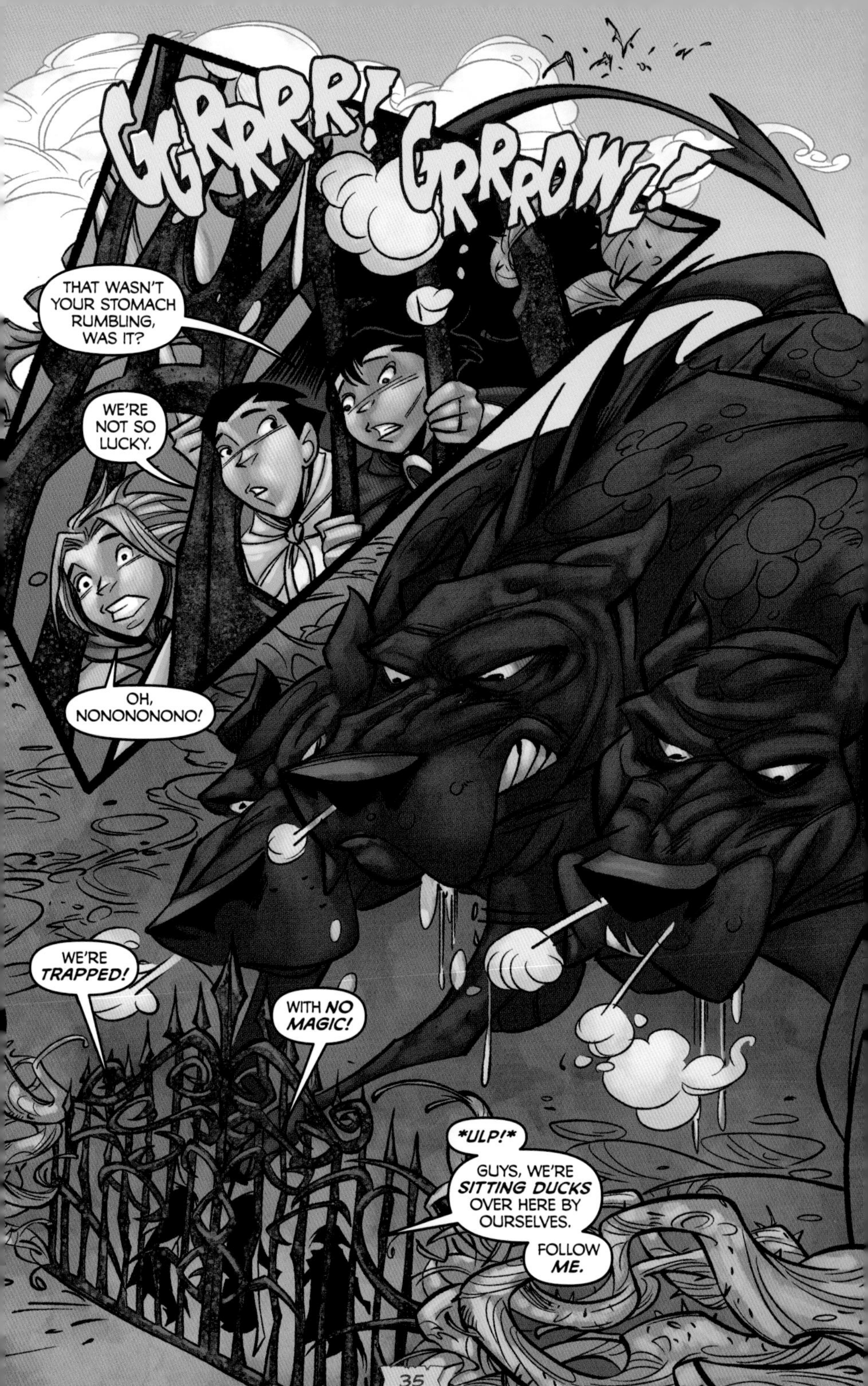
GGRRRR! GRRROWL!
THAT WASN'T YOUR STOMACH RUMBLING, WAS IT?
WE'RE NOT SO LUCKY.
OH, NONONONONO!
WE'RE *TRAPPED!*
WITH **NO MAGIC!**
ULP!
GUYS, WE'RE ***SITTING DUCKS*** OVER HERE BY OURSELVES.
FOLLOW ***ME.***

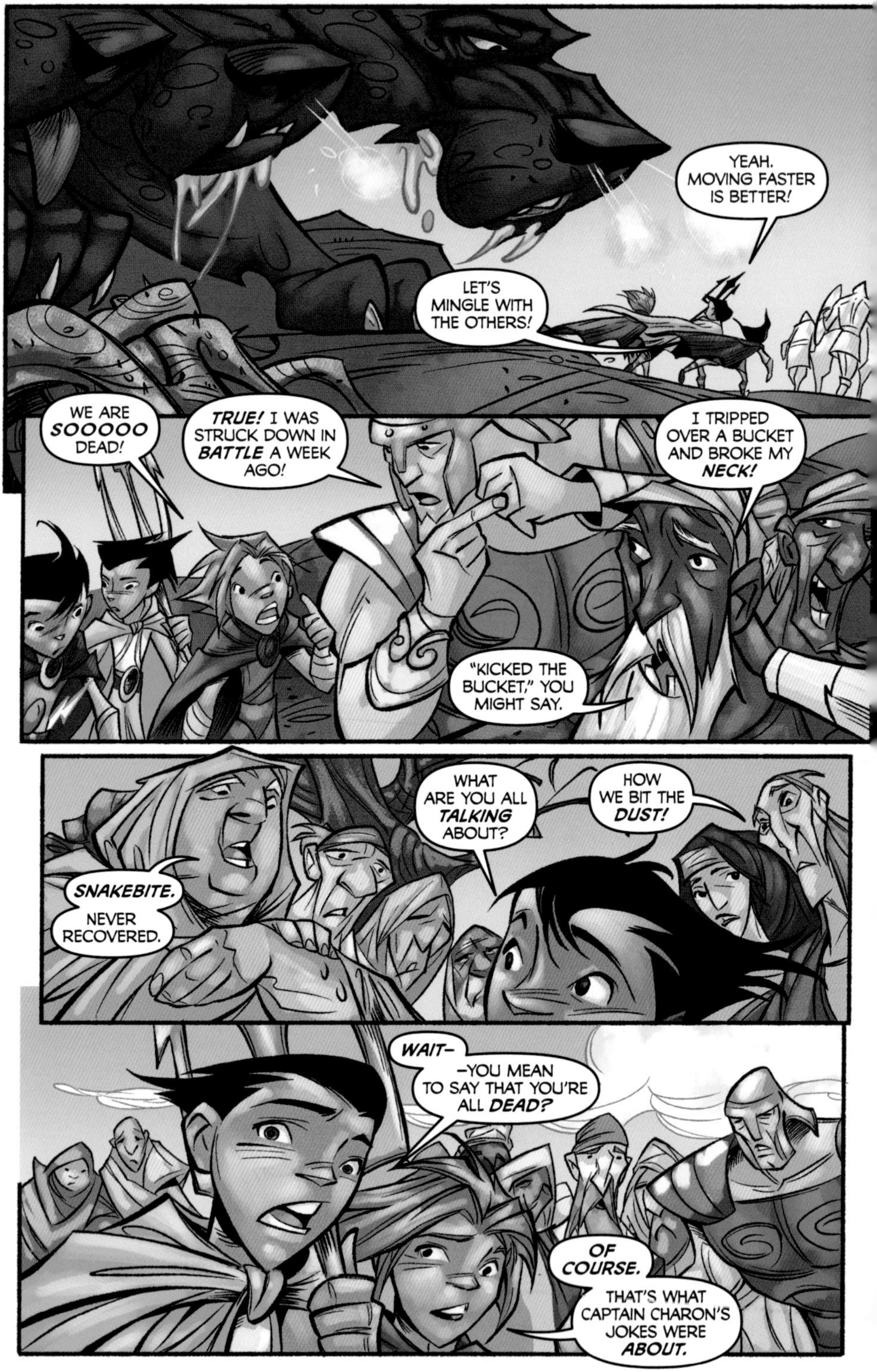
LET'S MINGLE WITH THE OTHERS!
YEAH. MOVING FASTER IS BETTER!
WE ARE SOOOOO DEAD!
TRUE! I WAS STRUCK DOWN IN BATTLE A WEEK AGO!
I TRIPPED OVER A BUCKET AND BROKE MY NECK!
"KICKED THE BUCKET," YOU MIGHT SAY.
SNAKEBITE.
NEVER RECOVERED.
WHAT ARE YOU ALL TALKING ABOUT?
HOW WE BIT THE DUST!
WAIT–
–YOU MEAN TO SAY THAT YOU'RE ALL DEAD?
OF COURSE.
THAT'S WHAT CAPTAIN CHARON'S JOKES WERE ABOUT.

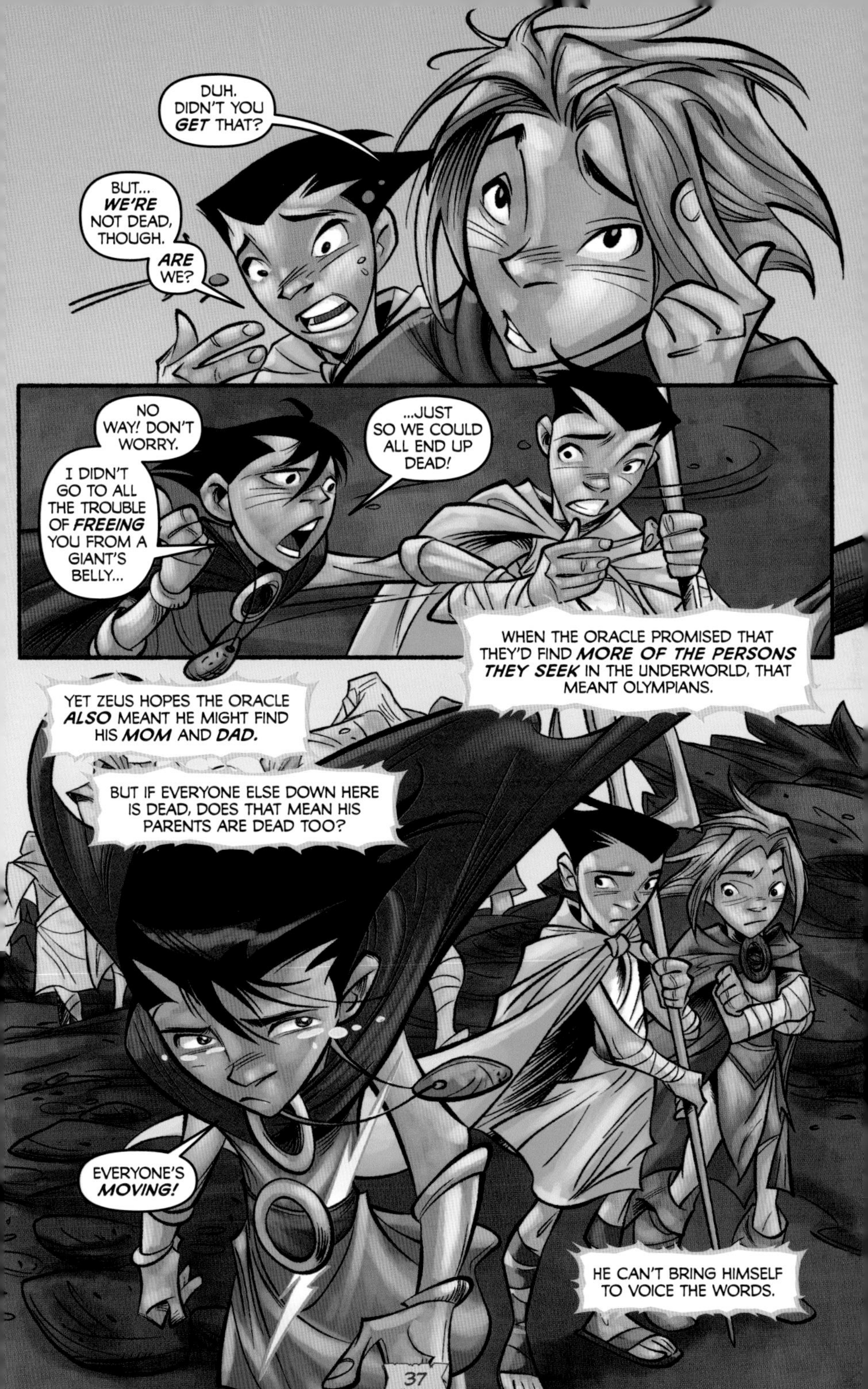
DUH. DIDN'T YOU GET THAT?
BUT... WE'RE NOT DEAD, THOUGH.
ARE WE?
NO WAY! DON'T WORRY.
I DIDN'T GO TO ALL THE TROUBLE OF FREEING YOU FROM A GIANT'S BELLY...
...JUST SO WE COULD ALL END UP DEAD!
WHEN THE ORACLE PROMISED THAT THEY'D FIND MORE OF THE PERSONS THEY SEEK IN THE UNDERWORLD, THAT MEANT OLYMPIANS.
YET ZEUS HOPES THE ORACLE ALSO MEANT HE MIGHT FIND HIS MOM AND DAD.
BUT IF EVERYONE ELSE DOWN HERE IS DEAD, DOES THAT MEAN HIS PARENTS ARE DEAD TOO?
EVERYONE'S MOVING!
HE CAN'T BRING HIMSELF TO VOICE THE WORDS.

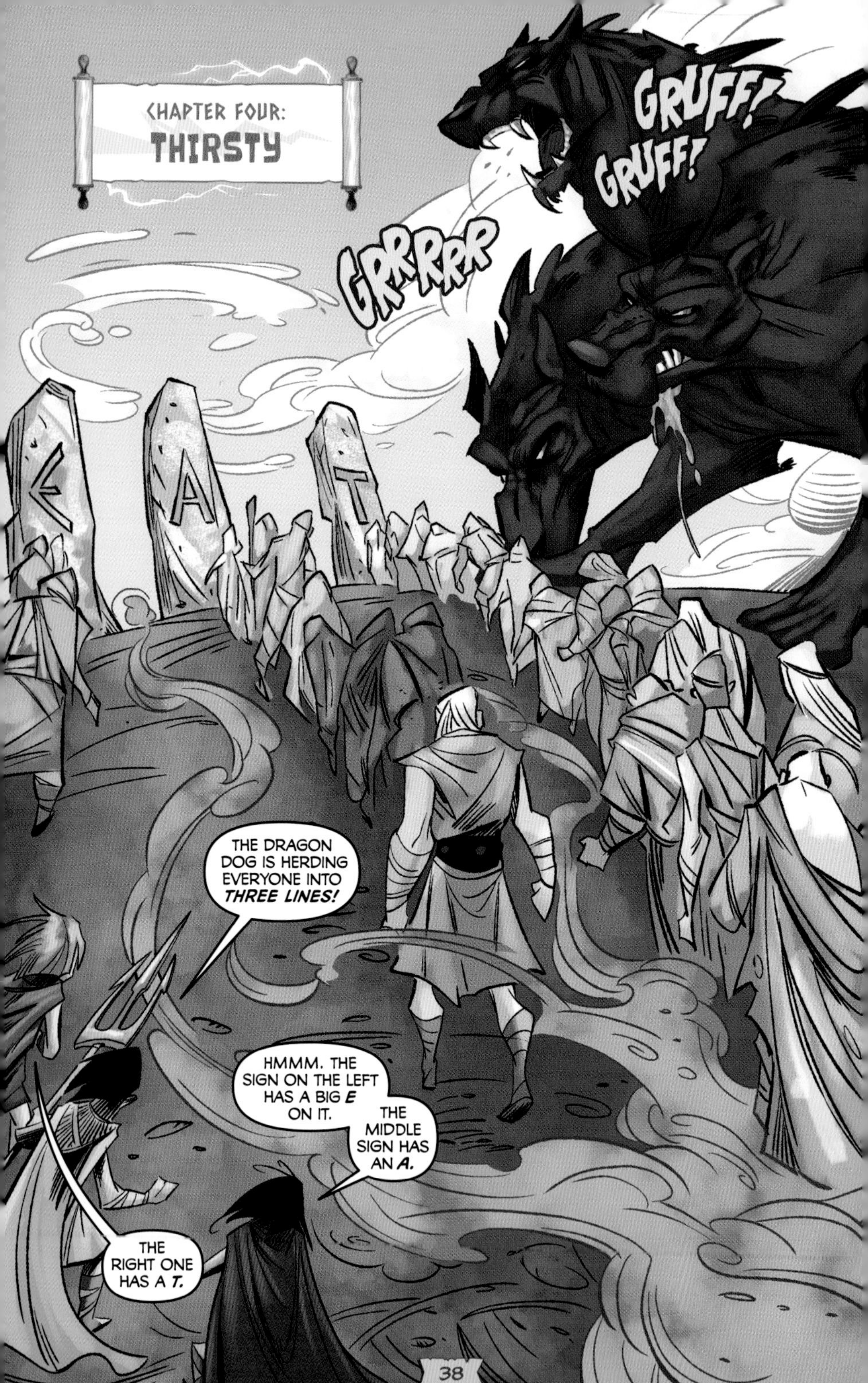
CHAPTER FOUR:
THIRSTY
GRUFF!
GRUFF!
GRRRRR
E
A
T
THE DRAGON DOG IS HERDING EVERYONE INTO *THREE LINES!*
HMMM. THE SIGN ON THE LEFT HAS A BIG *E* ON IT.
THE MIDDLE SIGN HAS AN *A.*
THE RIGHT ONE HAS A *T.*

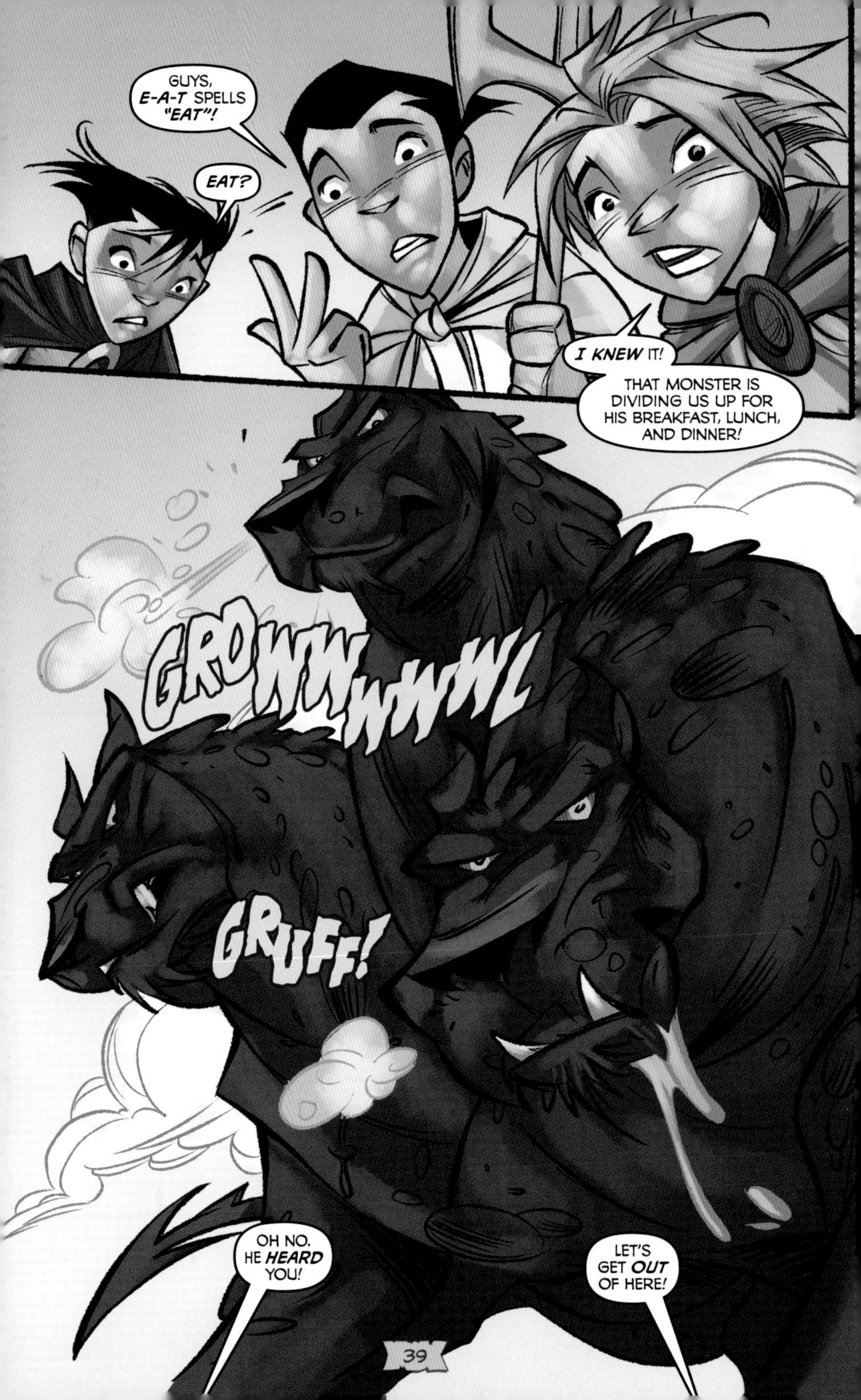
GUYS, E-A-T SPELLS "EAT"!
EAT?
I KNEW IT!
THAT MONSTER IS DIVIDING US UP FOR HIS BREAKFAST, LUNCH, AND DINNER!
GROWWWWWWL
GRUFF!
OH NO. HE HEARD YOU!
LET'S GET OUT OF HERE!

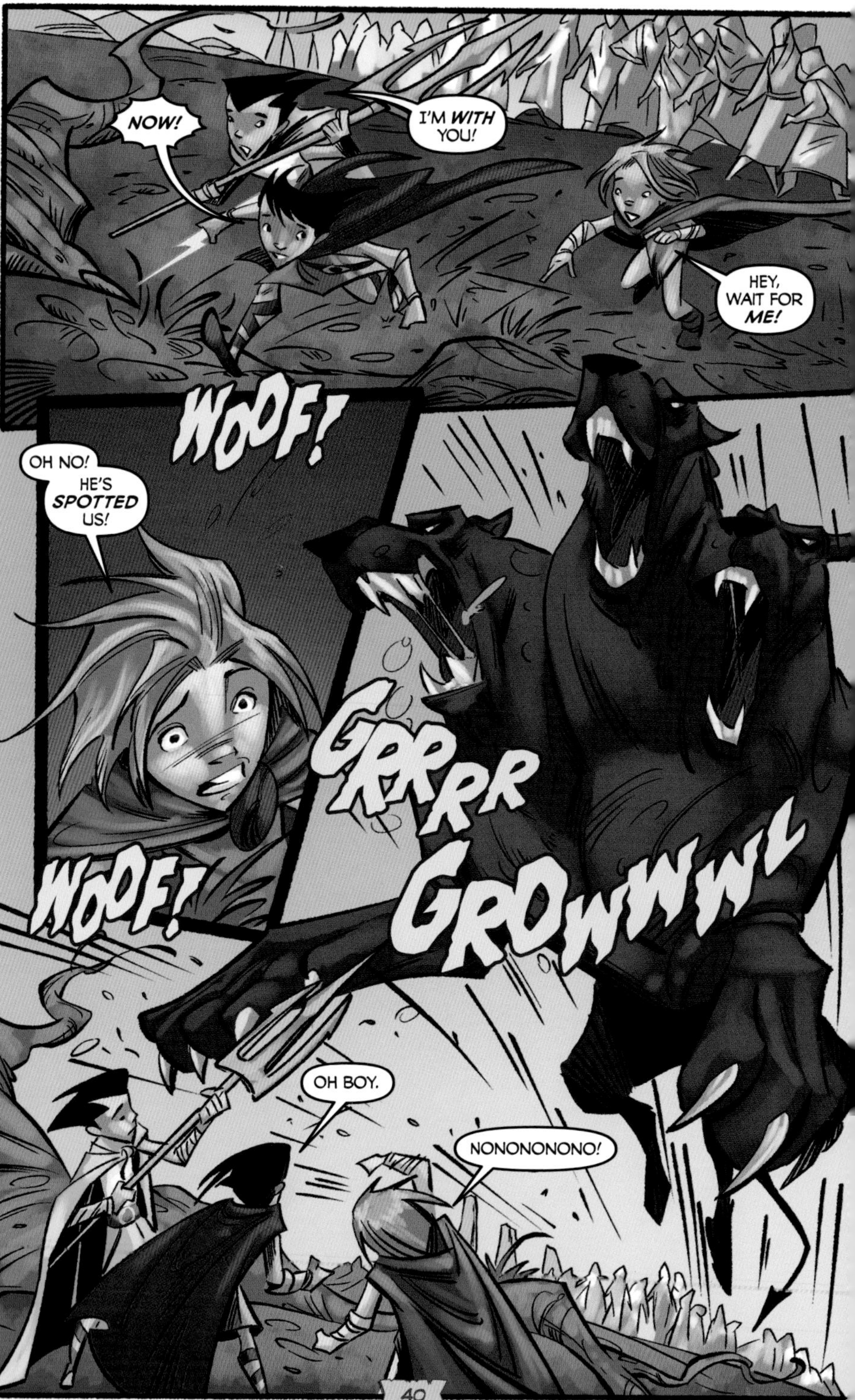
NOW!
I'M WITH YOU!
HEY, WAIT FOR ME!
WOOF!
OH NO! HE'S SPOTTED US!
GRRRR
WOOF!
GROWWWL
OH BOY.
NONONONONO!

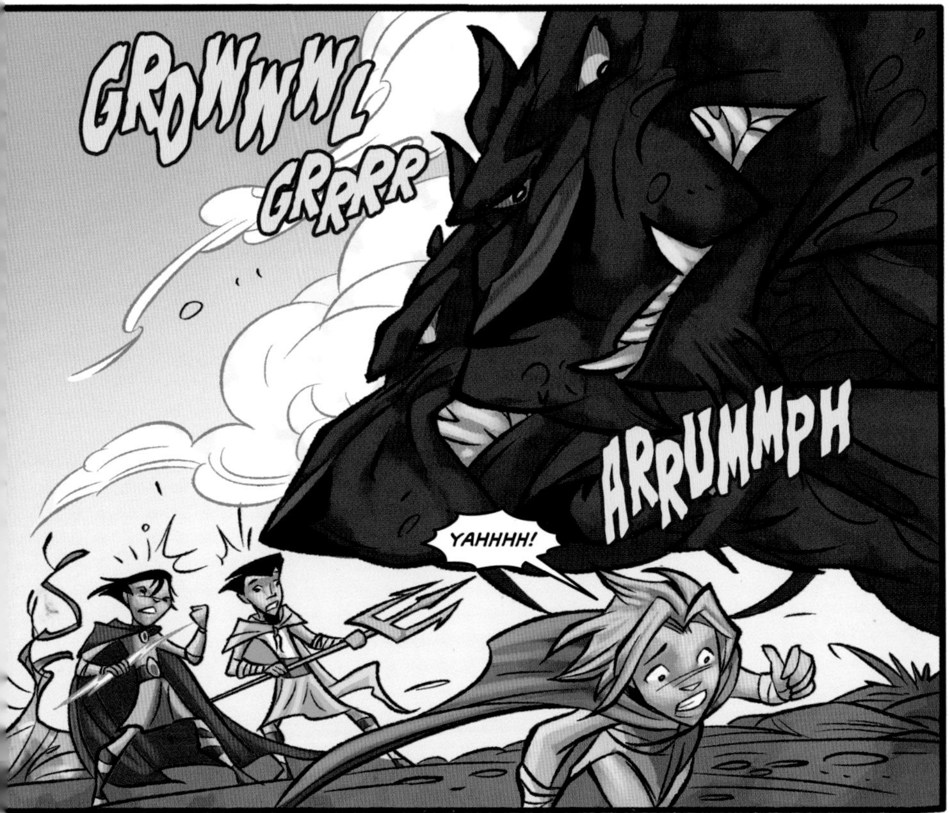
GROWWWL
GRRRR
ARRUMMPH
YAHHHH!

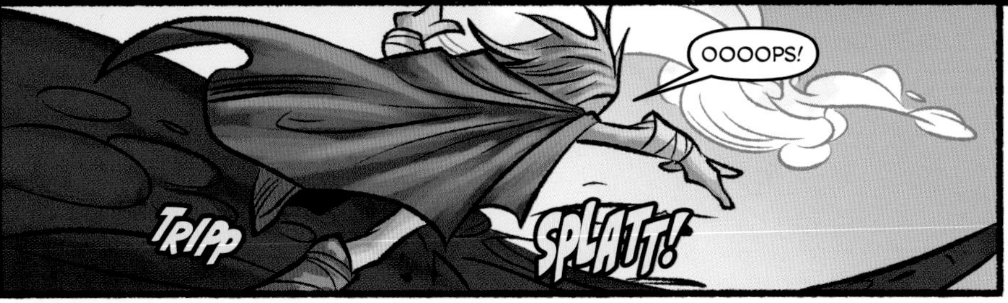
OOOOPS!
TRIPP
SPLATT!

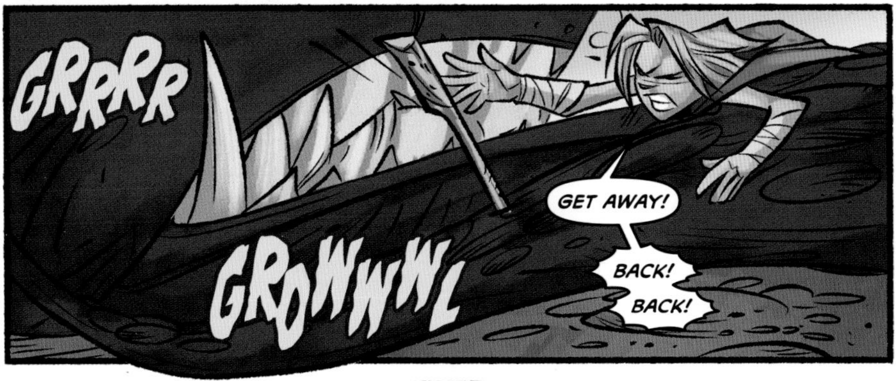
GRRRR
GET AWAY!
BACK!
BACK!
GROWWWL

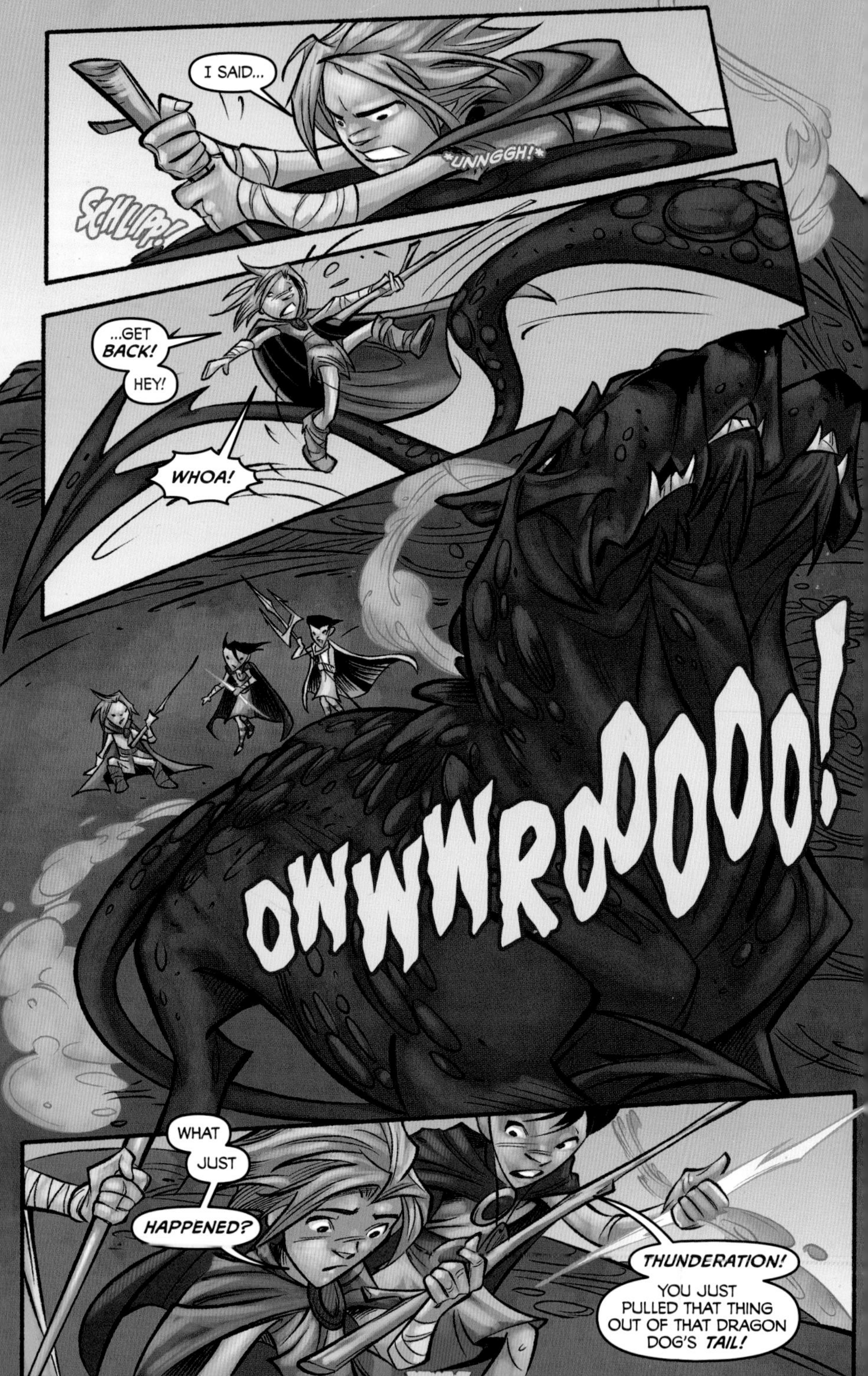
I SAID...
UNNGGH!
SCHLIPP!
...GET BACK!
HEY!
WHOA!
OWWWROOOOOO!
WHAT JUST HAPPENED?
THUNDERATION!
YOU JUST PULLED THAT THING OUT OF THAT DRAGON DOG'S TAIL!

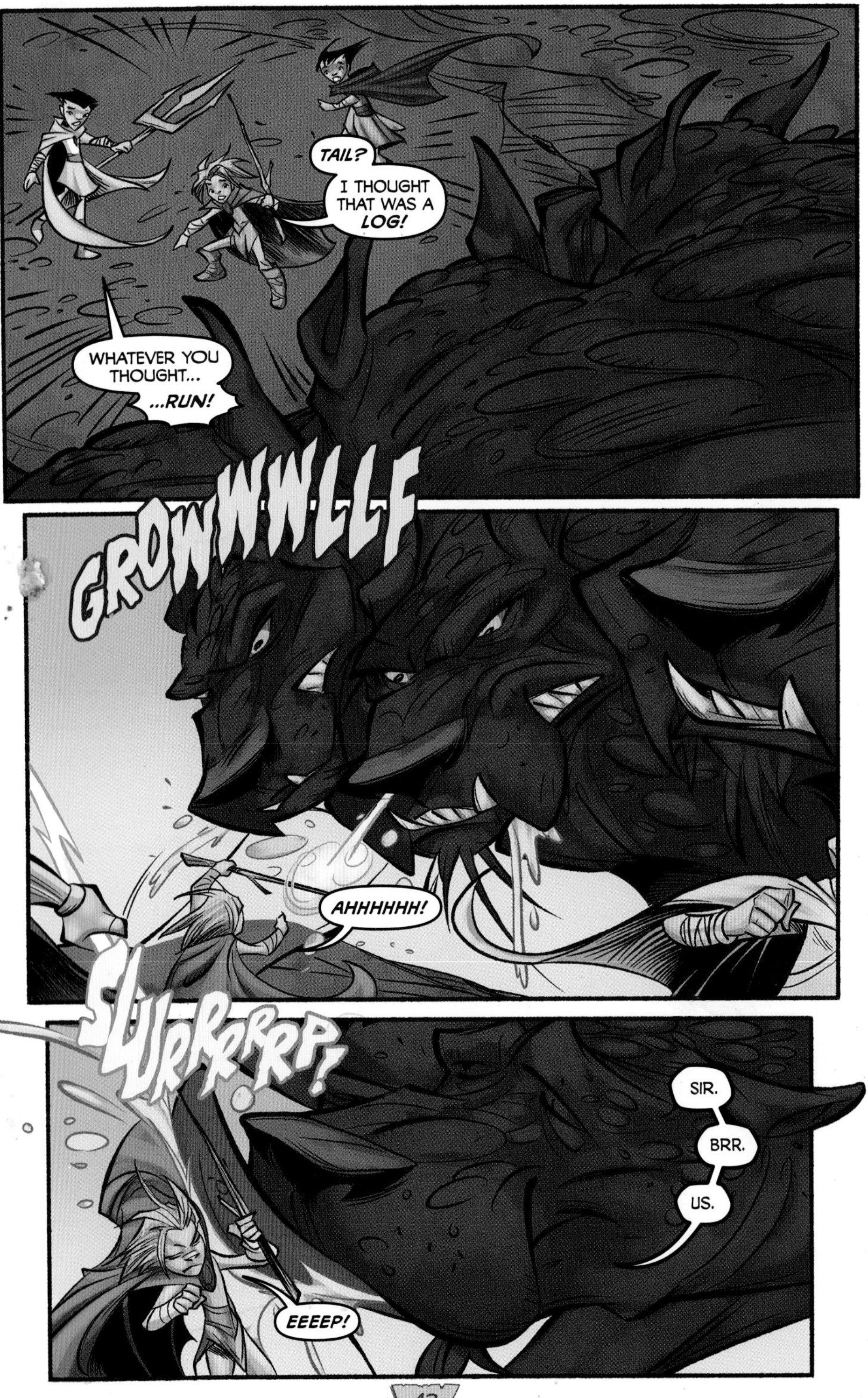
TAIL?
I THOUGHT THAT WAS A LOG!
WHATEVER YOU THOUGHT... ...RUN!
GROWWWLLF
AHHHHHH!
SLURRRRRP!
SIR.
BRR.
US.
EEEEP!

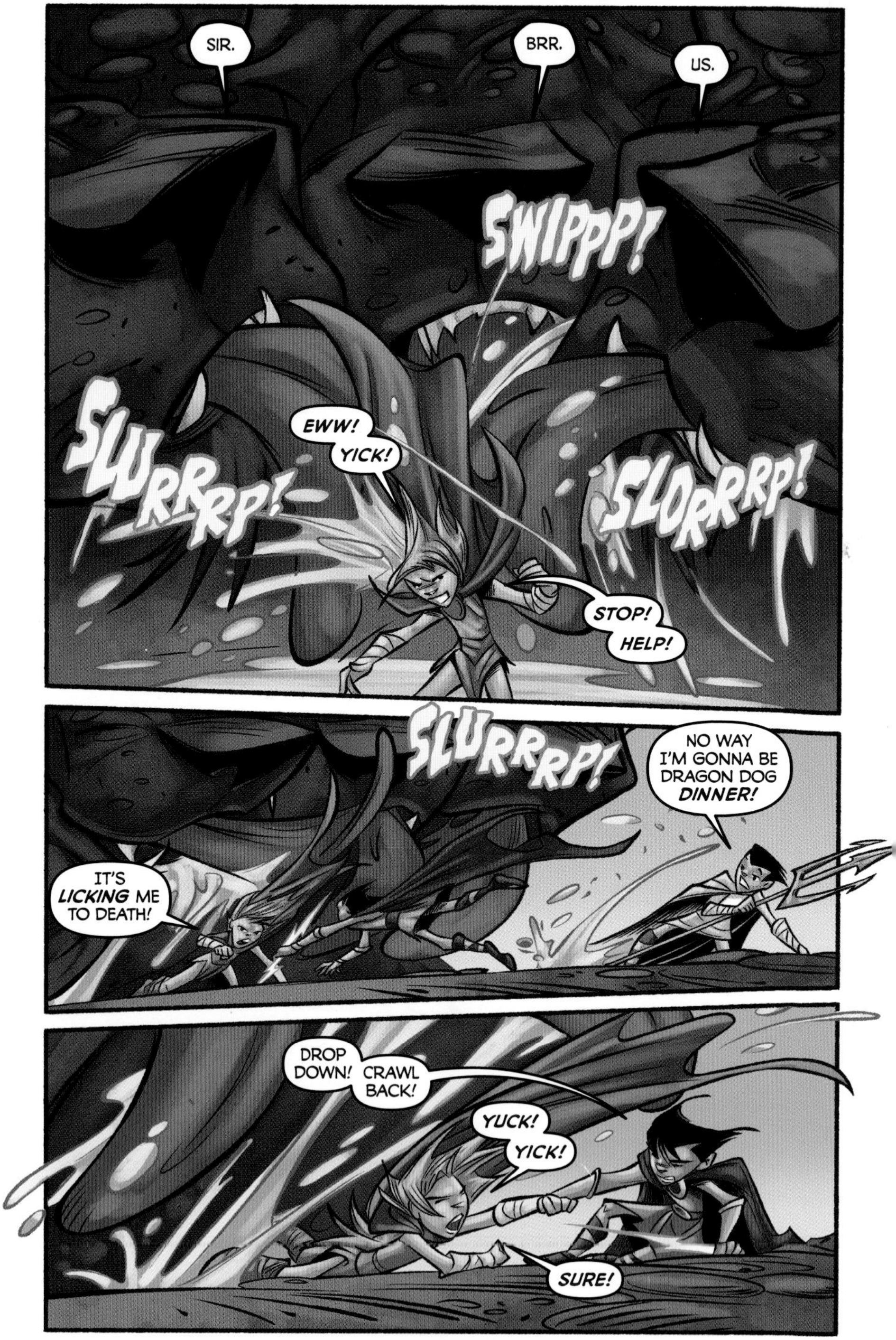
SIR.
BRR.
US.
SWIPPP!
EWW!
YICK!
SLURRRP!
SLORRRP!
STOP!
HELP!
SLURRRP!
NO WAY I'M GONNA BE DRAGON DOG *DINNER!*
IT'S *LICKING* ME TO DEATH!
DROP DOWN!
CRAWL BACK!
YUCK!
YICK!
SURE!

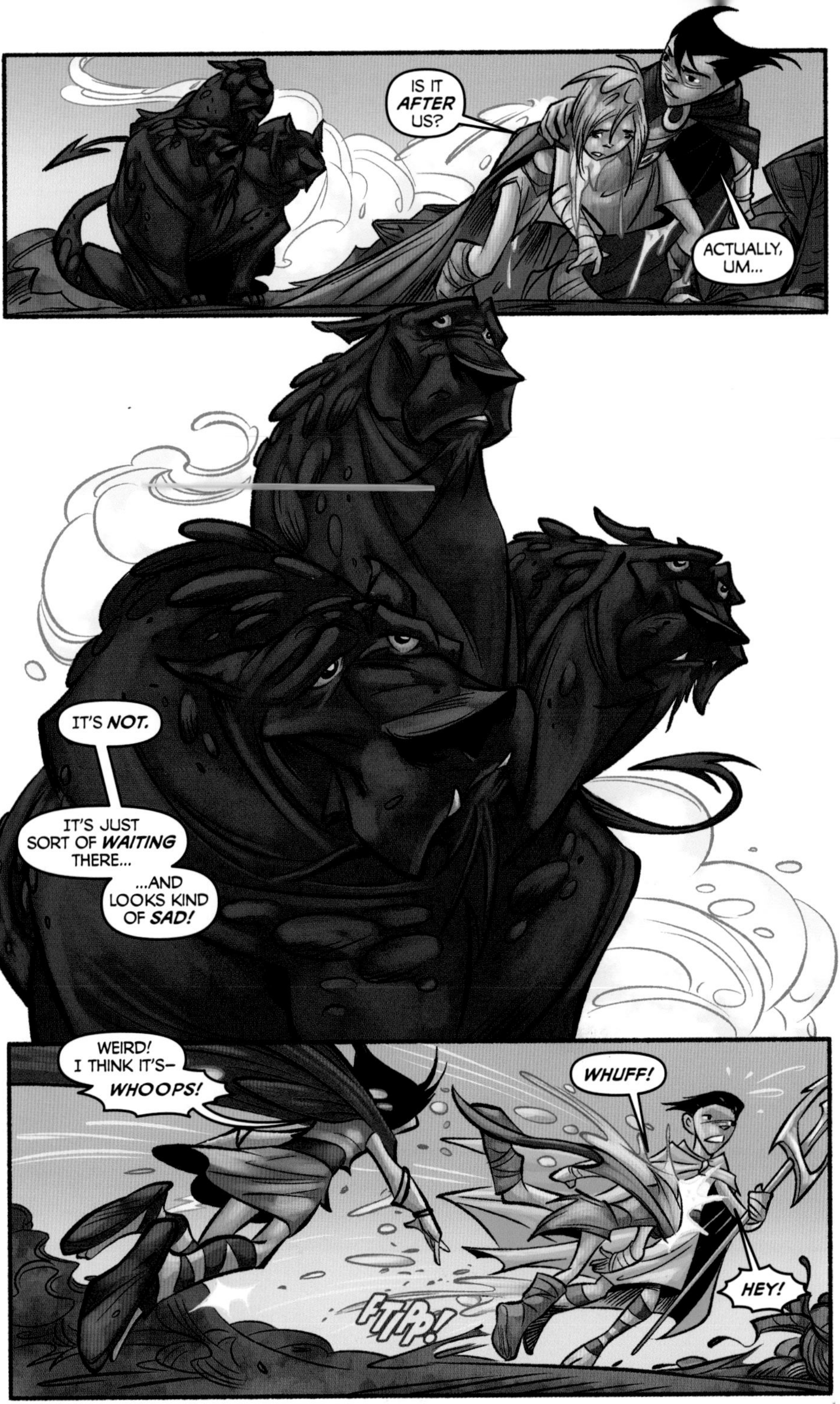
IS IT AFTER US?
ACTUALLY, UM...
IT'S NOT.
IT'S JUST SORT OF WAITING THERE...
...AND LOOKS KIND OF SAD!
WEIRD! I THINK IT'S— WHOOPS!
WHUFF!
FTIPP!
HEY!

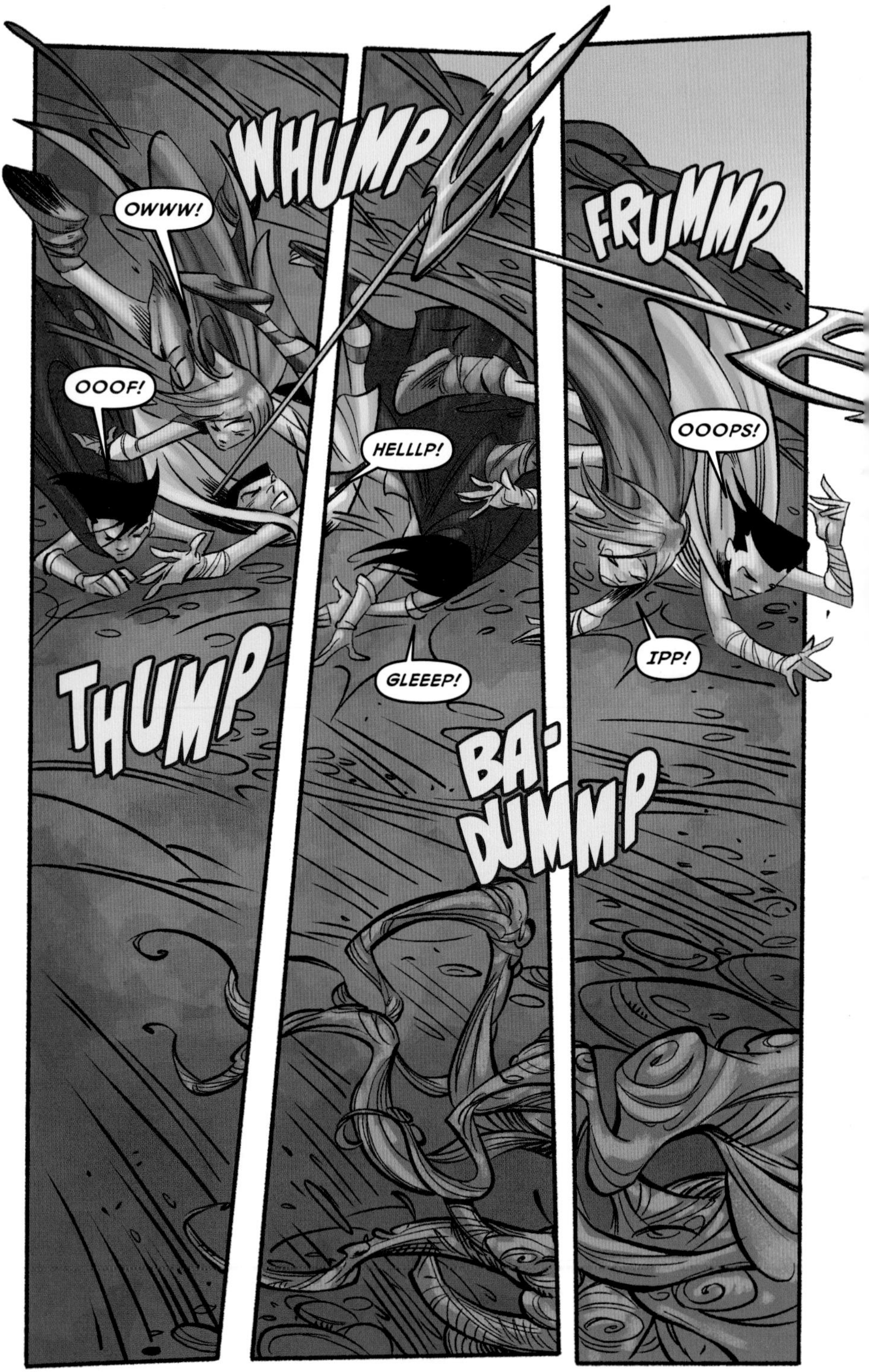
WHUMP
OWWW!
OOOF!
THUMP
HELLLP!
GLEEEP!
FRUMMP
OOOPS!
IPP!
BA-DUMMP

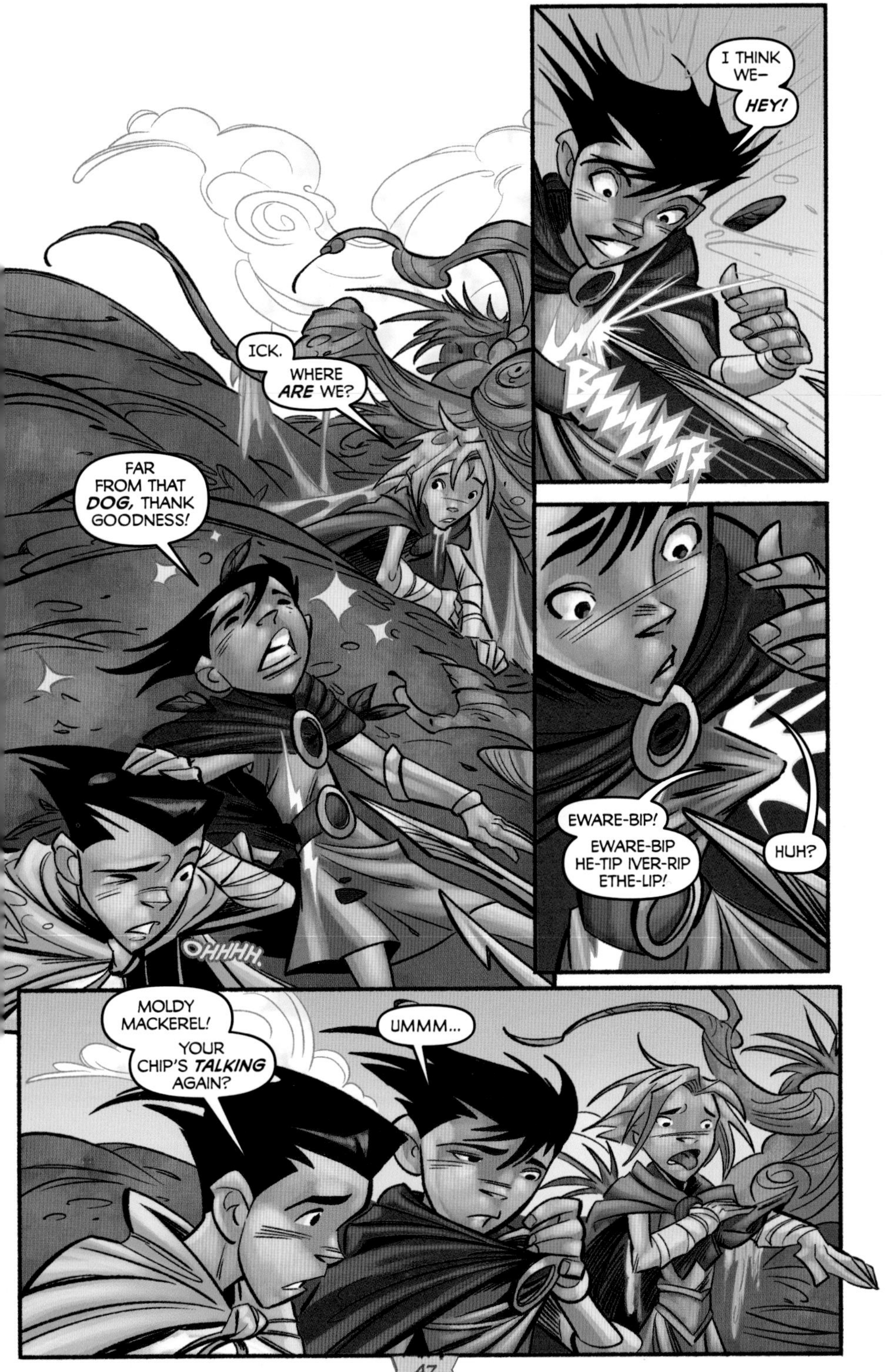
ICK.
WHERE ARE WE?
FAR FROM THAT DOG, THANK GOODNESS!
OHHHH.
I THINK WE– HEY!
BZZZZT!
EWARE-BIP!
EWARE-BIP HE-TIP IVER-RIP ETHE-LIP!
HUH?
MOLDY MACKEREL!
YOUR CHIP'S TALKING AGAIN?
UMMM...

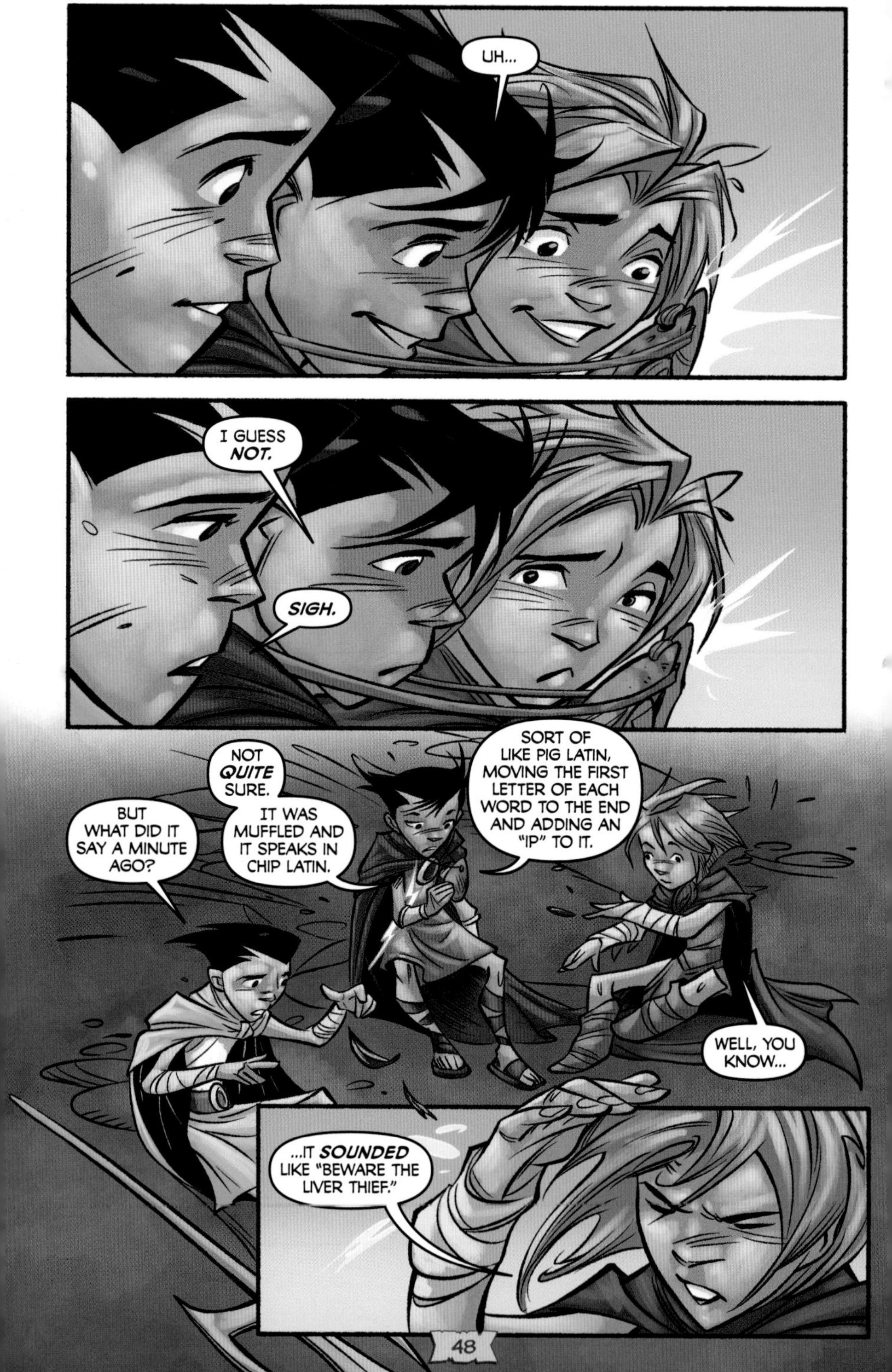
UH...
I GUESS NOT.
SIGH.
BUT WHAT DID IT SAY A MINUTE AGO?
NOT QUITE SURE.
IT WAS MUFFLED AND IT SPEAKS IN CHIP LATIN.
SORT OF LIKE PIG LATIN, MOVING THE FIRST LETTER OF EACH WORD TO THE END AND ADDING AN "IP" TO IT.
WELL, YOU KNOW...
...IT SOUNDED LIKE "BEWARE THE LIVER THIEF."

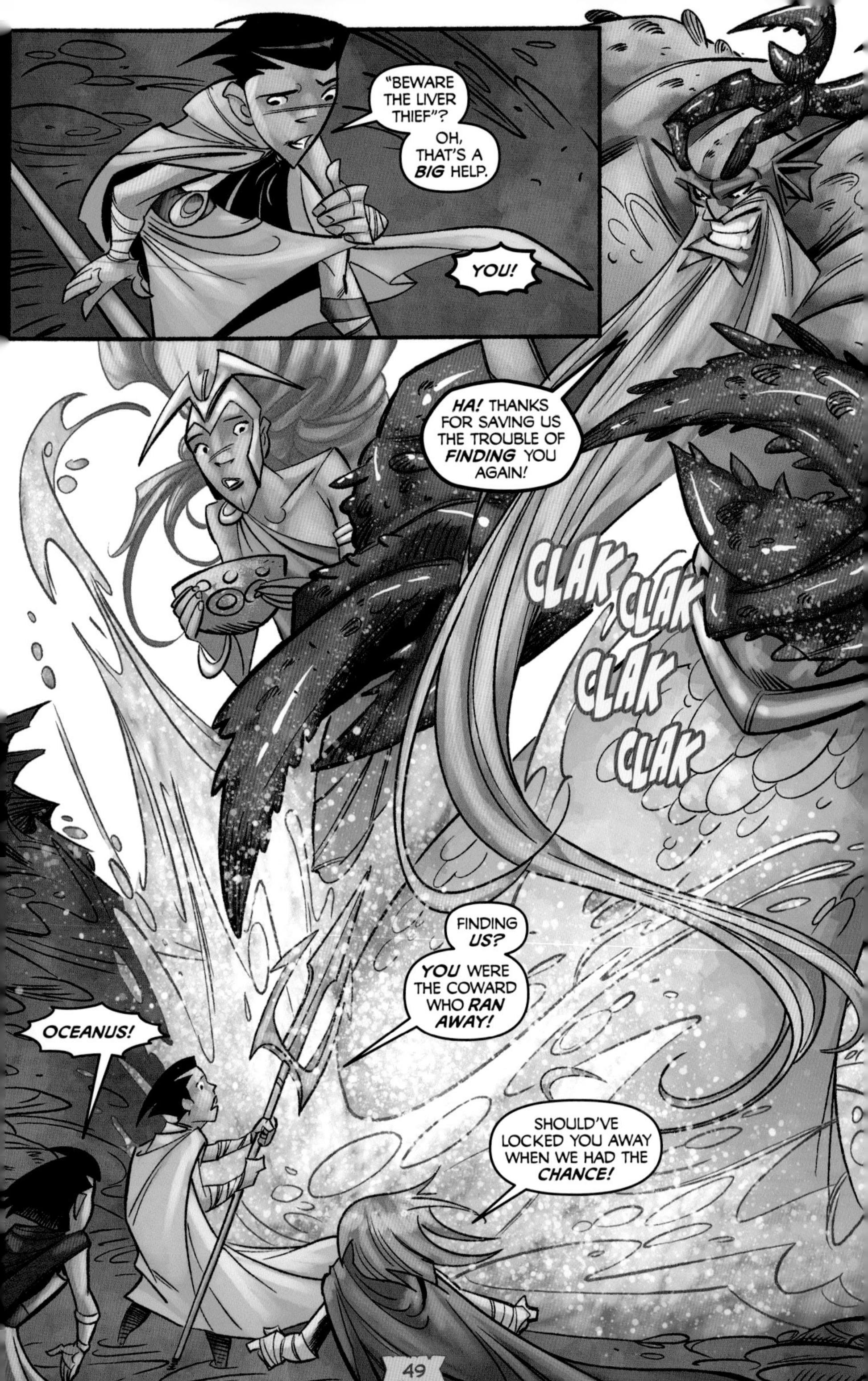
"BEWARE THE LIVER THIEF"?
OH, THAT'S A BIG HELP.
YOU!
HA! THANKS FOR SAVING US THE TROUBLE OF FINDING YOU AGAIN!
CLAK CLAK CLAK CLAK
FINDING US?
YOU WERE THE COWARD WHO RAN AWAY!
OCEANUS!
SHOULD'VE LOCKED YOU AWAY WHEN WE HAD THE CHANCE!

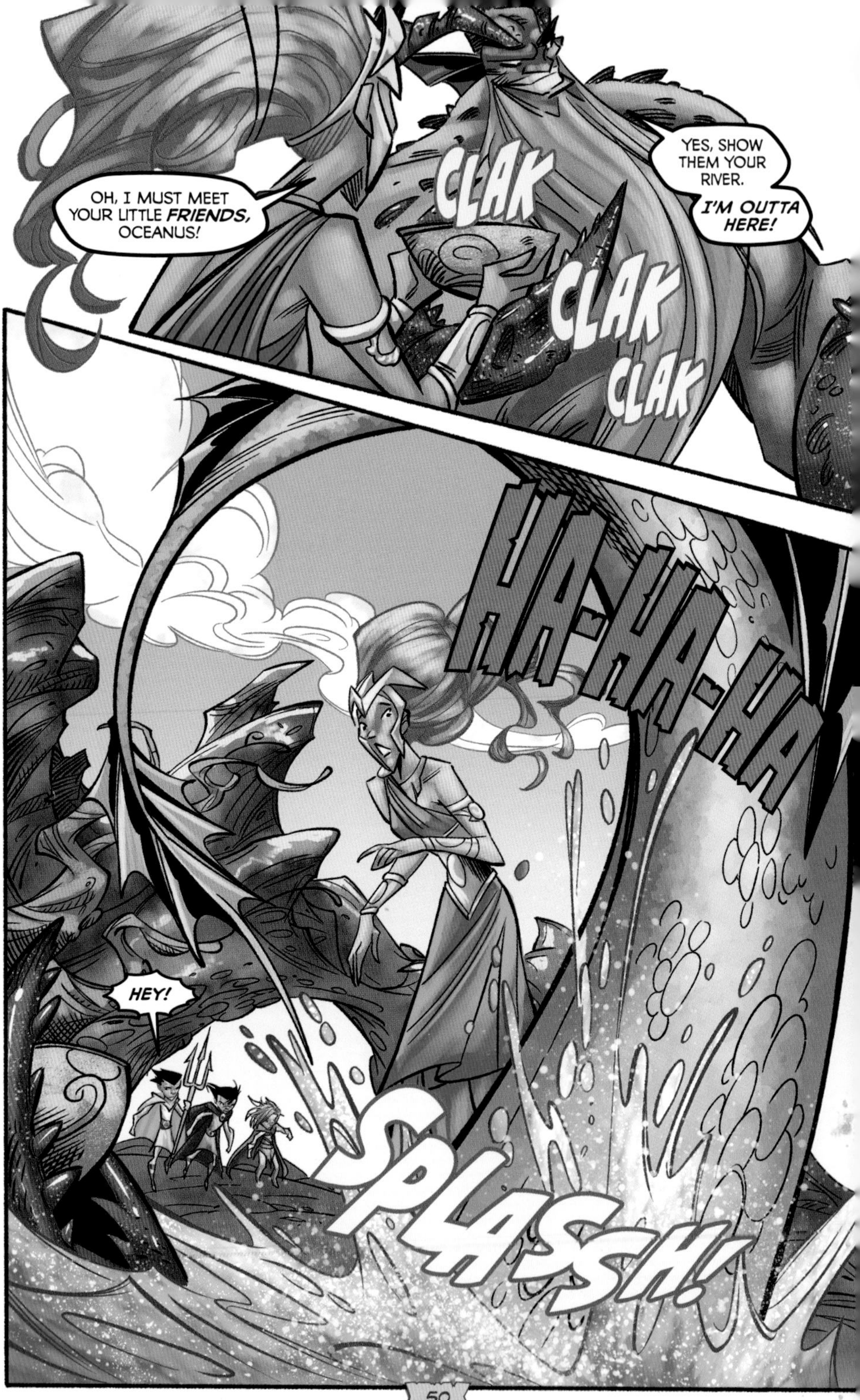
OH, I MUST MEET YOUR LITTLE *FRIENDS,* OCEANUS!
CLAK
CLAK
CLAK
YES, SHOW THEM YOUR RIVER.
I'M OUTTA HERE!
HA-HA-HA-HA
HEY!
SPLASH!

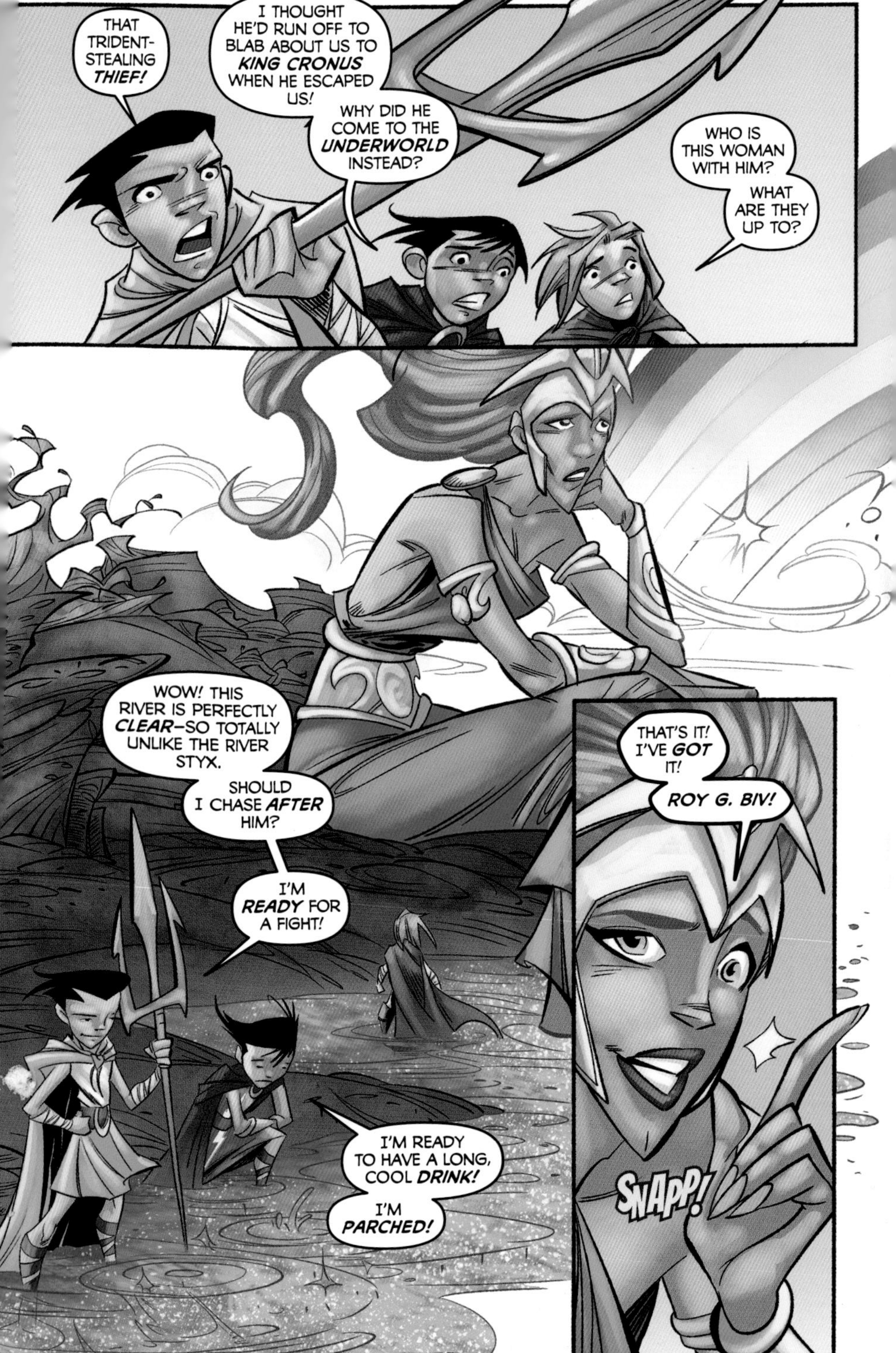
THAT TRIDENT-STEALING THIEF!
I THOUGHT HE'D RUN OFF TO BLAB ABOUT US TO KING CRONUS WHEN HE ESCAPED US!
WHY DID HE COME TO THE UNDERWORLD INSTEAD?
WHO IS THIS WOMAN WITH HIM?
WHAT ARE THEY UP TO?
WOW! THIS RIVER IS PERFECTLY CLEAR—SO TOTALLY UNLIKE THE RIVER STYX.
SHOULD I CHASE AFTER HIM?
I'M READY FOR A FIGHT!
I'M READY TO HAVE A LONG, COOL DRINK!
I'M PARCHED!
THAT'S IT! I'VE GOT IT!
ROY G. BIV!
SNAPP!

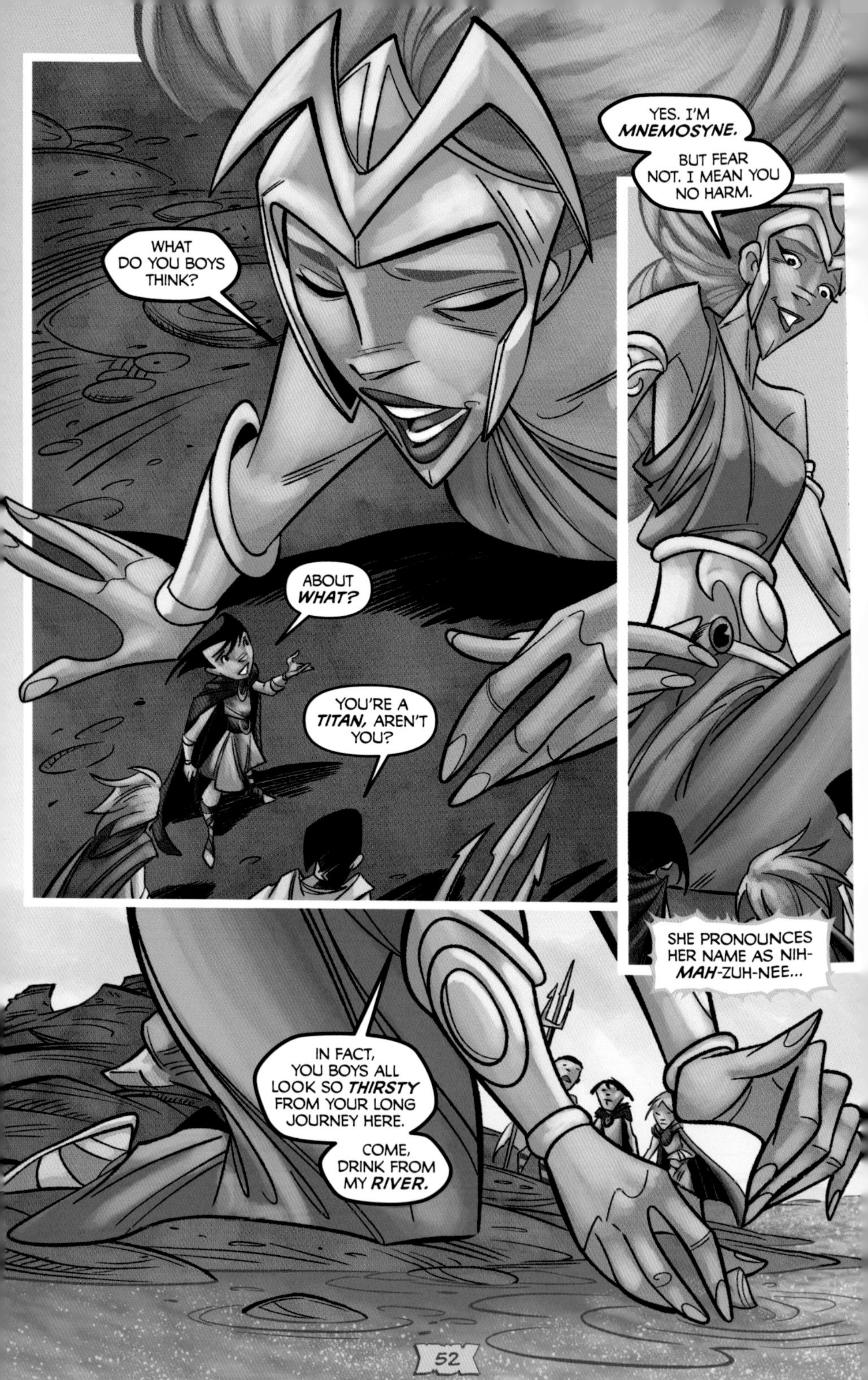
WHAT DO YOU BOYS THINK?
ABOUT *WHAT?*
YOU'RE A *TITAN,* AREN'T YOU?
YES. I'M *MNEMOSYNE.*
BUT FEAR NOT. I MEAN YOU NO HARM.
SHE PRONOUNCES HER NAME AS NIH-*MAH*-ZUH-NEE...
IN FACT, YOU BOYS ALL LOOK SO *THIRSTY* FROM YOUR LONG JOURNEY HERE.
COME, DRINK FROM MY *RIVER.*

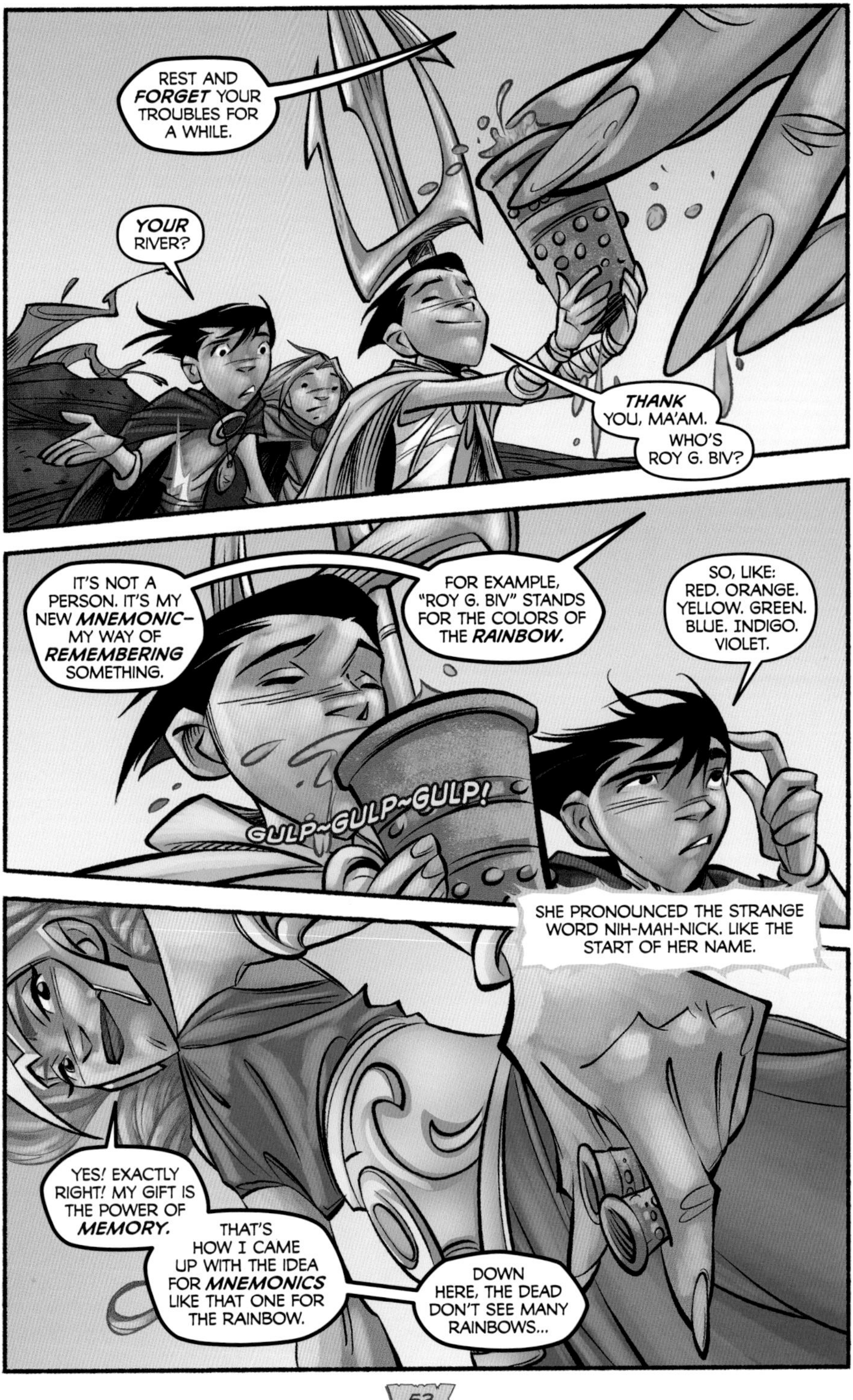
REST AND FORGET YOUR TROUBLES FOR A WHILE.
YOUR RIVER?
THANK YOU, MA'AM.
WHO'S ROY G. BIV?
IT'S NOT A PERSON. IT'S MY NEW MNEMONIC– MY WAY OF REMEMBERING SOMETHING.
FOR EXAMPLE, "ROY G. BIV" STANDS FOR THE COLORS OF THE RAINBOW.
SO, LIKE: RED. ORANGE. YELLOW. GREEN. BLUE. INDIGO. VIOLET.
GULP~GULP~GULP!
SHE PRONOUNCED THE STRANGE WORD NIH-MAH-NICK, LIKE THE START OF HER NAME.
YES! EXACTLY RIGHT! MY GIFT IS THE POWER OF MEMORY.
THAT'S HOW I CAME UP WITH THE IDEA FOR MNEMONICS LIKE THAT ONE FOR THE RAINBOW.
DOWN HERE, THE DEAD DON'T SEE MANY RAINBOWS...

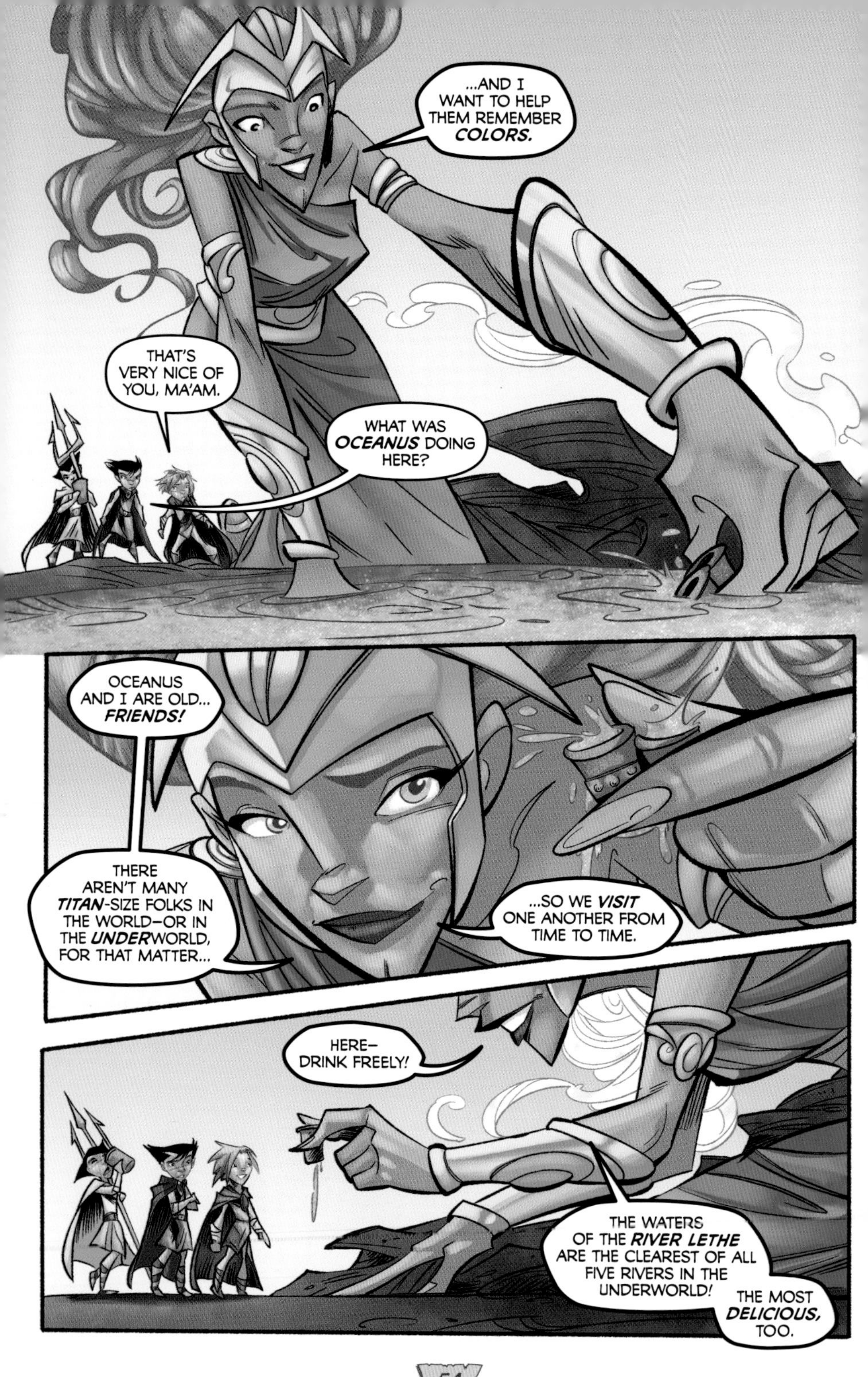
...AND I WANT TO HELP THEM REMEMBER *COLORS.*
THAT'S VERY NICE OF YOU, MA'AM.
WHAT WAS *OCEANUS* DOING HERE?
OCEANUS AND I ARE OLD... *FRIENDS!*
THERE AREN'T MANY *TITAN*-SIZE FOLKS IN THE WORLD—OR IN THE *UNDER*WORLD, FOR THAT MATTER...
...SO WE *VISIT* ONE ANOTHER FROM TIME TO TIME.
HERE— DRINK FREELY!
THE WATERS OF THE *RIVER LETHE* ARE THE CLEAREST OF ALL FIVE RIVERS IN THE UNDERWORLD!
THE MOST *DELICIOUS,* TOO.

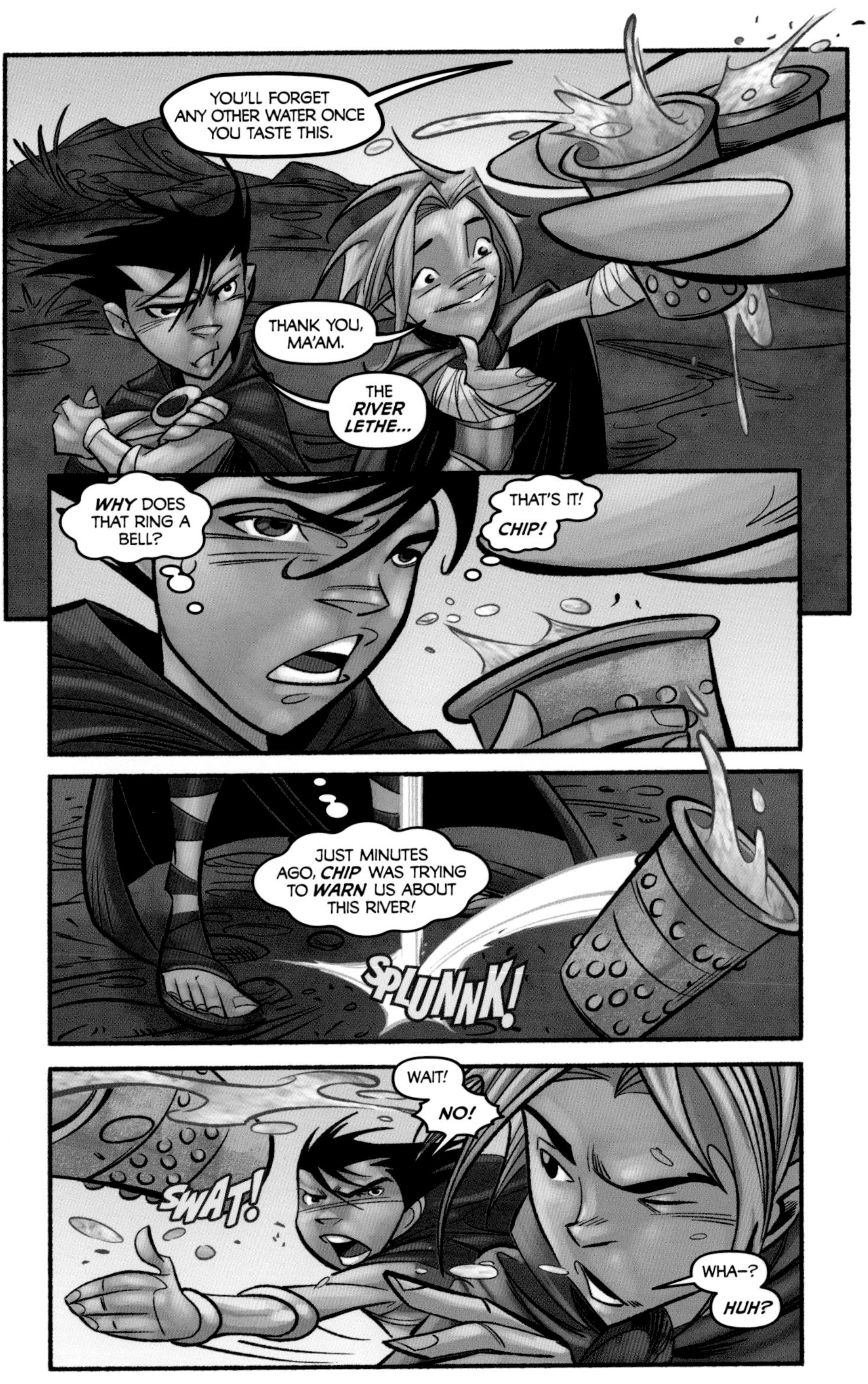
YOU'LL FORGET ANY OTHER WATER ONCE YOU TASTE THIS.
THANK YOU, MA'AM.
THE *RIVER LETHE...*
WHY DOES THAT RING A BELL?
THAT'S IT! *CHIP!*
JUST MINUTES AGO, *CHIP* WAS TRYING TO *WARN* US ABOUT THIS RIVER!
SPLUNNK!
WAIT! *NO!*
SWAT!
WHA–? *HUH?*

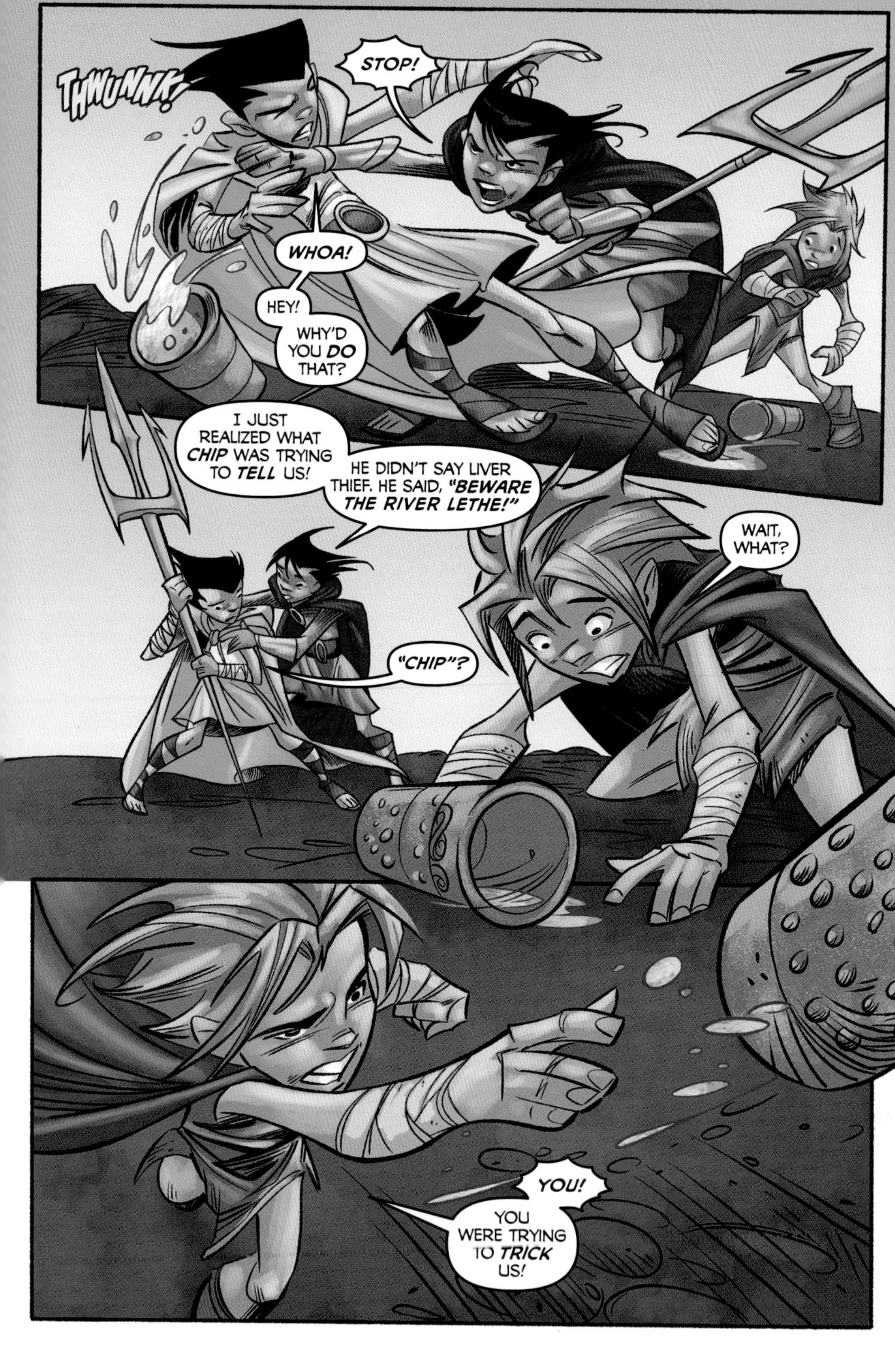
THWUNNK!
STOP!
WHOA!
HEY!
WHY'D YOU DO THAT?
I JUST REALIZED WHAT CHIP WAS TRYING TO TELL US!
HE DIDN'T SAY LIVER THIEF. HE SAID, "BEWARE THE RIVER LETHE!"
WAIT, WHAT?
"CHIP"?
YOU!
YOU WERE TRYING TO TRICK US!

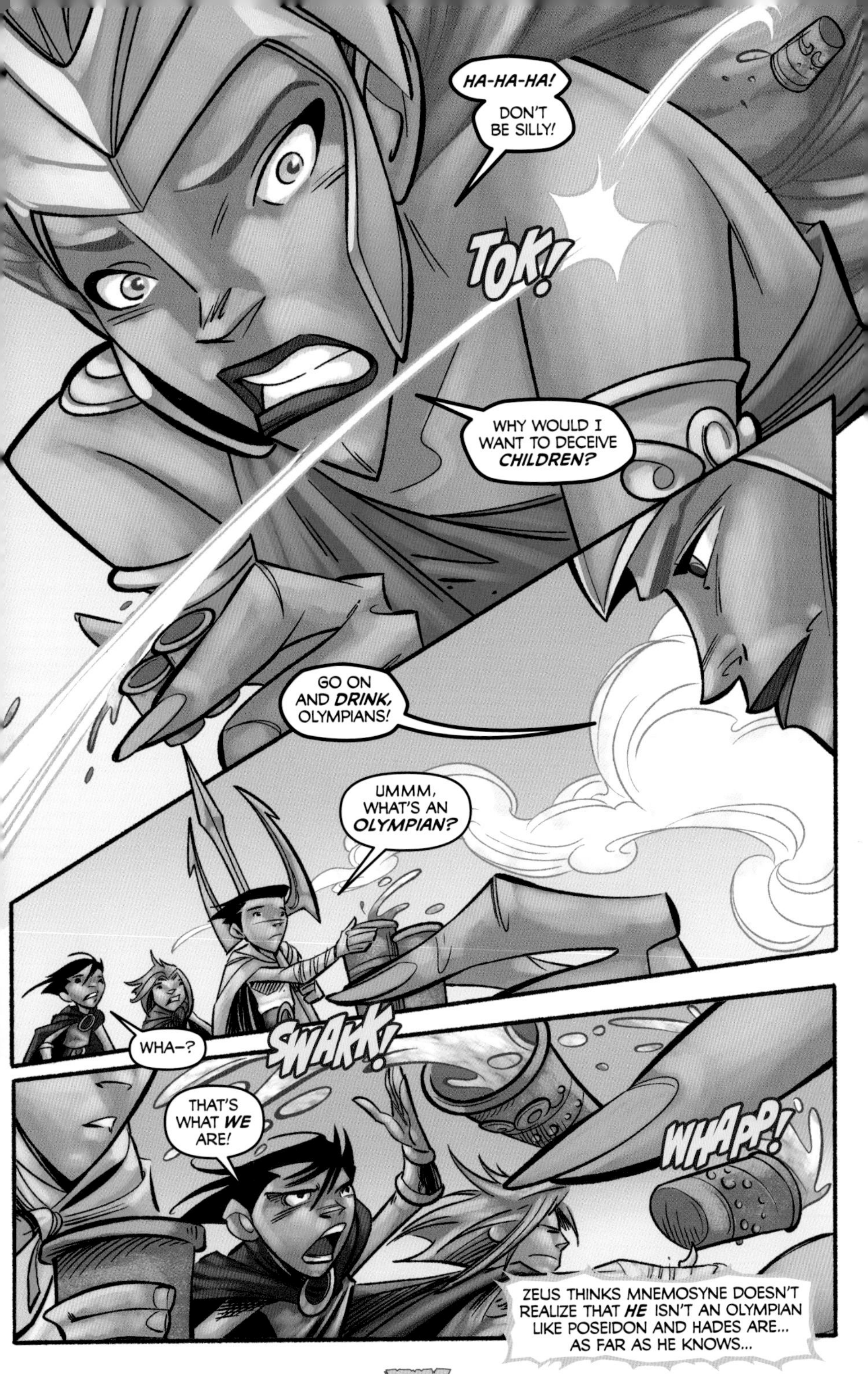
HA-HA-HA!
DON'T BE SILLY!
TOK!
WHY WOULD I WANT TO DECEIVE CHILDREN?
GO ON AND DRINK, OLYMPIANS!
UMMM, WHAT'S AN OLYMPIAN?
WHA-?
SWAKK!
THAT'S WHAT WE ARE!
WHAPP!
ZEUS THINKS MNEMOSYNE DOESN'T REALIZE THAT HE ISN'T AN OLYMPIAN LIKE POSEIDON AND HADES ARE... AS FAR AS HE KNOWS...

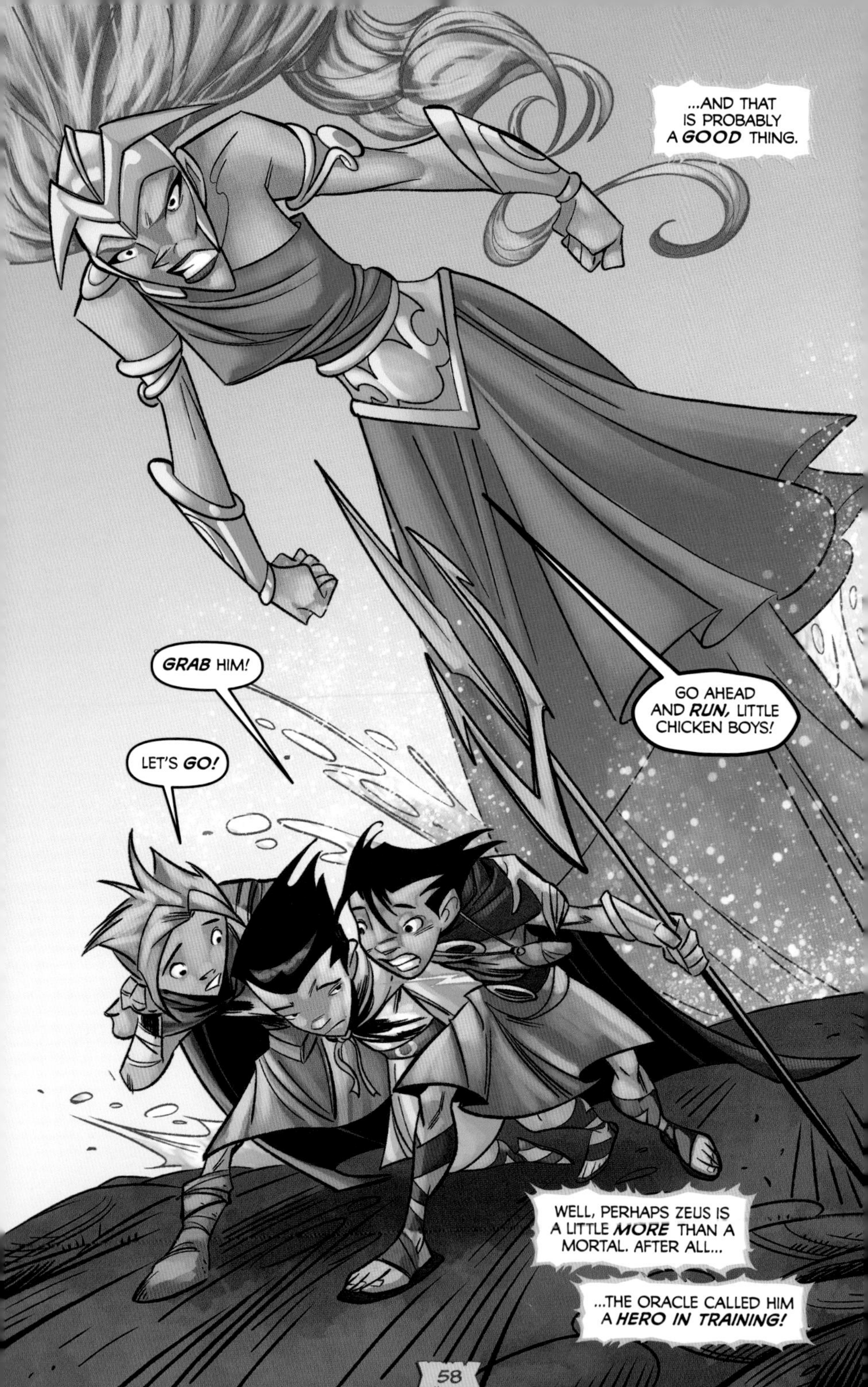
...AND THAT IS PROBABLY A GOOD THING.
GRAB HIM!
GO AHEAD AND RUN, LITTLE CHICKEN BOYS!
LET'S GO!
WELL, PERHAPS ZEUS IS A LITTLE MORE THAN A MORTAL. AFTER ALL...
...THE ORACLE CALLED HIM A HERO IN TRAINING!

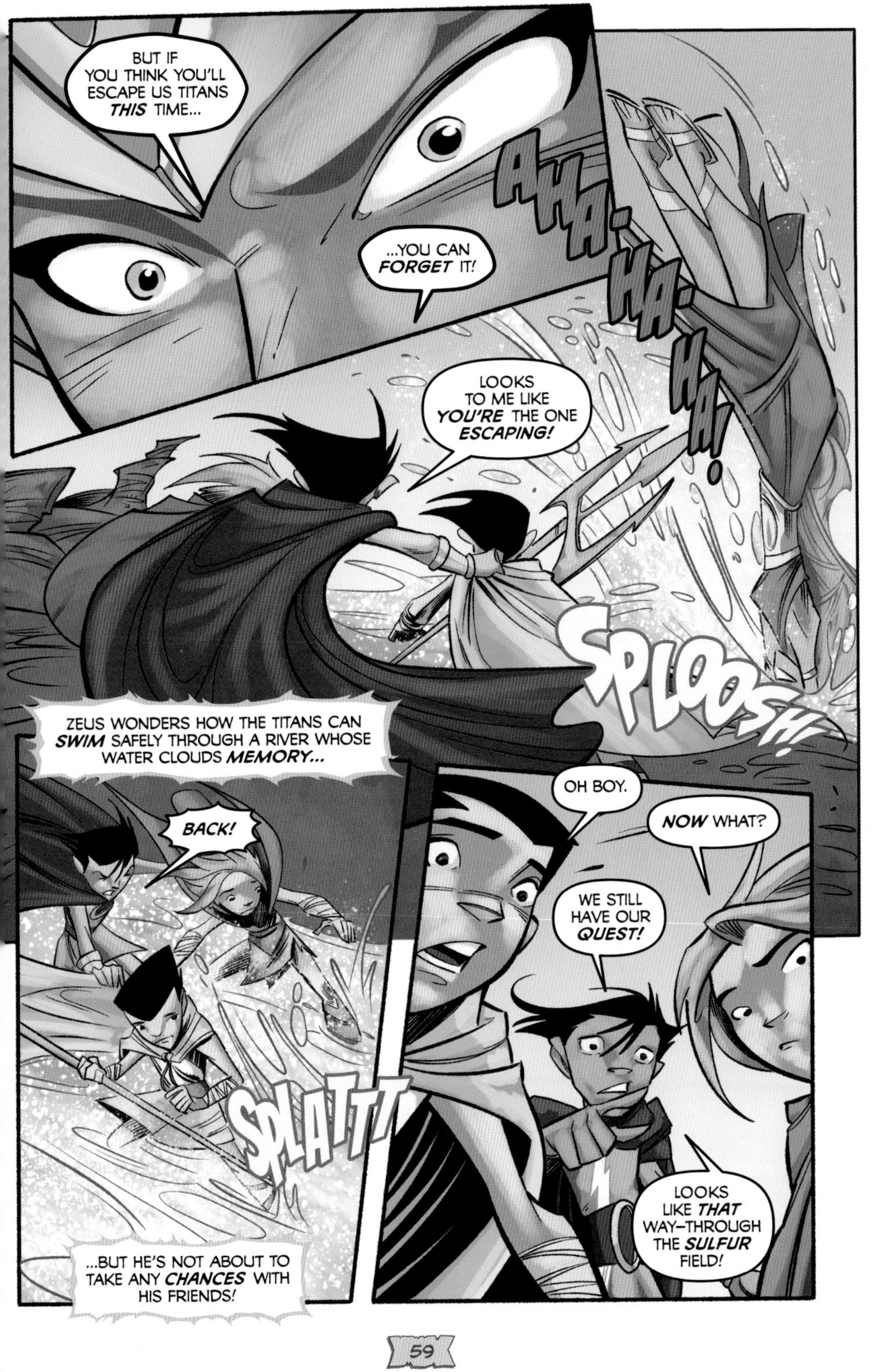

BUT IF YOU THINK YOU'LL ESCAPE US TITANS *THIS* TIME...
...YOU CAN *FORGET* IT!
AHHA-HA-HA-HA!
LOOKS TO ME LIKE *YOU'RE* THE ONE *ESCAPING!*
SPLOOSH!
ZEUS WONDERS HOW THE TITANS CAN *SWIM* SAFELY THROUGH A RIVER WHOSE WATER CLOUDS *MEMORY...*
BACK!
SPLATTT
...BUT HE'S NOT ABOUT TO TAKE ANY *CHANCES* WITH HIS FRIENDS!
OH BOY.
NOW WHAT?
WE STILL HAVE OUR *QUEST!*
LOOKS LIKE *THAT* WAY—THROUGH THE *SULFUR* FIELD!

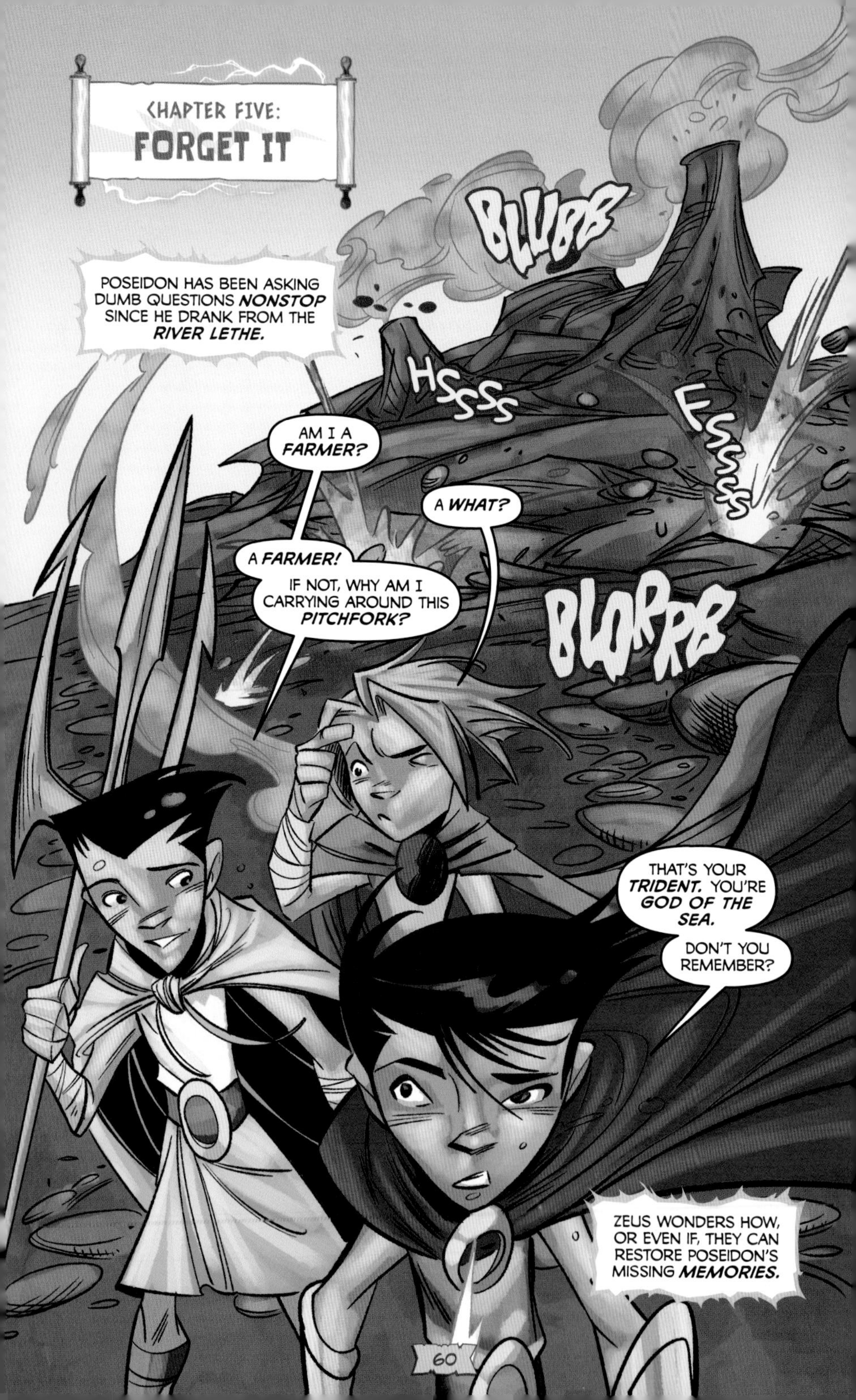
CHAPTER FIVE:
FORGET IT
POSEIDON HAS BEEN ASKING DUMB QUESTIONS NONSTOP SINCE HE DRANK FROM THE RIVER LETHE.
BLUBB
HSSSS
AM I A FARMER?
A WHAT?
A FARMER!
IF NOT, WHY AM I CARRYING AROUND THIS PITCHFORK?
BLORRB
THAT'S YOUR TRIDENT. YOU'RE GOD OF THE SEA.
DON'T YOU REMEMBER?
ZEUS WONDERS HOW, OR EVEN IF, THEY CAN RESTORE POSEIDON'S MISSING MEMORIES.

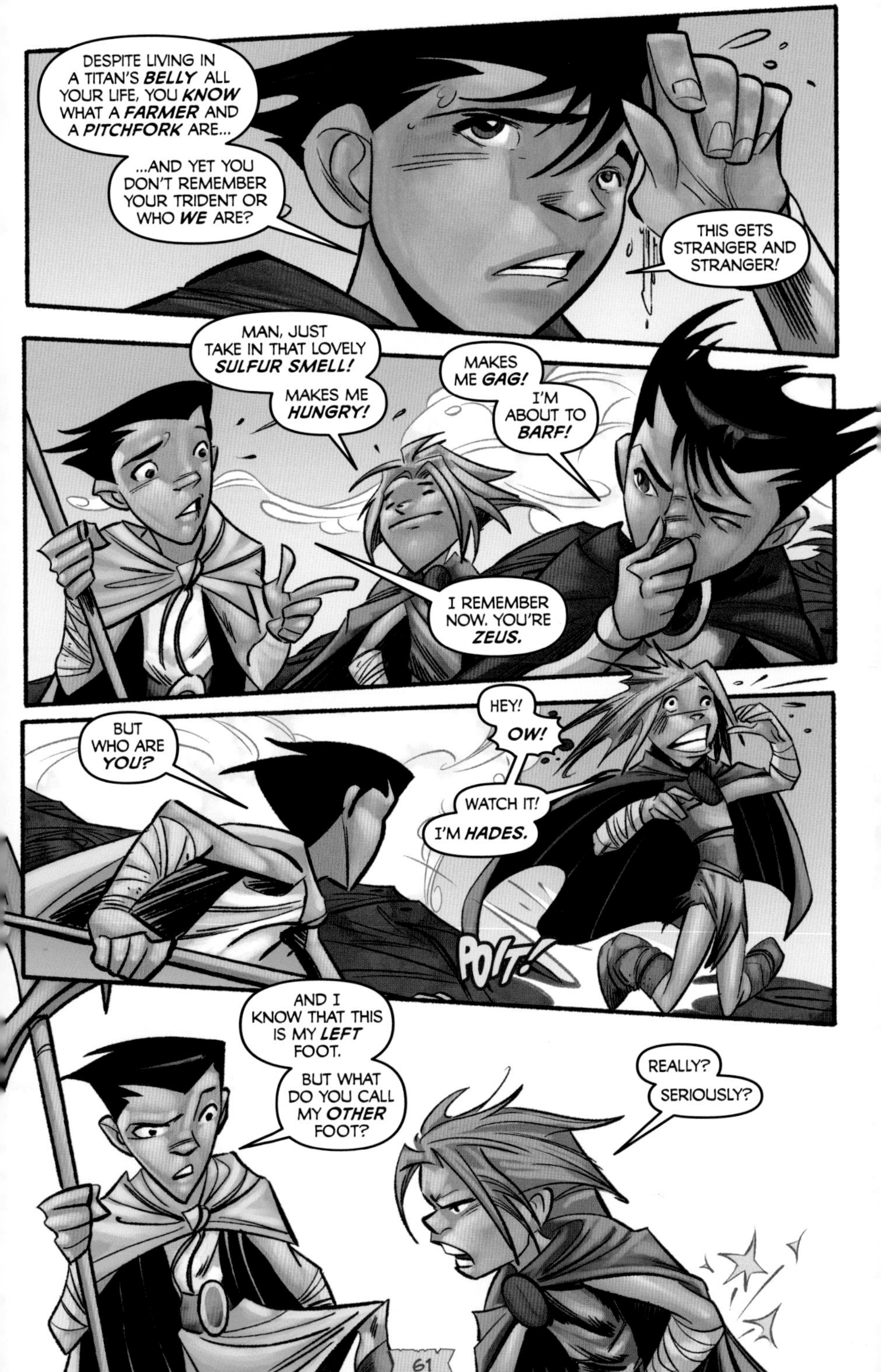
DESPITE LIVING IN A TITAN'S BELLY ALL YOUR LIFE, YOU KNOW WHAT A FARMER AND A PITCHFORK ARE...
...AND YET YOU DON'T REMEMBER YOUR TRIDENT OR WHO WE ARE?
THIS GETS STRANGER AND STRANGER!
MAN, JUST TAKE IN THAT LOVELY SULFUR SMELL!
MAKES ME HUNGRY!
MAKES ME GAG!
I'M ABOUT TO BARF!
I REMEMBER NOW. YOU'RE ZEUS.
BUT WHO ARE YOU?
HEY!
OW!
WATCH IT!
I'M HADES.
POIT!
AND I KNOW THAT THIS IS MY LEFT FOOT.
BUT WHAT DO YOU CALL MY OTHER FOOT?
REALLY?
SERIOUSLY?

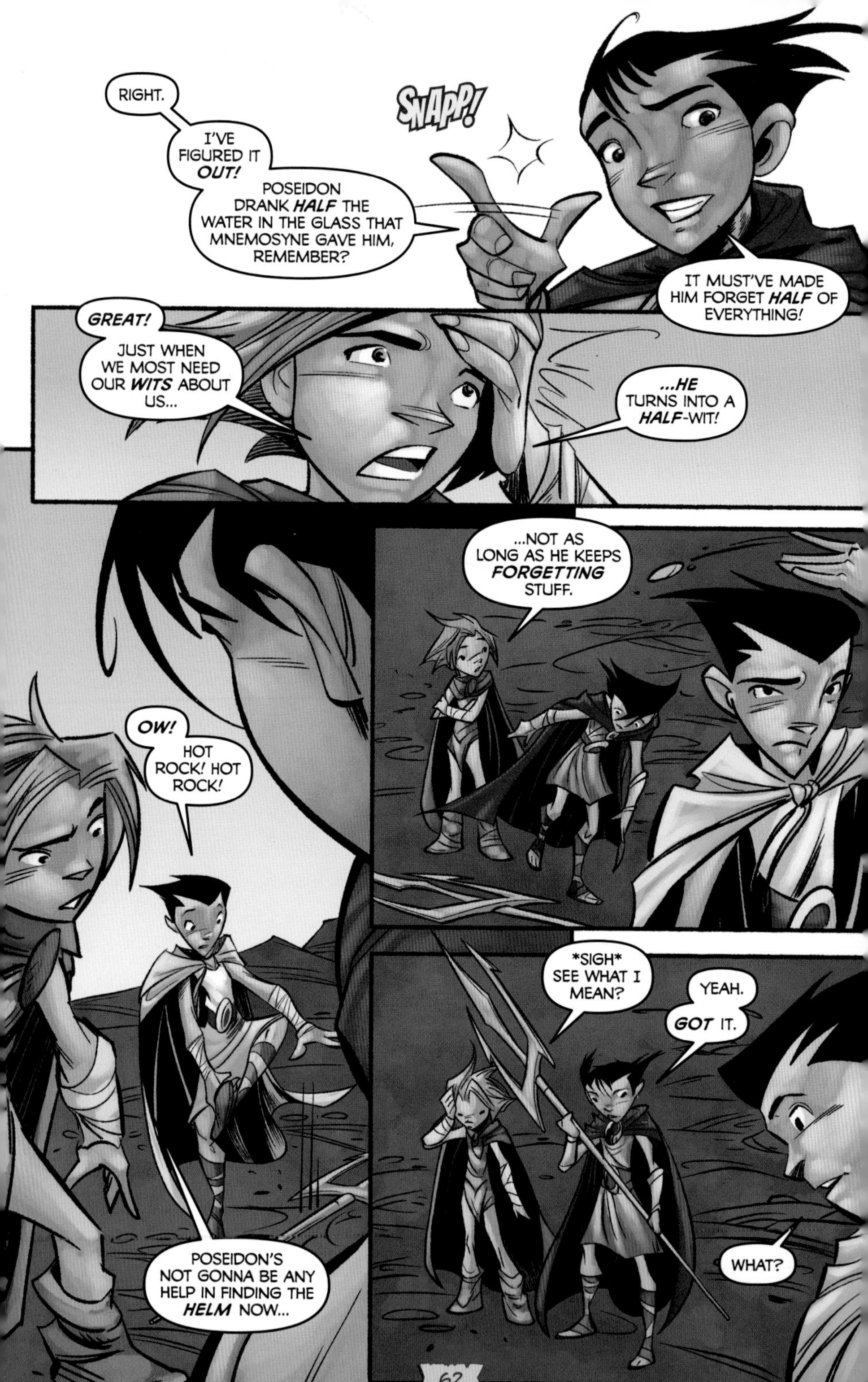
RIGHT.
I'VE FIGURED IT OUT!
POSEIDON DRANK HALF THE WATER IN THE GLASS THAT MNEMOSYNE GAVE HIM, REMEMBER?
SNAPP!
IT MUST'VE MADE HIM FORGET HALF OF EVERYTHING!
GREAT!
JUST WHEN WE MOST NEED OUR WITS ABOUT US...
...HE TURNS INTO A HALF-WIT!
OW!
HOT ROCK! HOT ROCK!
POSEIDON'S NOT GONNA BE ANY HELP IN FINDING THE HELM NOW...
...NOT AS LONG AS HE KEEPS FORGETTING STUFF.
SIGH SEE WHAT I MEAN?
YEAH.
GOT IT.
WHAT?

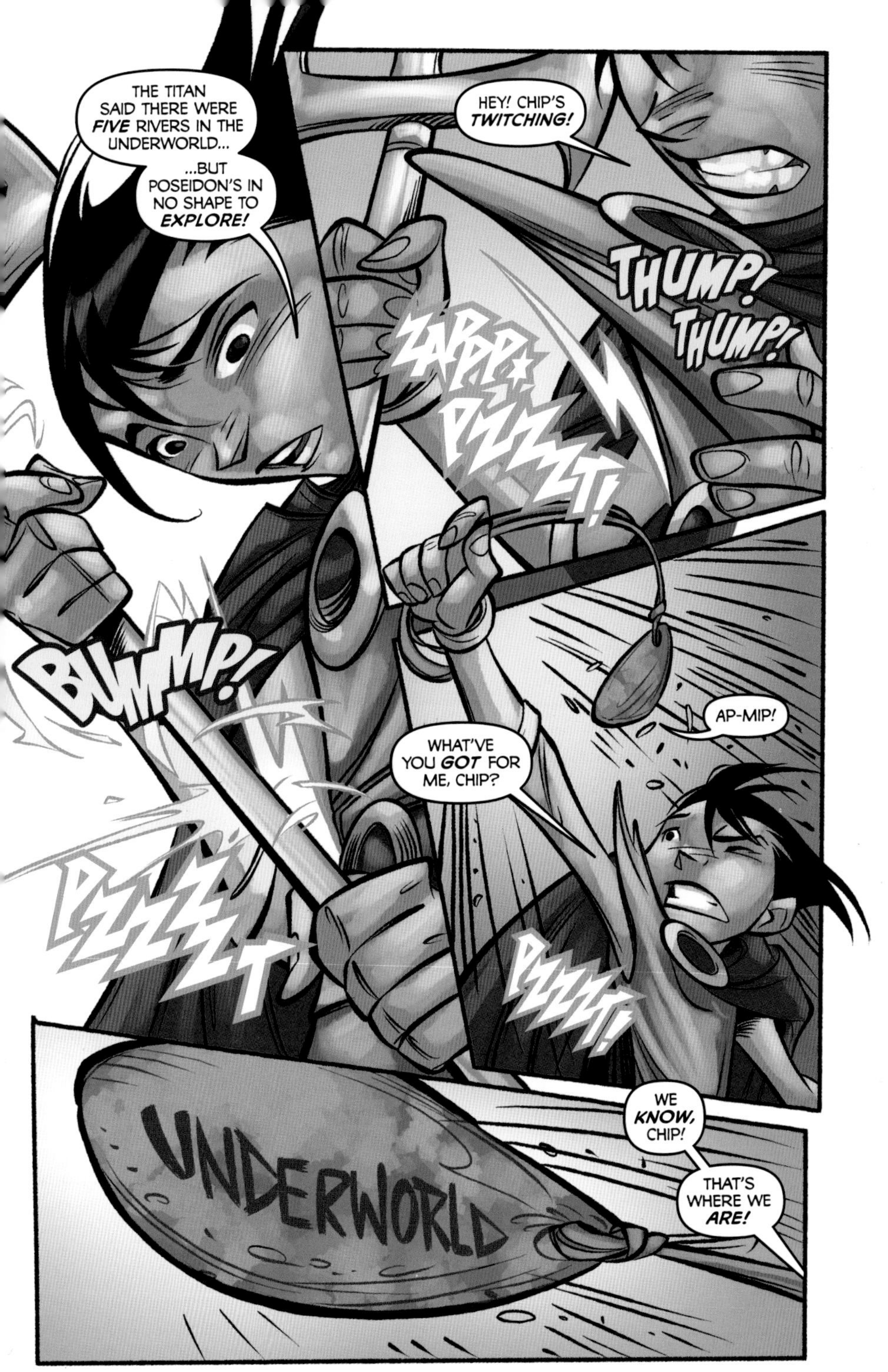
THE TITAN SAID THERE WERE *FIVE* RIVERS IN THE UNDERWORLD...
...BUT POSEIDON'S IN NO SHAPE TO *EXPLORE!*
HEY! CHIP'S *TWITCHING!*
THUMP! THUMP!
ZAPP☆ PZZZZT!
BUMMP!
PZZZZZT
AP-MIP!
WHAT'VE YOU *GOT* FOR ME, CHIP?
PZZZT!
UNDERWORLD
WE *KNOW,* CHIP!
THAT'S WHERE WE *ARE!*

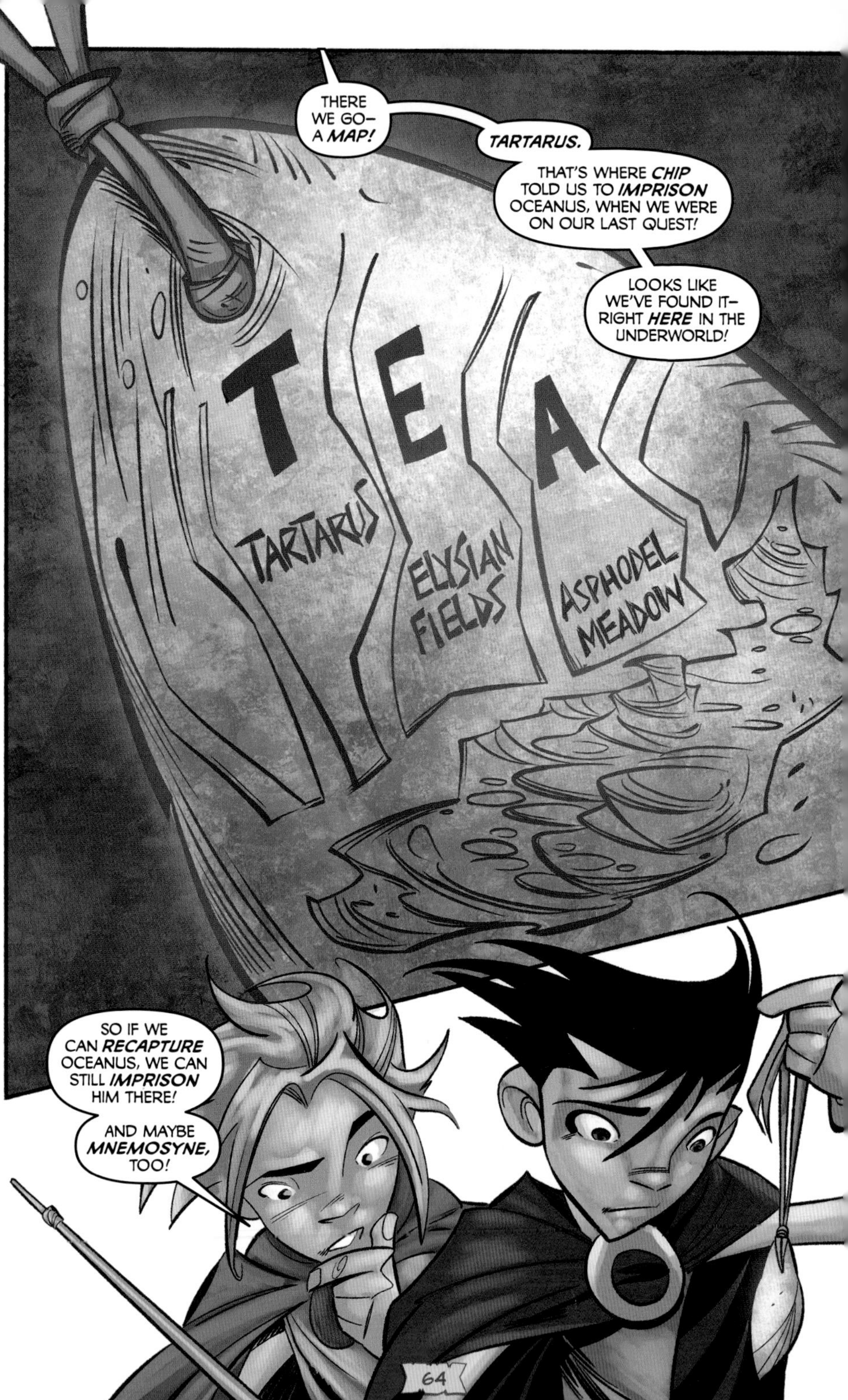

THERE WE GO— A *MAP!*
TARTARUS.
THAT'S WHERE *CHIP* TOLD US TO *IMPRISON* OCEANUS, WHEN WE WERE ON OUR LAST QUEST!
LOOKS LIKE WE'VE FOUND IT— RIGHT *HERE* IN THE UNDERWORLD!
T
E
A
TARTARUS
ELYSIAN FIELDS
ASPHODEL MEADOW
SO IF WE CAN *RECAPTURE* OCEANUS, WE CAN STILL *IMPRISON* HIM THERE!
AND MAYBE *MNEMOSYNE,* TOO!

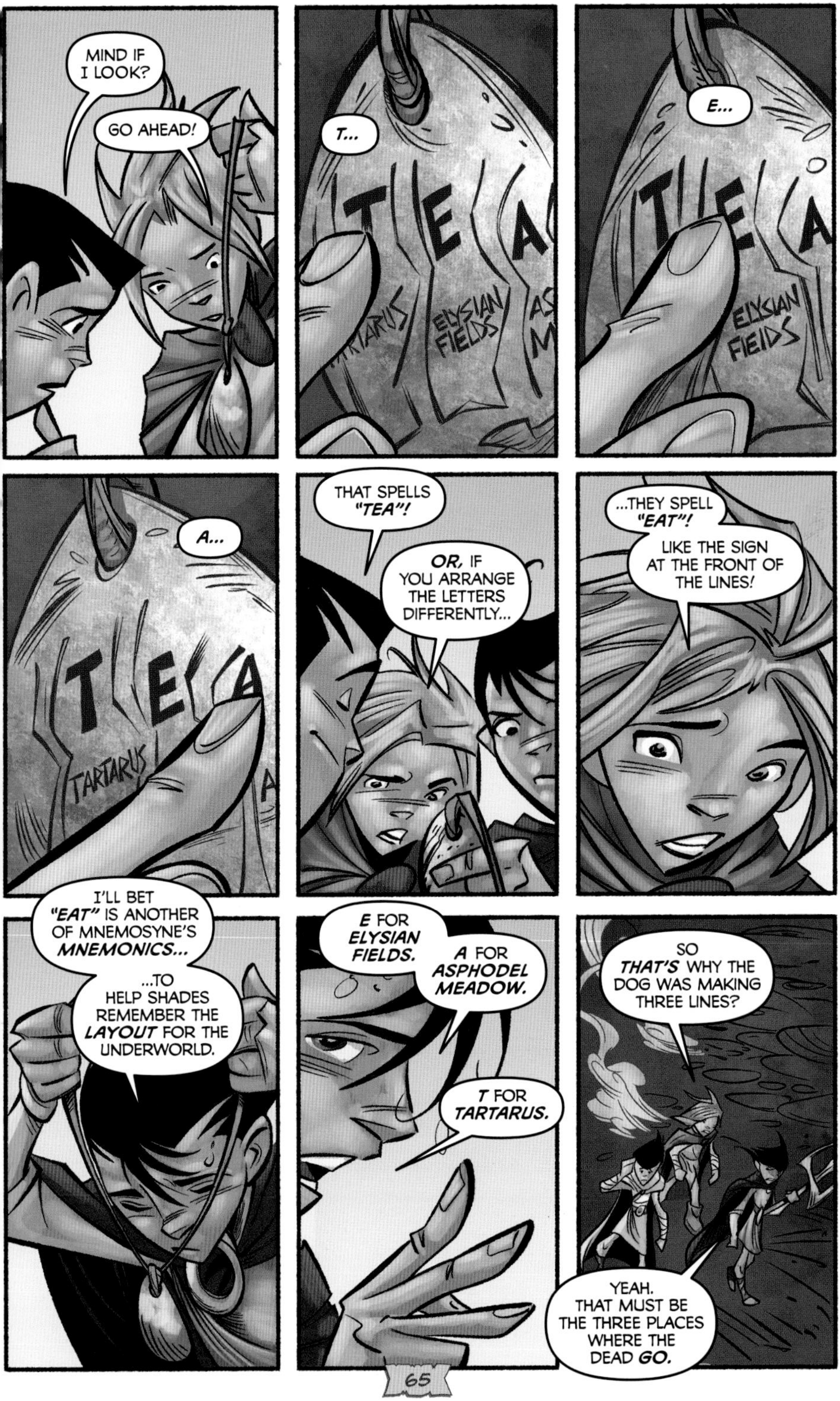
MIND IF I LOOK?
GO AHEAD!
T...
TEA
TARTARUS
ELYSIAN FIELDS
E...
A...
THAT SPELLS "TEA"!
OR, IF YOU ARRANGE THE LETTERS DIFFERENTLY...
...THEY SPELL "EAT"!
LIKE THE SIGN AT THE FRONT OF THE LINES!
I'LL BET "EAT" IS ANOTHER OF MNEMOSYNE'S MNEMONICS...
...TO HELP SHADES REMEMBER THE LAYOUT FOR THE UNDERWORLD.
E FOR ELYSIAN FIELDS.
A FOR ASPHODEL MEADOW.
T FOR TARTARUS.
SO THAT'S WHY THE DOG WAS MAKING THREE LINES?
YEAH. THAT MUST BE THE THREE PLACES WHERE THE DEAD GO.

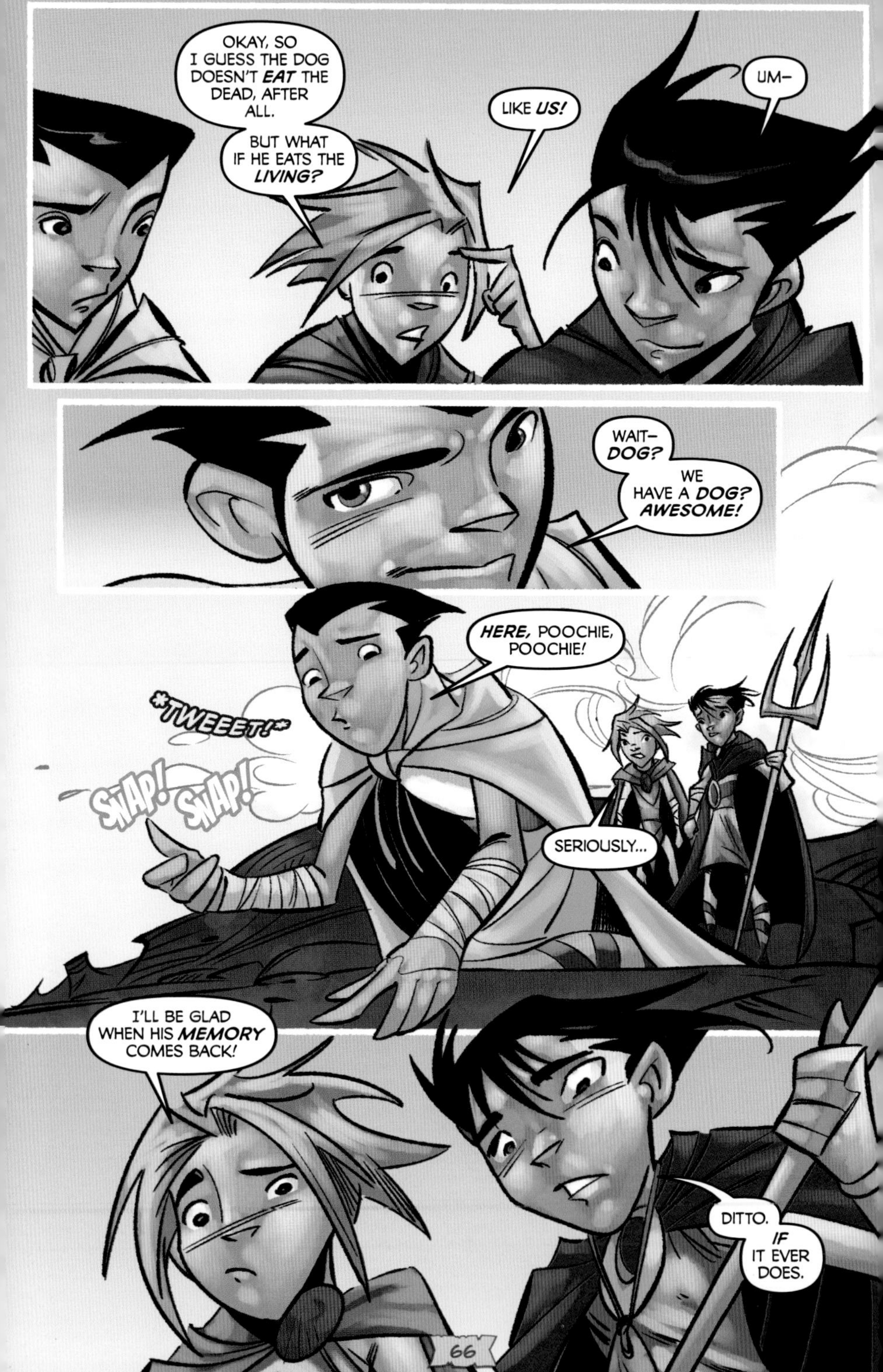
OKAY, SO I GUESS THE DOG DOESN'T *EAT* THE DEAD, AFTER ALL.
BUT WHAT IF HE EATS THE *LIVING?*
LIKE *US!*
UM–
WAIT– *DOG?*
WE HAVE A *DOG? AWESOME!*
HERE, POOCHIE, POOCHIE!
TWEEEET!
SNAP! SNAP!
SERIOUSLY...
I'LL BE GLAD WHEN HIS *MEMORY* COMES BACK!
DITTO. *IF* IT EVER DOES.

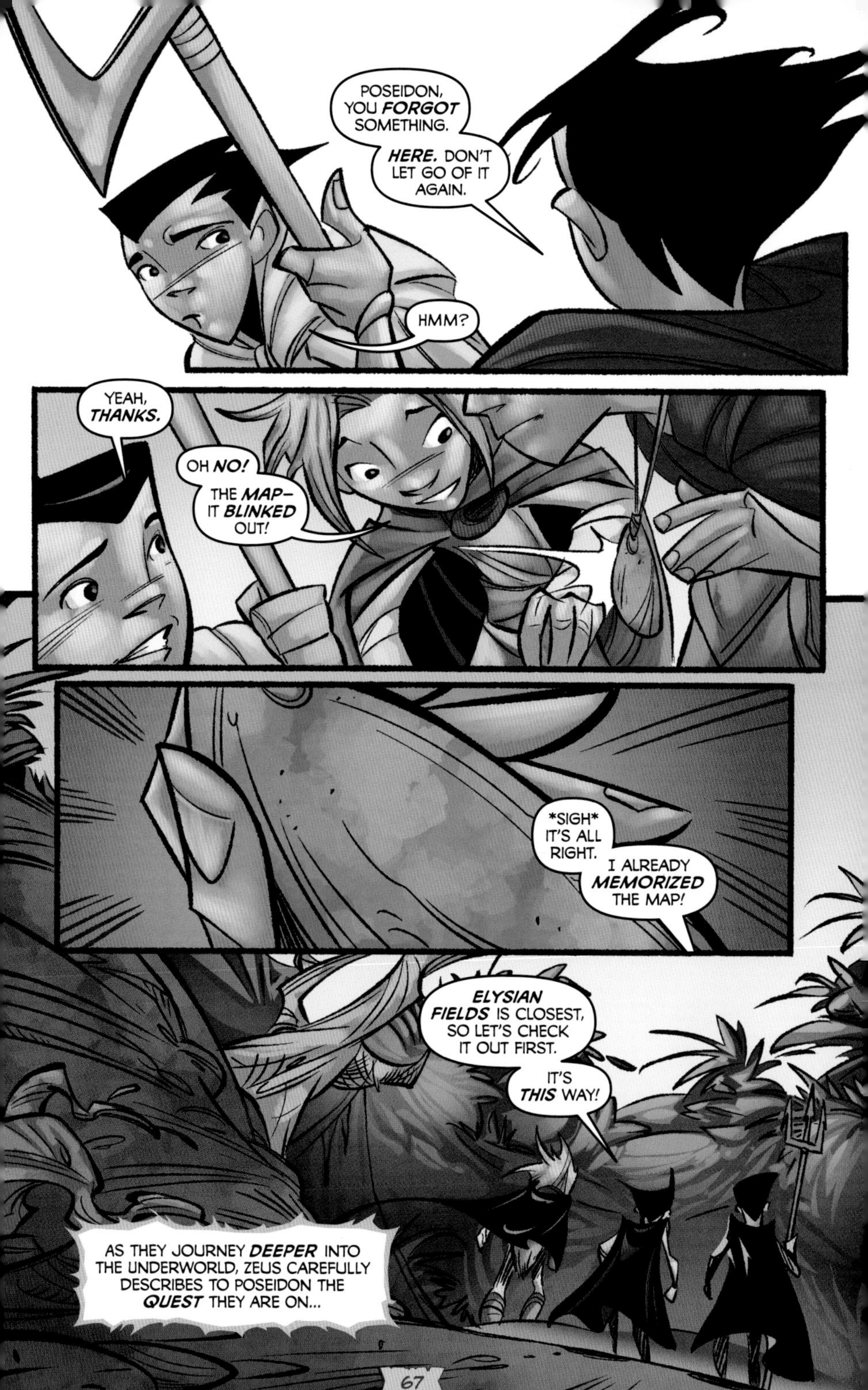
POSEIDON, YOU **FORGOT** SOMETHING.
HERE. DON'T LET GO OF IT AGAIN.
HMM?
YEAH, **THANKS.**
OH **NO!**
THE **MAP**— IT **BLINKED** OUT!
SIGH IT'S ALL RIGHT.
I ALREADY **MEMORIZED** THE MAP!
ELYSIAN FIELDS IS CLOSEST, SO LET'S CHECK IT OUT FIRST.
IT'S **THIS** WAY!
AS THEY JOURNEY **DEEPER** INTO THE UNDERWORLD, ZEUS CAREFULLY DESCRIBES TO POSEIDON THE **QUEST** THEY ARE ON...

CHAPTER SIX:
GOOD, AND DEAD

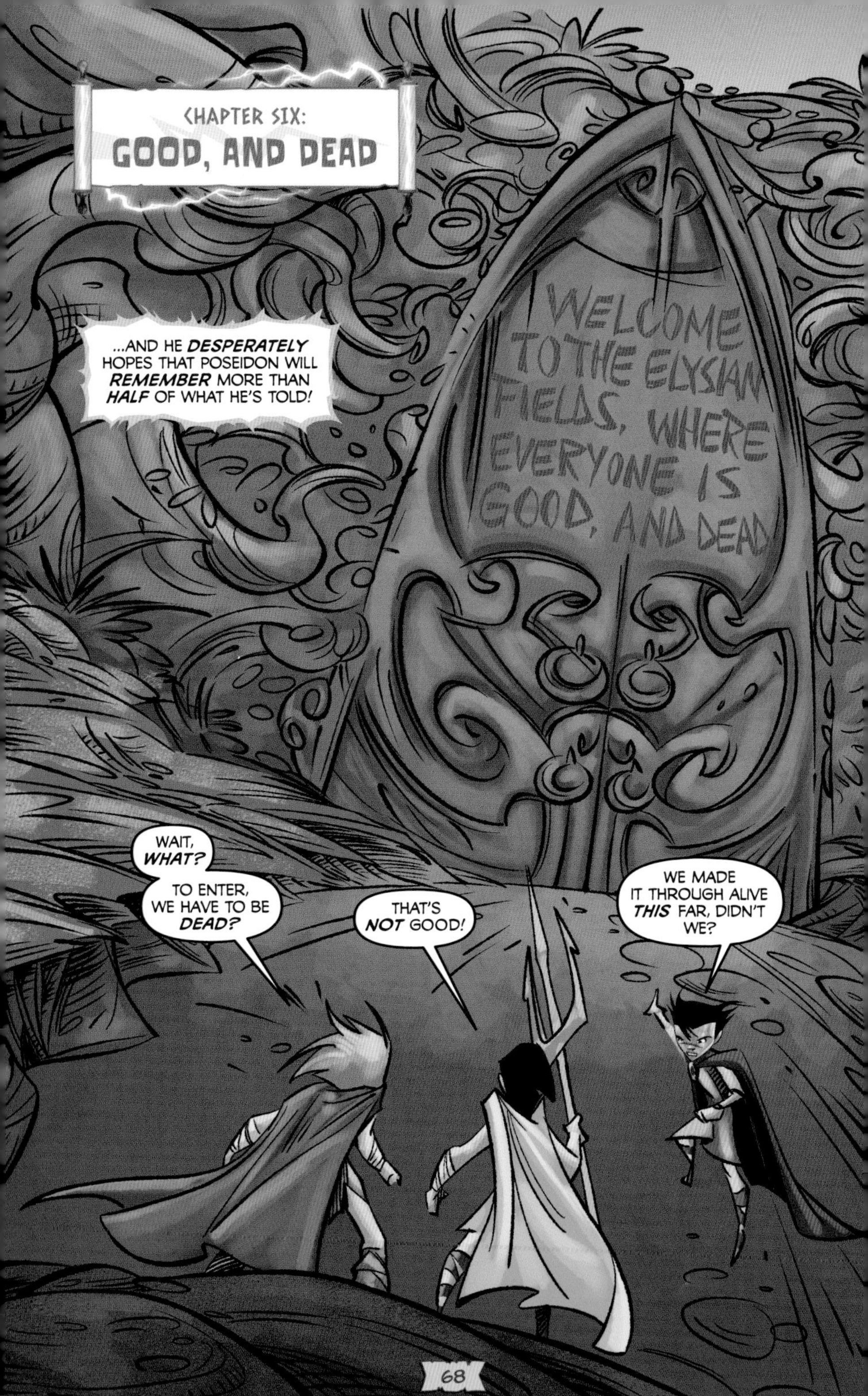

...AND HE DESPERATELY HOPES THAT POSEIDON WILL REMEMBER MORE THAN HALF OF WHAT HE'S TOLD!
WELCOME TO THE ELYSIAN FIELDS, WHERE EVERYONE IS GOOD, AND DEAD
WAIT, WHAT?
TO ENTER, WE HAVE TO BE DEAD?
THAT'S NOT GOOD!
WE MADE IT THROUGH ALIVE THIS FAR, DIDN'T WE?

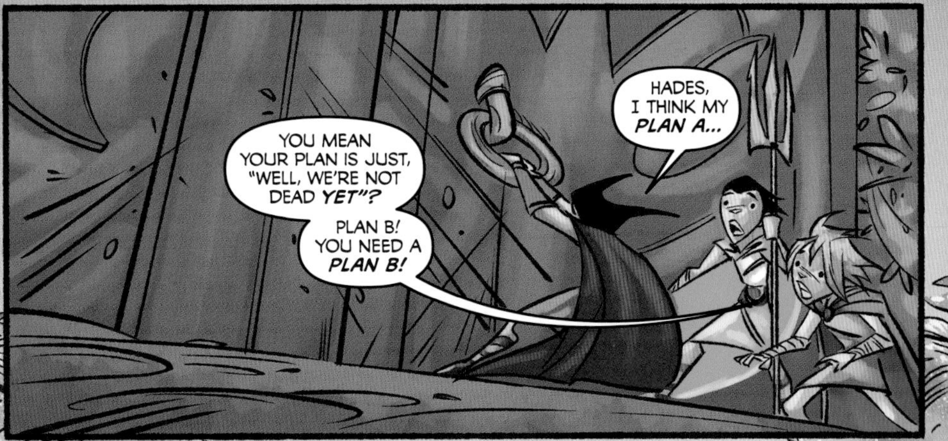
HADES, I THINK MY *PLAN A...*
YOU MEAN YOUR PLAN IS JUST, "WELL, WE'RE NOT DEAD *YET*"?
PLAN B! YOU NEED A *PLAN B!*

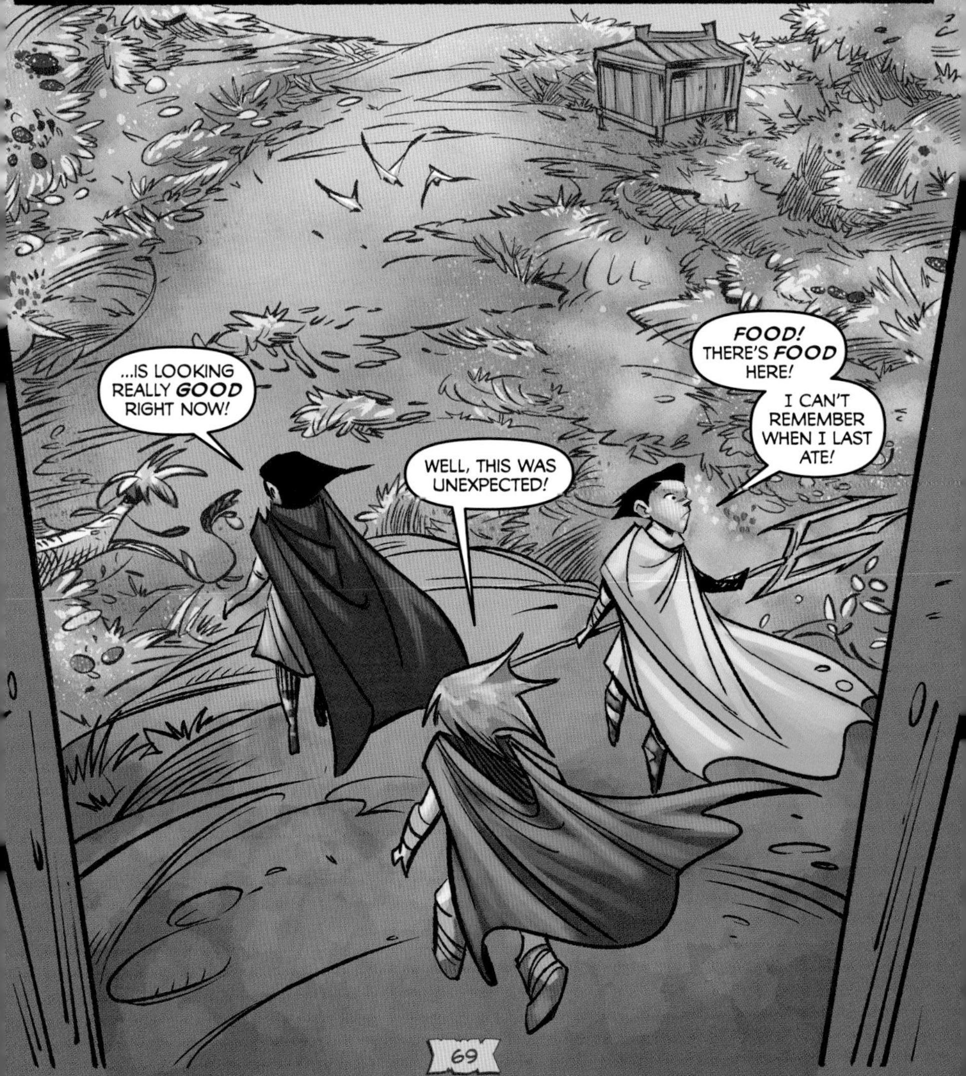
...IS LOOKING REALLY *GOOD* RIGHT NOW!
WELL, THIS WAS UNEXPECTED!
FOOD! THERE'S *FOOD* HERE!
I CAN'T REMEMBER WHEN I LAST ATE!

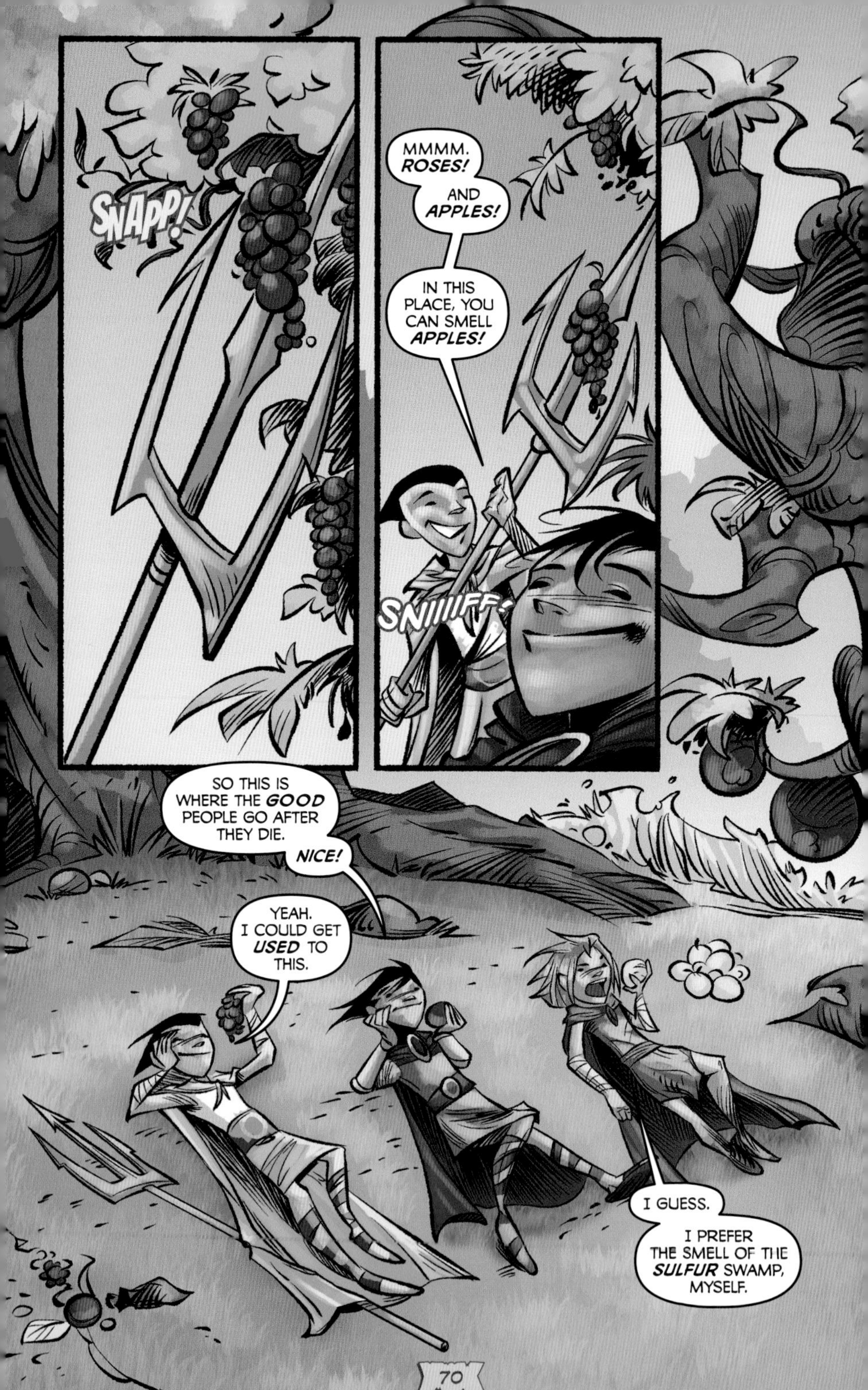
SNAPP!
MMMM. ROSES!
AND APPLES!
IN THIS PLACE, YOU CAN SMELL APPLES!
SNIIIIFF!
SO THIS IS WHERE THE GOOD PEOPLE GO AFTER THEY DIE.
NICE!
YEAH. I COULD GET USED TO THIS.
I GUESS.
I PREFER THE SMELL OF THE SULFUR SWAMP, MYSELF.

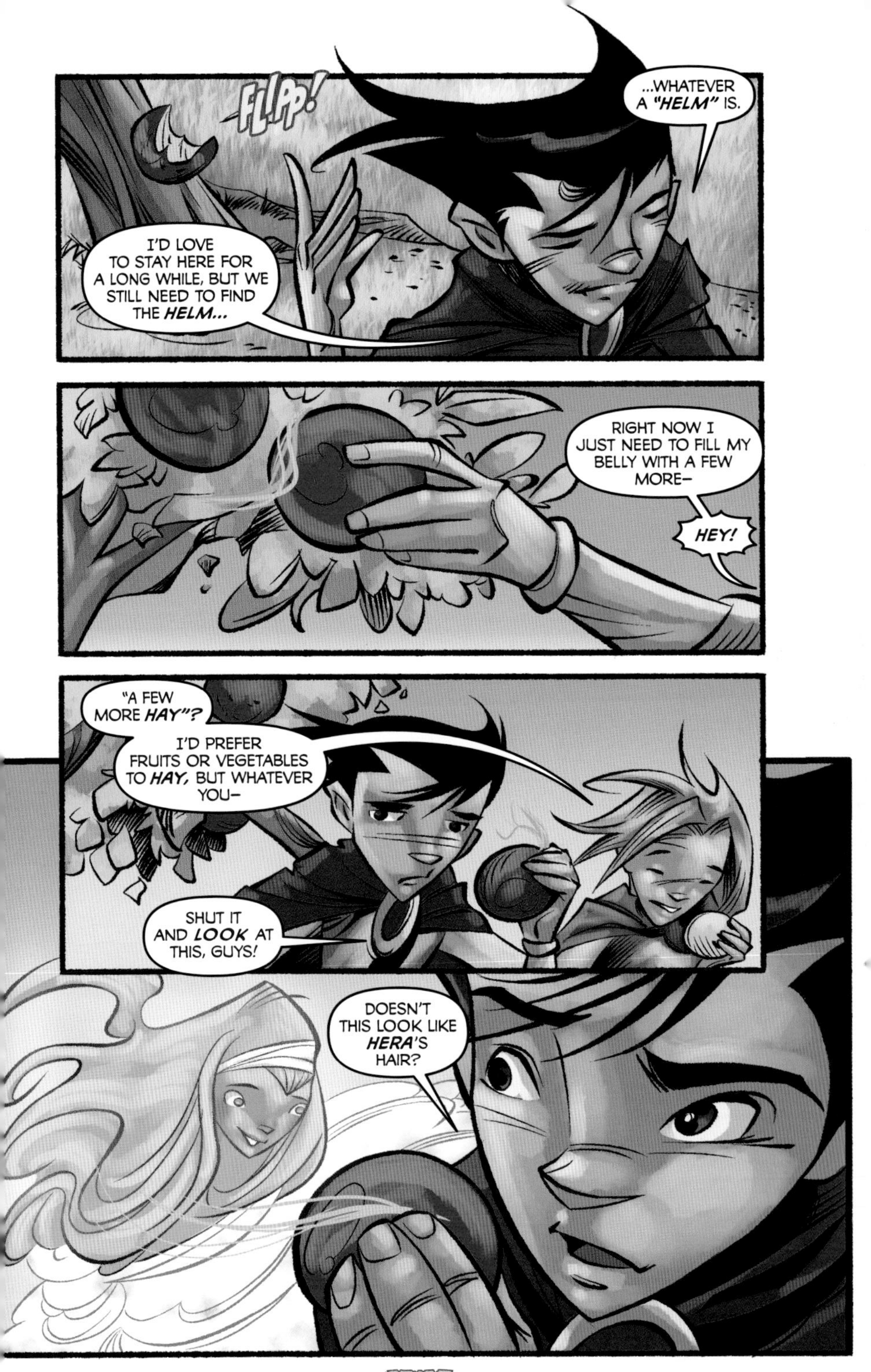
FL!PP!
...WHATEVER A "HELM" IS.
I'D LOVE TO STAY HERE FOR A LONG WHILE, BUT WE STILL NEED TO FIND THE HELM...
RIGHT NOW I JUST NEED TO FILL MY BELLY WITH A FEW MORE–
HEY!
"A FEW MORE HAY"?
I'D PREFER FRUITS OR VEGETABLES TO HAY, BUT WHATEVER YOU–
SHUT IT AND LOOK AT THIS, GUYS!
DOESN'T THIS LOOK LIKE HERA'S HAIR?

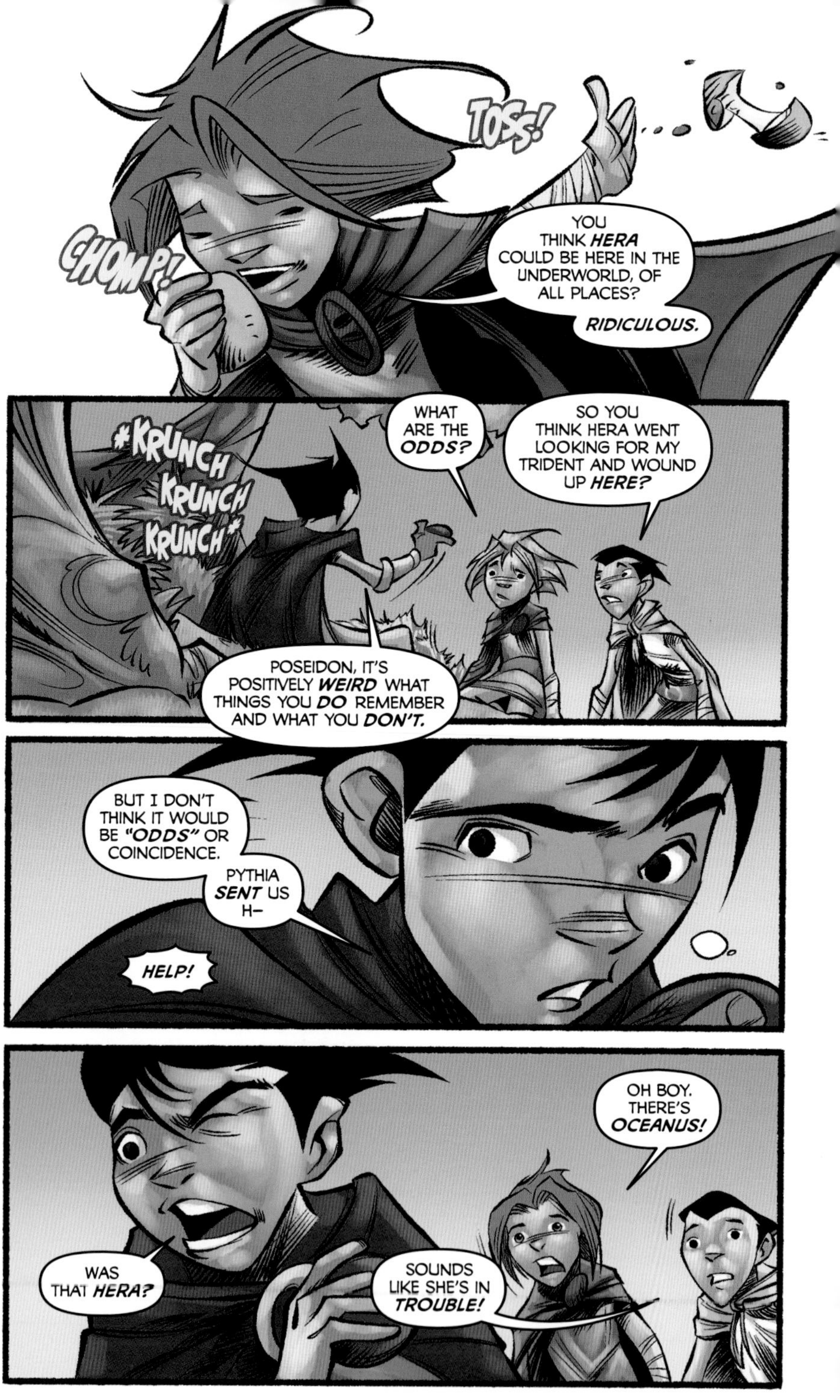
TOSS!
CHOMP!
YOU THINK HERA COULD BE HERE IN THE UNDERWORLD, OF ALL PLACES?
RIDICULOUS.
KRUNCH KRUNCH KRUNCH
WHAT ARE THE ODDS?
SO YOU THINK HERA WENT LOOKING FOR MY TRIDENT AND WOUND UP HERE?
POSEIDON, IT'S POSITIVELY WEIRD WHAT THINGS YOU DO REMEMBER AND WHAT YOU DON'T.
BUT I DON'T THINK IT WOULD BE "ODDS" OR COINCIDENCE.
PYTHIA SENT US H–
HELP!
WAS THAT HERA?
SOUNDS LIKE SHE'S IN TROUBLE!
OH BOY. THERE'S OCEANUS!

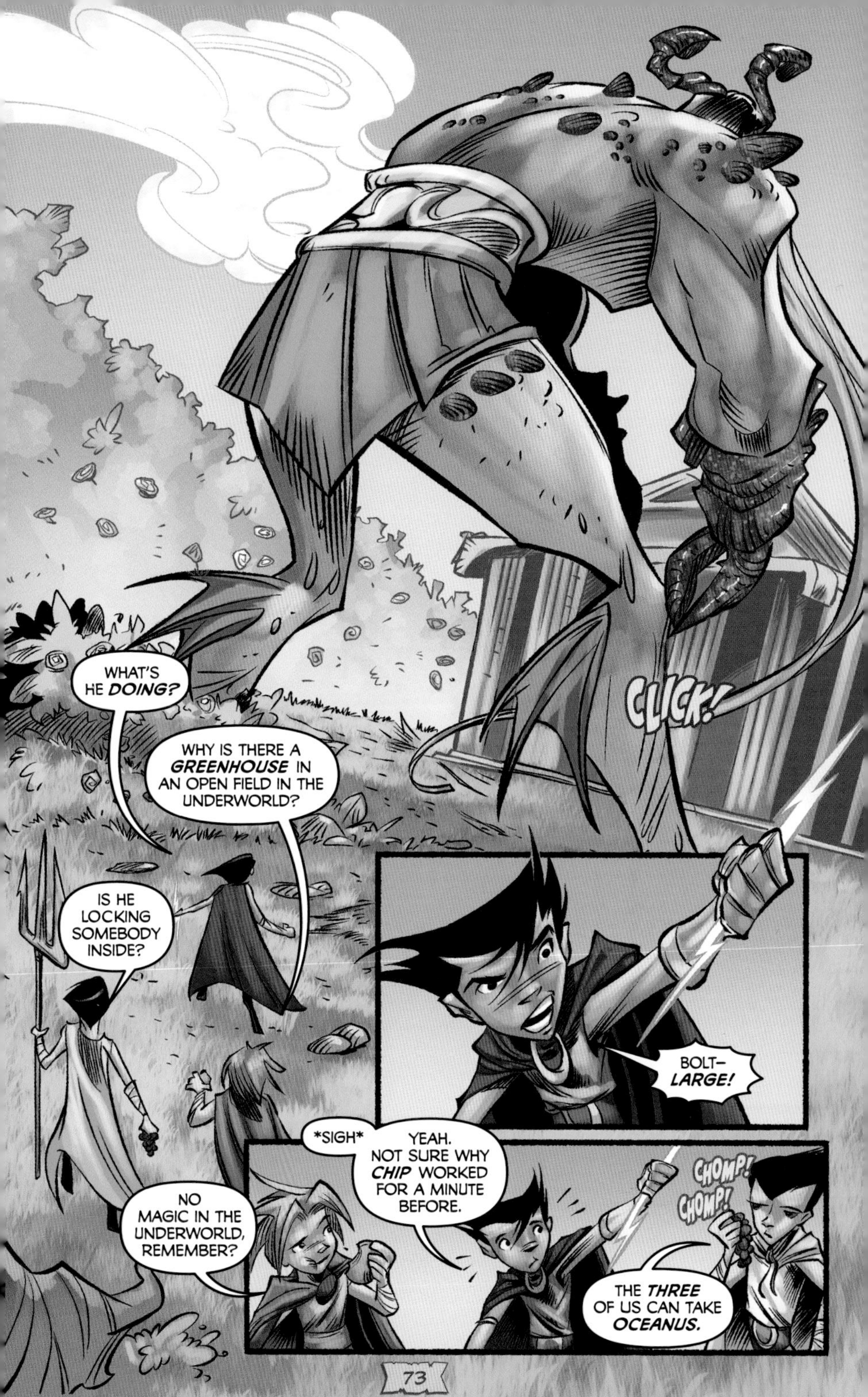
WHAT'S HE *DOING?*
CLICK!
WHY IS THERE A *GREENHOUSE* IN AN OPEN FIELD IN THE UNDERWORLD?
IS HE LOCKING SOMEBODY INSIDE?
BOLT— *LARGE!*
SIGH
YEAH. NOT SURE WHY *CHIP* WORKED FOR A MINUTE BEFORE.
NO MAGIC IN THE UNDERWORLD, REMEMBER?
CHOMP! CHOMP!
THE *THREE* OF US CAN TAKE *OCEANUS.*

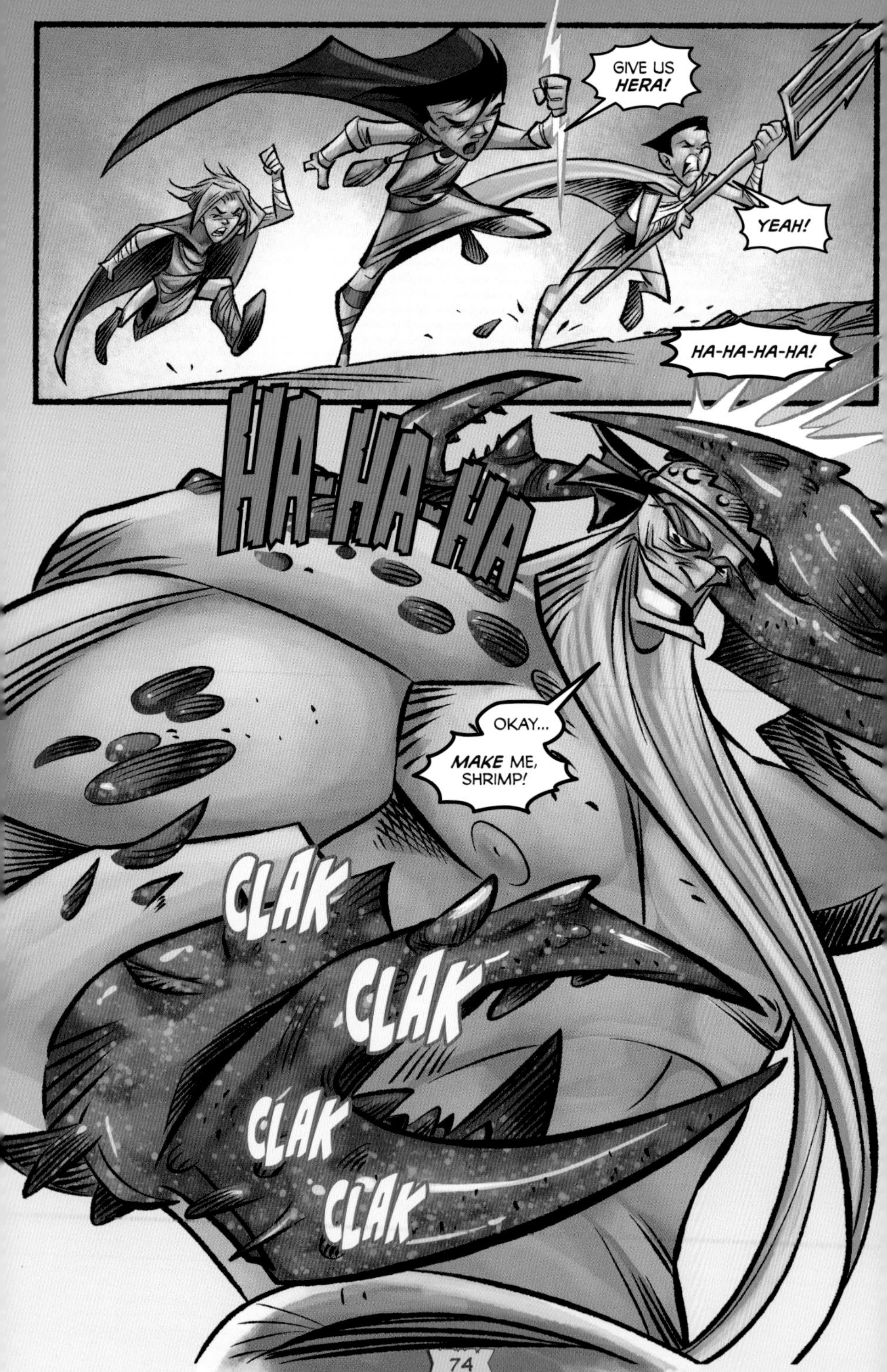
GIVE US HERA!
YEAH!
HA-HA-HA-HA!
HA-HA-HA
OKAY... MAKE ME, SHRIMP!
CLAK
CLAK
CLAK
CLAK

CHAPTER SEVEN:
THE HELM

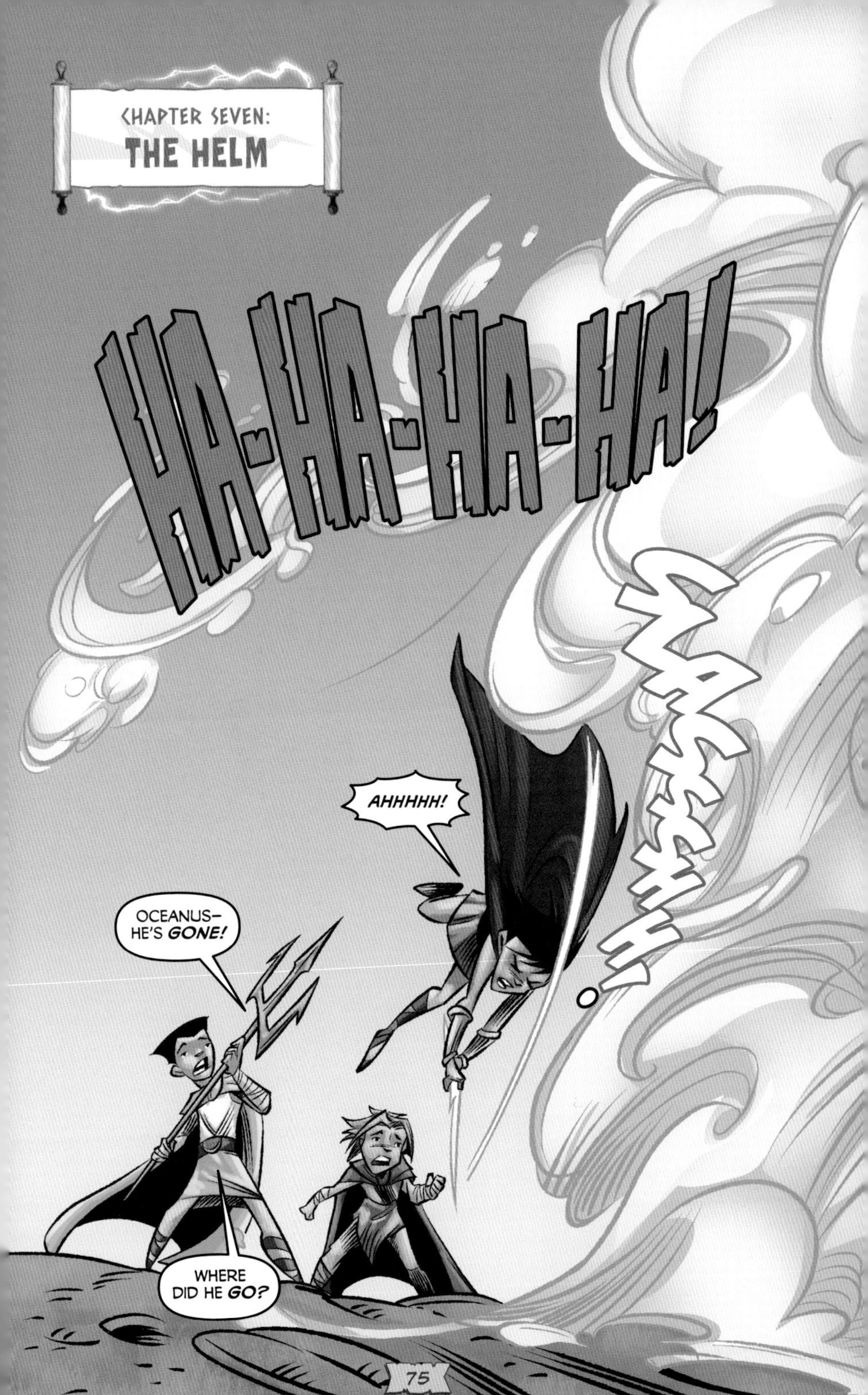
HA-HA-HA-HA!
SHASSHH!
AHHHHH!
OCEANUS—HE'S GONE!
WHERE DID HE GO?

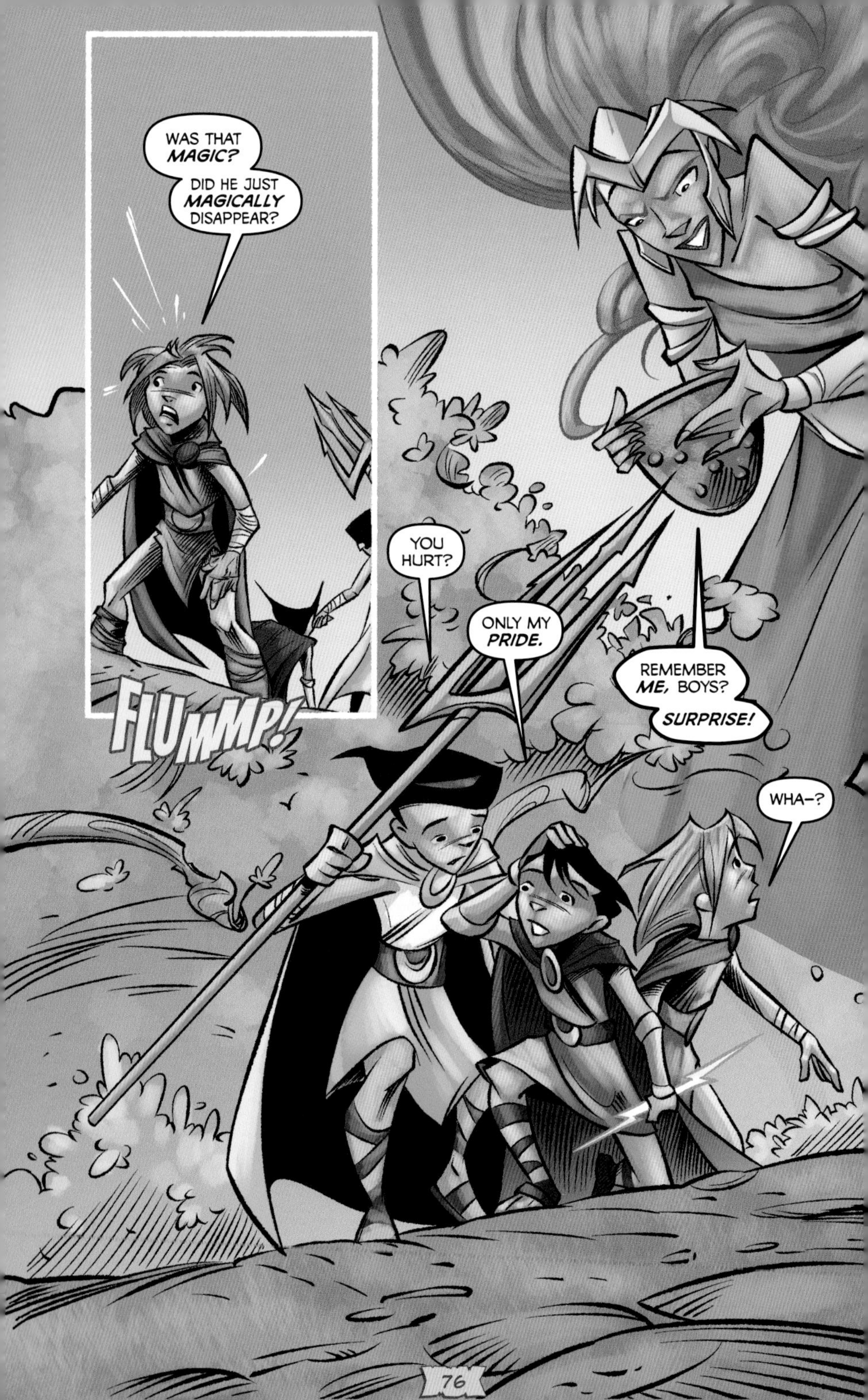
WAS THAT *MAGIC?*
DID HE JUST *MAGICALLY* DISAPPEAR?
FLUMMP!
YOU HURT?
ONLY MY *PRIDE.*
REMEMBER *ME,* BOYS?
SURPRISE!
WHA-?

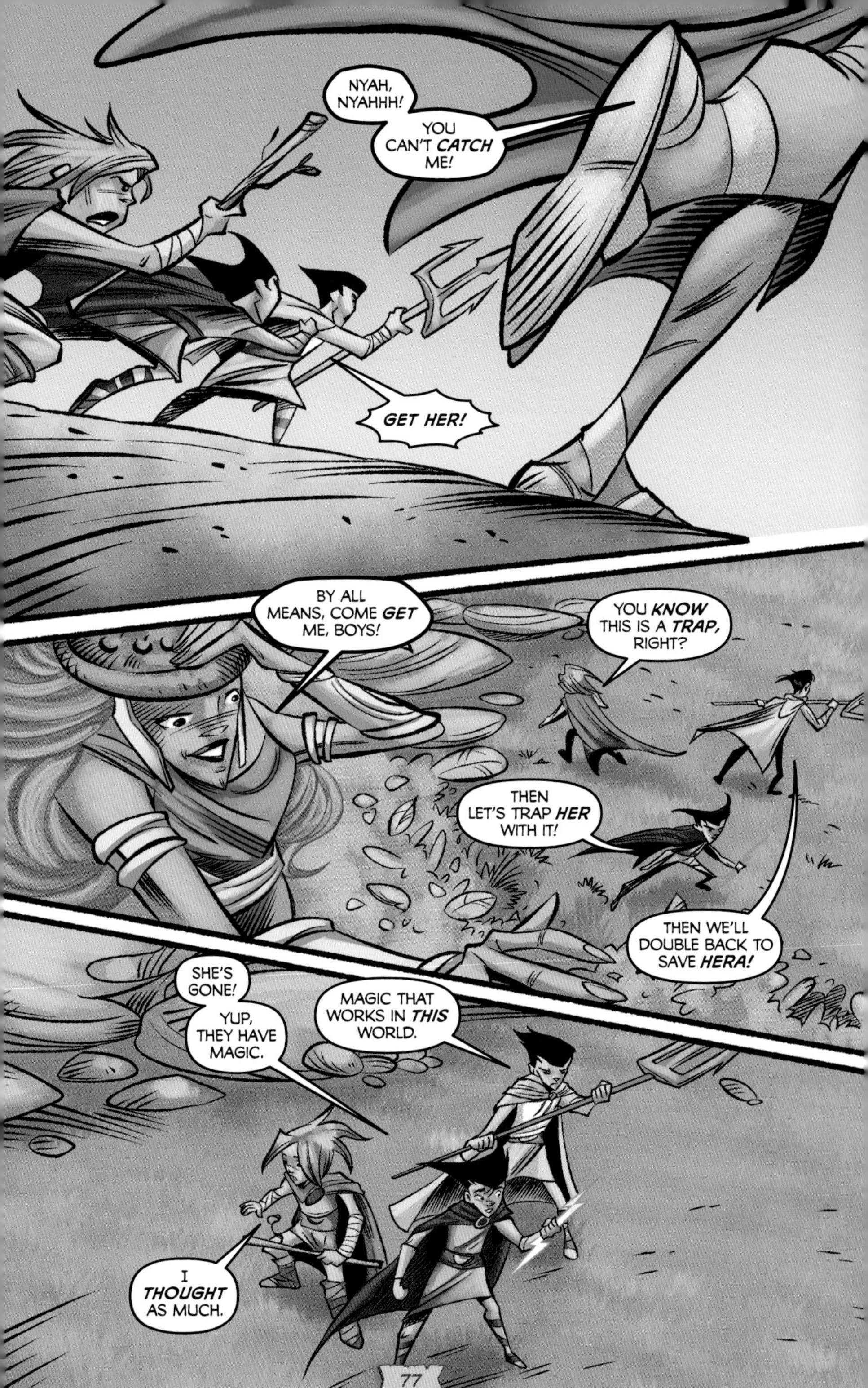
NYAH, NYAHHH!
YOU CAN'T *CATCH* ME!
GET HER!
BY ALL MEANS, COME *GET* ME, BOYS!
YOU *KNOW* THIS IS A *TRAP,* RIGHT?
THEN LET'S TRAP *HER* WITH IT!
THEN WE'LL DOUBLE BACK TO SAVE *HERA!*
SHE'S GONE!
YUP, THEY HAVE MAGIC.
MAGIC THAT WORKS IN *THIS* WORLD.
I *THOUGHT* AS MUCH.

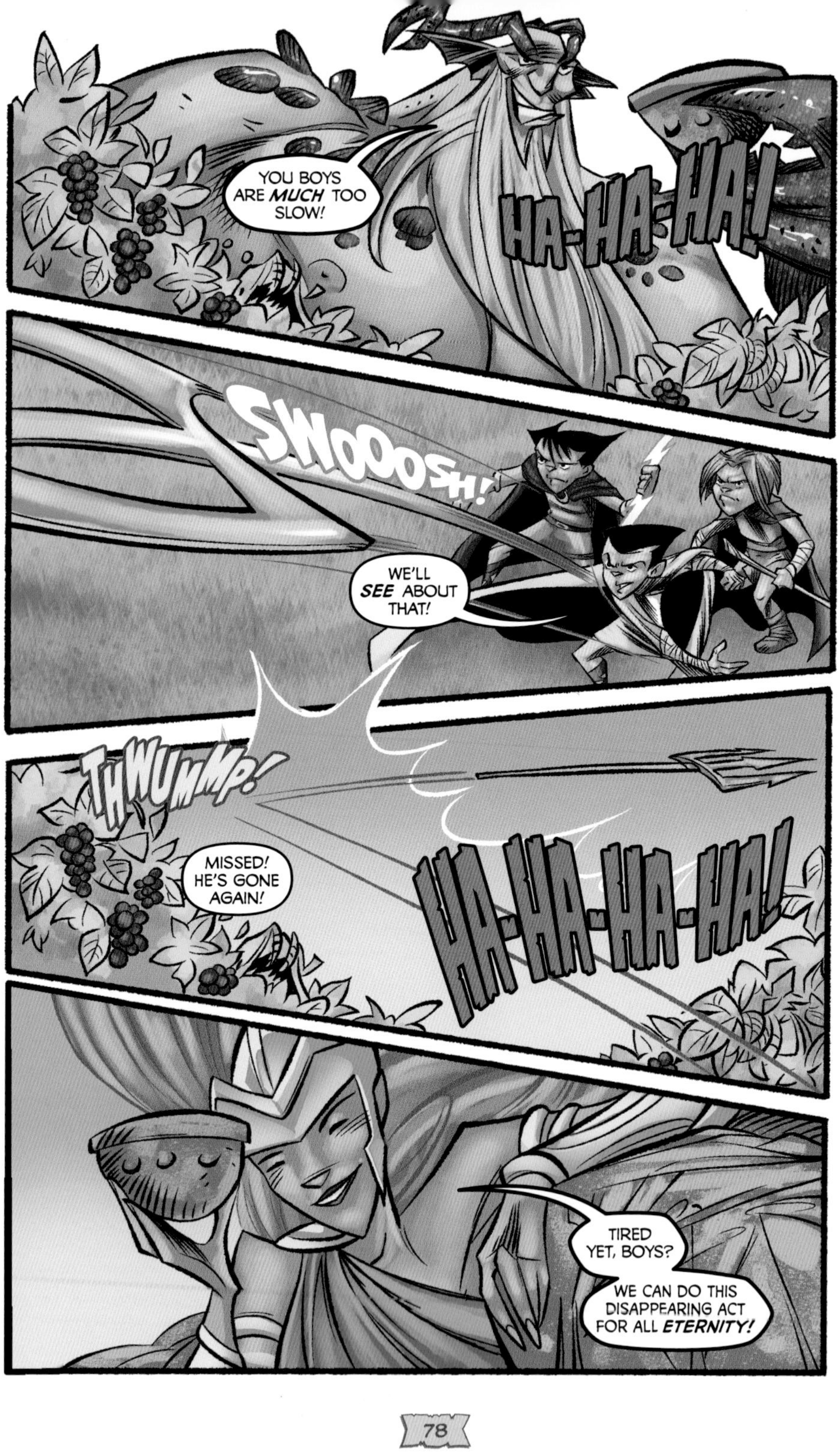
YOU BOYS ARE *MUCH* TOO SLOW!
HA-HA-HA!
SWOOOSH!
WE'LL *SEE* ABOUT THAT!
THWUMMP!
MISSED! HE'S GONE AGAIN!
HA-HA-HA-HA!
TIRED YET, BOYS?
WE CAN DO THIS DISAPPEARING ACT FOR ALL *ETERNITY!*

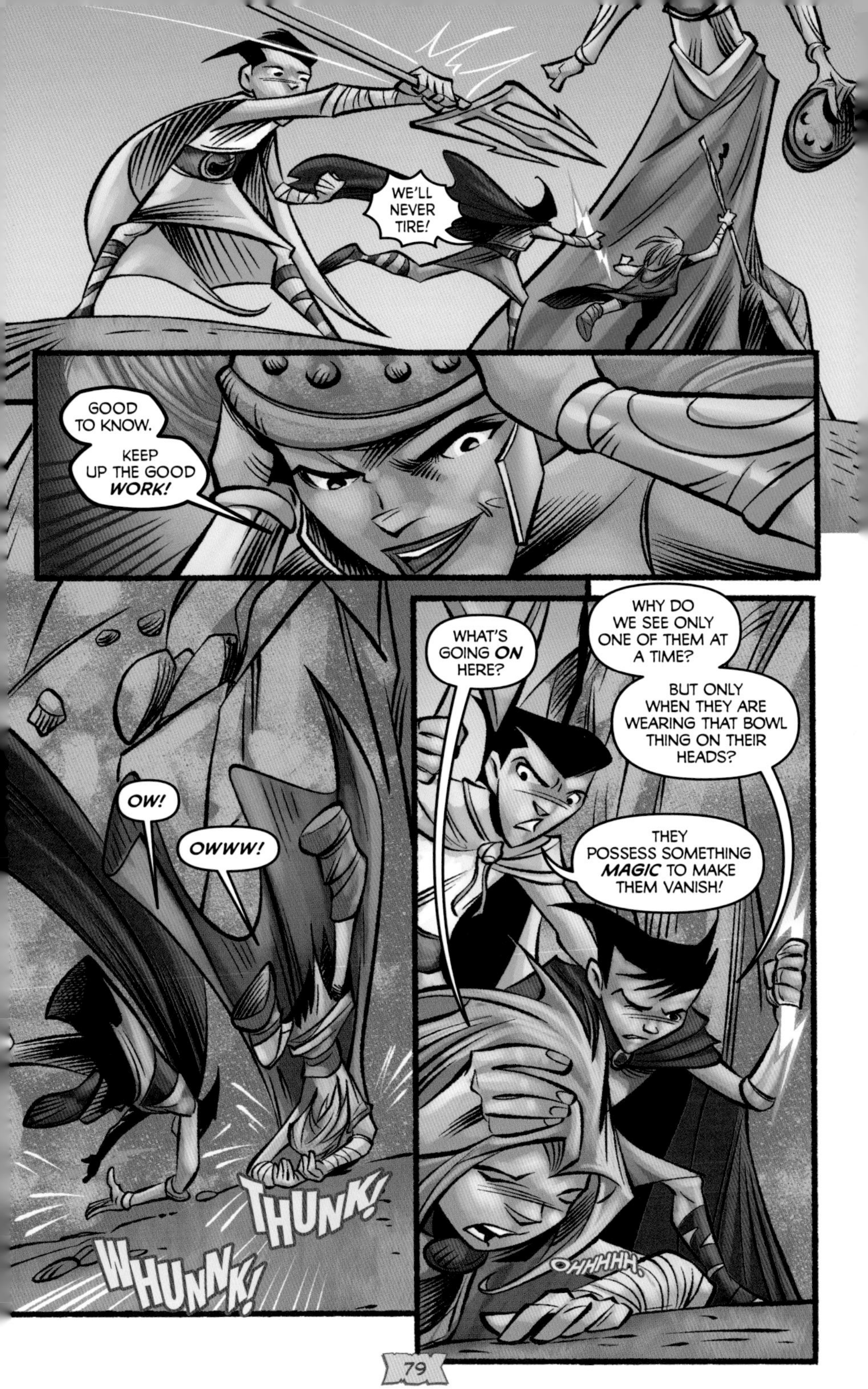
WE'LL NEVER TIRE!
GOOD TO KNOW.
KEEP UP THE GOOD WORK!
OW!
OWWW!
THUNK!
WHUNNK!
WHAT'S GOING ON HERE?
WHY DO WE SEE ONLY ONE OF THEM AT A TIME?
BUT ONLY WHEN THEY ARE WEARING THAT BOWL THING ON THEIR HEADS?
THEY POSSESS SOMETHING MAGIC TO MAKE THEM VANISH!
OHHHHH.

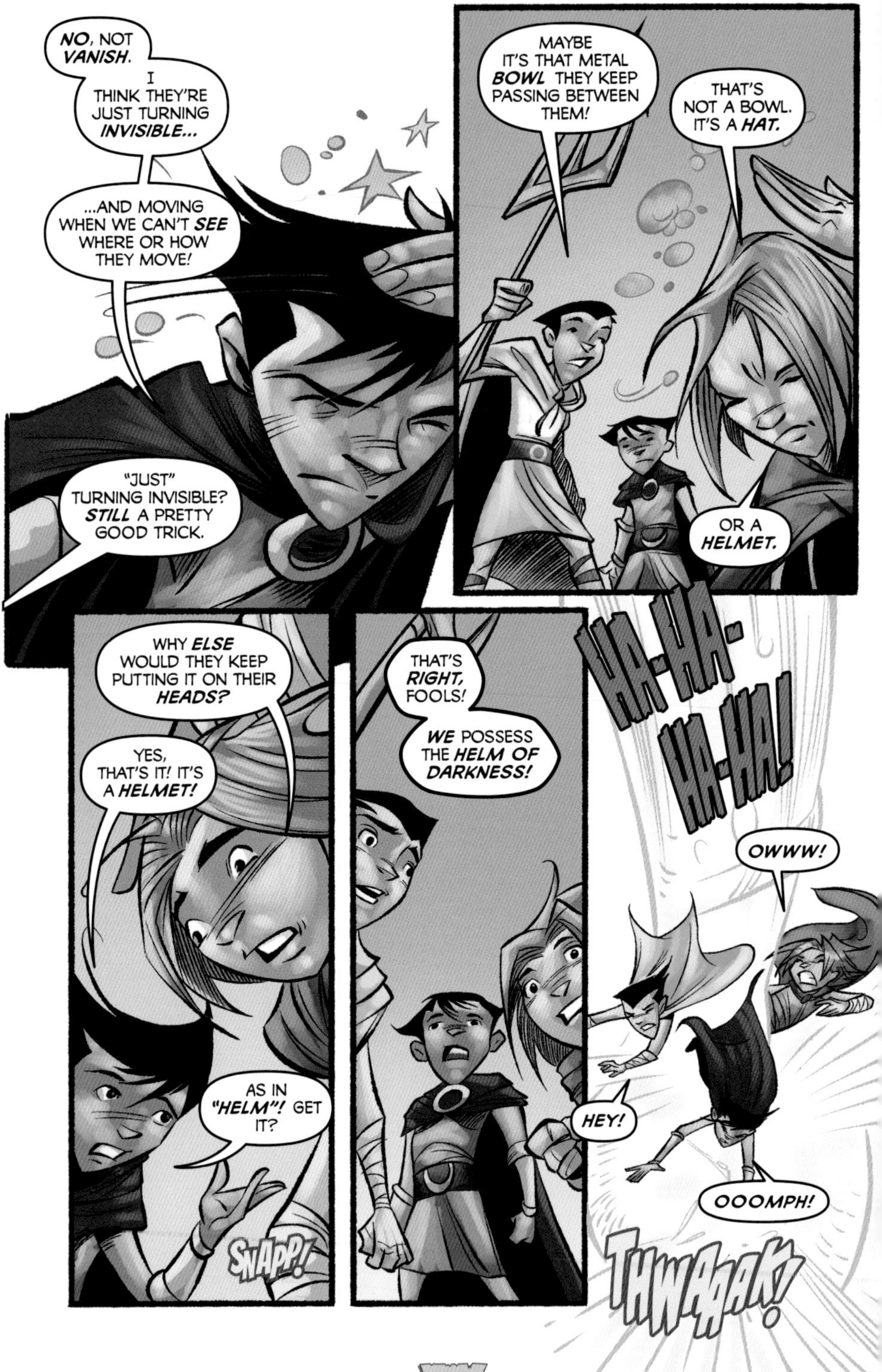
NO, NOT VANISH.
I THINK THEY'RE JUST TURNING INVISIBLE...
...AND MOVING WHEN WE CAN'T SEE WHERE OR HOW THEY MOVE!
"JUST" TURNING INVISIBLE? STILL A PRETTY GOOD TRICK.
MAYBE IT'S THAT METAL BOWL THEY KEEP PASSING BETWEEN THEM!
THAT'S NOT A BOWL. IT'S A HAT.
OR A HELMET.
WHY ELSE WOULD THEY KEEP PUTTING IT ON THEIR HEADS?
YES, THAT'S IT! IT'S A HELMET!
AS IN "HELM"! GET IT?
SNAPP!
THAT'S RIGHT, FOOLS!
WE POSSESS THE HELM OF DARKNESS!
HA-HA-HA-HA!
OWWW!
HEY!
OOOMPH!
THWAAAK!

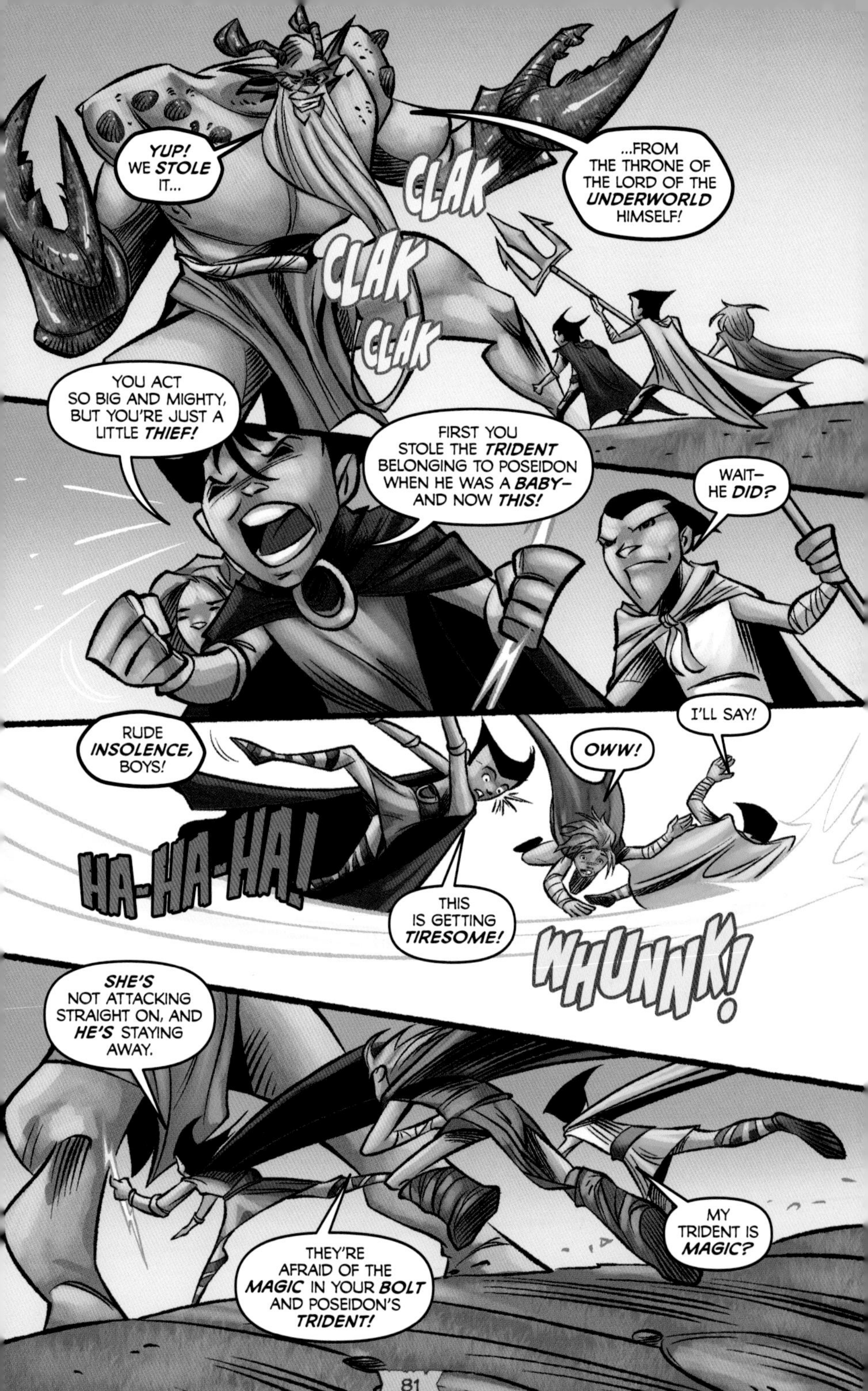
YUP! WE STOLE IT...
...FROM THE THRONE OF THE LORD OF THE UNDERWORLD HIMSELF!
CLAK
CLAK
CLAK
YOU ACT SO BIG AND MIGHTY, BUT YOU'RE JUST A LITTLE THIEF!
FIRST YOU STOLE THE TRIDENT BELONGING TO POSEIDON WHEN HE WAS A BABY— AND NOW THIS!
WAIT— HE DID?
RUDE INSOLENCE, BOYS!
OWW!
I'LL SAY!
HA-HA-HA!
THIS IS GETTING TIRESOME!
WHUNNK!
SHE'S NOT ATTACKING STRAIGHT ON, AND HE'S STAYING AWAY.
THEY'RE AFRAID OF THE MAGIC IN YOUR BOLT AND POSEIDON'S TRIDENT!
MY TRIDENT IS MAGIC?

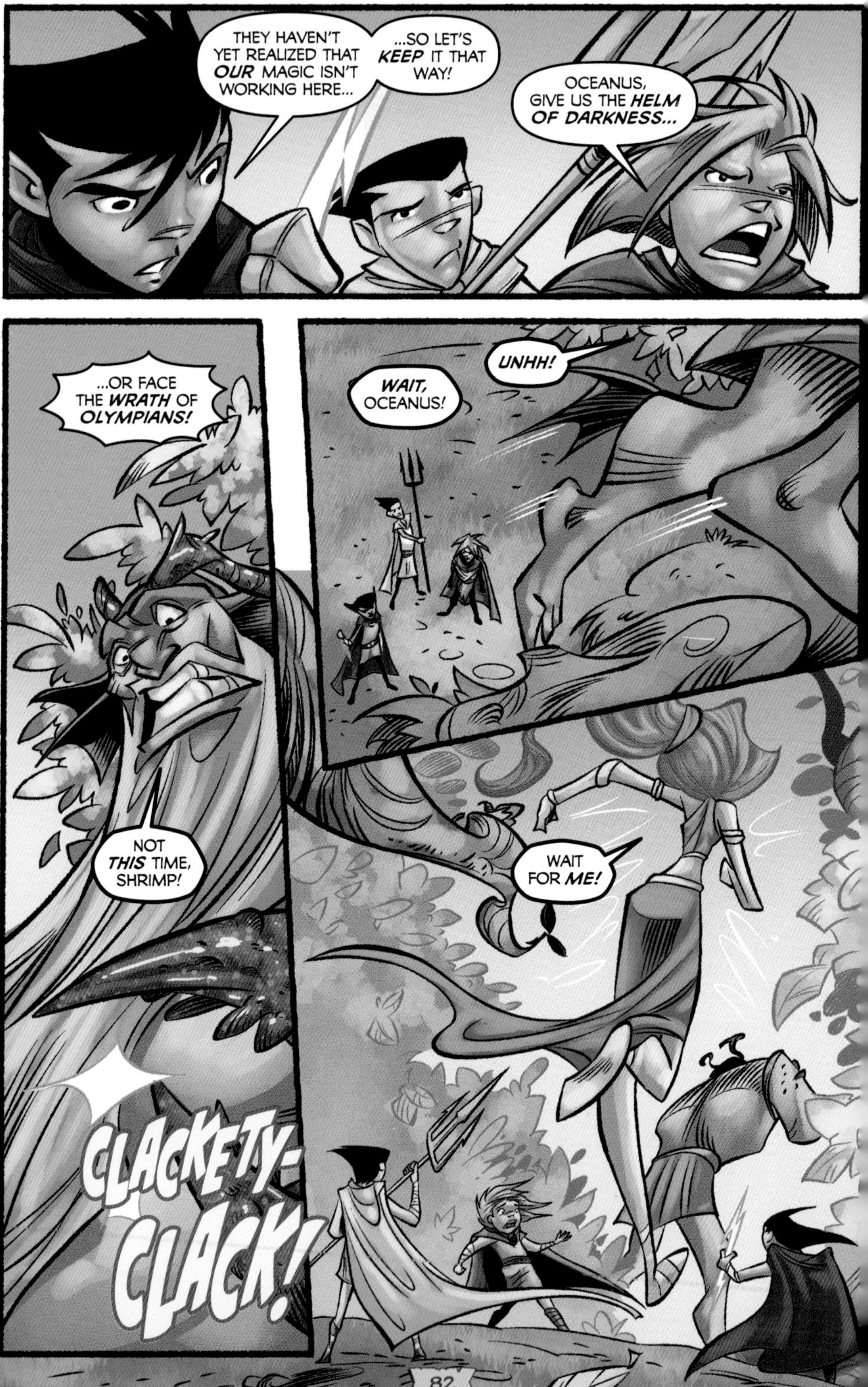
THEY HAVEN'T YET REALIZED THAT OUR MAGIC ISN'T WORKING HERE...
...SO LET'S KEEP IT THAT WAY!
OCEANUS, GIVE US THE HELM OF DARKNESS...
...OR FACE THE WRATH OF OLYMPIANS!
NOT THIS TIME, SHRIMP!
CLACKETY-CLACK!
UNHH!
WAIT, OCEANUS!
WAIT FOR ME!

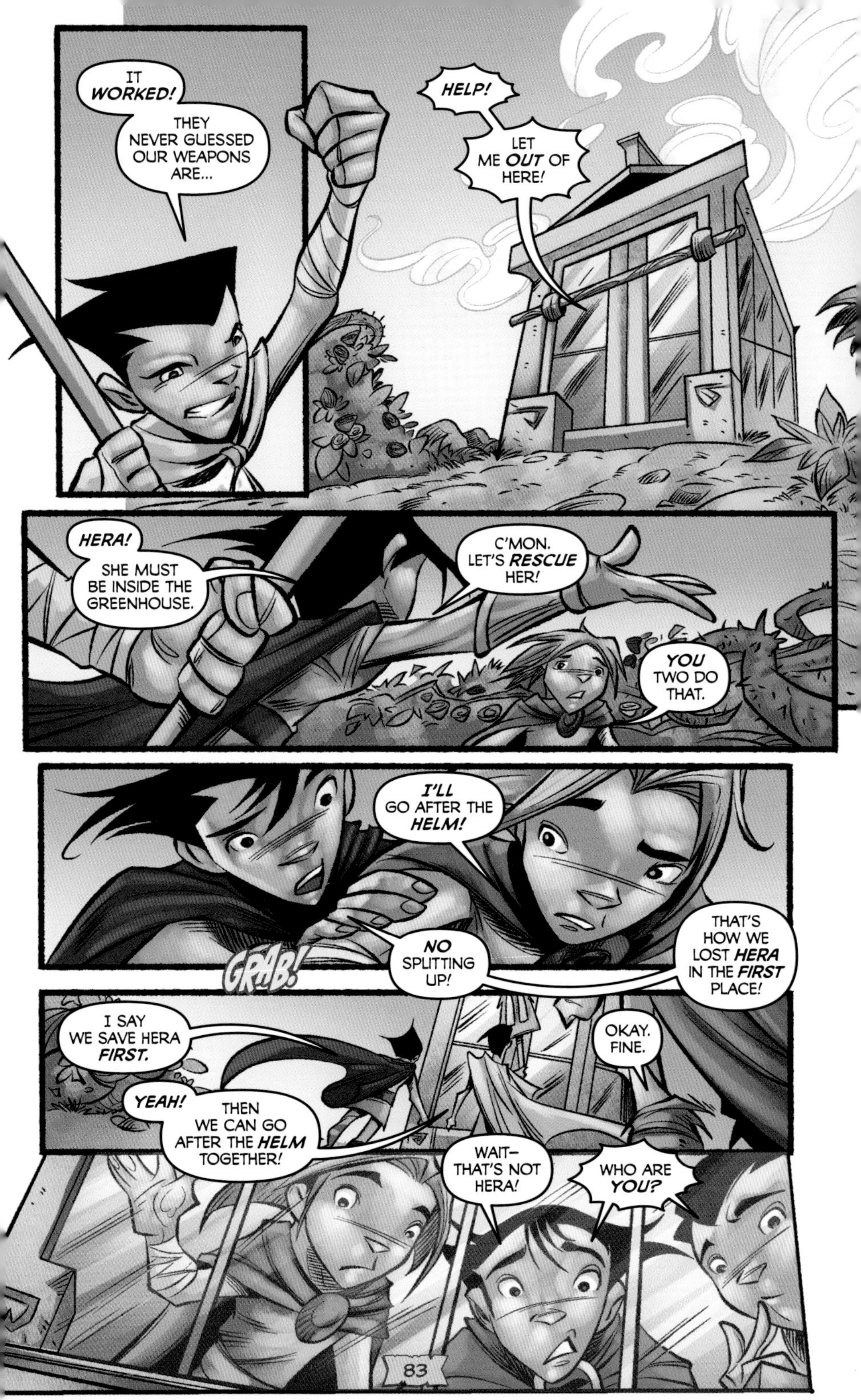
IT WORKED!
THEY NEVER GUESSED OUR WEAPONS ARE...
HELP!
LET ME OUT OF HERE!
HERA!
SHE MUST BE INSIDE THE GREENHOUSE.
C'MON. LET'S RESCUE HER!
YOU TWO DO THAT.
I'LL GO AFTER THE HELM!
GRAB!
NO SPLITTING UP!
THAT'S HOW WE LOST HERA IN THE FIRST PLACE!
I SAY WE SAVE HERA FIRST.
OKAY. FINE.
YEAH!
THEN WE CAN GO AFTER THE HELM TOGETHER!
WAIT— THAT'S NOT HERA!
WHO ARE YOU?

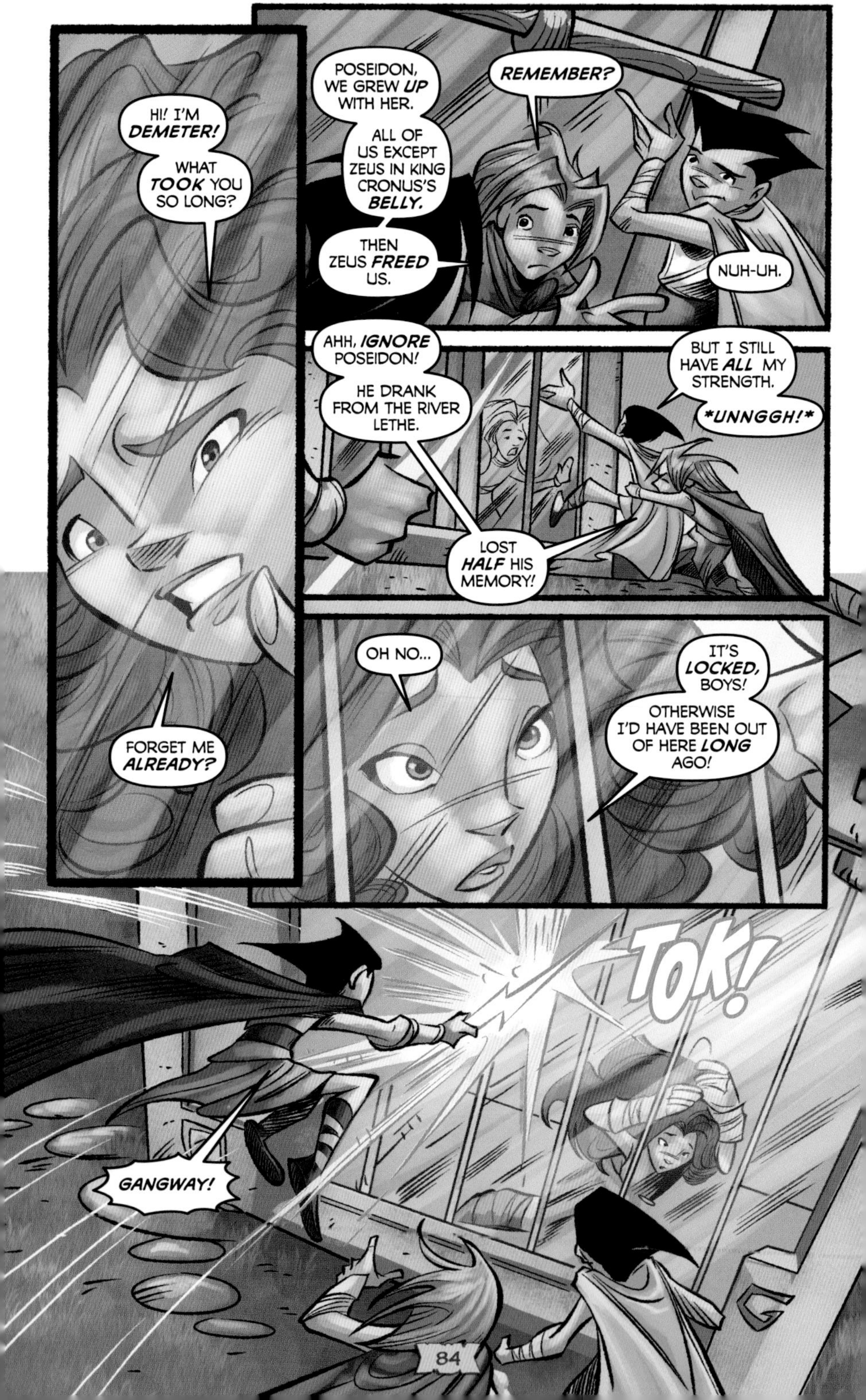

HI! I'M DEMETER!
WHAT TOOK YOU SO LONG?
FORGET ME ALREADY?
POSEIDON, WE GREW UP WITH HER.
ALL OF US EXCEPT ZEUS IN KING CRONUS'S BELLY.
THEN ZEUS FREED US.
REMEMBER?
NUH-UH.
AHH, IGNORE POSEIDON!
HE DRANK FROM THE RIVER LETHE.
LOST HALF HIS MEMORY!
BUT I STILL HAVE ALL MY STRENGTH.
UNNGGH!
OH NO...
IT'S LOCKED, BOYS!
OTHERWISE I'D HAVE BEEN OUT OF HERE LONG AGO!
TOK!
GANGWAY!

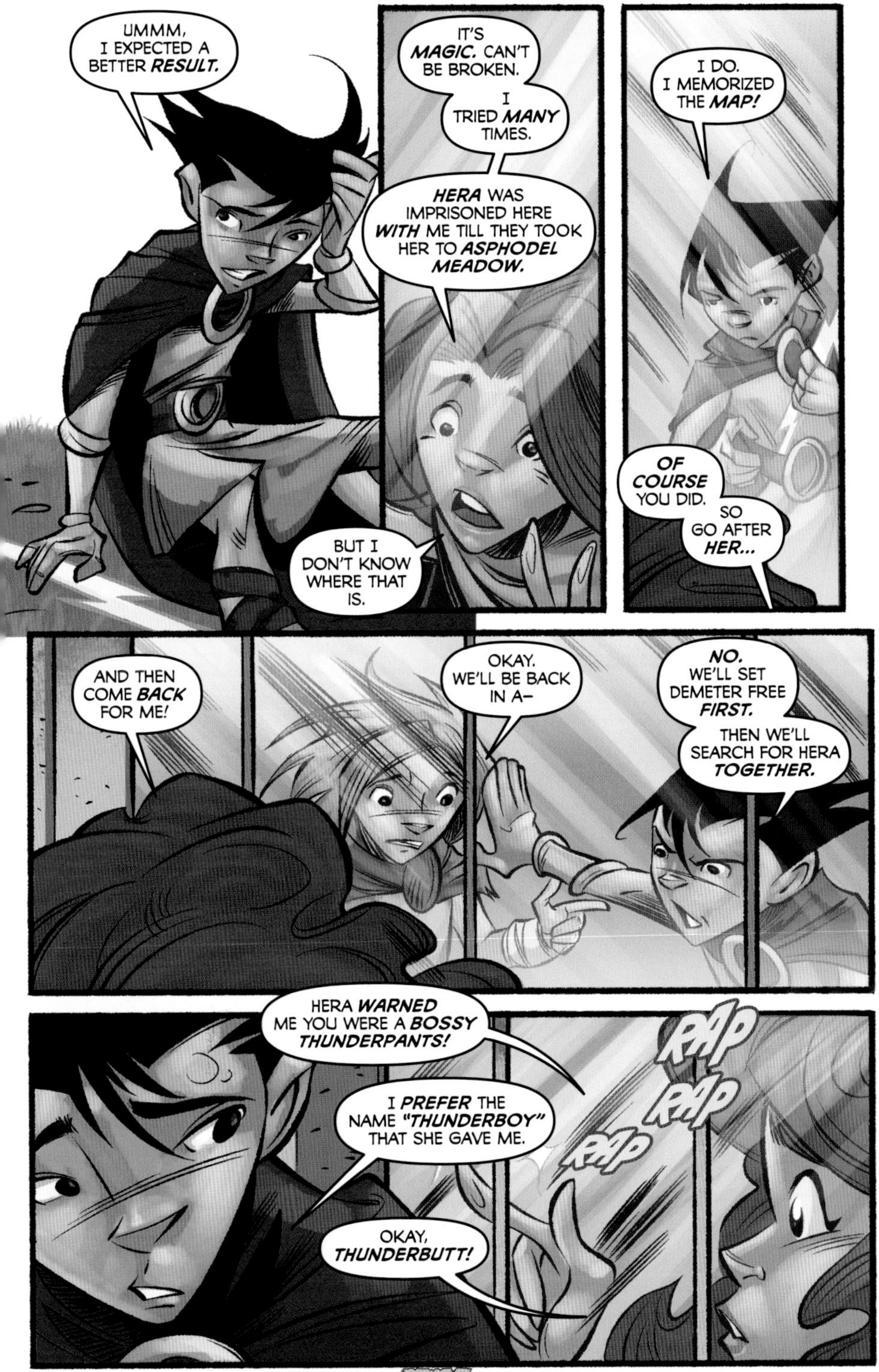
UMMM, I EXPECTED A BETTER RESULT.
IT'S MAGIC. CAN'T BE BROKEN.
I TRIED MANY TIMES.
HERA WAS IMPRISONED HERE WITH ME TILL THEY TOOK HER TO ASPHODEL MEADOW.
BUT I DON'T KNOW WHERE THAT IS.
I DO. I MEMORIZED THE MAP!
OF COURSE YOU DID.
SO GO AFTER HER...
AND THEN COME BACK FOR ME!
OKAY. WE'LL BE BACK IN A–
NO. WE'LL SET DEMETER FREE FIRST.
THEN WE'LL SEARCH FOR HERA TOGETHER.
HERA WARNED ME YOU WERE A BOSSY THUNDERPANTS!
I PREFER THE NAME "THUNDERBOY" THAT SHE GAVE ME.
RAP RAP RAP
OKAY, THUNDERBUTT!

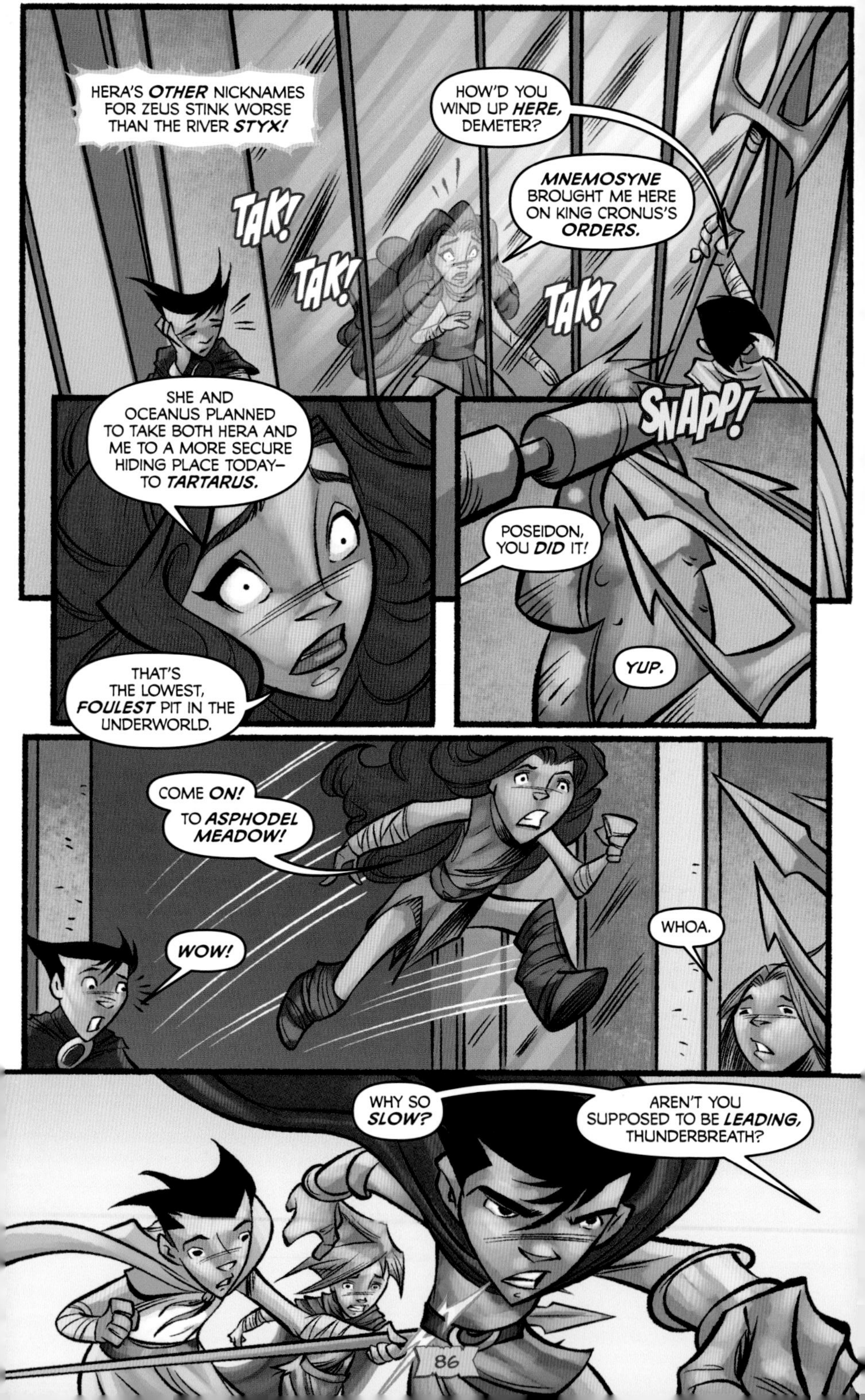
HERA'S *OTHER* NICKNAMES FOR ZEUS STINK WORSE THAN THE RIVER *STYX!*
HOW'D YOU WIND UP *HERE,* DEMETER?
MNEMOSYNE BROUGHT ME HERE ON KING CRONUS'S *ORDERS.*
TAK!
TAK!
TAK!
SHE AND OCEANUS PLANNED TO TAKE BOTH HERA AND ME TO A MORE SECURE HIDING PLACE TODAY— TO *TARTARUS.*
THAT'S THE LOWEST, *FOULEST* PIT IN THE UNDERWORLD.
SNAPP!
POSEIDON, YOU *DID* IT!
YUP.
COME *ON!* TO *ASPHODEL MEADOW!*
WOW!
WHOA.
WHY SO *SLOW?*
AREN'T YOU SUPPOSED TO BE *LEADING,* THUNDERBREATH?

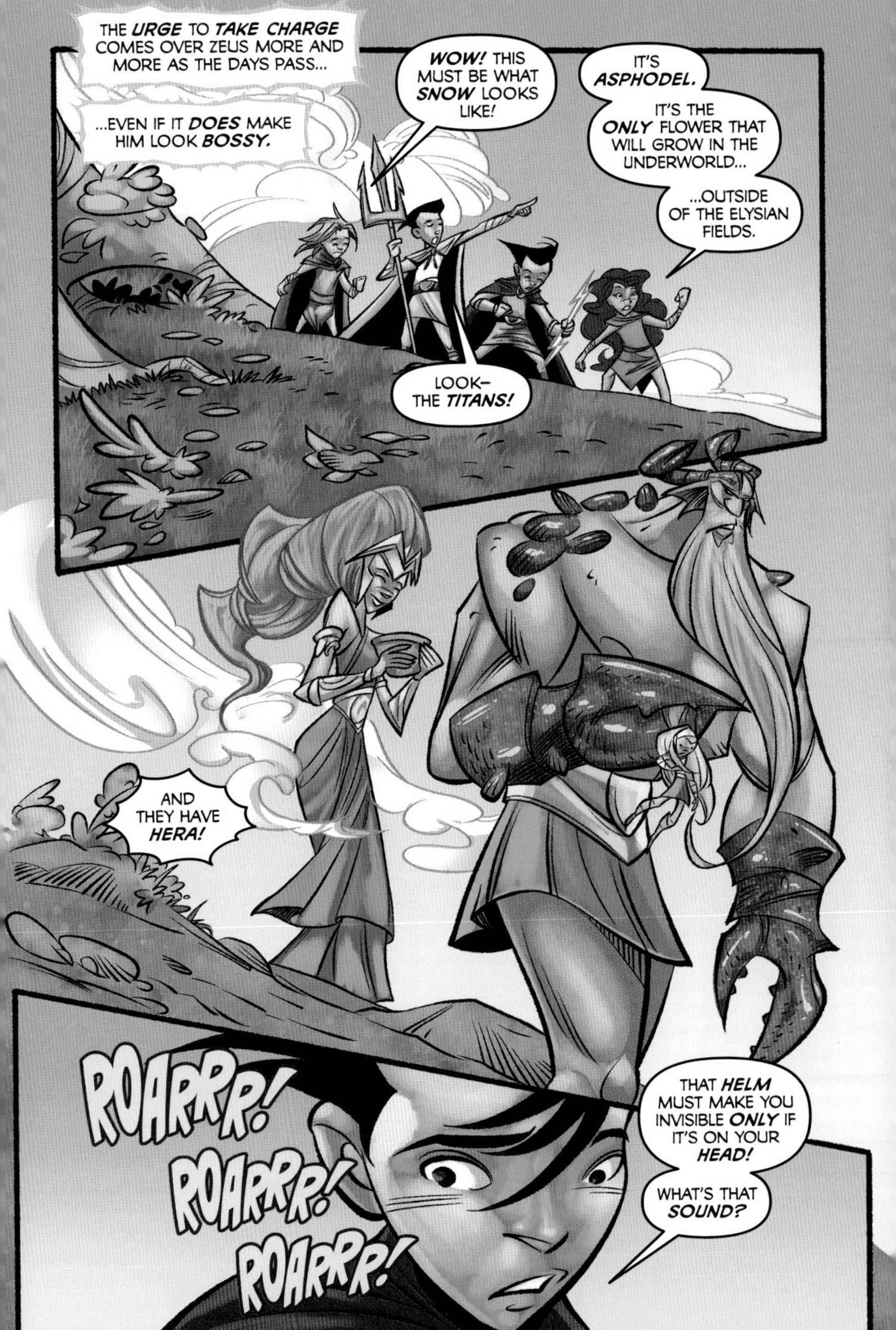
THE URGE TO TAKE CHARGE COMES OVER ZEUS MORE AND MORE AS THE DAYS PASS...
...EVEN IF IT DOES MAKE HIM LOOK BOSSY.
WOW! THIS MUST BE WHAT SNOW LOOKS LIKE!
IT'S ASPHODEL.
IT'S THE ONLY FLOWER THAT WILL GROW IN THE UNDERWORLD...
...OUTSIDE OF THE ELYSIAN FIELDS.
LOOK— THE TITANS!
AND THEY HAVE HERA!
ROARRR! ROARRR! ROARRR!
THAT HELM MUST MAKE YOU INVISIBLE ONLY IF IT'S ON YOUR HEAD!
WHAT'S THAT SOUND?

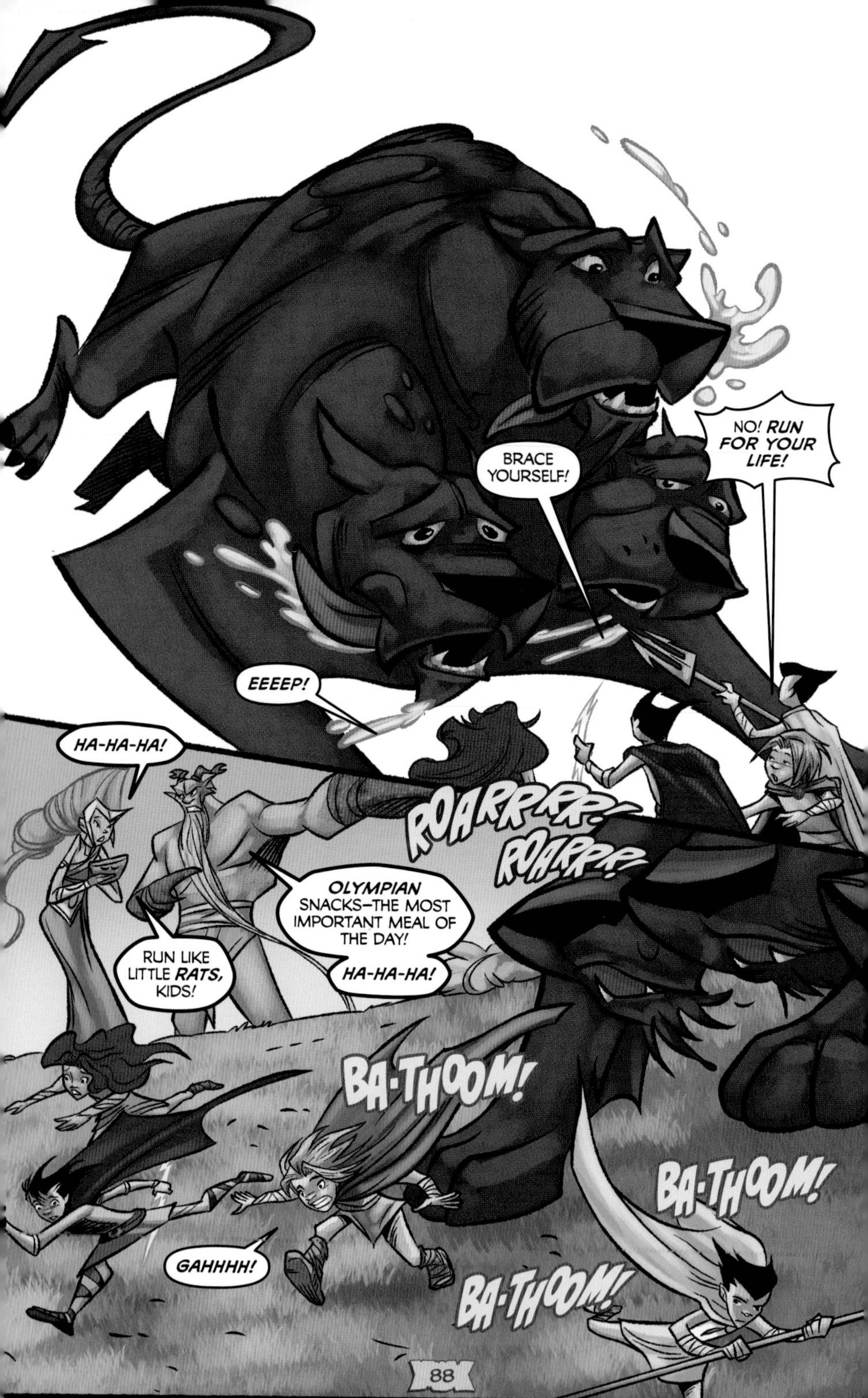
BRACE YOURSELF!
NO! RUN FOR YOUR LIFE!
EEEEP!
HA-HA-HA!
ROARRRR!
ROARRR!
OLYMPIAN SNACKS—THE MOST IMPORTANT MEAL OF THE DAY!
HA-HA-HA!
RUN LIKE LITTLE RATS, KIDS!
BA-THOOM!
BA-THOOM!
GAHHHH!
BA-THOOM!

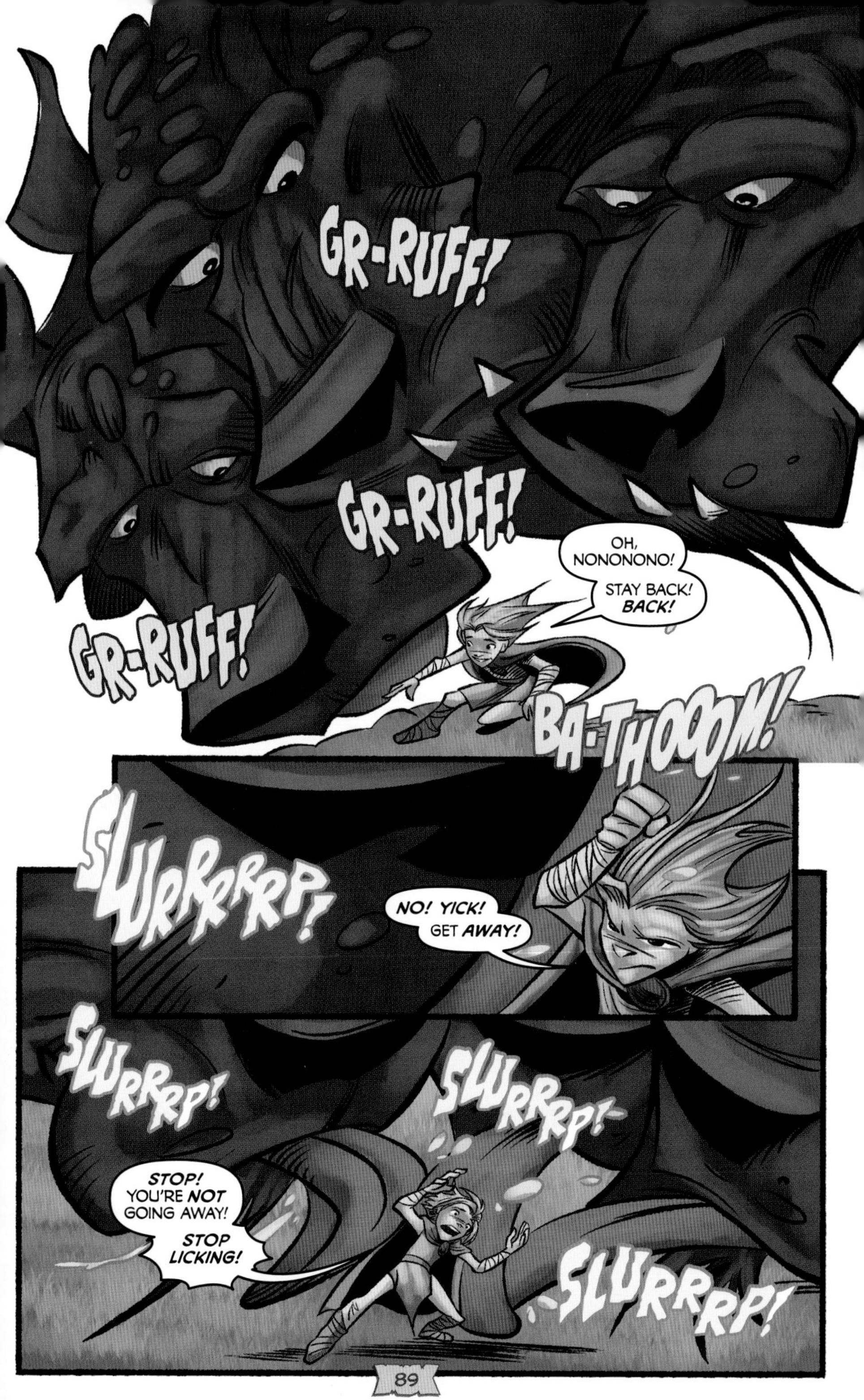
GR-RUFF!
GR-RUFF!
GR-RUFF!
OH, NONONONO!
STAY BACK! BACK!
BA-THOOOM!
SLURRRRP!
NO! YICK! GET AWAY!
SLURRRP!
SLURRRP!
STOP! YOU'RE NOT GOING AWAY!
STOP LICKING!
SLURRRP!

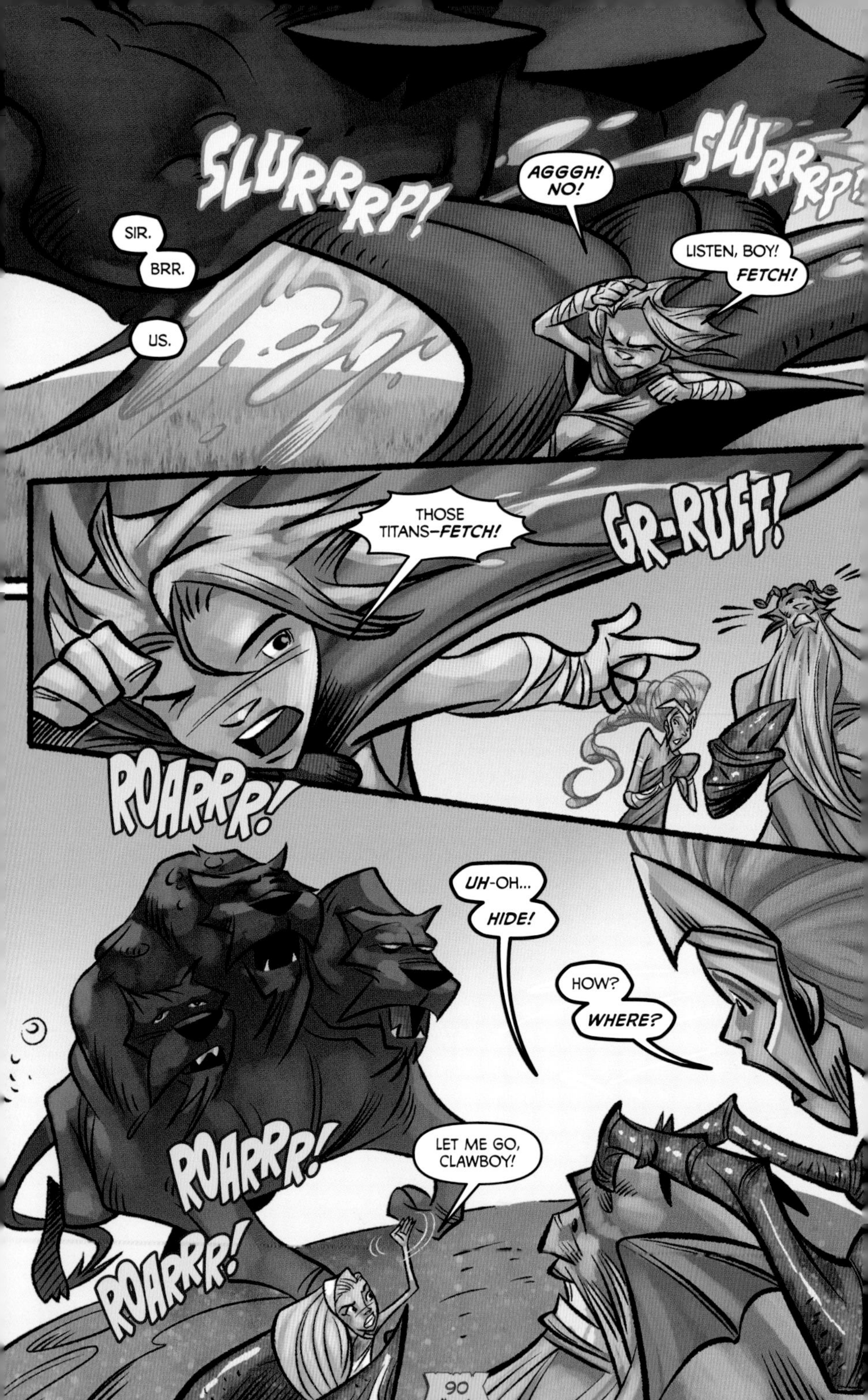
SLURRRP!
AGGGH! NO!
SLURRRP!
SIR.
BRR.
US.
LISTEN, BOY! FETCH!
THOSE TITANS—FETCH!
GR-RUFF!
ROARRR!
UH-OH... HIDE!
HOW? WHERE?
ROARRR!
LET ME GO, CLAWBOY!
ROARRR!

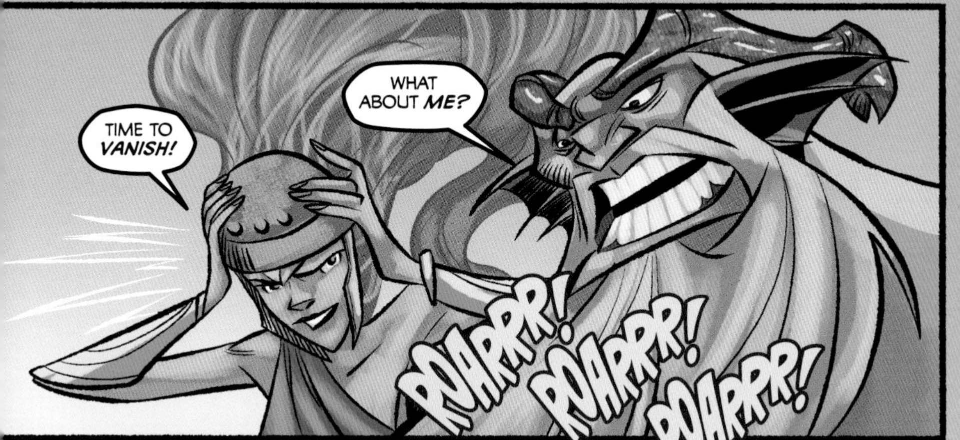
TIME TO VANISH!
WHAT ABOUT ME?
ROARRR! ROARRR! ROARRR!

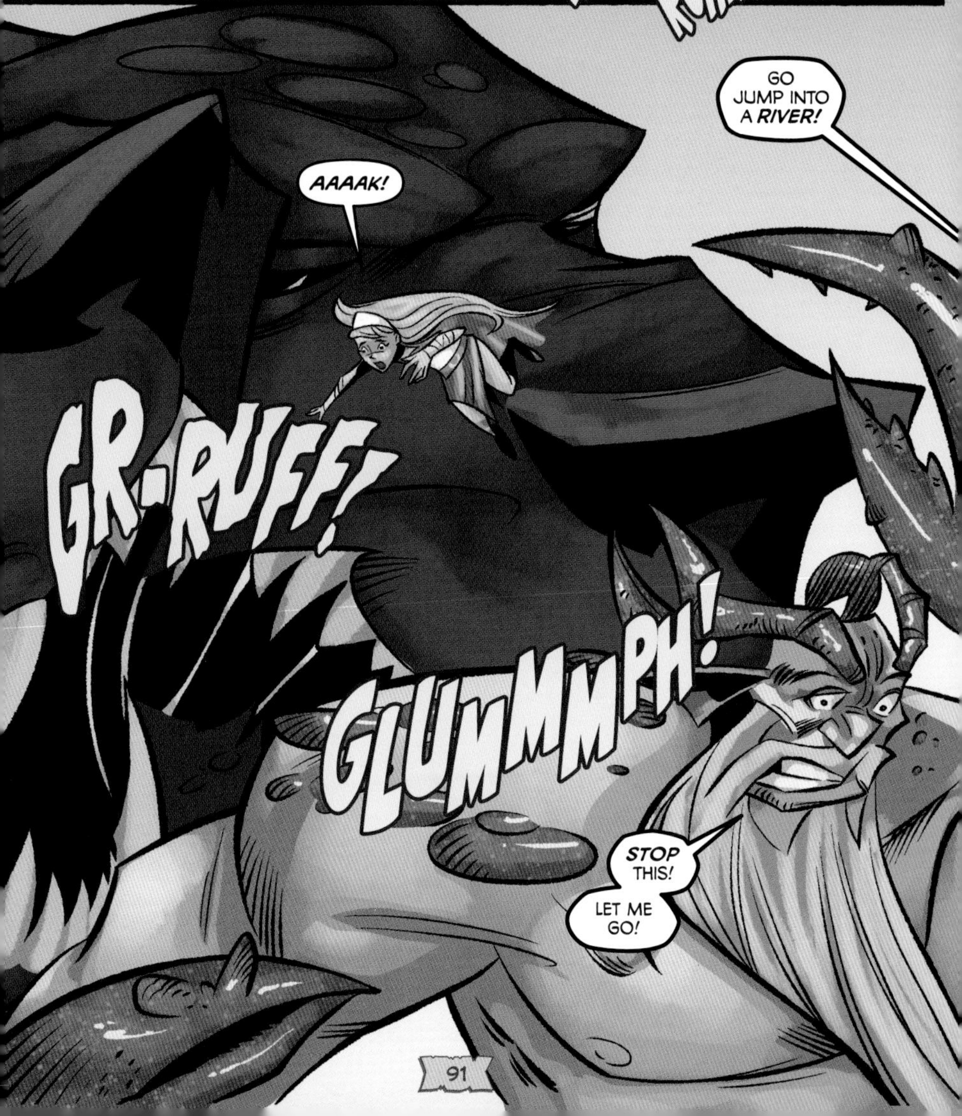
GO JUMP INTO A RIVER!
AAAAK!
GR-RUFF!
GLUMMMPH!
STOP THIS!
LET ME GO!

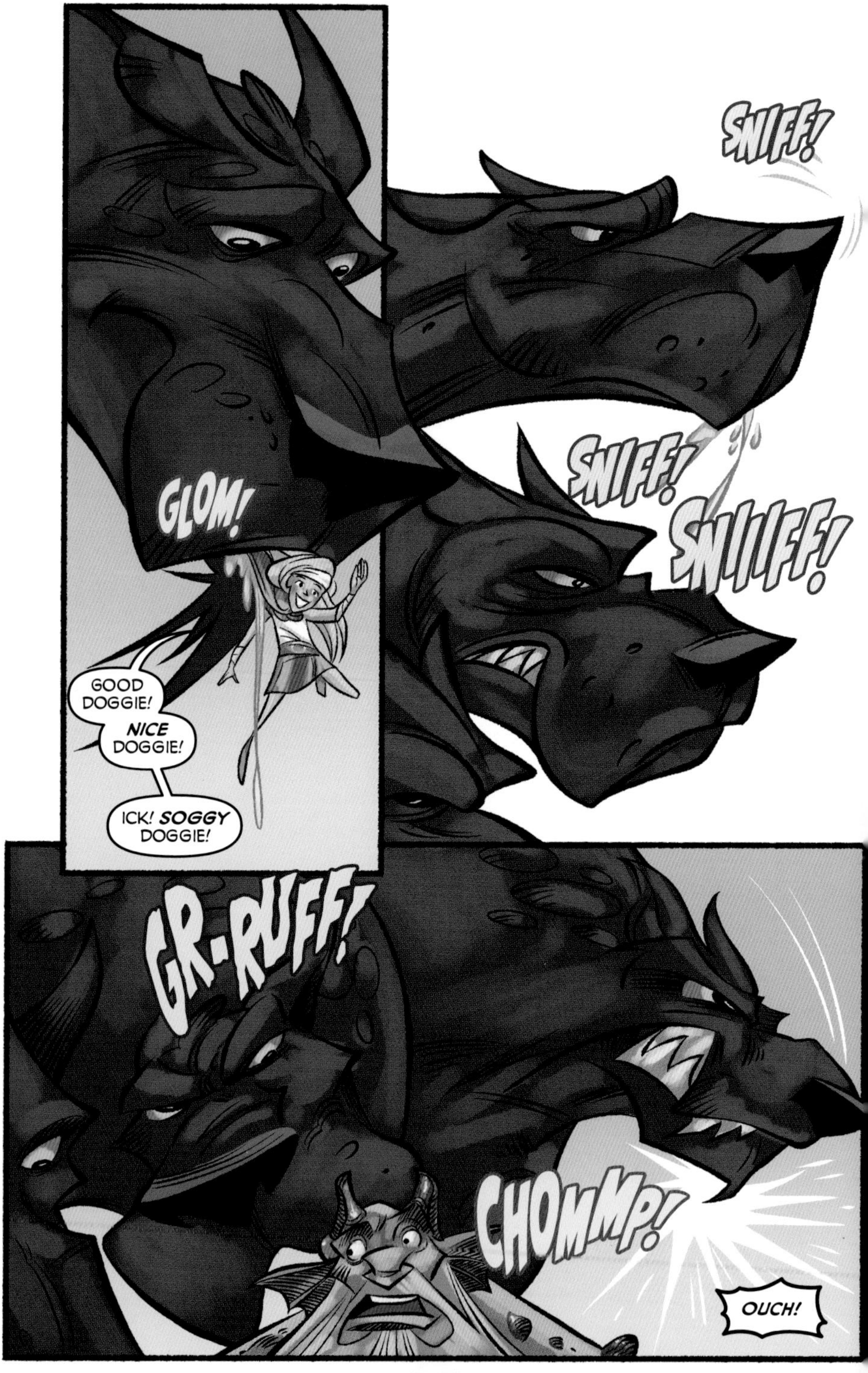
SNIFF!
GLOM!
SNIFF!
SNIIIFF!
GOOD DOGGIE!
NICE DOGGIE!
ICK! SOGGY DOGGIE!
GR-RUFF!
CHOMMP!
OUCH!

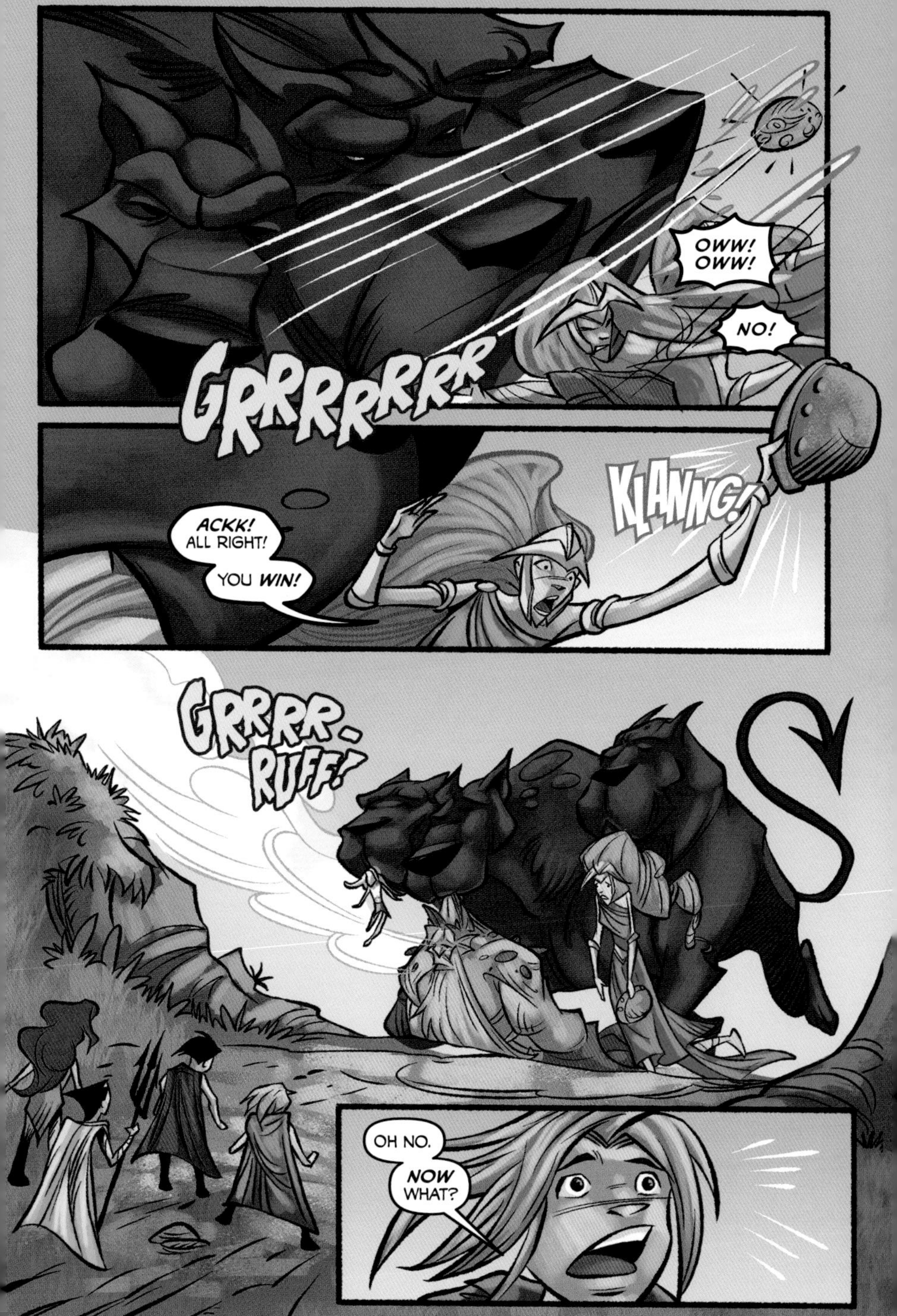

OWW!
OWW!
NO!
GRRRRRRR
KLANNG!
ACKK!
ALL RIGHT!
YOU WIN!
GRRRR-
RUFF!
OH NO.
NOW
WHAT?

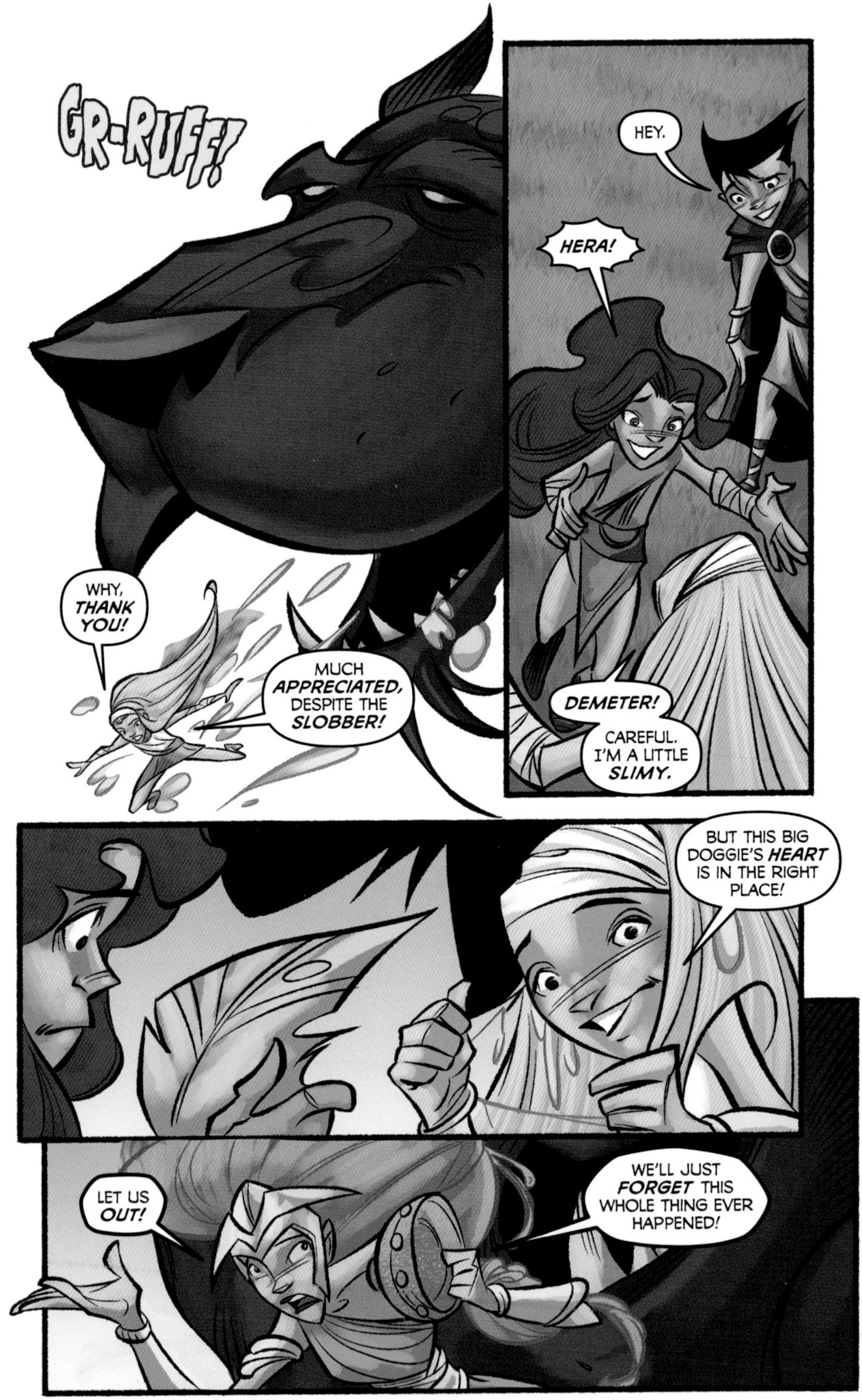
GR-RUFF!
HEY.
HERA!
WHY, THANK YOU!
MUCH APPRECIATED, DESPITE THE SLOBBER!
DEMETER!
CAREFUL. I'M A LITTLE SLIMY.
BUT THIS BIG DOGGIE'S HEART IS IN THE RIGHT PLACE!
LET US OUT!
WE'LL JUST FORGET THIS WHOLE THING EVER HAPPENED!

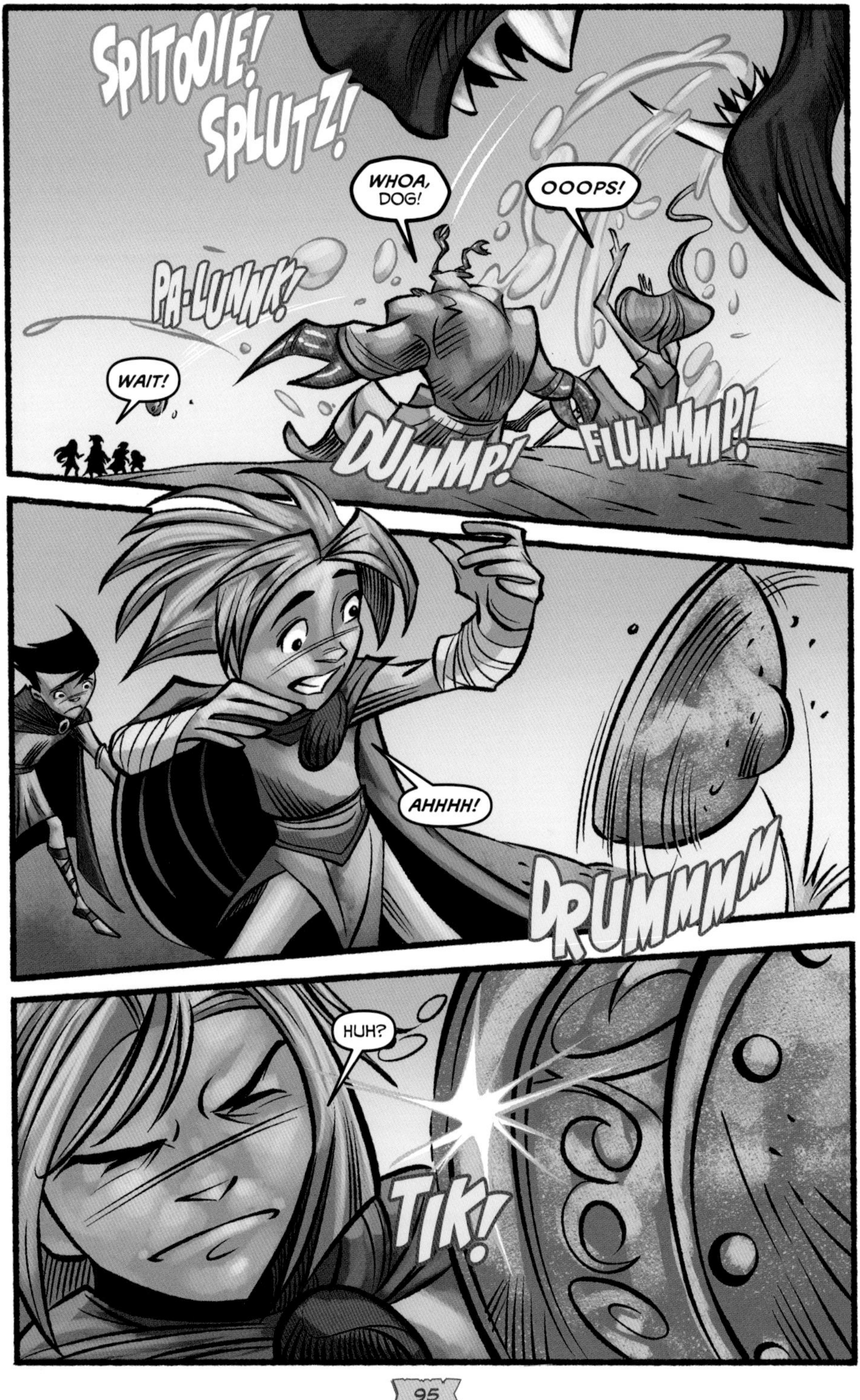
SPITOOIE!
SPLUTZ!
WHOA, DOG!
OOOPS!
PA-LUNNK!
WAIT!
DUMMP!
FLUMMMP!
AHHHH!
DRUMMMM
HUH?
TIK!

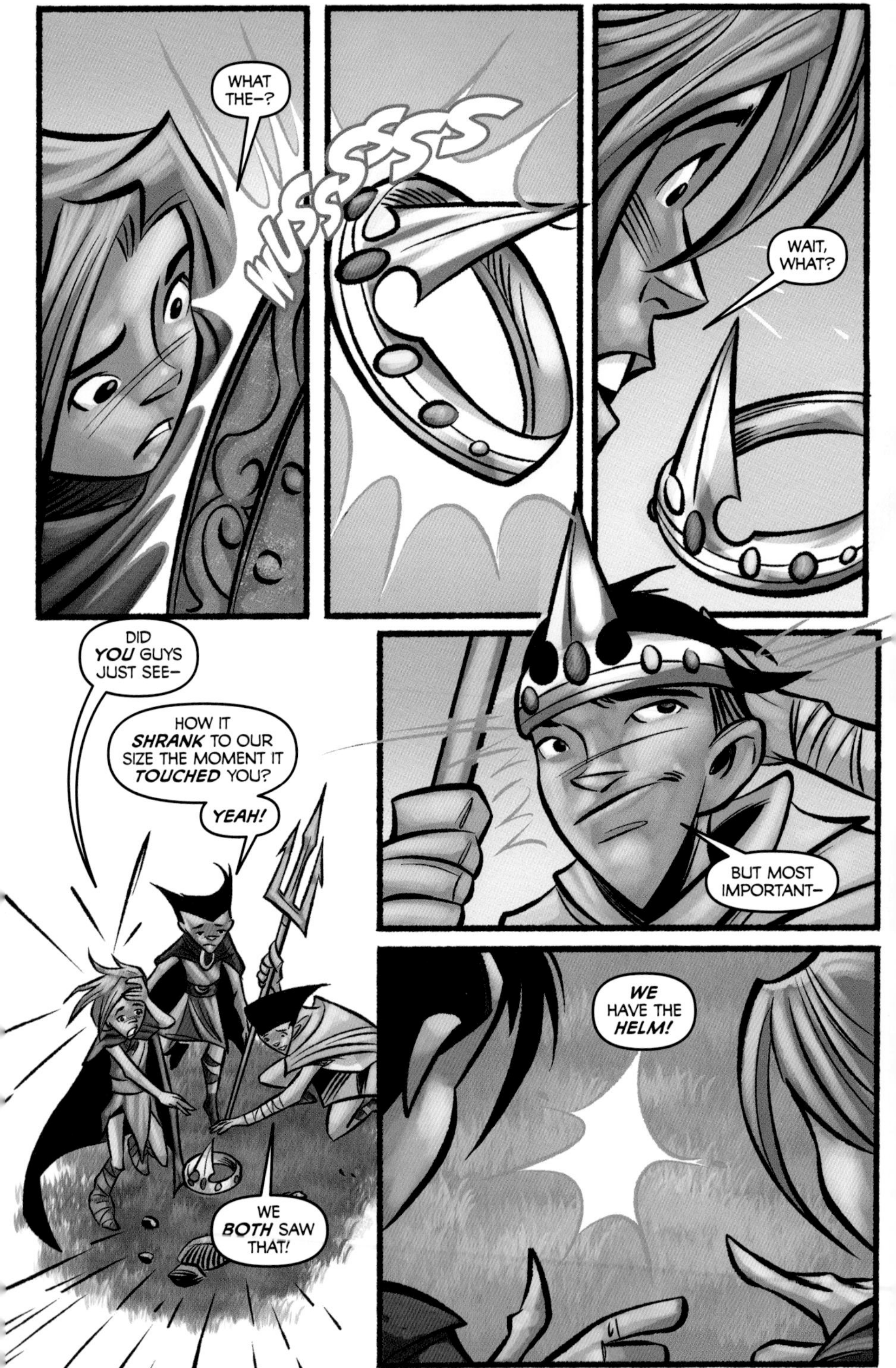
WHAT THE–?
WUSSSSSS
WAIT, WHAT?
DID YOU GUYS JUST SEE–
HOW IT SHRANK TO OUR SIZE THE MOMENT IT TOUCHED YOU?
YEAH!
WE BOTH SAW THAT!
BUT MOST IMPORTANT–
WE HAVE THE HELM!

CHAPTER EIGHT:
THE FURIES

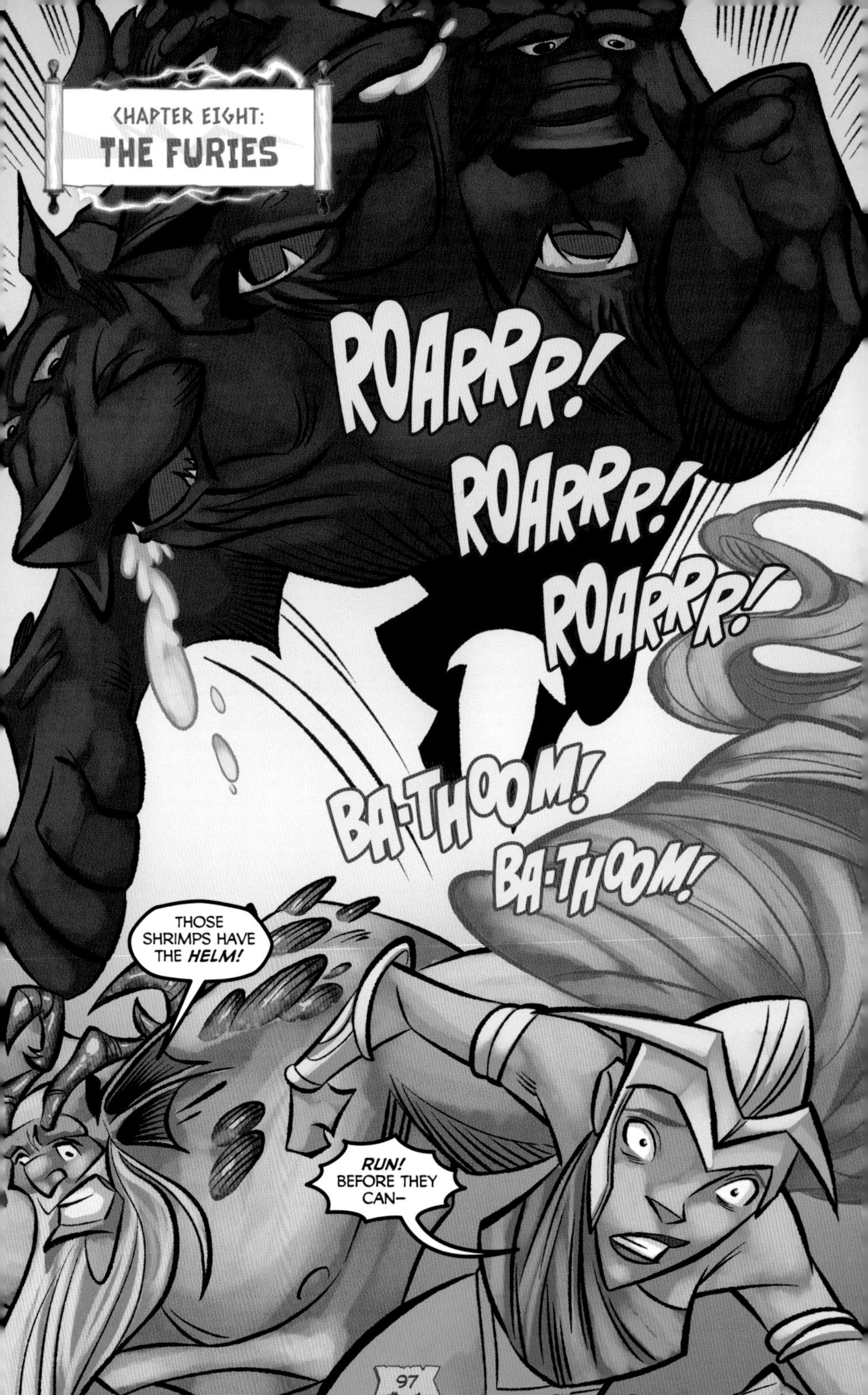
ROARRR!
ROARRR!
ROARRR!
BA-THOOM!
BA-THOOM!
THOSE SHRIMPS HAVE THE *HELM!*
RUN! BEFORE THEY CAN–

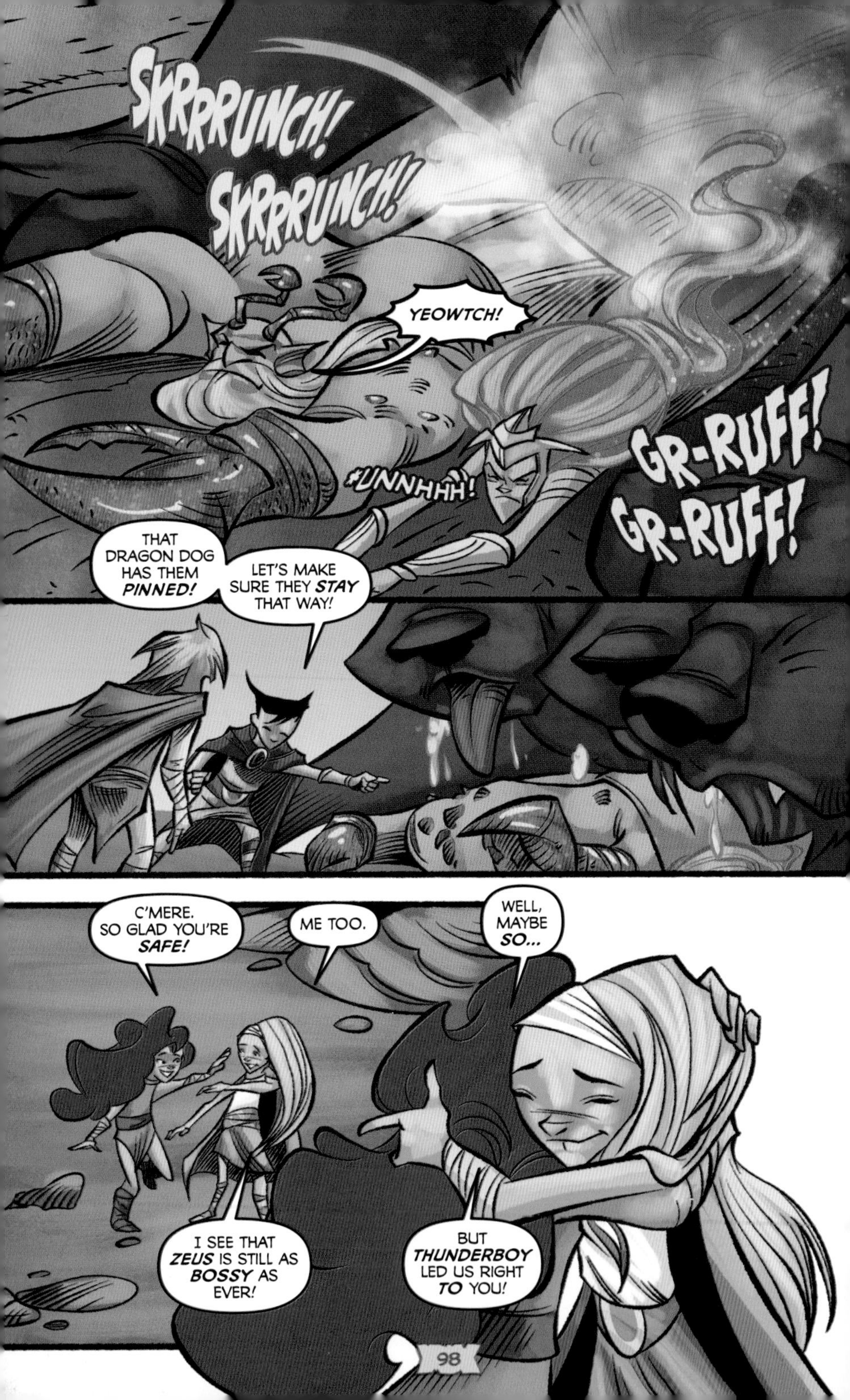
SKRRRUNCH!
SKRRRUNCH!
YEOWTCH!
UNNHHH!
GR-RUFF!
GR-RUFF!
THAT DRAGON DOG HAS THEM *PINNED!*
LET'S MAKE SURE THEY *STAY* THAT WAY!
C'MERE. SO GLAD YOU'RE *SAFE!*
ME TOO.
WELL, MAYBE *SO...*
I SEE THAT *ZEUS* IS STILL AS *BOSSY* AS EVER!
BUT *THUNDERBOY* LED US RIGHT *TO* YOU!

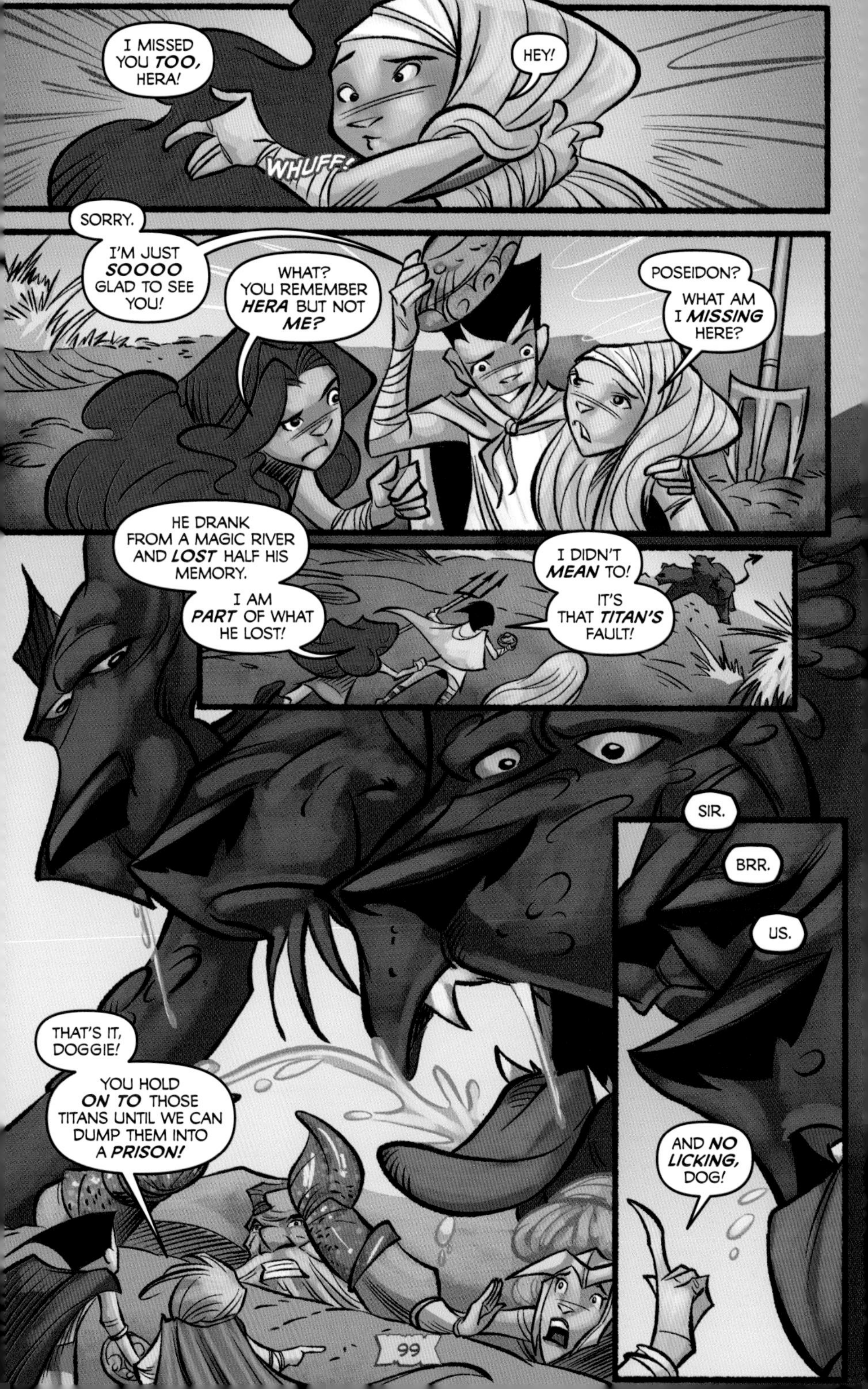
I MISSED YOU *TOO,* HERA!
HEY!
WHUFF!
SORRY.
I'M JUST *SOOOO* GLAD TO SEE YOU!
WHAT? YOU REMEMBER *HERA* BUT NOT *ME?*
POSEIDON?
WHAT AM I *MISSING* HERE?
HE DRANK FROM A MAGIC RIVER AND *LOST* HALF HIS MEMORY.
I AM *PART* OF WHAT HE LOST!
I DIDN'T *MEAN* TO!
IT'S THAT *TITAN'S* FAULT!
SIR.
BRR.
US.
THAT'S IT, DOGGIE!
YOU HOLD *ON TO* THOSE TITANS UNTIL WE CAN DUMP THEM INTO A *PRISON!*
AND *NO LICKING,* DOG!

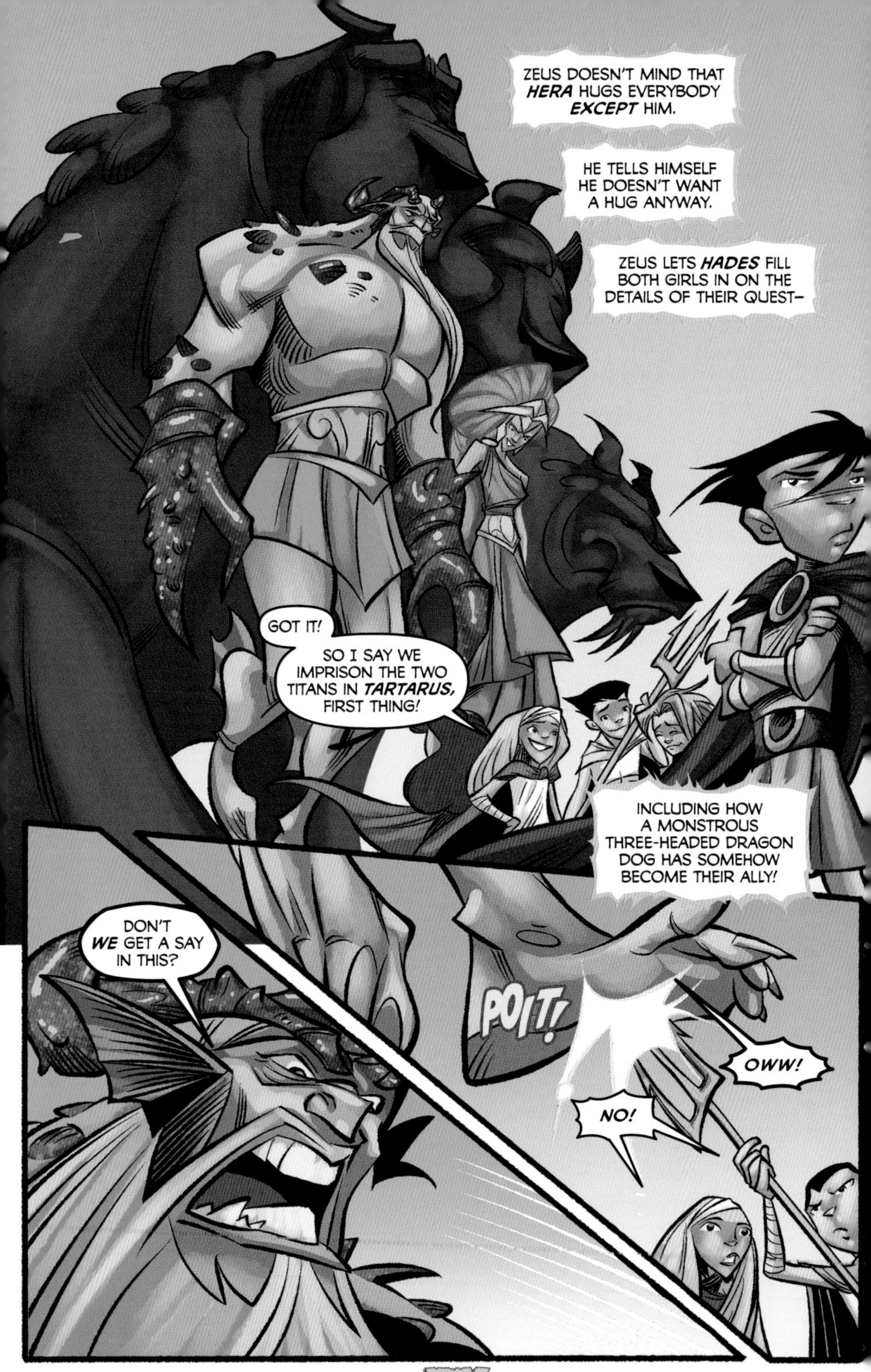
ZEUS DOESN'T MIND THAT HERA HUGS EVERYBODY EXCEPT HIM.
HE TELLS HIMSELF HE DOESN'T WANT A HUG ANYWAY.
ZEUS LETS HADES FILL BOTH GIRLS IN ON THE DETAILS OF THEIR QUEST–
GOT IT!
SO I SAY WE IMPRISON THE TWO TITANS IN TARTARUS, FIRST THING!
INCLUDING HOW A MONSTROUS THREE-HEADED DRAGON DOG HAS SOMEHOW BECOME THEIR ALLY!
DON'T WE GET A SAY IN THIS?
POIT!
OWW!
NO!

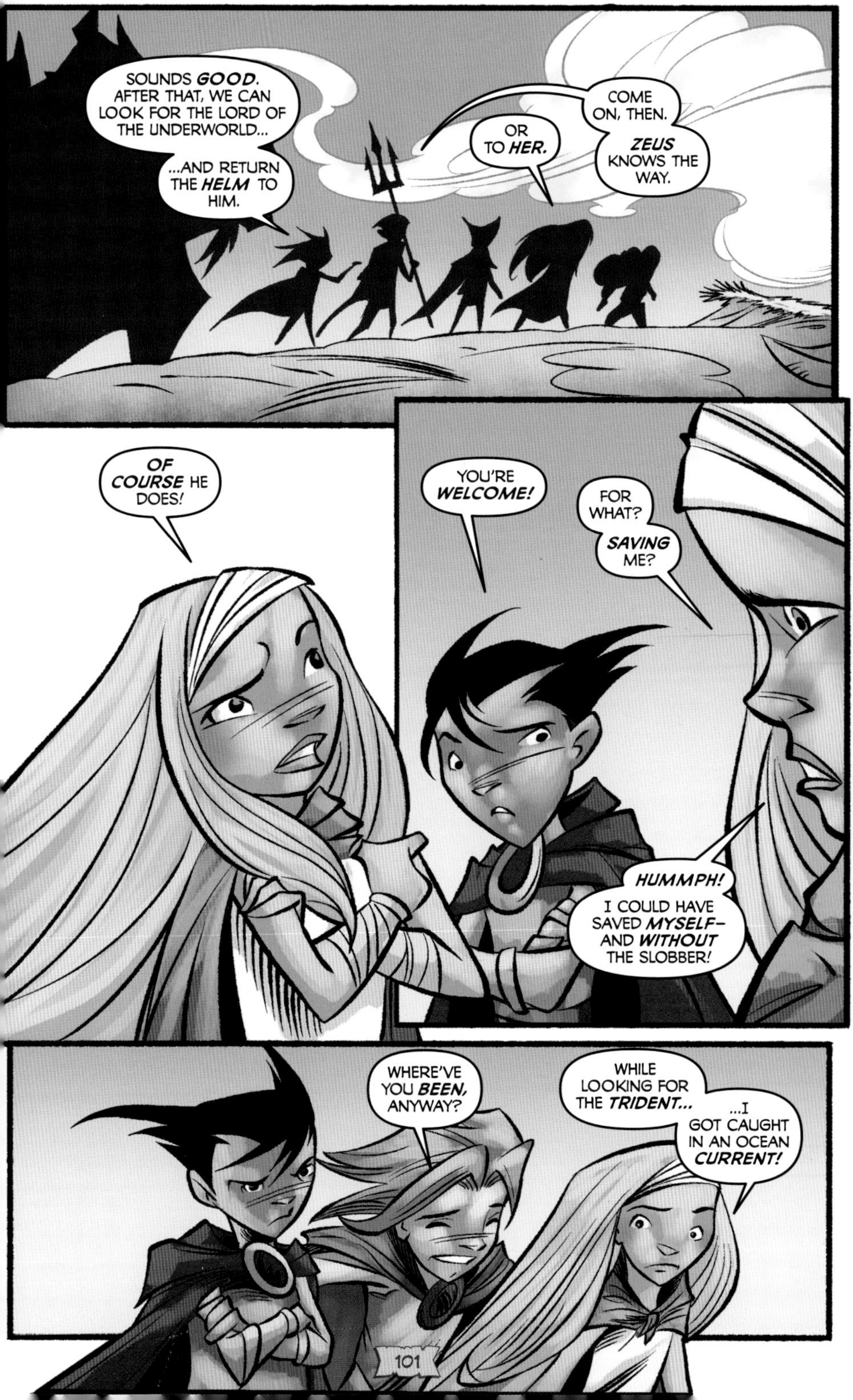
SOUNDS GOOD. AFTER THAT, WE CAN LOOK FOR THE LORD OF THE UNDERWORLD...
...AND RETURN THE HELM TO HIM.
OR TO HER.
COME ON, THEN.
ZEUS KNOWS THE WAY.
OF COURSE HE DOES!
YOU'RE WELCOME!
FOR WHAT?
SAVING ME?
HUMMPH!
I COULD HAVE SAVED MYSELF— AND WITHOUT THE SLOBBER!
WHERE'VE YOU BEEN, ANYWAY?
WHILE LOOKING FOR THE TRIDENT...
...I GOT CAUGHT IN AN OCEAN CURRENT!

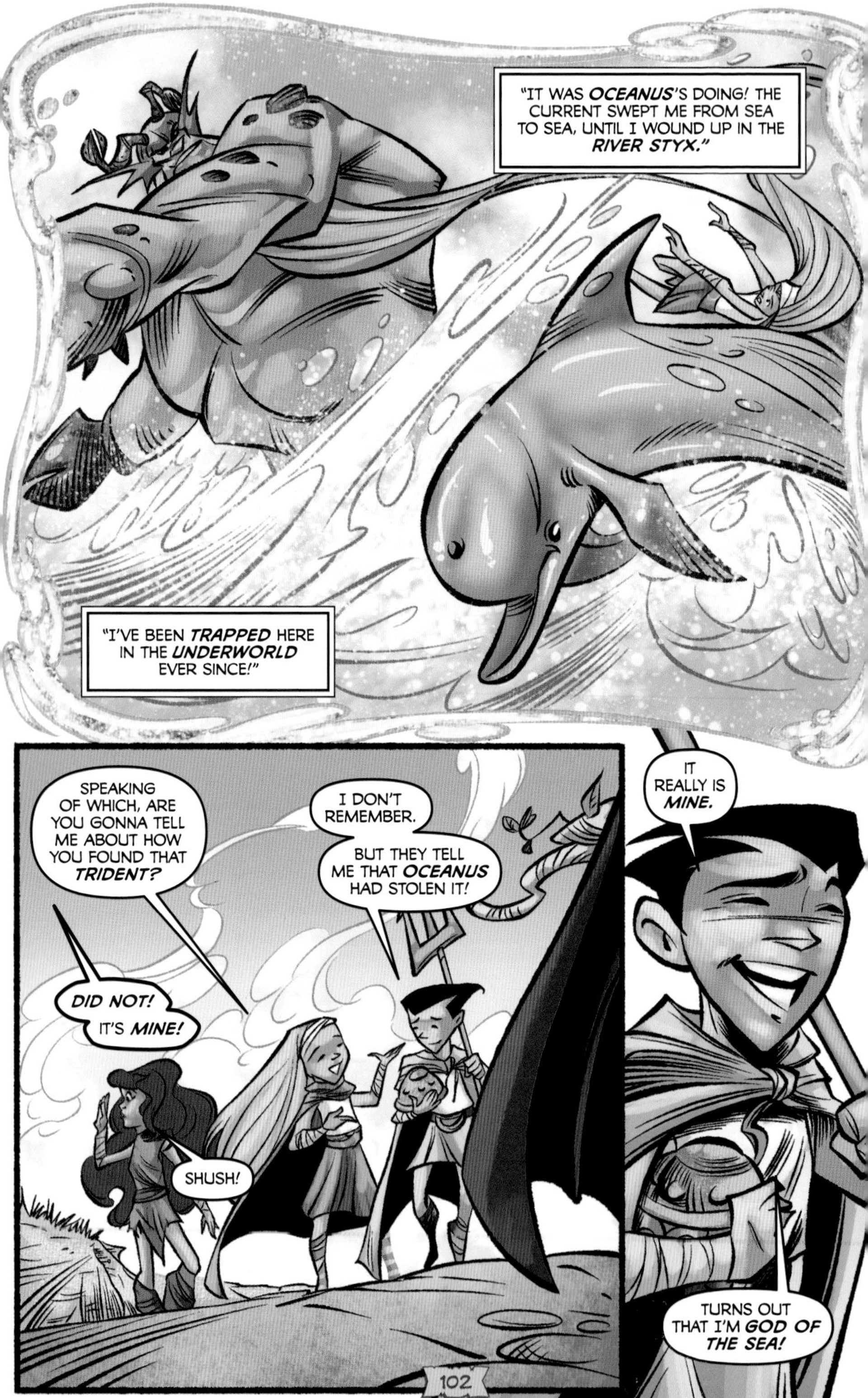
"IT WAS OCEANUS'S DOING! THE CURRENT SWEPT ME FROM SEA TO SEA, UNTIL I WOUND UP IN THE RIVER STYX."
"I'VE BEEN TRAPPED HERE IN THE UNDERWORLD EVER SINCE!"
SPEAKING OF WHICH, ARE YOU GONNA TELL ME ABOUT HOW YOU FOUND THAT TRIDENT?
I DON'T REMEMBER.
BUT THEY TELL ME THAT OCEANUS HAD STOLEN IT!
DID NOT!
IT'S MINE!
SHUSH!
IT REALLY IS MINE.
TURNS OUT THAT I'M GOD OF THE SEA!

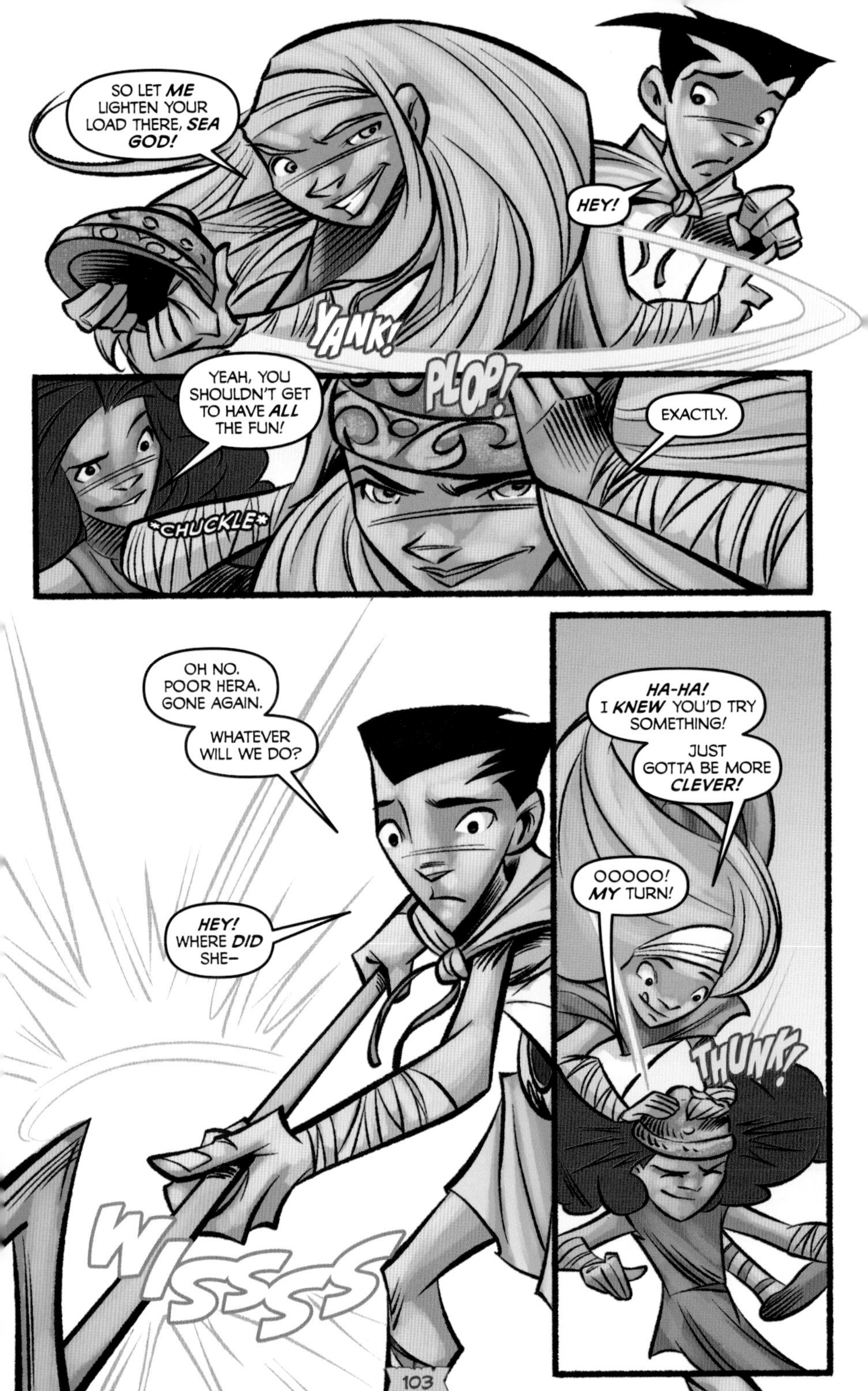
SO LET ME LIGHTEN YOUR LOAD THERE, SEA GOD!
HEY!
YANK!
PLOP!
YEAH, YOU SHOULDN'T GET TO HAVE ALL THE FUN!
CHUCKLE
EXACTLY.
OH NO. POOR HERA. GONE AGAIN.
WHATEVER WILL WE DO?
HEY! WHERE DID SHE–
WISSS
HA-HA! I KNEW YOU'D TRY SOMETHING!
JUST GOTTA BE MORE CLEVER!
OOOOO! MY TURN!
THUNK!

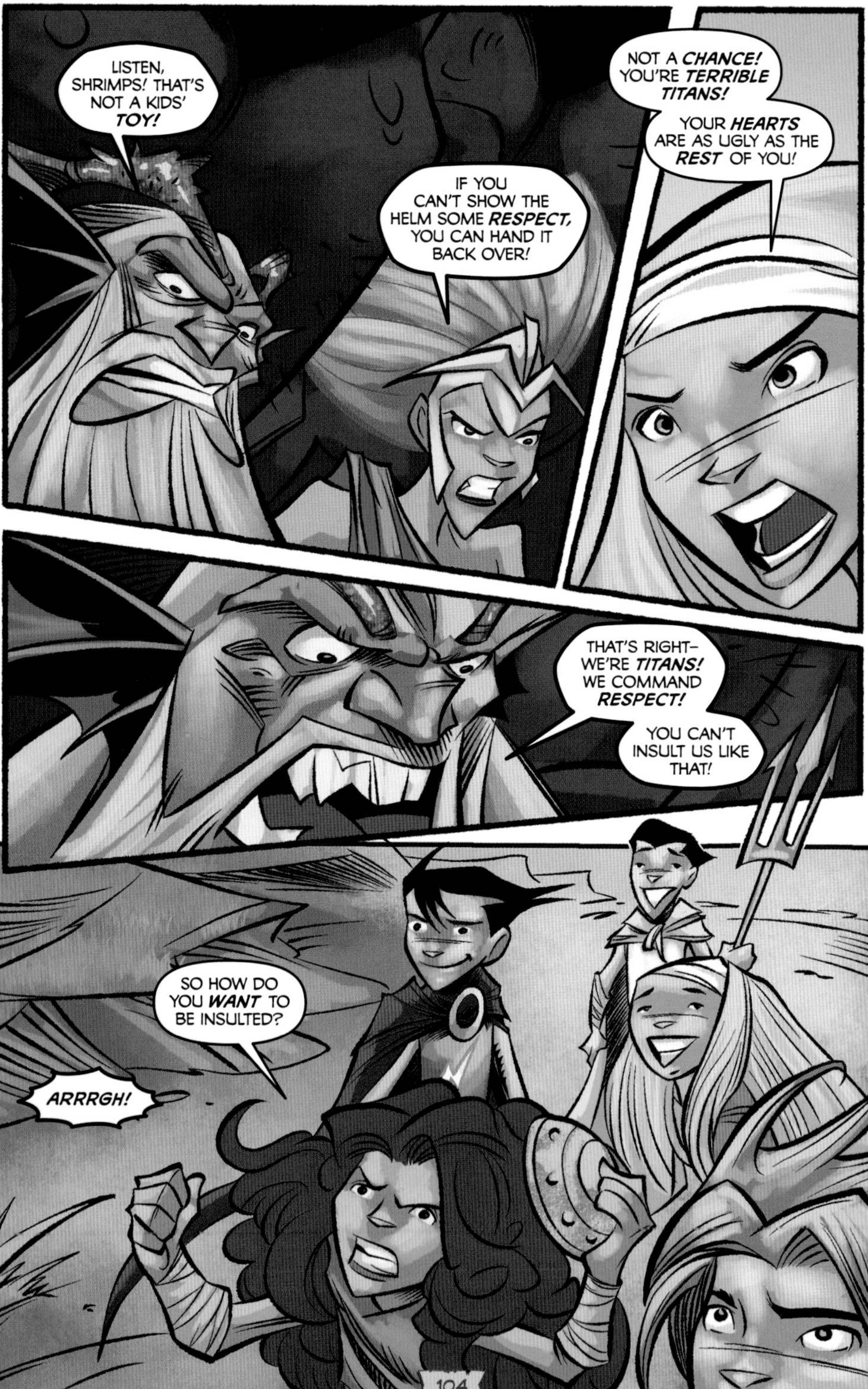
LISTEN, SHRIMPS! THAT'S NOT A KIDS' TOY!
IF YOU CAN'T SHOW THE HELM SOME RESPECT, YOU CAN HAND IT BACK OVER!
NOT A CHANCE! YOU'RE TERRIBLE TITANS!
YOUR HEARTS ARE AS UGLY AS THE REST OF YOU!
THAT'S RIGHT– WE'RE TITANS! WE COMMAND RESPECT!
YOU CAN'T INSULT US LIKE THAT!
SO HOW DO YOU WANT TO BE INSULTED?
ARRRGH!

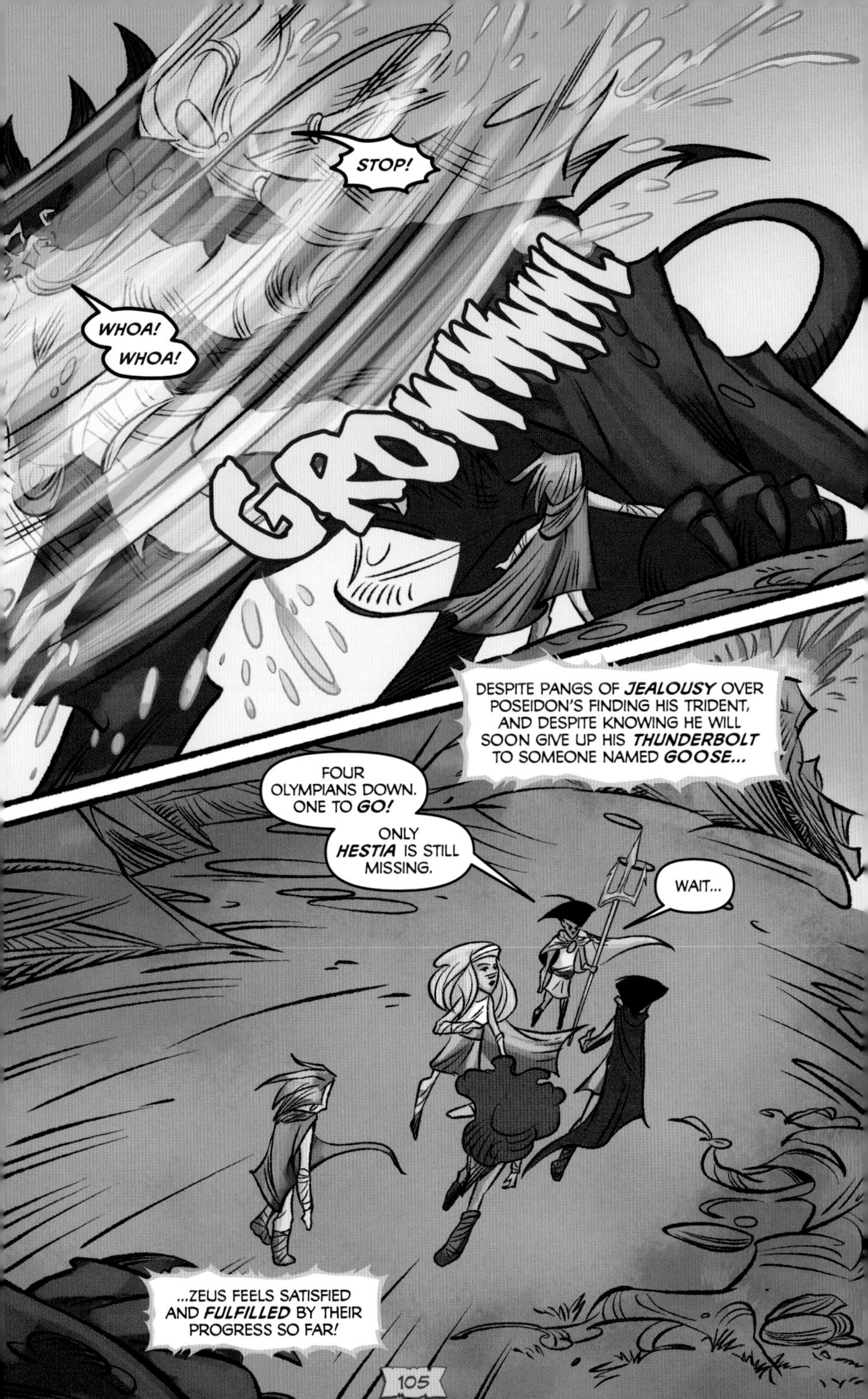
STOP!
WHOA! WHOA!
DESPITE PANGS OF ***JEALOUSY*** OVER POSEIDON'S FINDING HIS TRIDENT, AND DESPITE KNOWING HE WILL SOON GIVE UP HIS ***THUNDERBOLT*** TO SOMEONE NAMED ***GOOSE...***
FOUR OLYMPIANS DOWN. ONE TO ***GO!***
ONLY ***HESTIA*** IS STILL MISSING.
WAIT...
...ZEUS FEELS SATISFIED AND ***FULFILLED*** BY THEIR PROGRESS SO FAR!

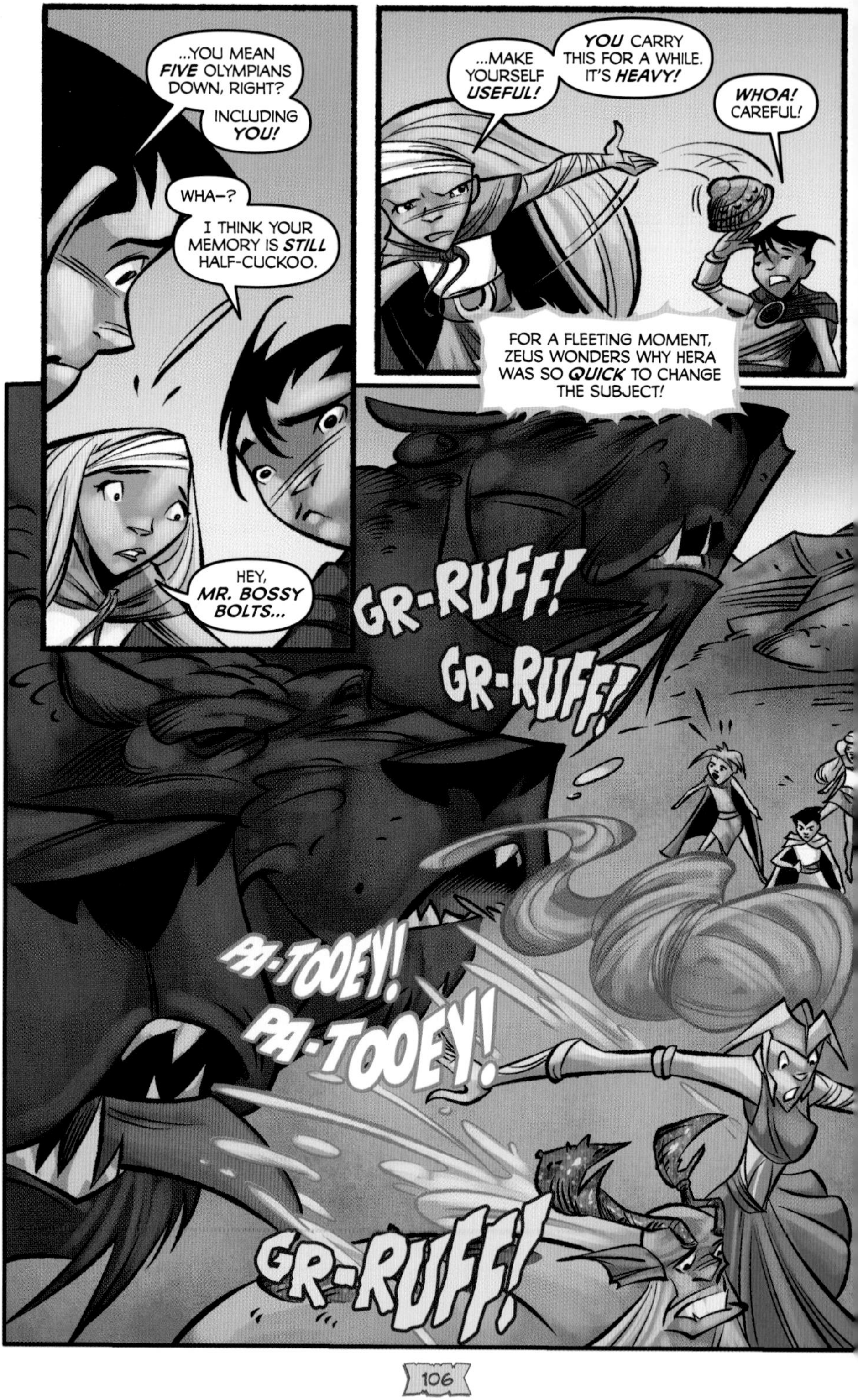

...YOU MEAN *FIVE* OLYMPIANS DOWN, RIGHT?
INCLUDING *YOU!*
WHA–?
I THINK YOUR MEMORY IS *STILL* HALF-CUCKOO.
HEY, *MR. BOSSY BOLTS...*
...MAKE YOURSELF *USEFUL!*
YOU CARRY THIS FOR A WHILE. IT'S *HEAVY!*
WHOA! CAREFUL!
FOR A FLEETING MOMENT, ZEUS WONDERS WHY HERA WAS SO *QUICK* TO CHANGE THE SUBJECT!
GR-RUFF!
GR-RUFF!
PA-TOOEY!
PA-TOOEY!
GR-RUFF!

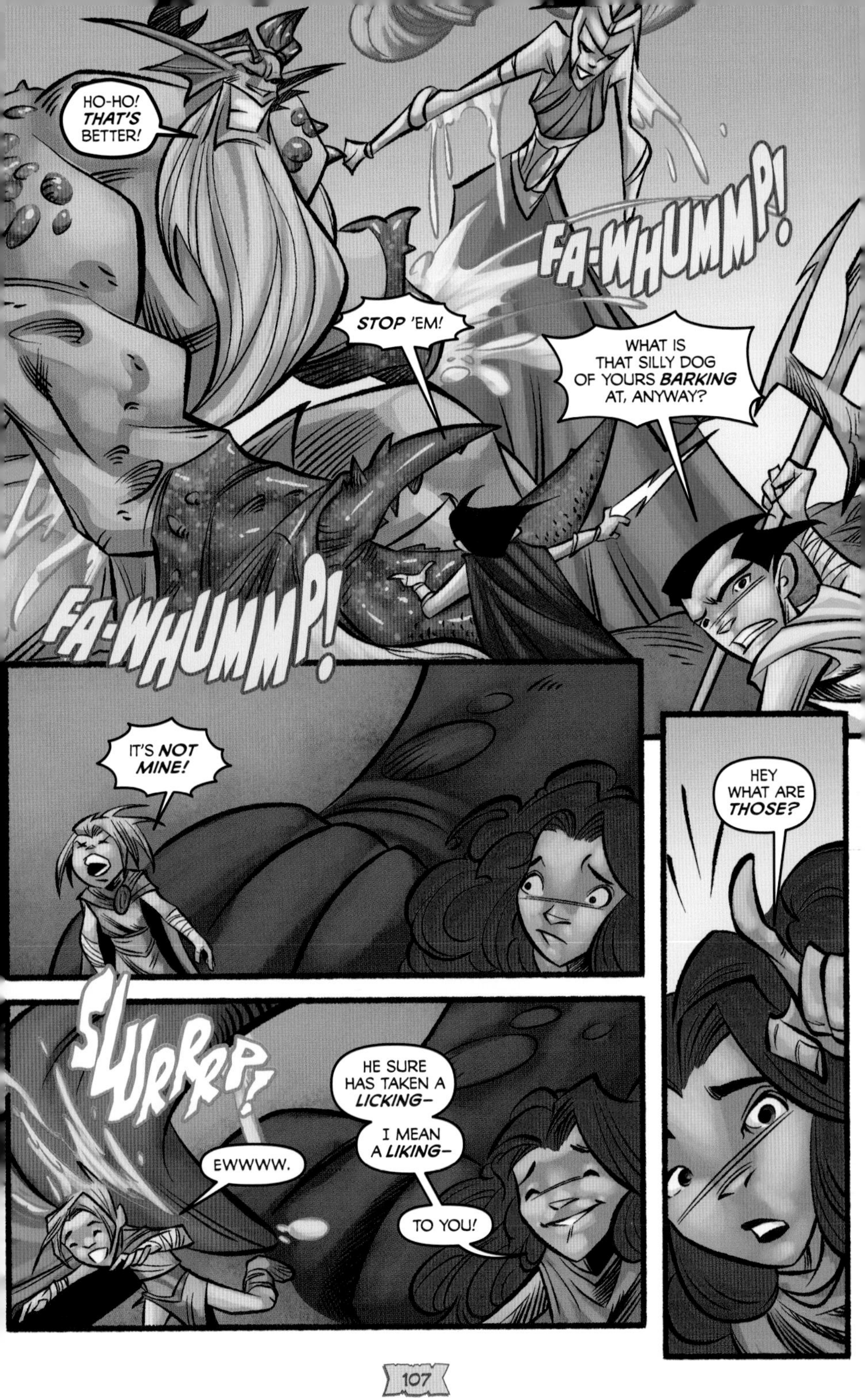

HO-HO! *THAT'S* BETTER!
FA-WHUMMP!
STOP 'EM!
WHAT IS THAT SILLY DOG OF YOURS *BARKING* AT, ANYWAY?
FA-WHUMMP!
IT'S *NOT MINE!*
HEY WHAT ARE *THOSE?*
SLURRRP!
HE SURE HAS TAKEN A *LICKING*–
I MEAN A *LIKING*–
EWWWW.
TO YOU!

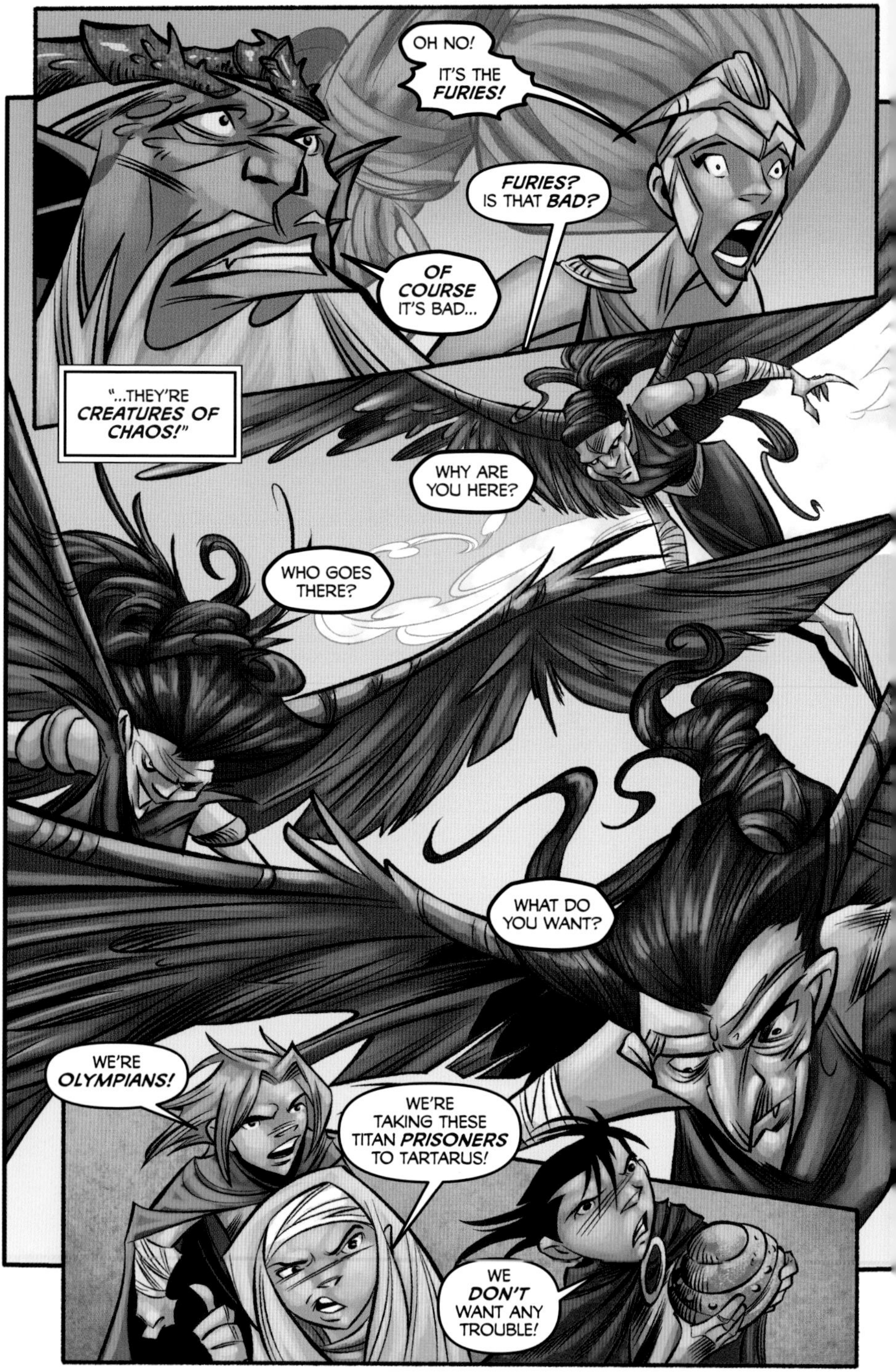

OH NO!
IT'S THE *FURIES!*
FURIES? IS THAT *BAD?*
OF COURSE IT'S BAD...
"...THEY'RE *CREATURES OF CHAOS!*"
WHY ARE YOU HERE?
WHO GOES THERE?
WHAT DO YOU WANT?
WE'RE *OLYMPIANS!*
WE'RE TAKING THESE TITAN *PRISONERS* TO TARTARUS!
WE *DON'T* WANT ANY TROUBLE!

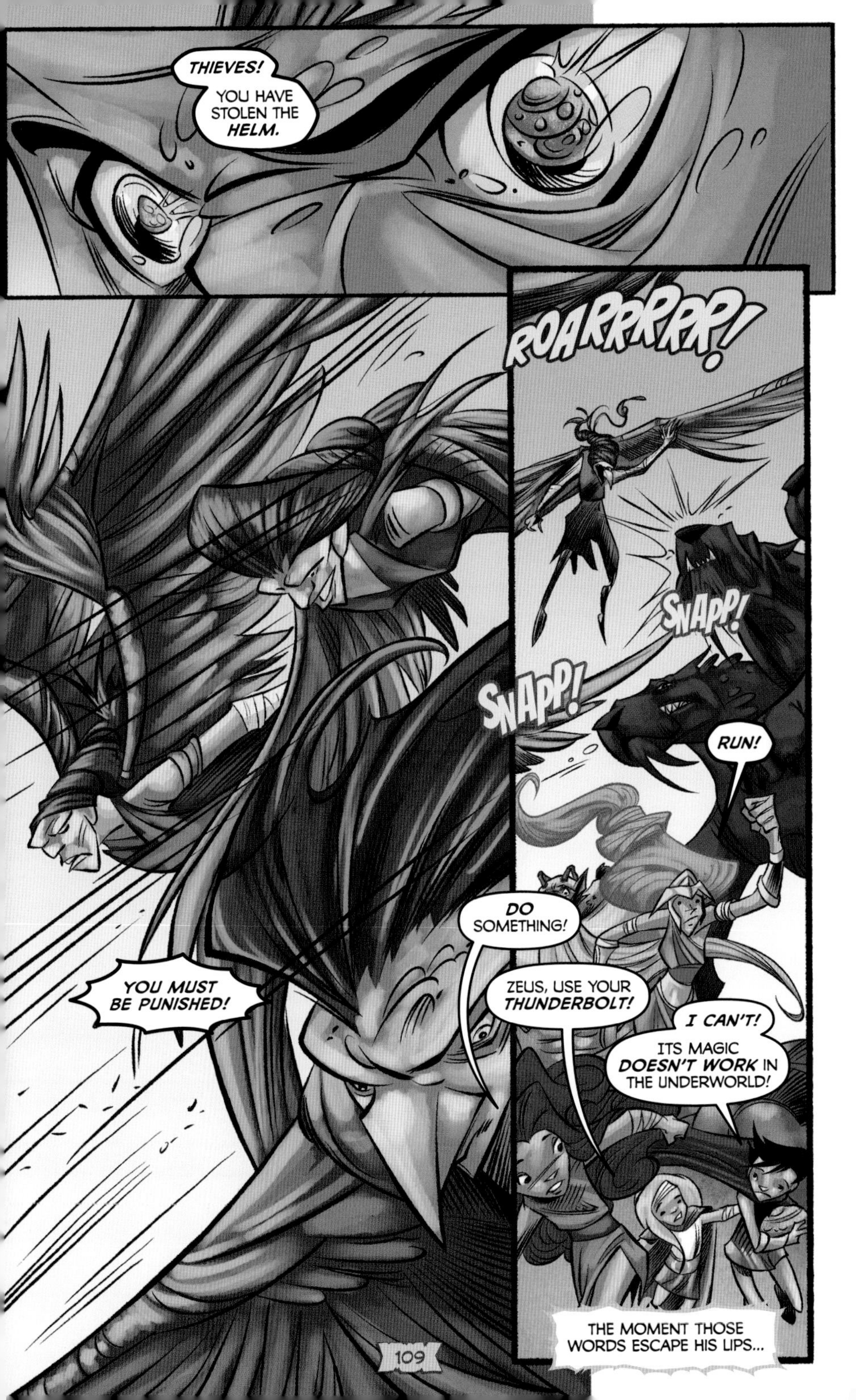
THIEVES!
YOU HAVE STOLEN THE HELM.
ROARRRRRP!
SNAPP!
SNAPP!
RUN!
DO SOMETHING!
YOU MUST BE PUNISHED!
ZEUS, USE YOUR THUNDERBOLT!
I CAN'T!
ITS MAGIC DOESN'T WORK IN THE UNDERWORLD!
THE MOMENT THOSE WORDS ESCAPE HIS LIPS...

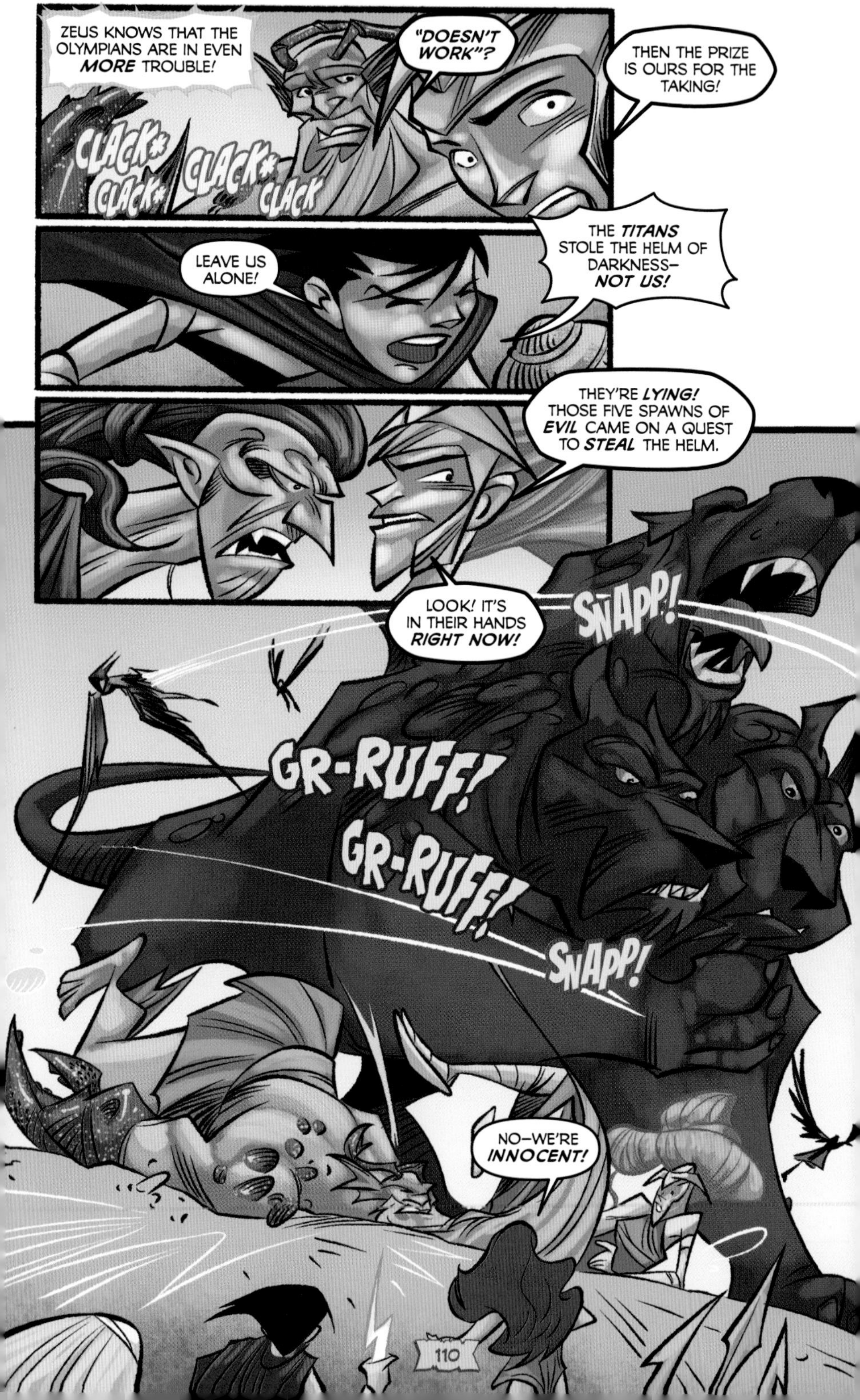

ZEUS KNOWS THAT THE OLYMPIANS ARE IN EVEN MORE TROUBLE!
"DOESN'T WORK"?
THEN THE PRIZE IS OURS FOR THE TAKING!
CLACK* CLACK* CLACK* CLACK
LEAVE US ALONE!
THE TITANS STOLE THE HELM OF DARKNESS— NOT US!
THEY'RE LYING! THOSE FIVE SPAWNS OF EVIL CAME ON A QUEST TO STEAL THE HELM.
LOOK! IT'S IN THEIR HANDS RIGHT NOW!
SNAPP!
GR-RUFF!
GR-RUFF!
SNAPP!
NO—WE'RE INNOCENT!

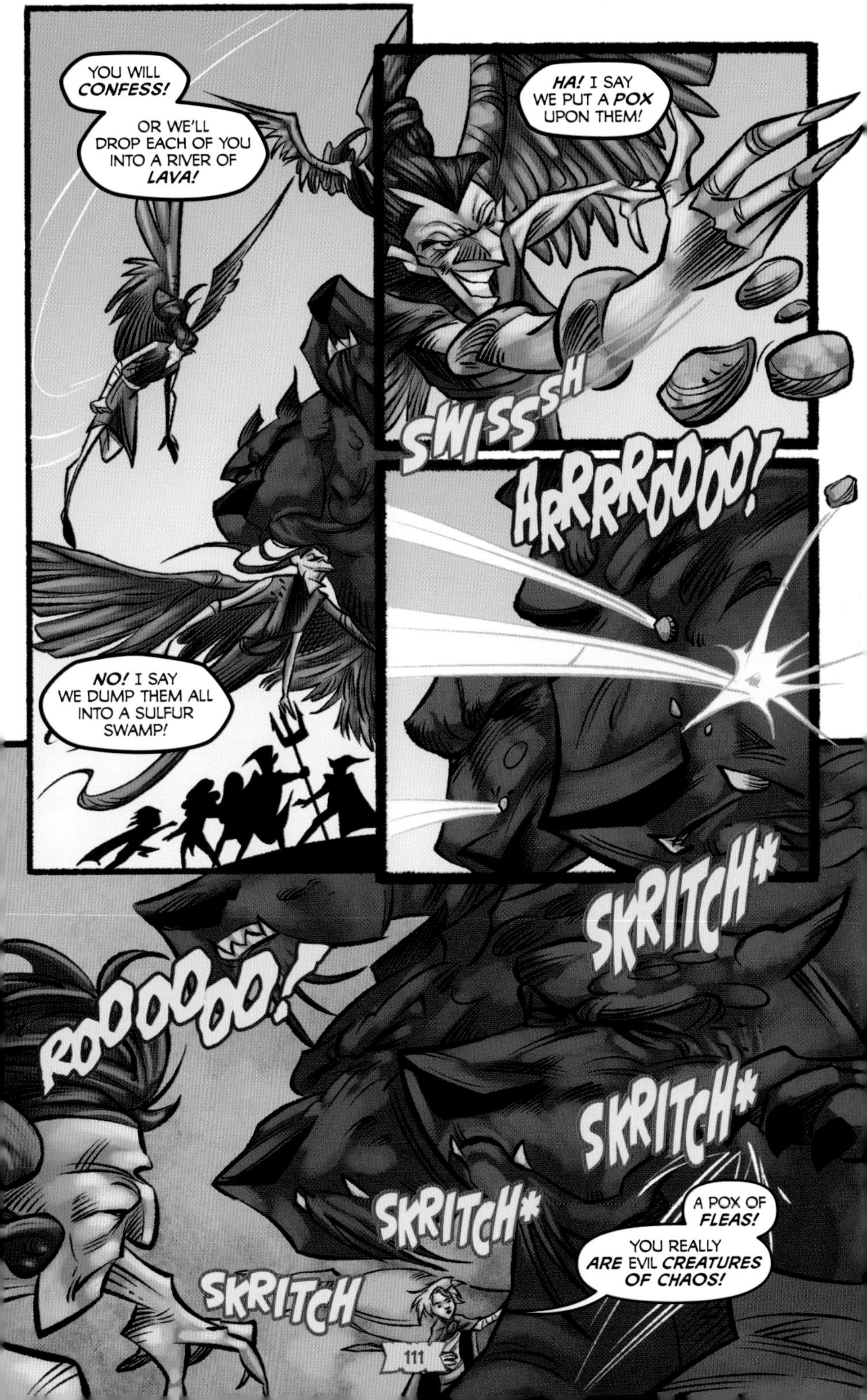
YOU WILL CONFESS!
OR WE'LL DROP EACH OF YOU INTO A RIVER OF LAVA!
NO! I SAY WE DUMP THEM ALL INTO A SULFUR SWAMP!
HA! I SAY WE PUT A POX UPON THEM!
SWISSSH
ARRRROOOOO!
ROOOOOO!
SKRITCH*
SKRITCH*
SKRITCH*
SKRITCH
A POX OF FLEAS!
YOU REALLY ARE EVIL CREATURES OF CHAOS!

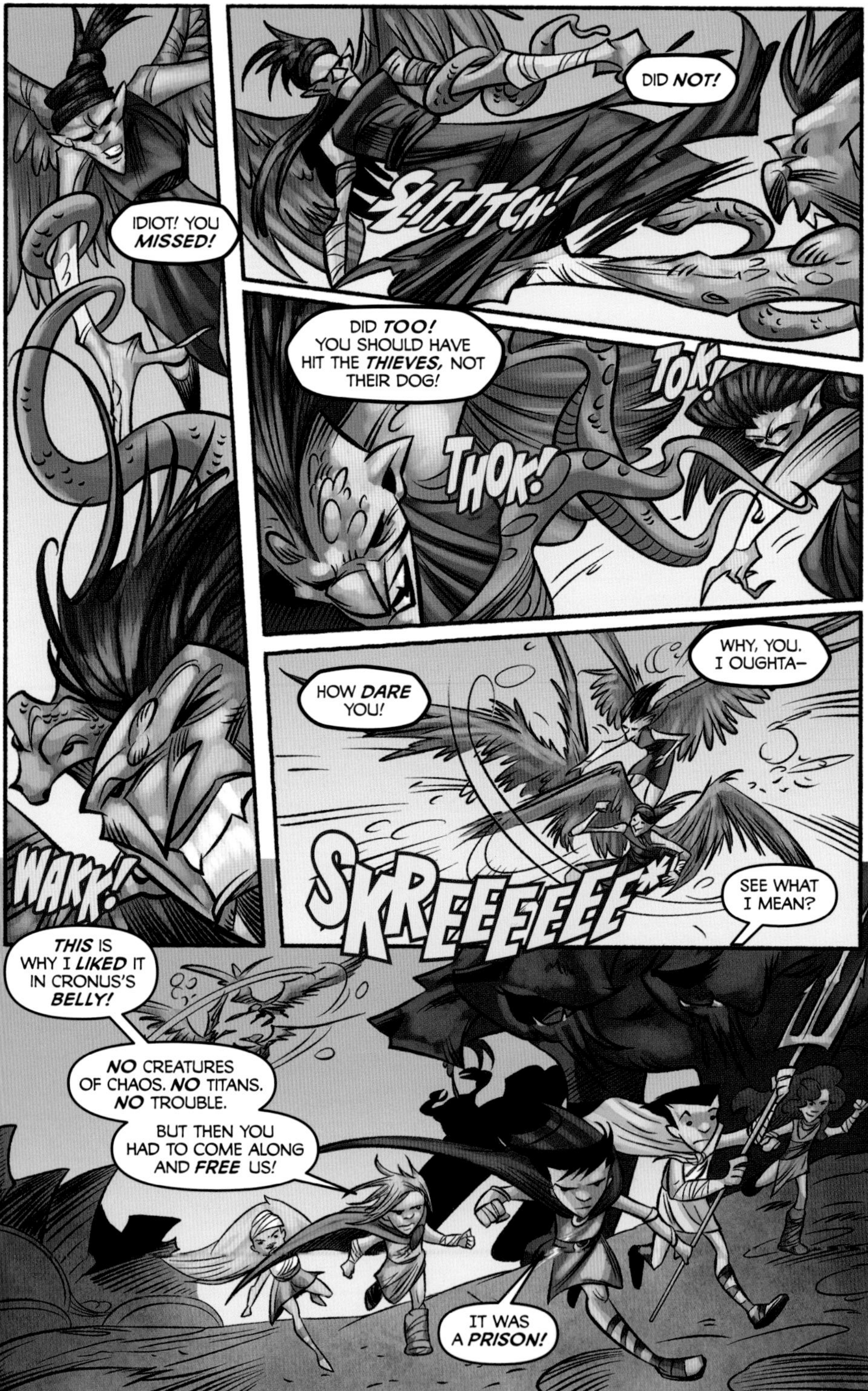
IDIOT! YOU MISSED!
SLITTTCH!
DID NOT!
DID TOO! YOU SHOULD HAVE HIT THE THIEVES, NOT THEIR DOG!
TOK!
THOK!
WAKK!
HOW DARE YOU!
WHY, YOU. I OUGHTA–
SKREEEEEEE*
SEE WHAT I MEAN?
THIS IS WHY I LIKED IT IN CRONUS'S BELLY!
NO CREATURES OF CHAOS. NO TITANS. NO TROUBLE.
BUT THEN YOU HAD TO COME ALONG AND FREE US!
IT WAS A PRISON!

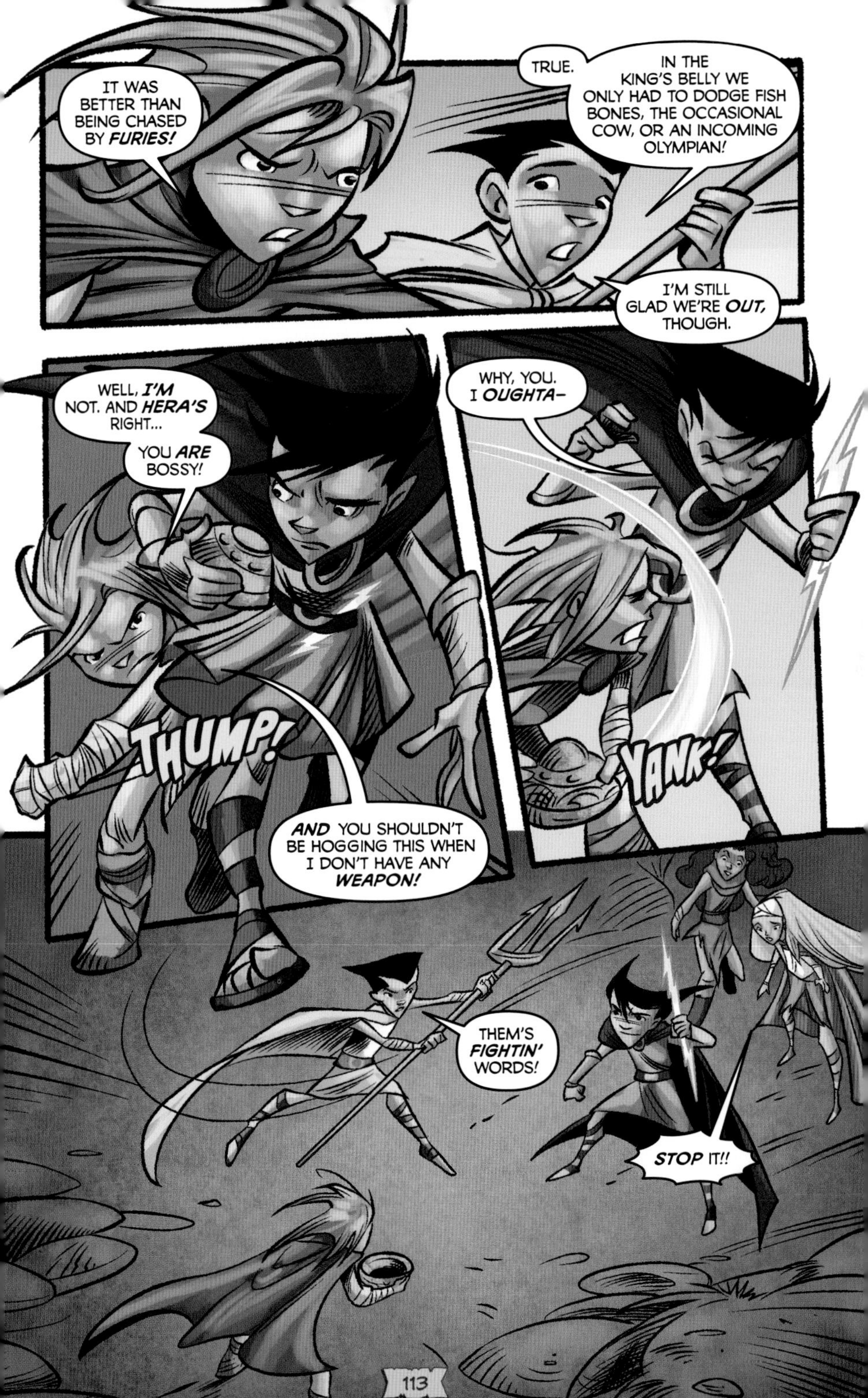
IT WAS BETTER THAN BEING CHASED BY ***FURIES!***
TRUE.
IN THE KING'S BELLY WE ONLY HAD TO DODGE FISH BONES, THE OCCASIONAL COW, OR AN INCOMING OLYMPIAN!
I'M STILL GLAD WE'RE ***OUT,*** THOUGH.
WELL, ***I'M*** NOT. AND ***HERA'S*** RIGHT...
YOU ***ARE*** BOSSY!
THUMP!
AND YOU SHOULDN'T BE HOGGING THIS WHEN I DON'T HAVE ANY ***WEAPON!***
WHY, YOU. I ***OUGHTA–***
YANK!
THEM'S ***FIGHTIN'*** WORDS!
STOP IT!!

CHAPTER NINE:
TAG! YOU'RE DEAD

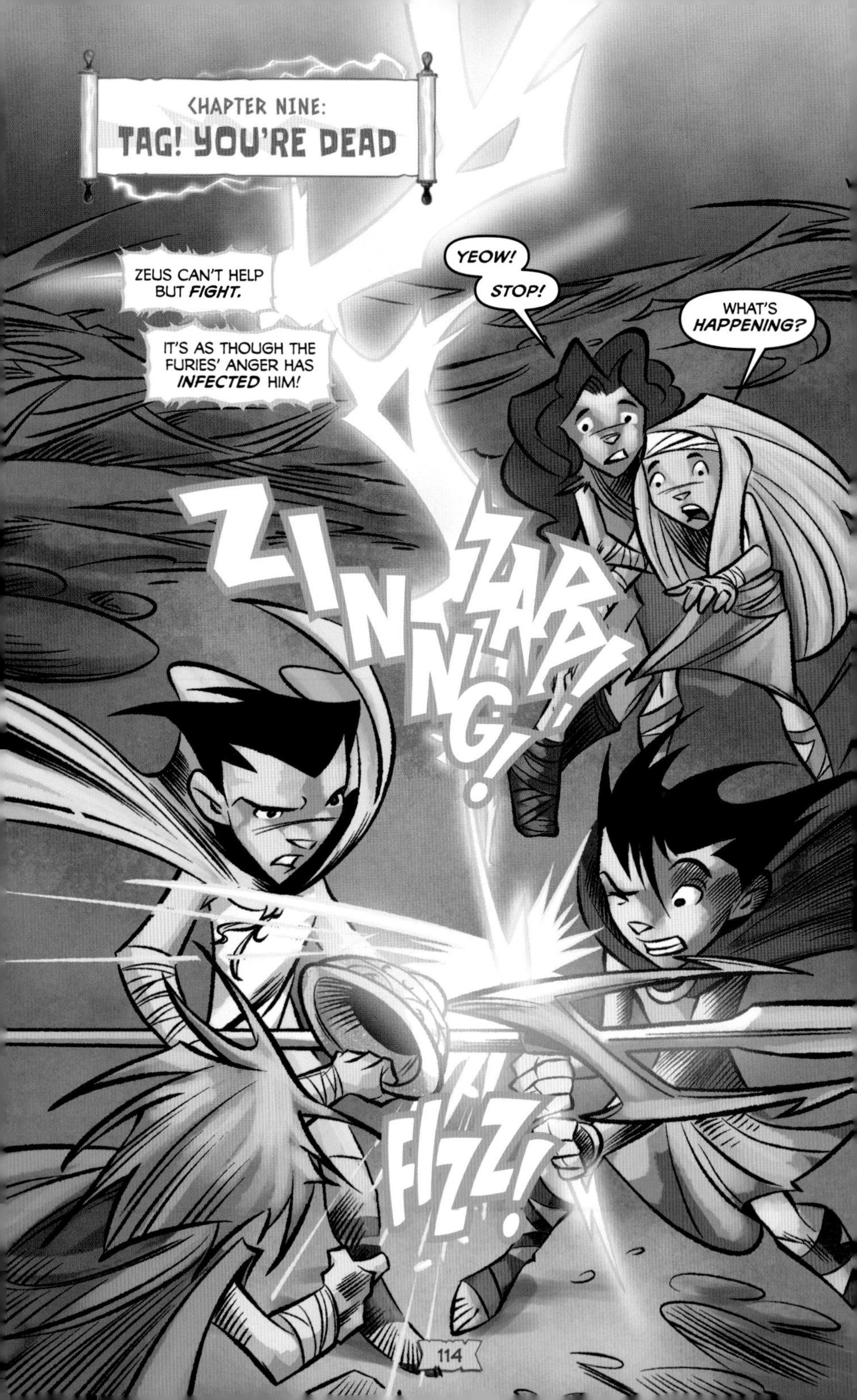
ZEUS CAN'T HELP BUT *FIGHT.*
IT'S AS THOUGH THE FURIES' ANGER HAS *INFECTED* HIM!
YEOW!
STOP!
WHAT'S *HAPPENING?*
ZINNNG!
ZAP!
FIZZ!

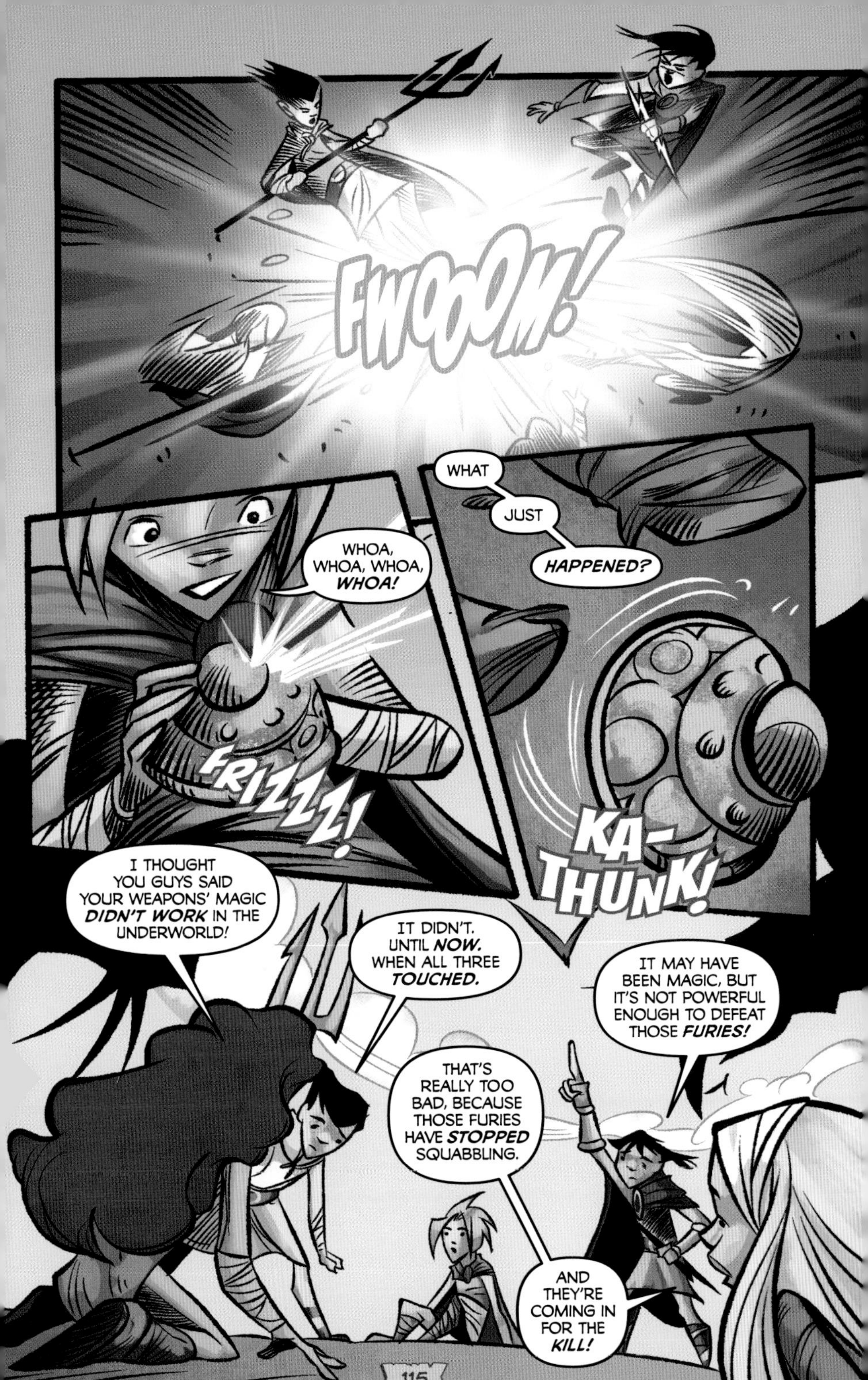
FWOOOM!
WHOA, WHOA, WHOA, WHOA!
FRIZZZ!
WHAT
JUST
HAPPENED?
KA-THUNK!
I THOUGHT YOU GUYS SAID YOUR WEAPONS' MAGIC DIDN'T WORK IN THE UNDERWORLD!
IT DIDN'T. UNTIL NOW. WHEN ALL THREE TOUCHED.
IT MAY HAVE BEEN MAGIC, BUT IT'S NOT POWERFUL ENOUGH TO DEFEAT THOSE FURIES!
THAT'S REALLY TOO BAD, BECAUSE THOSE FURIES HAVE STOPPED SQUABBLING.
AND THEY'RE COMING IN FOR THE KILL!

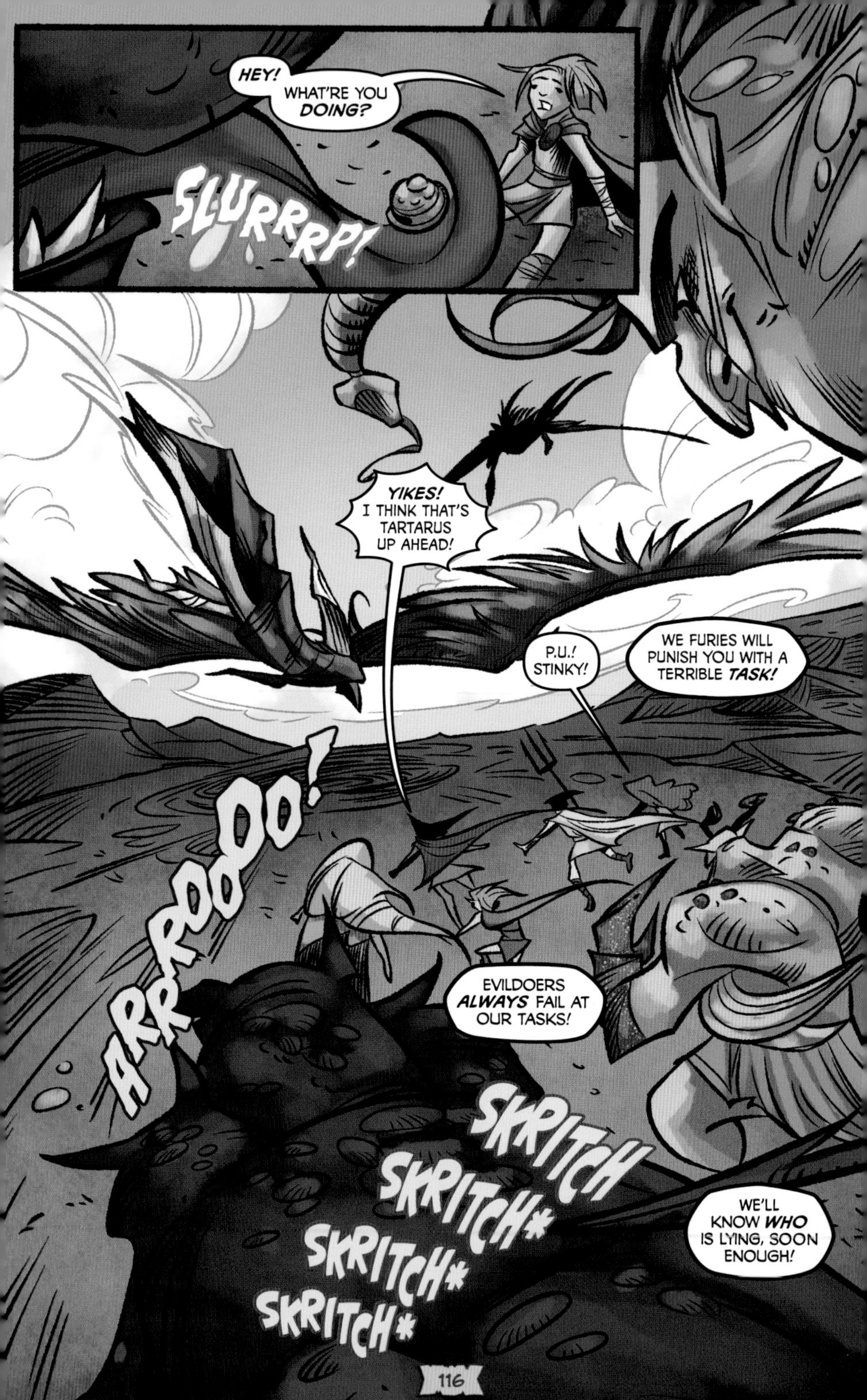
HEY!
WHAT'RE YOU DOING?
SLURRRP!
YIKES! I THINK THAT'S TARTARUS UP AHEAD!
P.U.! STINKY!
WE FURIES WILL PUNISH YOU WITH A TERRIBLE TASK!
ARROOOO!
EVILDOERS ALWAYS FAIL AT OUR TASKS!
SKRITCH
SKRITCH*
SKRITCH*
SKRITCH*
WE'LL KNOW WHO IS LYING, SOON ENOUGH!

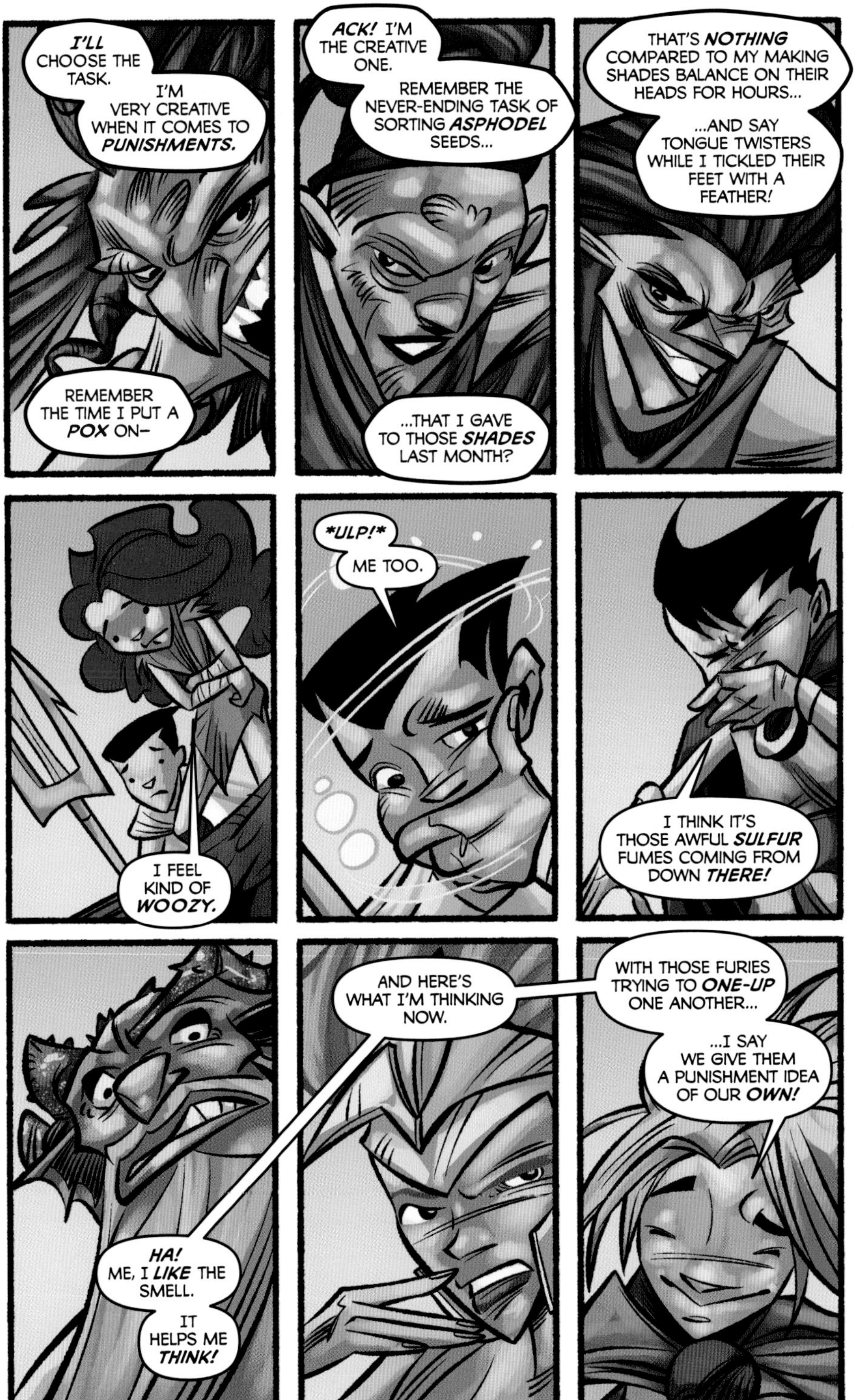
I'LL CHOOSE THE TASK.
I'M VERY CREATIVE WHEN IT COMES TO PUNISHMENTS.
REMEMBER THE TIME I PUT A POX ON–
ACK! I'M THE CREATIVE ONE.
REMEMBER THE NEVER-ENDING TASK OF SORTING ASPHODEL SEEDS...
...THAT I GAVE TO THOSE SHADES LAST MONTH?
THAT'S NOTHING COMPARED TO MY MAKING SHADES BALANCE ON THEIR HEADS FOR HOURS...
...AND SAY TONGUE TWISTERS WHILE I TICKLED THEIR FEET WITH A FEATHER!
I FEEL KIND OF WOOZY.
ULP!
ME TOO.
I THINK IT'S THOSE AWFUL SULFUR FUMES COMING FROM DOWN THERE!
HA! ME, I LIKE THE SMELL.
IT HELPS ME THINK!
AND HERE'S WHAT I'M THINKING NOW.
WITH THOSE FURIES TRYING TO ONE-UP ONE ANOTHER...
...I SAY WE GIVE THEM A PUNISHMENT IDEA OF OUR OWN!

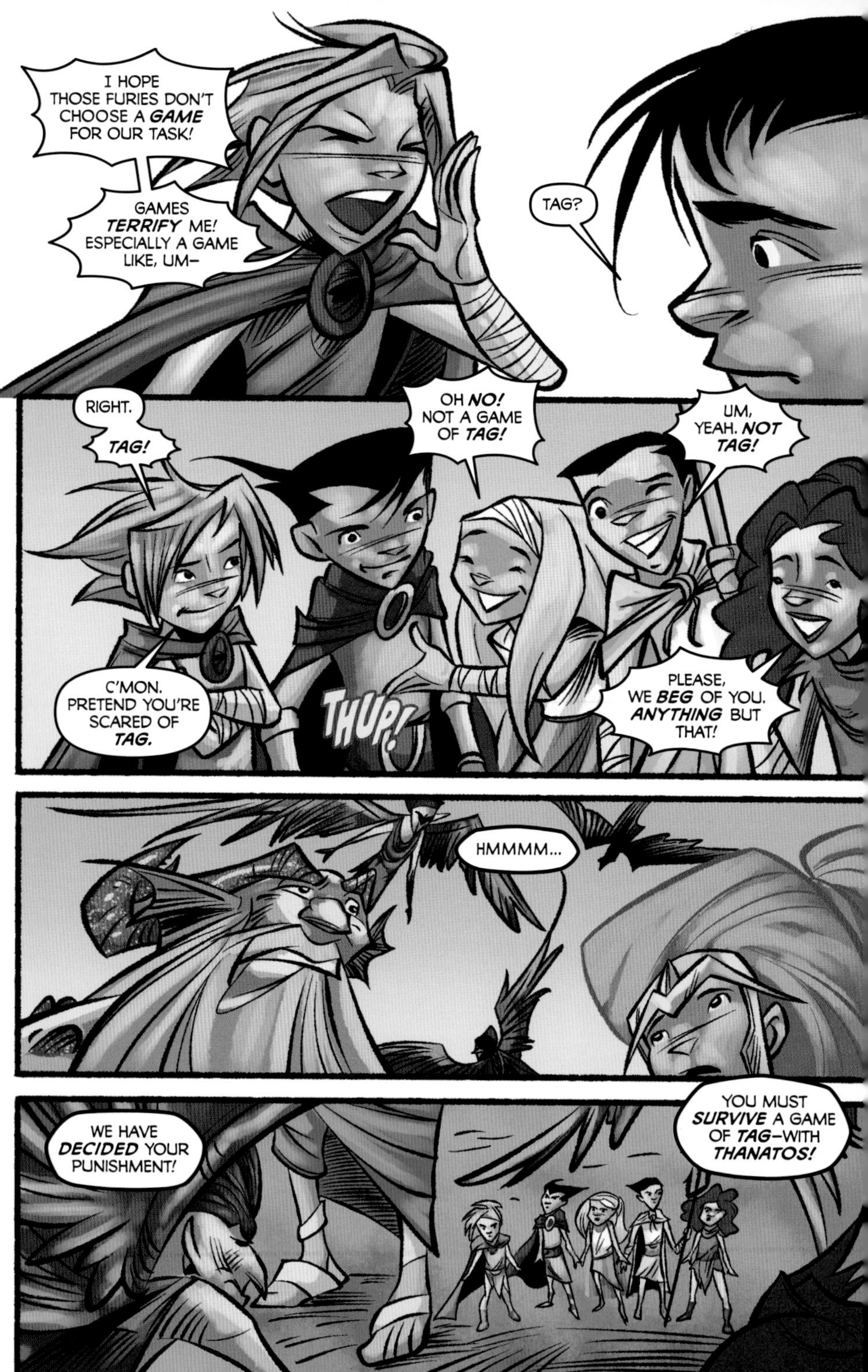
I HOPE THOSE FURIES DON'T CHOOSE A *GAME* FOR OUR TASK!
GAMES *TERRIFY* ME! ESPECIALLY A GAME LIKE, UM–
TAG?
RIGHT.
TAG!
OH *NO!* NOT A GAME OF *TAG!*
UM, YEAH. *NOT TAG!*
C'MON. PRETEND YOU'RE SCARED OF *TAG.*
THUP!
PLEASE, WE *BEG* OF YOU. *ANYTHING* BUT THAT!
HMMMM...
WE HAVE *DECIDED* YOUR PUNISHMENT!
YOU MUST *SURVIVE* A GAME OF *TAG*–WITH *THANATOS!*

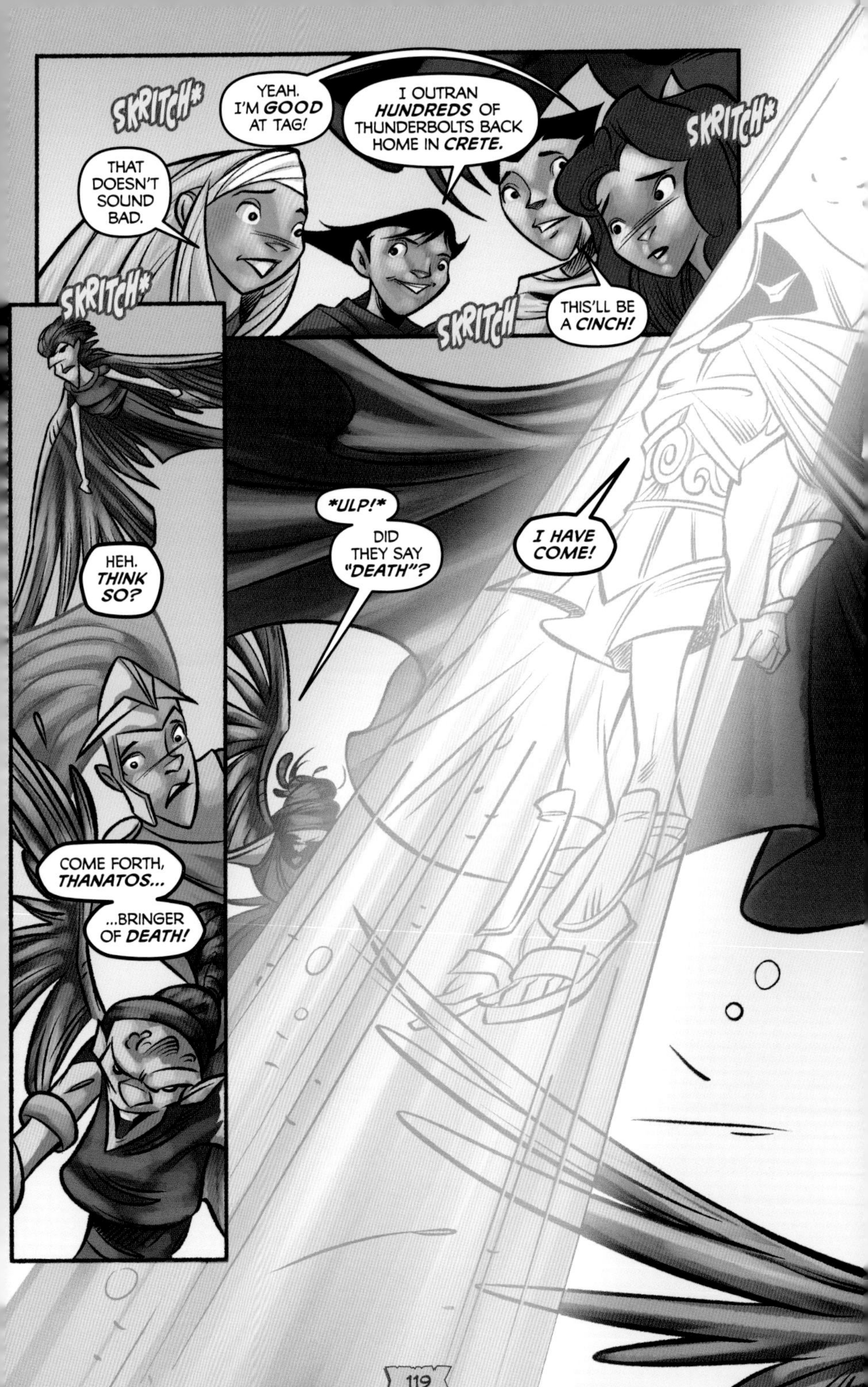
SKRITCH*
YEAH. I'M GOOD AT TAG!
I OUTRAN HUNDREDS OF THUNDERBOLTS BACK HOME IN CRETE.
SKRITCH*
THAT DOESN'T SOUND BAD.
SKRITCH*
SKRITCH
THIS'LL BE A CINCH!
HEH. THINK SO?
ULP! DID THEY SAY "DEATH"?
I HAVE COME!
COME FORTH, THANATOS...
...BRINGER OF DEATH!

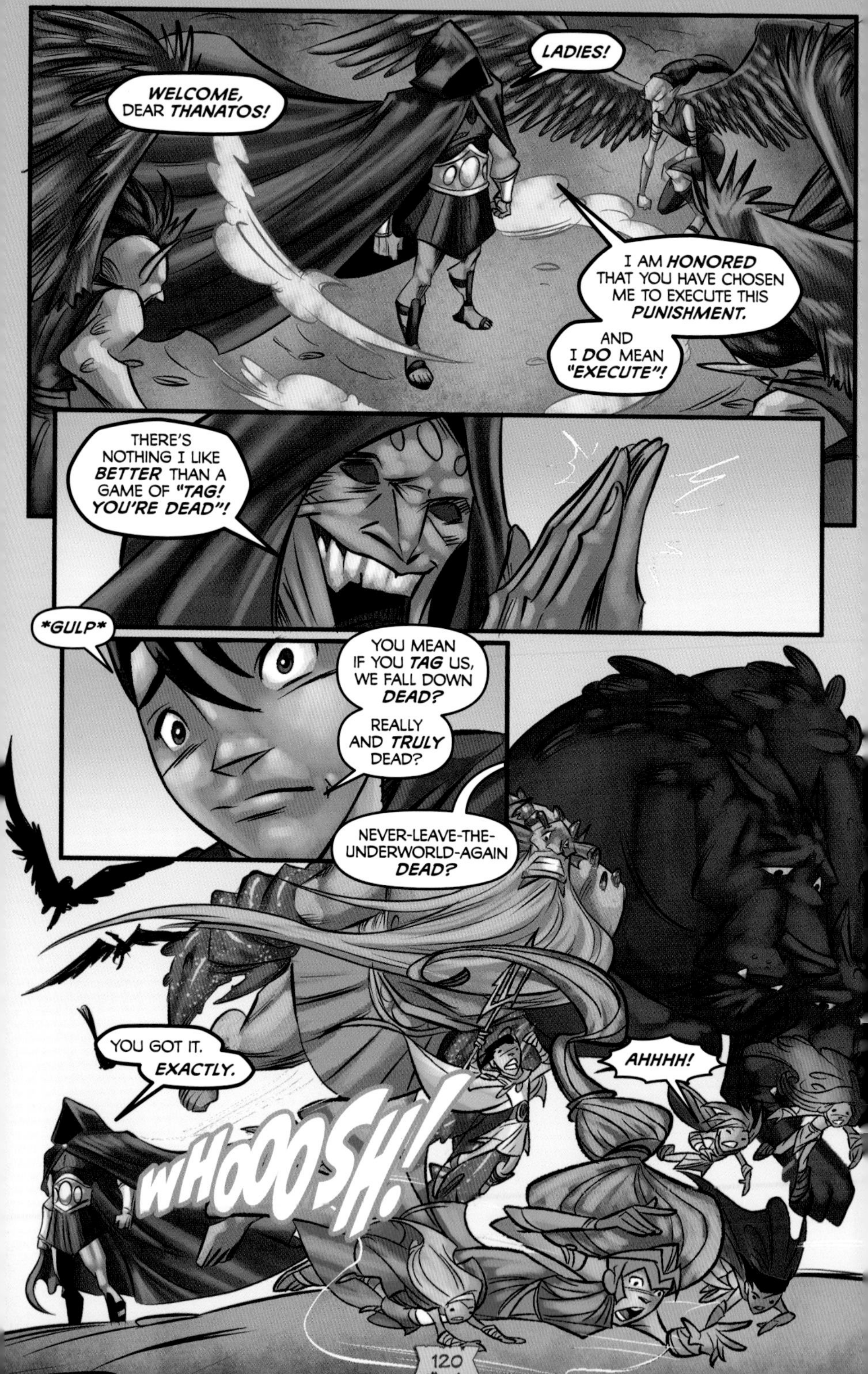
WELCOME, DEAR THANATOS!
LADIES!
I AM HONORED THAT YOU HAVE CHOSEN ME TO EXECUTE THIS PUNISHMENT.
AND I DO MEAN "EXECUTE"!
THERE'S NOTHING I LIKE BETTER THAN A GAME OF "TAG! YOU'RE DEAD"!
GULP
YOU MEAN IF YOU TAG US, WE FALL DOWN DEAD?
REALLY AND TRULY DEAD?
NEVER-LEAVE-THE-UNDERWORLD-AGAIN DEAD?
YOU GOT IT. EXACTLY.
AHHHH!
WHOOOSH!

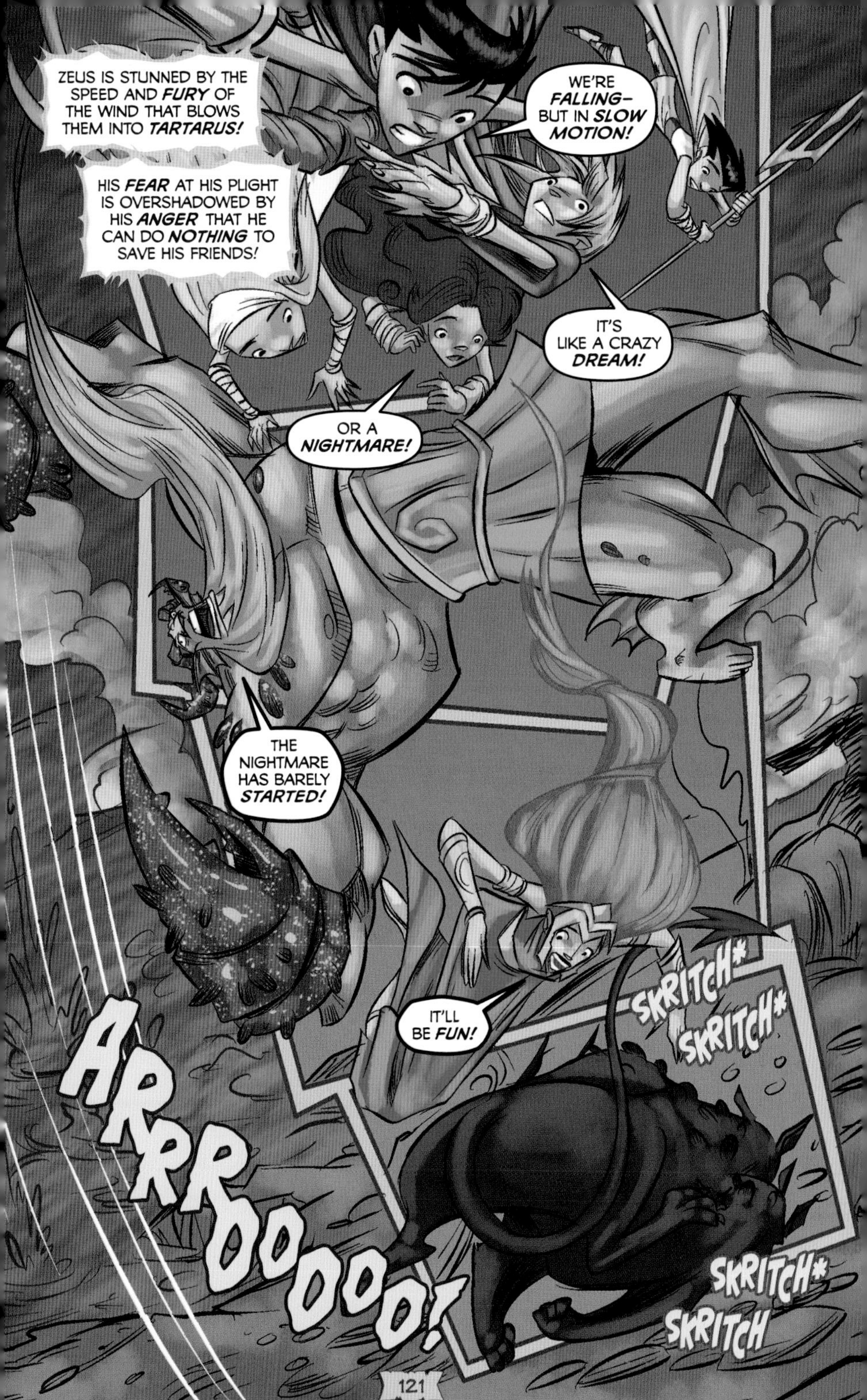

ZEUS IS STUNNED BY THE SPEED AND FURY OF THE WIND THAT BLOWS THEM INTO TARTARUS!
WE'RE FALLING— BUT IN SLOW MOTION!
HIS FEAR AT HIS PLIGHT IS OVERSHADOWED BY HIS ANGER THAT HE CAN DO NOTHING TO SAVE HIS FRIENDS!
IT'S LIKE A CRAZY DREAM!
OR A NIGHTMARE!
THE NIGHTMARE HAS BARELY STARTED!
IT'LL BE FUN!
SKRITCH* SKRITCH*
ARRROOOOO!
SKRITCH* SKRITCH

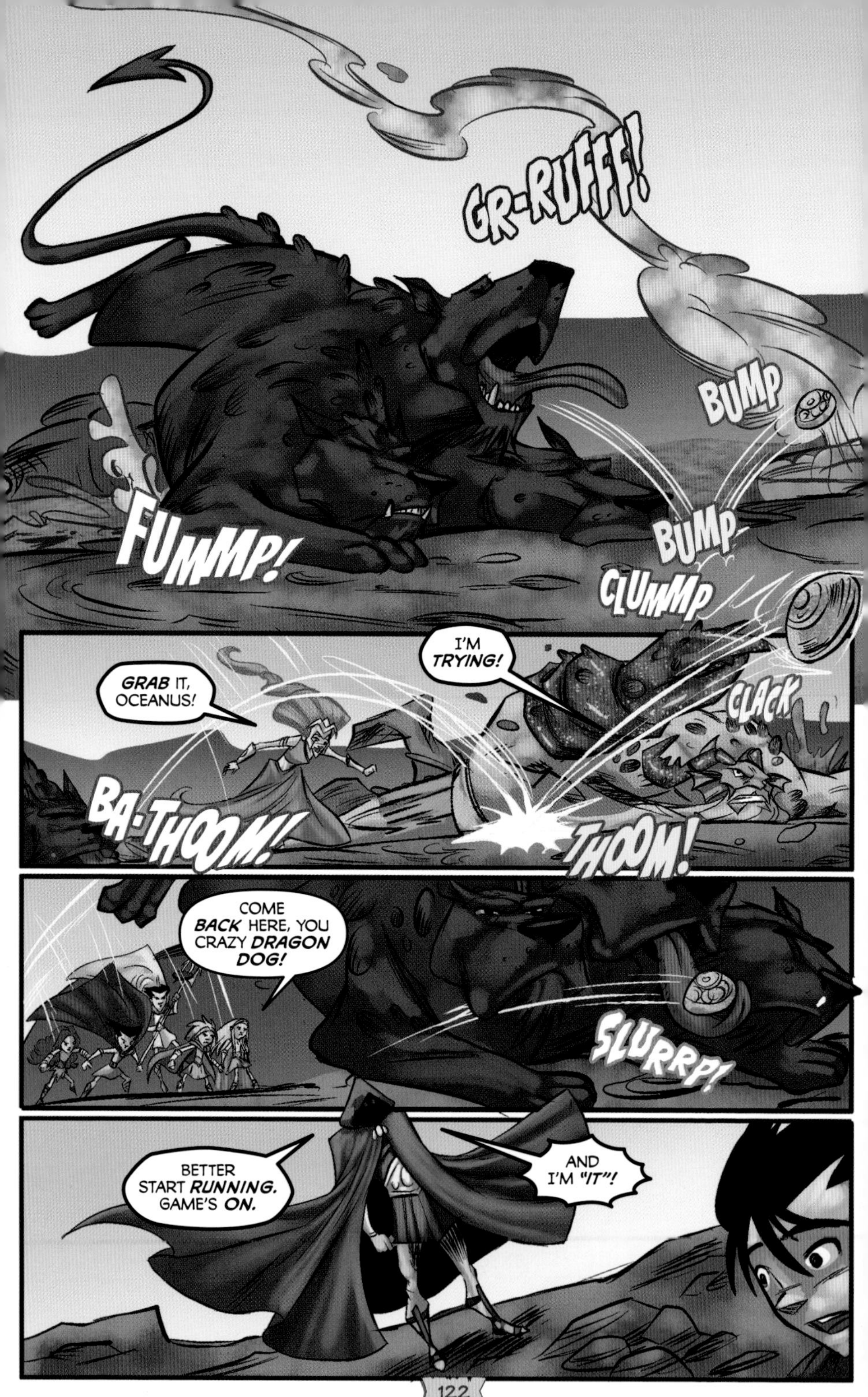
GR-RUFFF!
BUMP
FUMMP!
BUMP
CLUMMP
GRAB IT, OCEANUS!
I'M TRYING!
CLACK
BA-THOOM!
THOOM!
COME BACK HERE, YOU CRAZY DRAGON DOG!
SLURRP!
BETTER START RUNNING. GAME'S ON.
AND I'M "IT"!

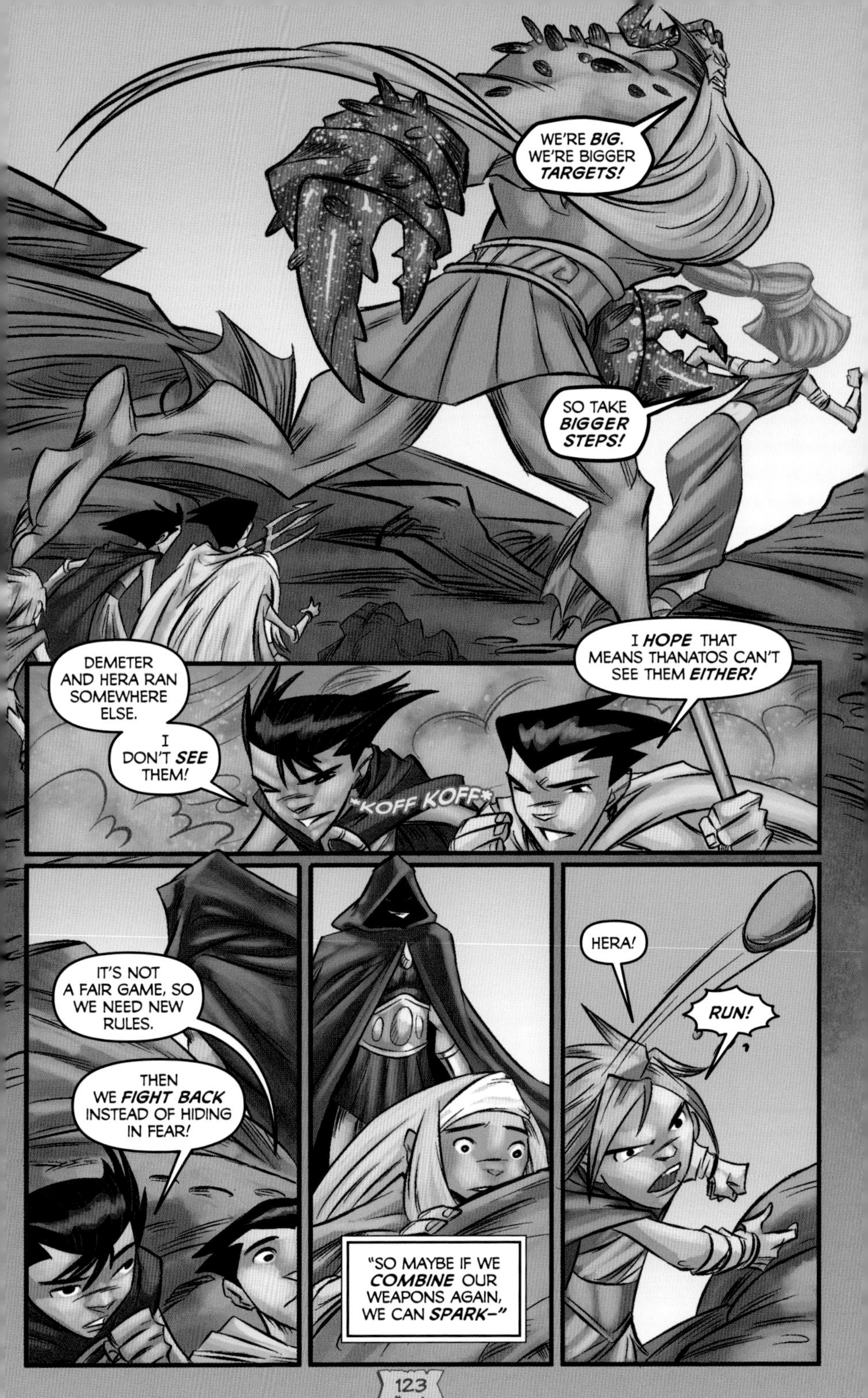
WE'RE BIG. WE'RE BIGGER TARGETS!
SO TAKE BIGGER STEPS!
DEMETER AND HERA RAN SOMEWHERE ELSE.
I DON'T SEE THEM!
I HOPE THAT MEANS THANATOS CAN'T SEE THEM EITHER!
KOFF KOFF
IT'S NOT A FAIR GAME, SO WE NEED NEW RULES.
THEN WE FIGHT BACK INSTEAD OF HIDING IN FEAR!
"SO MAYBE IF WE COMBINE OUR WEAPONS AGAIN, WE CAN SPARK–"
HERA!
RUN!

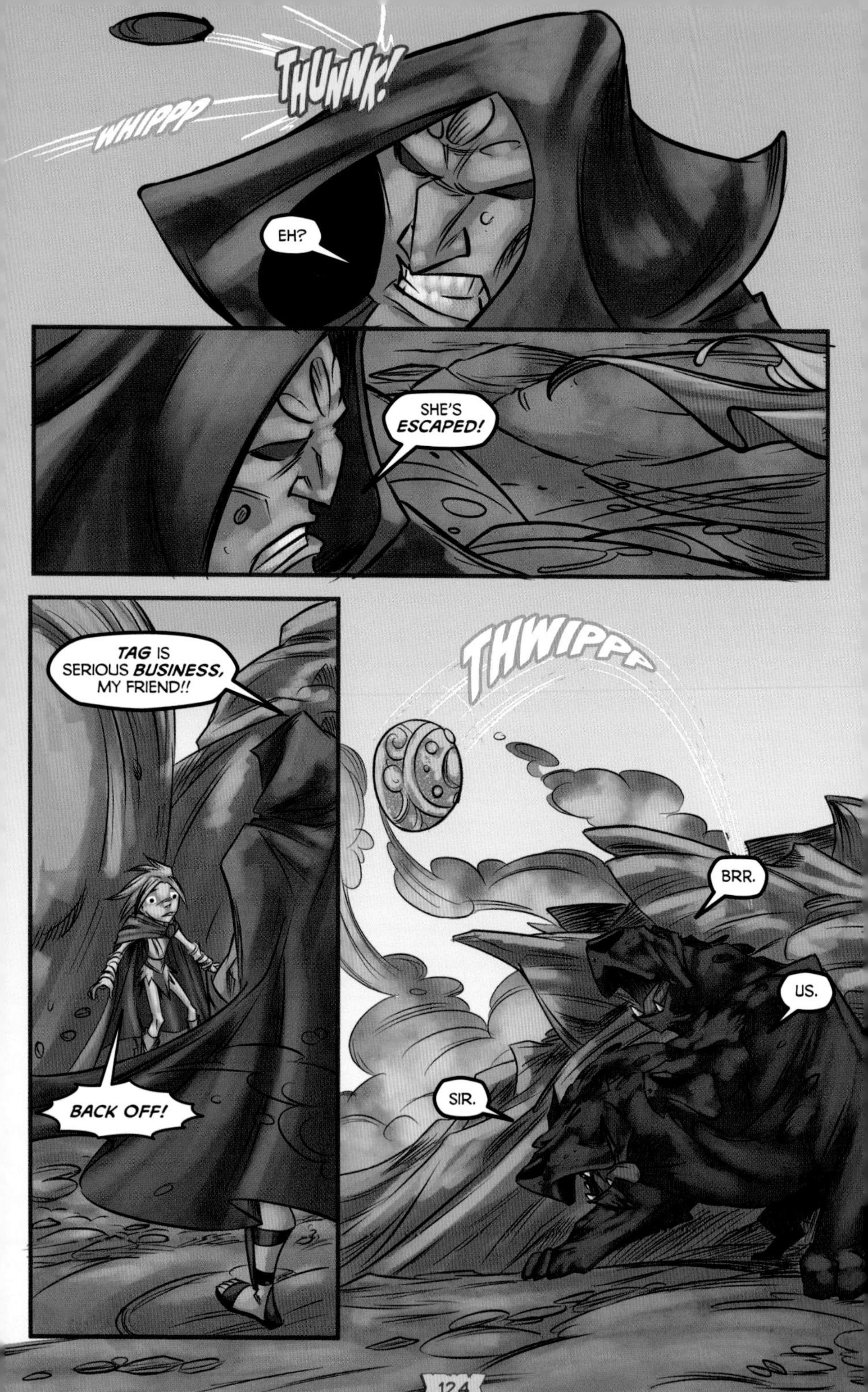
WHIPPP
THUNNK!
EH?
SHE'S ESCAPED!
TAG IS SERIOUS BUSINESS, MY FRIEND!!
BACK OFF!
THWIPPP
BRR.
US.
SIR.

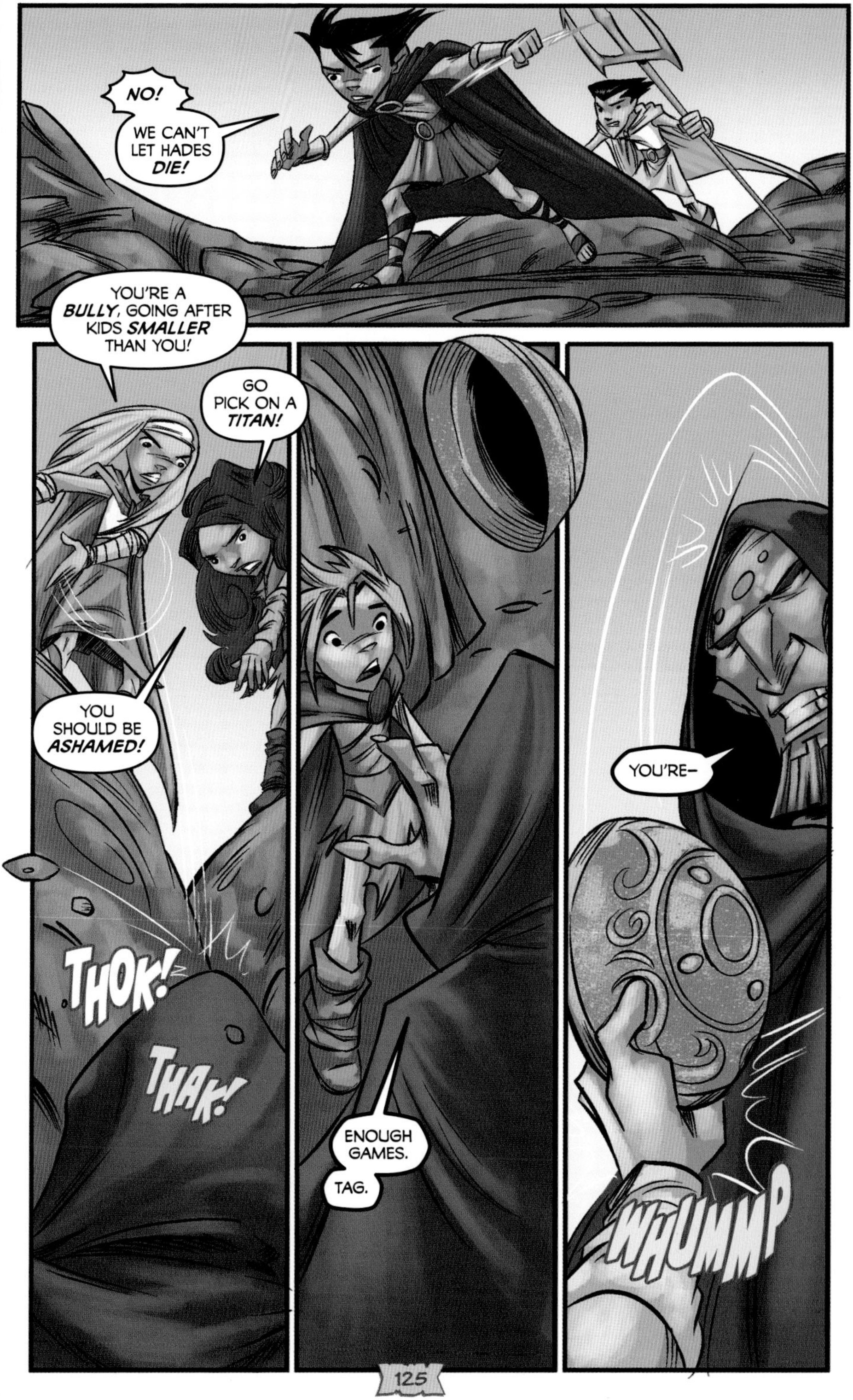
NO!
WE CAN'T LET HADES DIE!
YOU'RE A BULLY, GOING AFTER KIDS SMALLER THAN YOU!
GO PICK ON A TITAN!
YOU SHOULD BE ASHAMED!
THOK!
THAK!
ENOUGH GAMES.
TAG.
YOU'RE–
WHUMMP

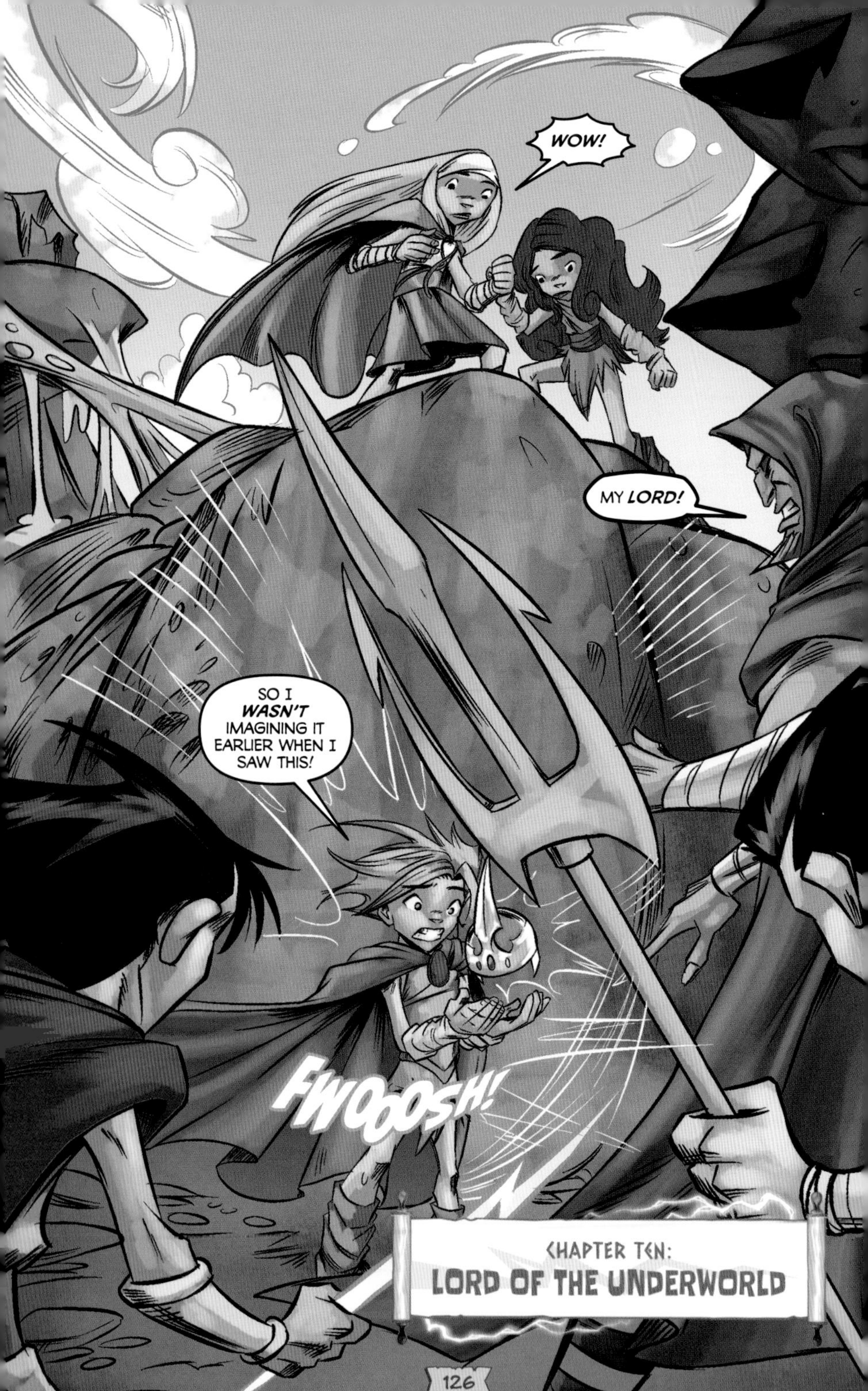
WOW!
MY LORD!
SO I WASN'T IMAGINING IT EARLIER WHEN I SAW THIS!
FWOOOSH!
CHAPTER TEN:
LORD OF THE UNDERWORLD

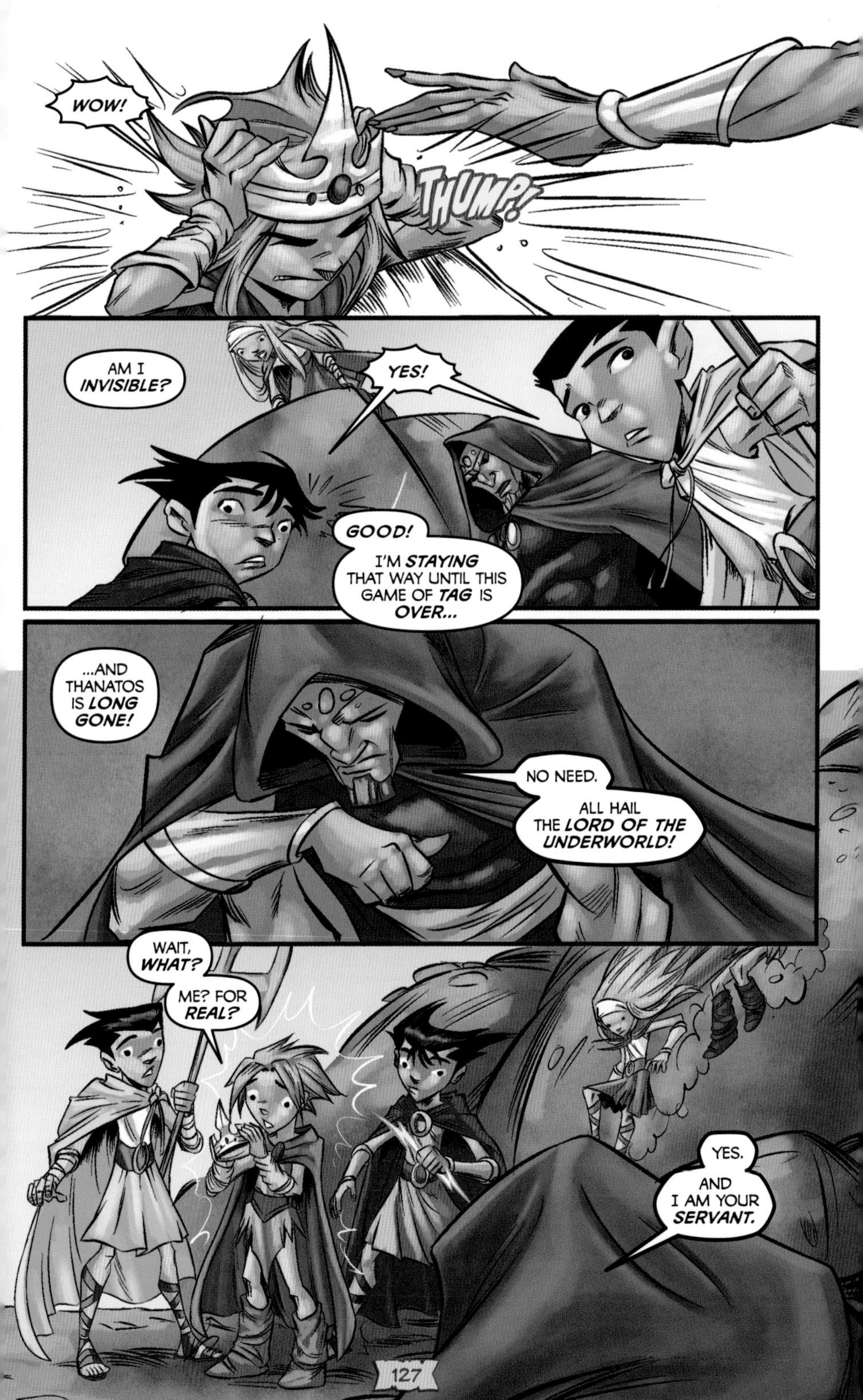
WOW!
THUMP!
AM I INVISIBLE?
YES!
GOOD!
I'M STAYING THAT WAY UNTIL THIS GAME OF TAG IS OVER...
...AND THANATOS IS LONG GONE!
NO NEED.
ALL HAIL THE LORD OF THE UNDERWORLD!
WAIT, WHAT?
ME? FOR REAL?
YES.
AND I AM YOUR SERVANT.

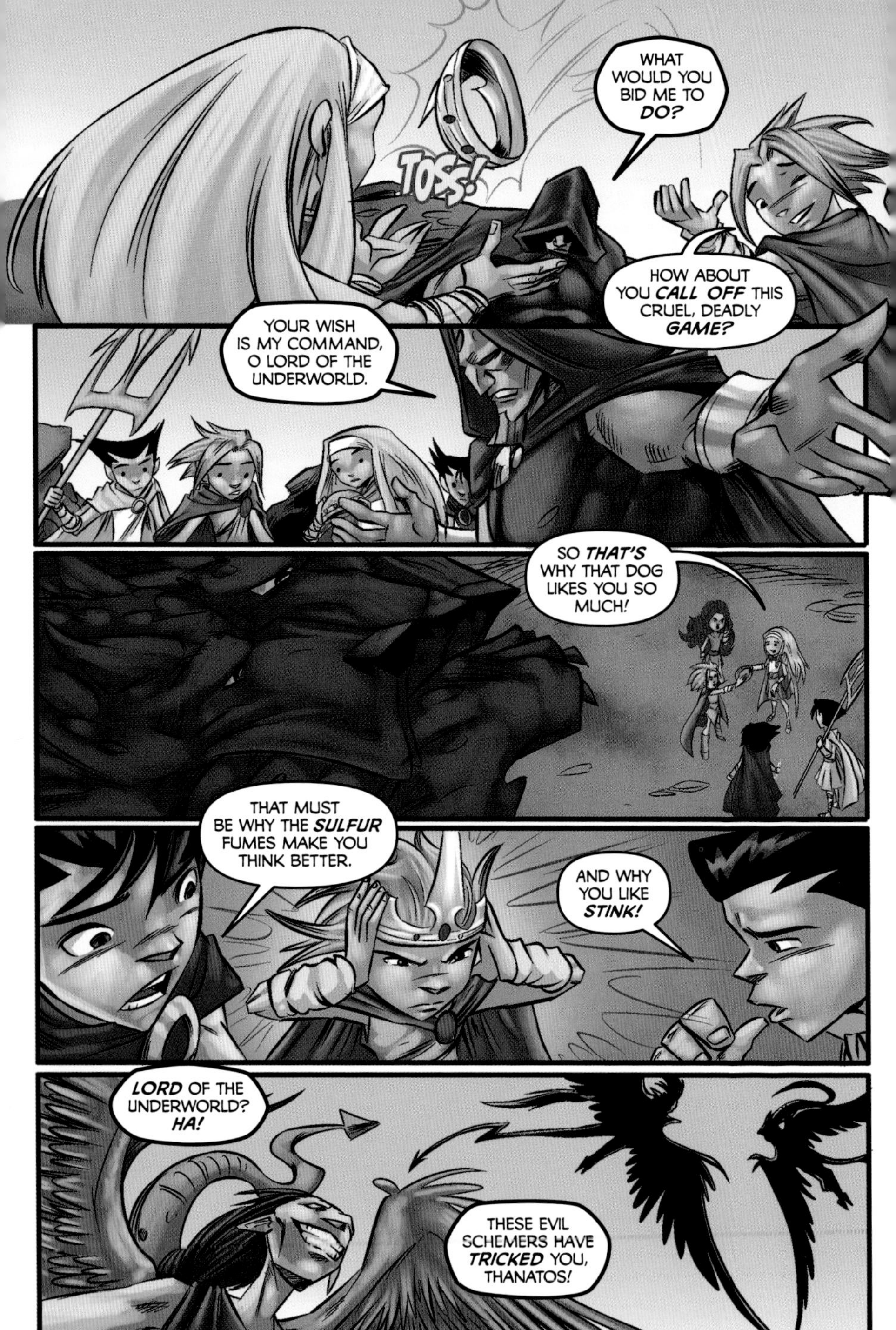
TOSS!
WHAT WOULD YOU BID ME TO *DO?*
HOW ABOUT YOU ***CALL OFF*** THIS CRUEL, DEADLY ***GAME?***
YOUR WISH IS MY COMMAND, O LORD OF THE UNDERWORLD.
SO ***THAT'S*** WHY THAT DOG LIKES YOU SO MUCH!
THAT MUST BE WHY THE ***SULFUR*** FUMES MAKE YOU THINK BETTER.
AND WHY YOU LIKE ***STINK!***
LORD OF THE UNDERWORLD? ***HA!***
THESE EVIL SCHEMERS HAVE ***TRICKED*** YOU, THANATOS!

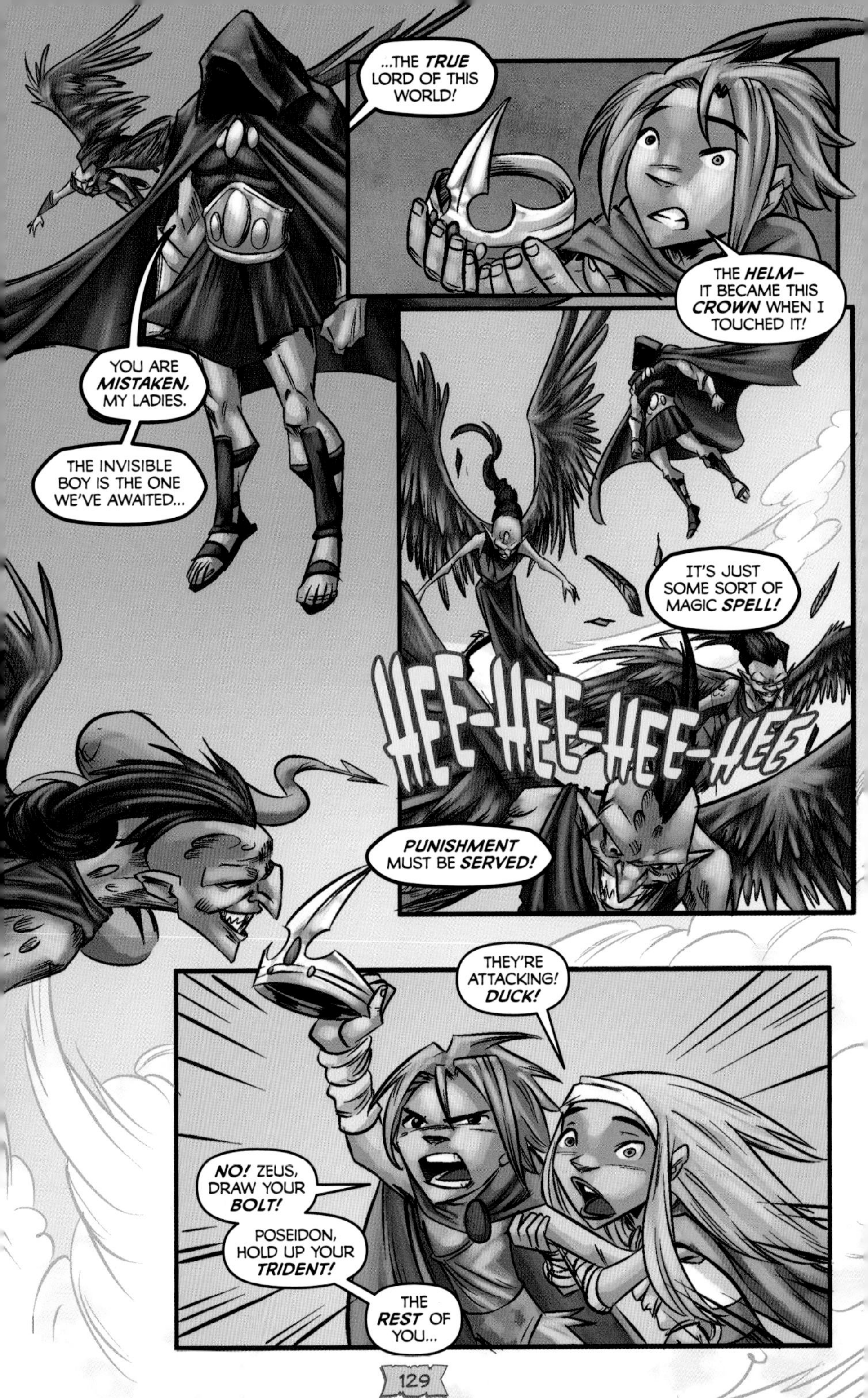
YOU ARE MISTAKEN, MY LADIES.
THE INVISIBLE BOY IS THE ONE WE'VE AWAITED...
...THE TRUE LORD OF THIS WORLD!
THE HELM— IT BECAME THIS CROWN WHEN I TOUCHED IT!
IT'S JUST SOME SORT OF MAGIC SPELL!
HEE-HEE-HEE-HEE
PUNISHMENT MUST BE SERVED!
THEY'RE ATTACKING! DUCK!
NO! ZEUS, DRAW YOUR BOLT!
POSEIDON, HOLD UP YOUR TRIDENT!
THE REST OF YOU...

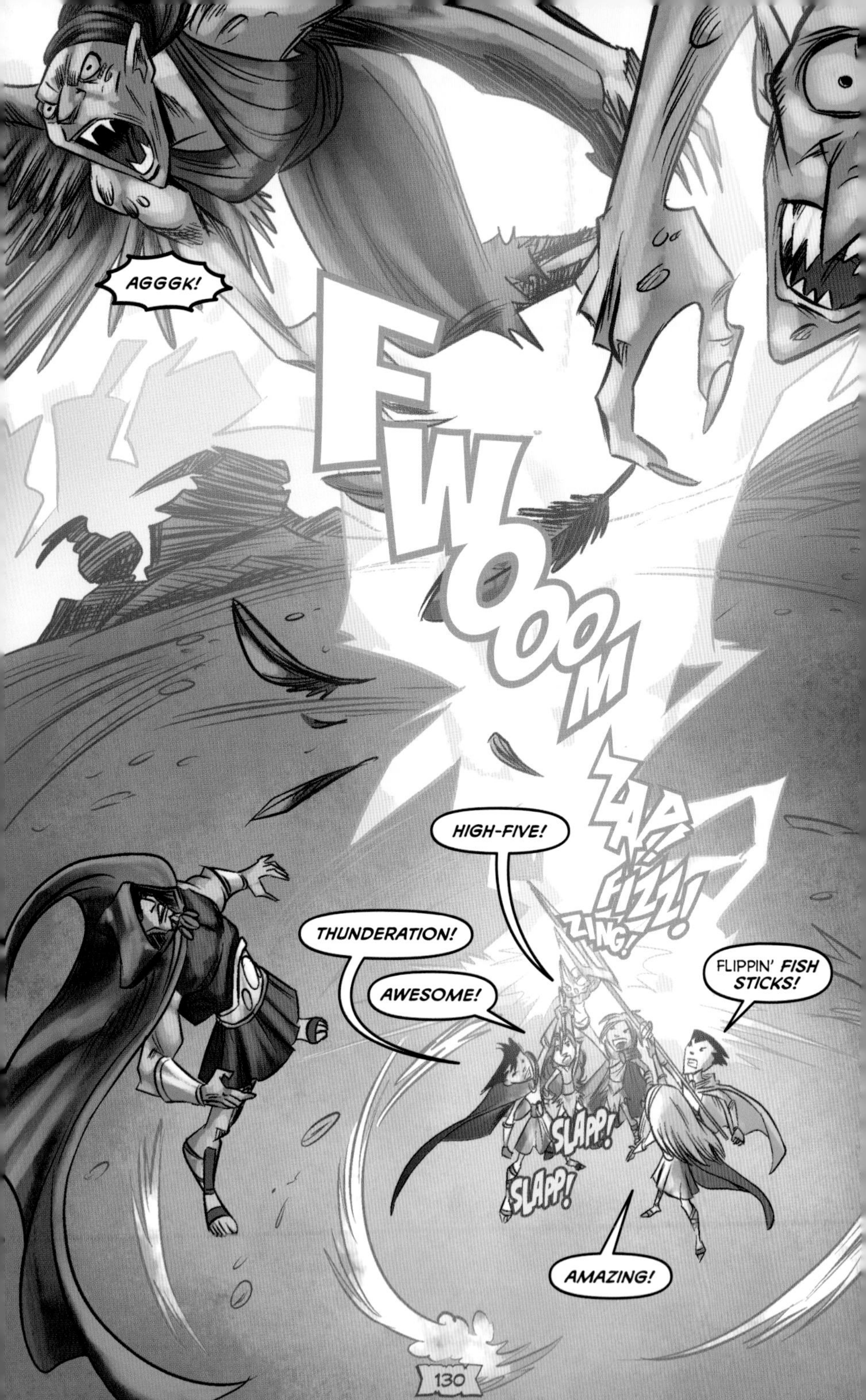
AGGGK!
FWOOOM
ZAP!
FIZZ!
ZING!
HIGH-FIVE!
THUNDERATION!
AWESOME!
FLIPPIN' *FISH STICKS!*
SLAPP!
SLAPP!
AMAZING!

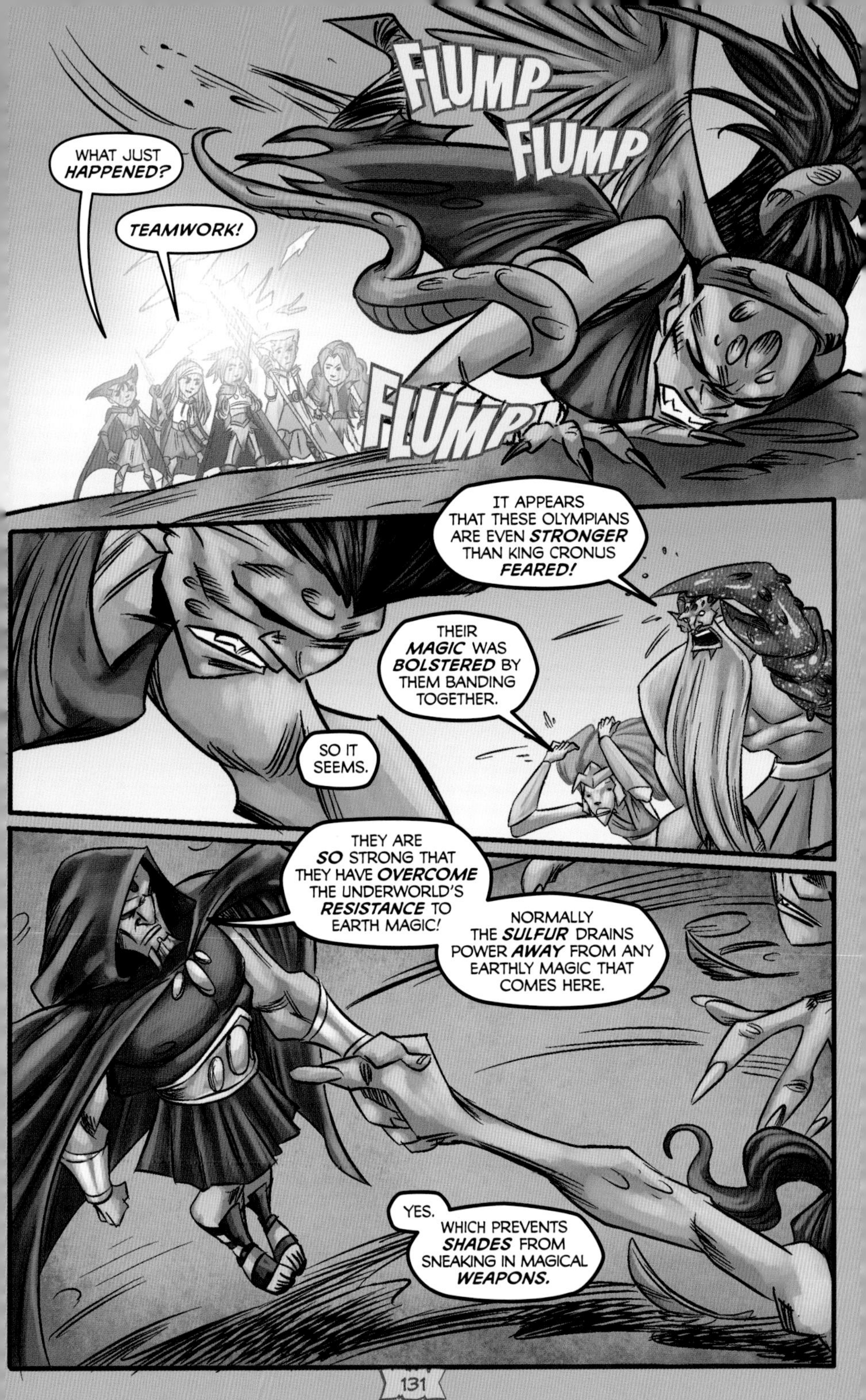
FLUMP
FLUMP
WHAT JUST HAPPENED?
TEAMWORK!
FLUMP
IT APPEARS THAT THESE OLYMPIANS ARE EVEN STRONGER THAN KING CRONUS FEARED!
THEIR MAGIC WAS BOLSTERED BY THEM BANDING TOGETHER.
SO IT SEEMS.
THEY ARE SO STRONG THAT THEY HAVE OVERCOME THE UNDERWORLD'S RESISTANCE TO EARTH MAGIC!
NORMALLY THE SULFUR DRAINS POWER AWAY FROM ANY EARTHLY MAGIC THAT COMES HERE.
YES.
WHICH PREVENTS SHADES FROM SNEAKING IN MAGICAL WEAPONS.

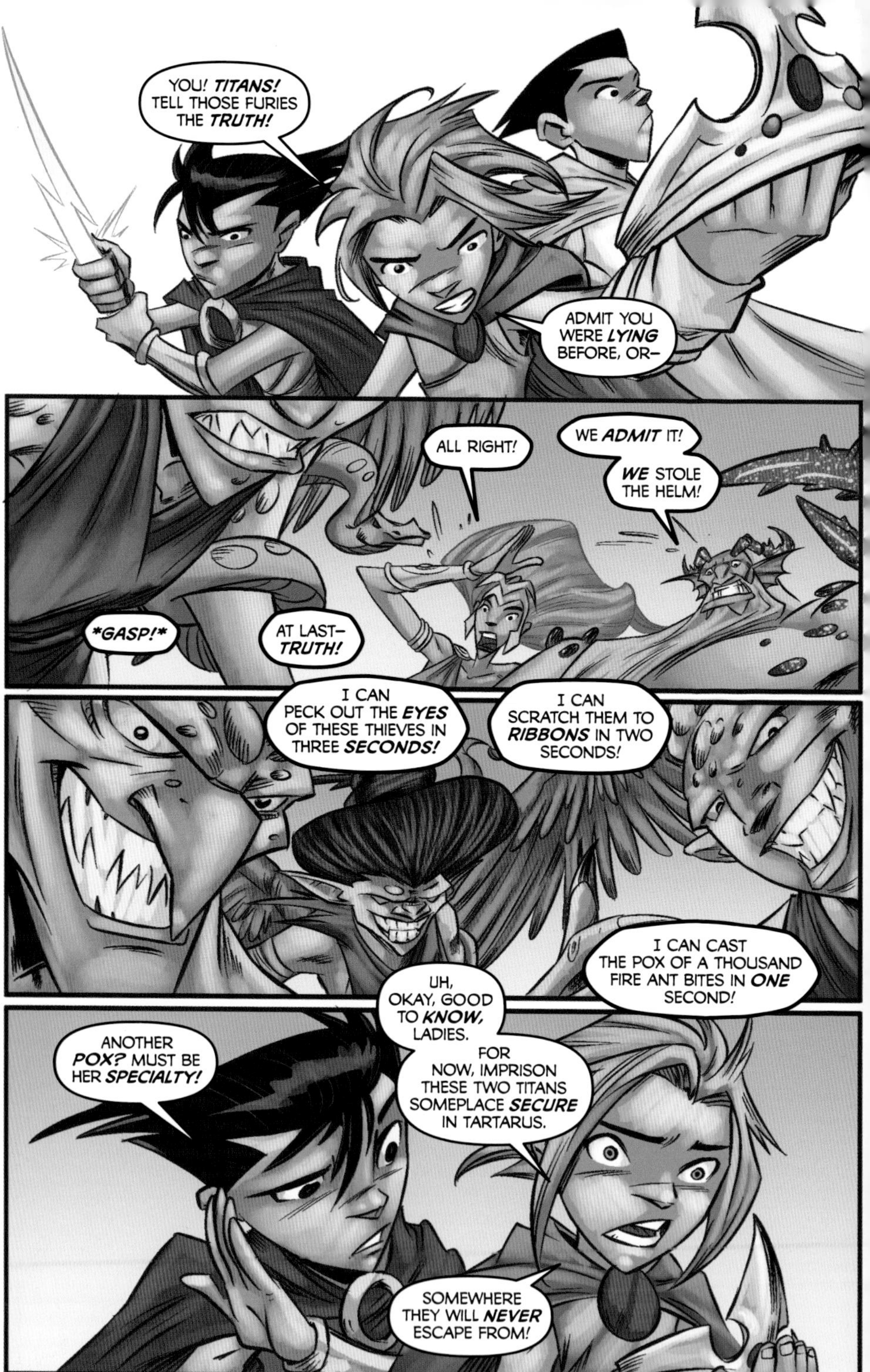
YOU! TITANS! TELL THOSE FURIES THE TRUTH!
ADMIT YOU WERE LYING BEFORE, OR–
ALL RIGHT!
WE ADMIT IT!
WE STOLE THE HELM!
GASP!
AT LAST– TRUTH!
I CAN PECK OUT THE EYES OF THESE THIEVES IN THREE SECONDS!
I CAN SCRATCH THEM TO RIBBONS IN TWO SECONDS!
I CAN CAST THE POX OF A THOUSAND FIRE ANT BITES IN ONE SECOND!
UH, OKAY, GOOD TO KNOW, LADIES.
FOR NOW, IMPRISON THESE TWO TITANS SOMEPLACE SECURE IN TARTARUS.
ANOTHER POX? MUST BE HER SPECIALTY!
SOMEWHERE THEY WILL NEVER ESCAPE FROM!

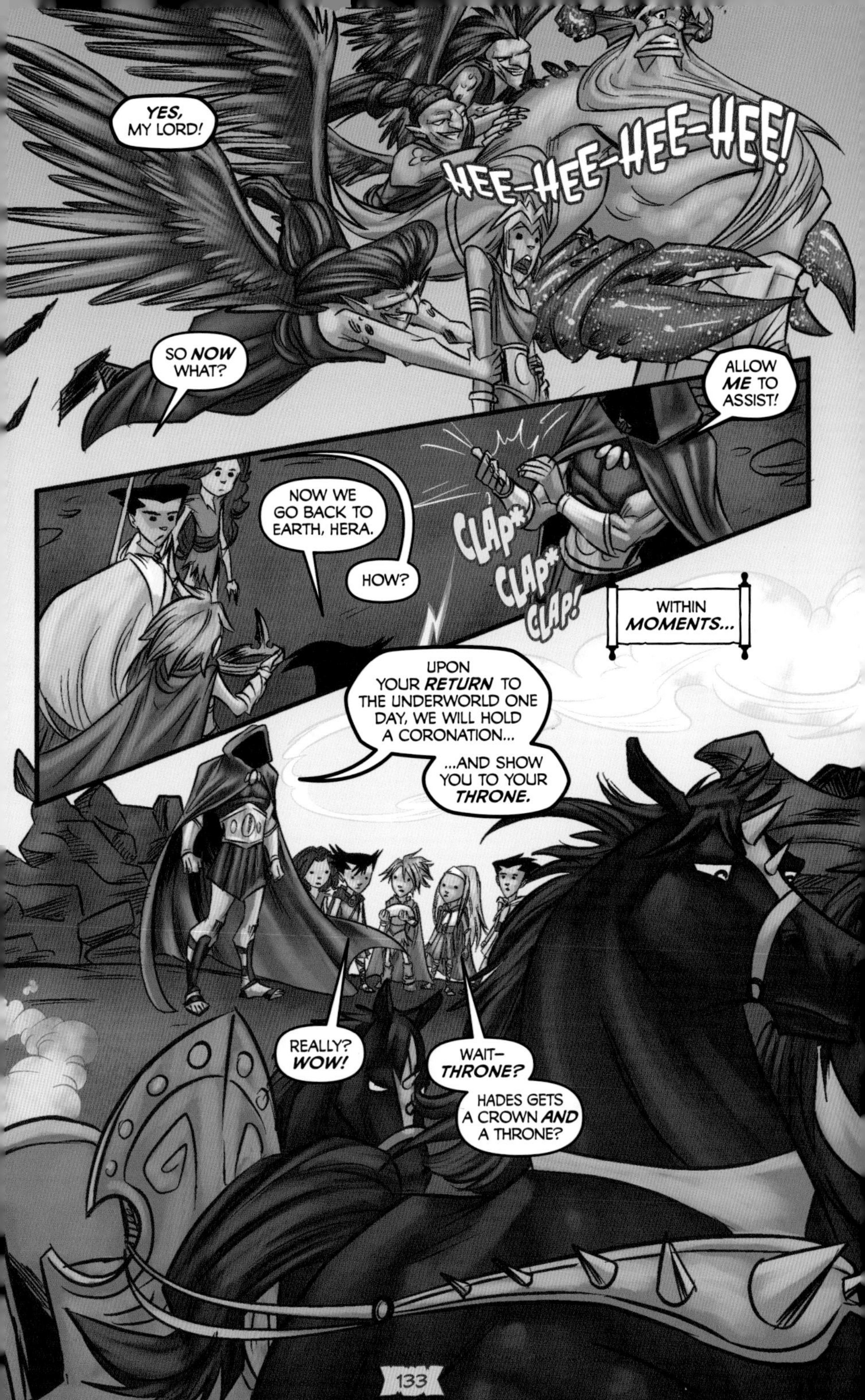
YES, MY LORD!
HEE-HEE-HEE-HEE!
SO NOW WHAT?
ALLOW ME TO ASSIST!
NOW WE GO BACK TO EARTH, HERA.
HOW?
CLAP* CLAP* CLAP!
WITHIN MOMENTS...
UPON YOUR RETURN TO THE UNDERWORLD ONE DAY, WE WILL HOLD A CORONATION...
...AND SHOW YOU TO YOUR THRONE.
REALLY? WOW!
WAIT— THRONE?
HADES GETS A CROWN AND A THRONE?

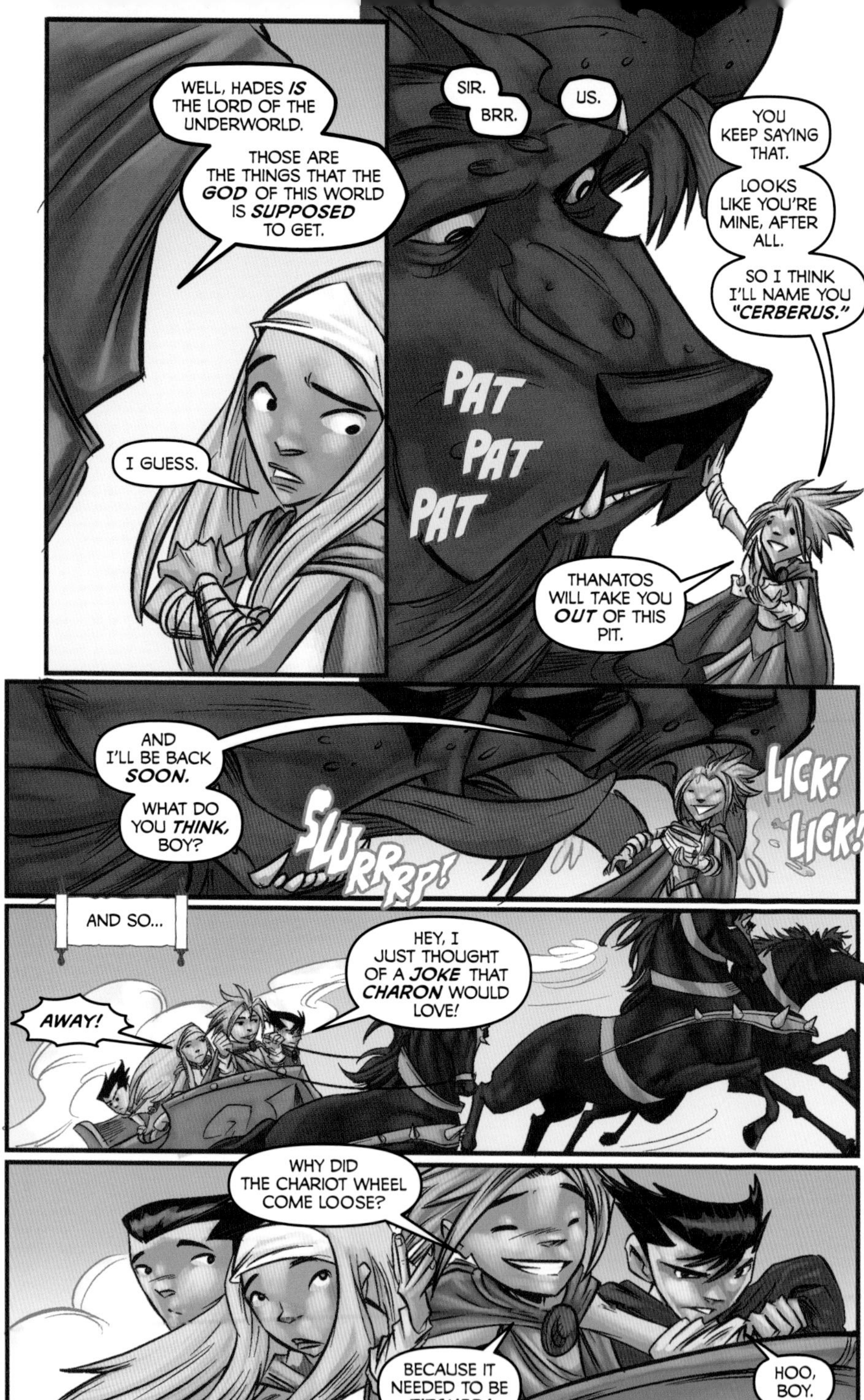

WELL, HADES *IS* THE LORD OF THE UNDERWORLD.
THOSE ARE THE THINGS THAT THE *GOD* OF THIS WORLD IS *SUPPOSED* TO GET.
I GUESS.
SIR.
BRR.
US.
YOU KEEP SAYING THAT.
LOOKS LIKE YOU'RE MINE, AFTER ALL.
SO I THINK I'LL NAME YOU *"CERBERUS."*
PAT PAT PAT
THANATOS WILL TAKE YOU *OUT* OF THIS PIT.
AND I'LL BE BACK *SOON.*
WHAT DO YOU *THINK,* BOY?
SLURRRRP!
LICK! LICK!
AND SO...
HEY, I JUST THOUGHT OF A *JOKE* THAT *CHARON* WOULD LOVE!
AWAY!
WHY DID THE CHARIOT WHEEL COME LOOSE?
BECAUSE IT NEEDED TO BE *TITANED!*
HOO, BOY.

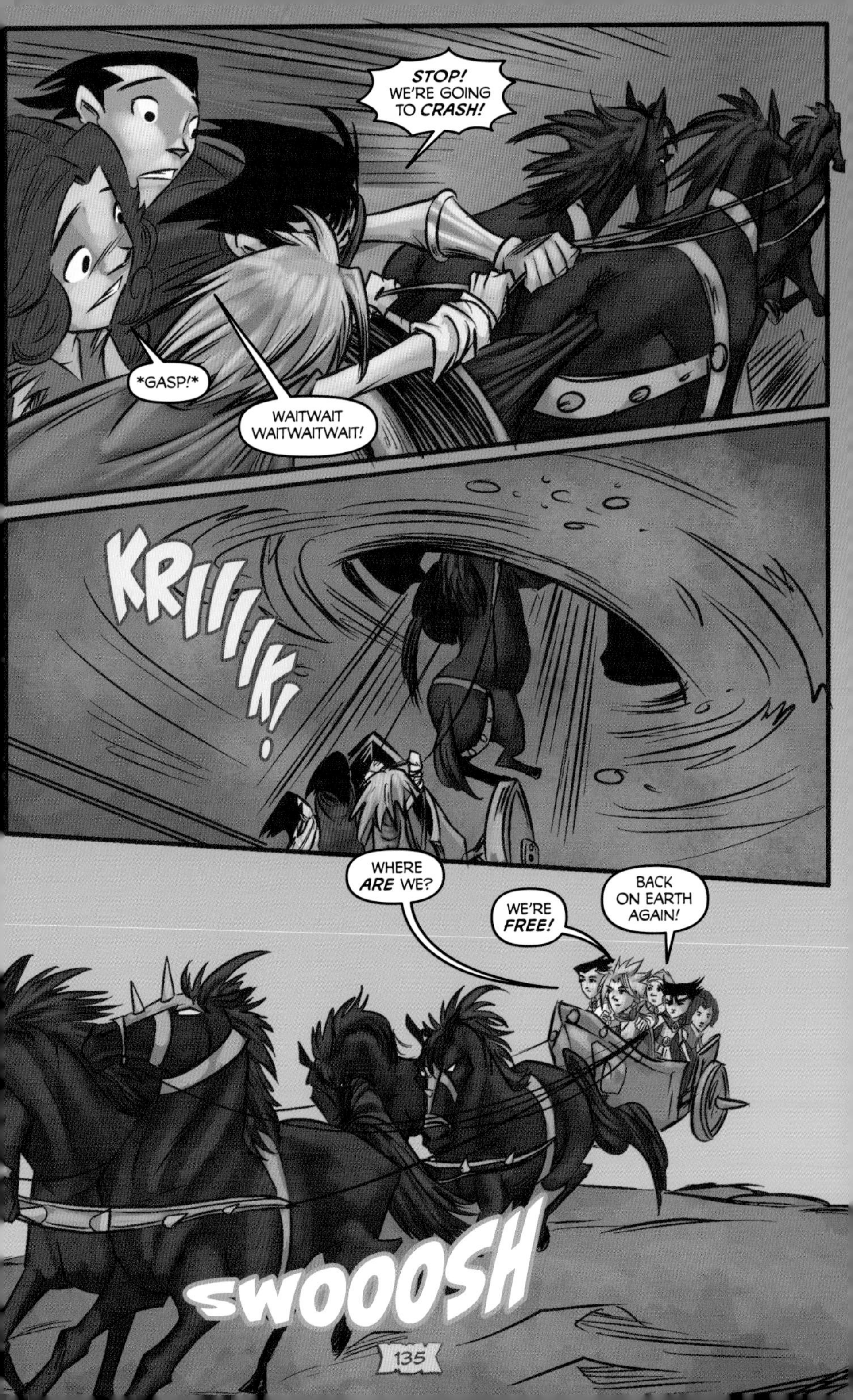
STOP! WE'RE GOING TO CRASH!
GASP!
WAITWAIT WAITWAITWAIT!
KRIIIIK!
WHERE ARE WE?
WE'RE FREE!
BACK ON EARTH AGAIN!
SWOOOSH

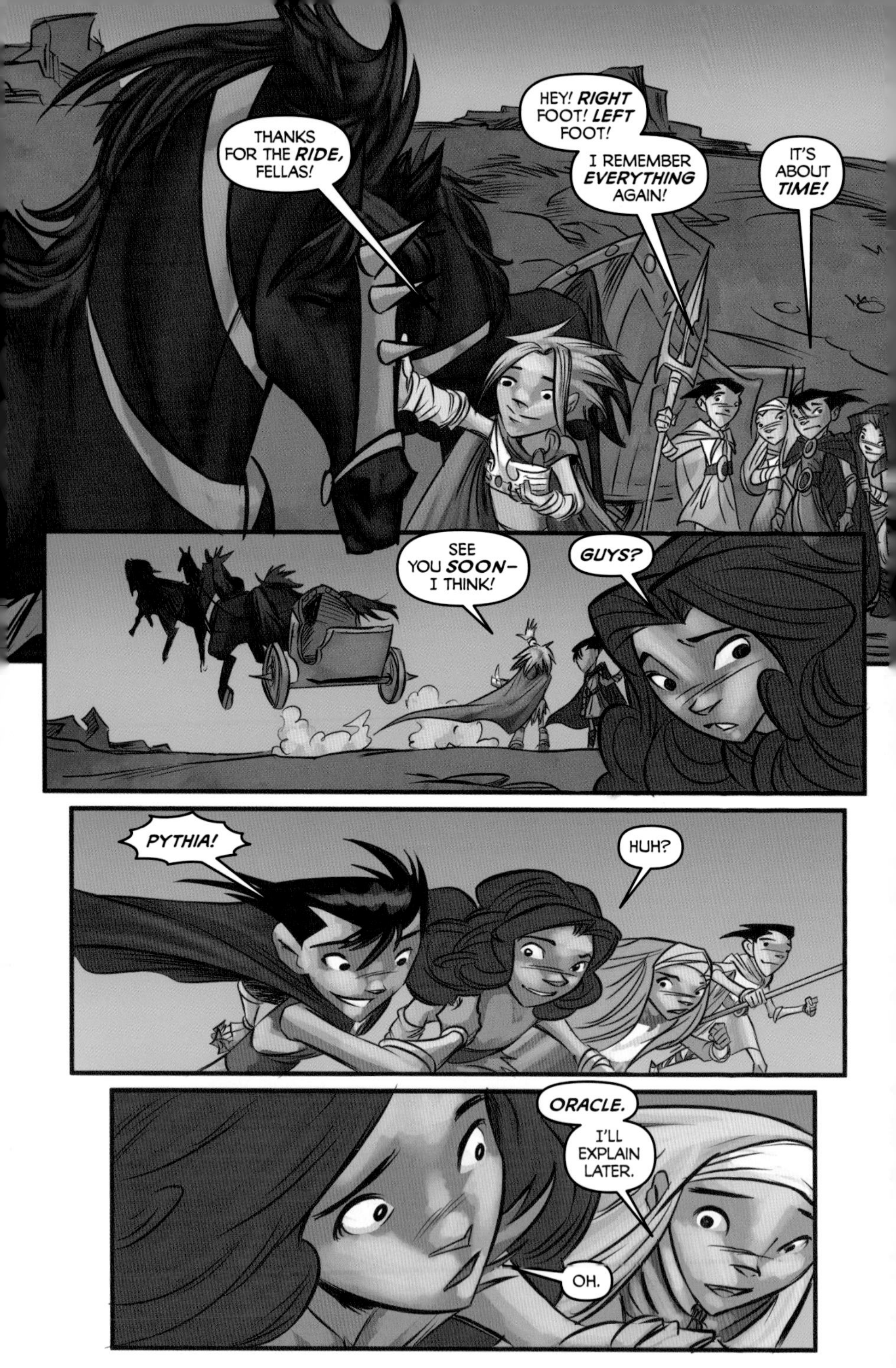
THANKS FOR THE RIDE, FELLAS!
HEY! RIGHT FOOT! LEFT FOOT!
I REMEMBER EVERYTHING AGAIN!
IT'S ABOUT TIME!
SEE YOU SOON– I THINK!
GUYS?
PYTHIA!
HUH?
ORACLE.
I'LL EXPLAIN LATER.
OH.

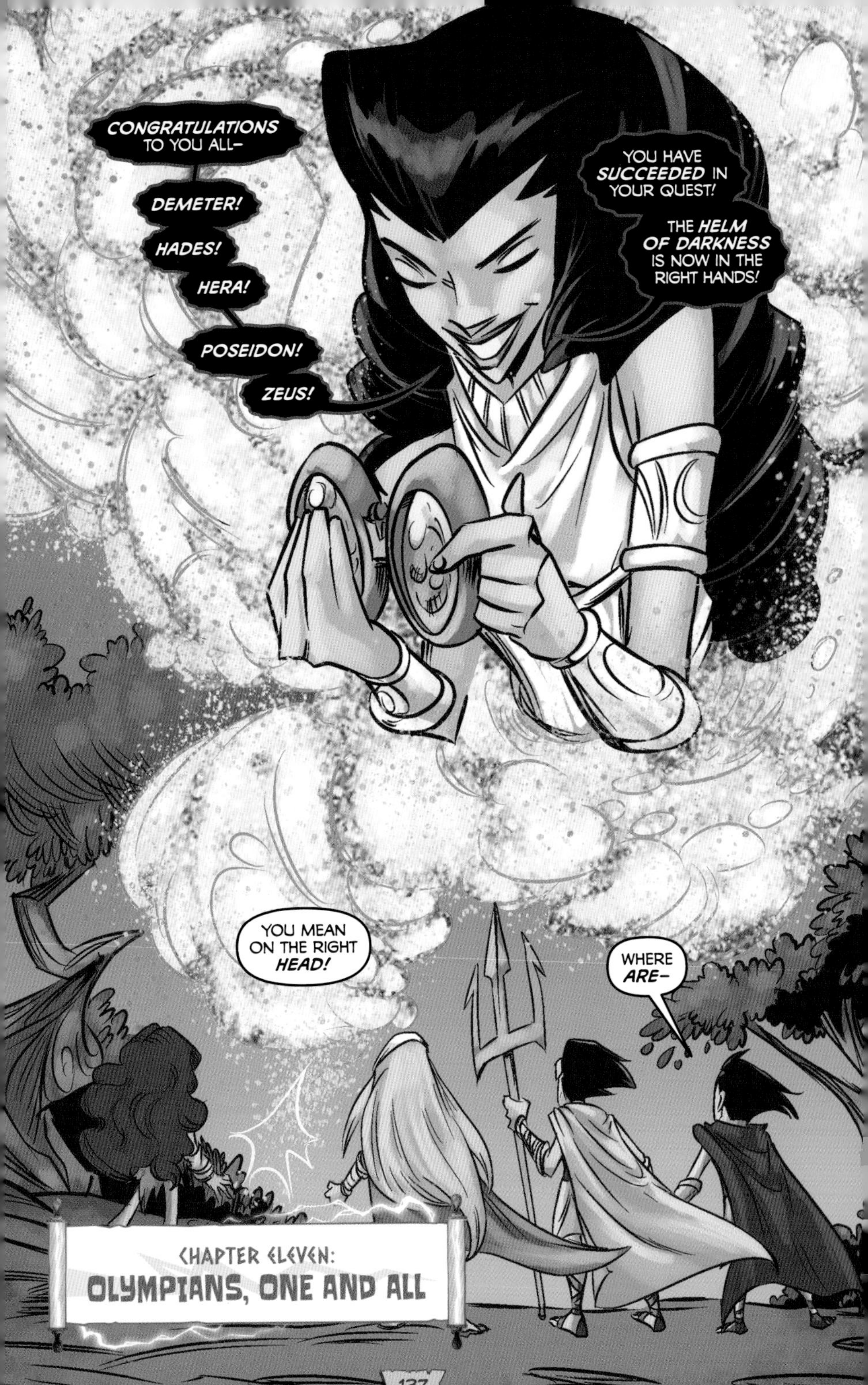
CONGRATULATIONS TO YOU ALL–
DEMETER!
HADES!
HERA!
POSEIDON!
ZEUS!
YOU HAVE SUCCEEDED IN YOUR QUEST!
THE HELM OF DARKNESS IS NOW IN THE RIGHT HANDS!
YOU MEAN ON THE RIGHT HEAD!
WHERE ARE–
CHAPTER ELEVEN:
OLYMPIANS, ONE AND ALL

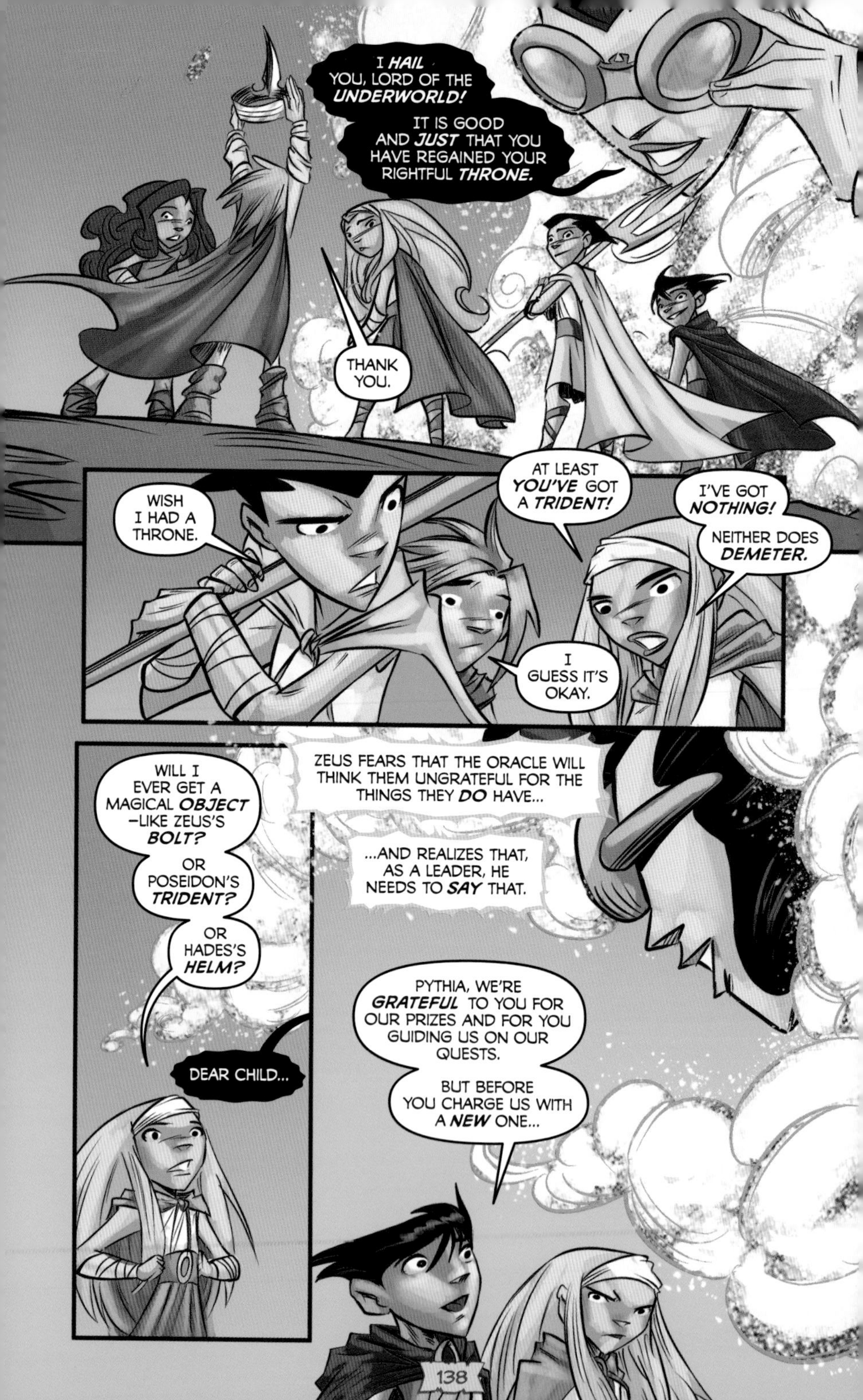
I HAIL YOU, LORD OF THE UNDERWORLD!
IT IS GOOD AND JUST THAT YOU HAVE REGAINED YOUR RIGHTFUL THRONE.
THANK YOU.
WISH I HAD A THRONE.
AT LEAST YOU'VE GOT A TRIDENT!
I'VE GOT NOTHING!
NEITHER DOES DEMETER.
I GUESS IT'S OKAY.
WILL I EVER GET A MAGICAL OBJECT —LIKE ZEUS'S BOLT?
OR POSEIDON'S TRIDENT?
OR HADES'S HELM?
ZEUS FEARS THAT THE ORACLE WILL THINK THEM UNGRATEFUL FOR THE THINGS THEY DO HAVE...
...AND REALIZES THAT, AS A LEADER, HE NEEDS TO SAY THAT.
DEAR CHILD...
PYTHIA, WE'RE GRATEFUL TO YOU FOR OUR PRIZES AND FOR YOU GUIDING US ON OUR QUESTS.
BUT BEFORE YOU CHARGE US WITH A NEW ONE...

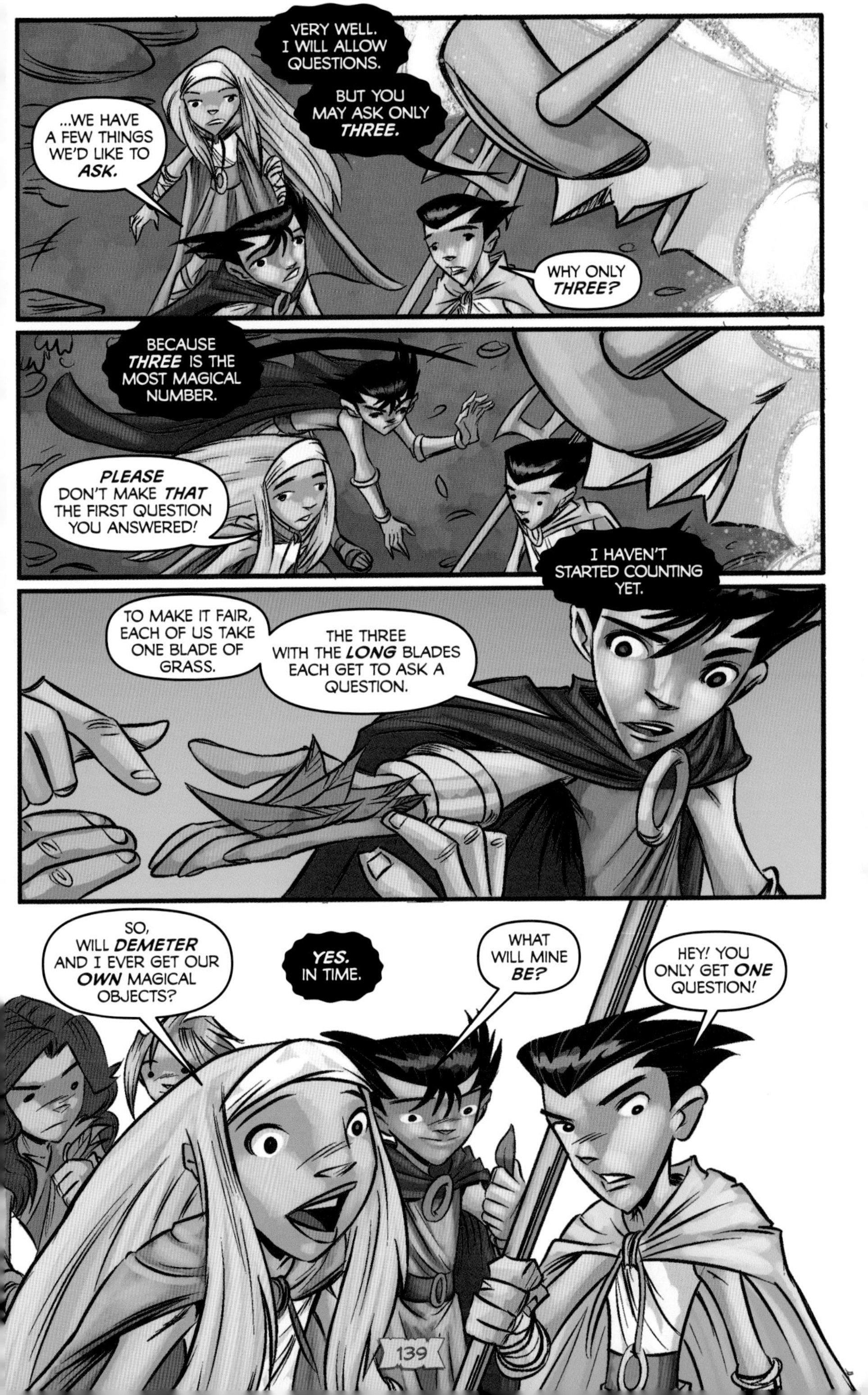
...WE HAVE A FEW THINGS WE'D LIKE TO *ASK.*
VERY WELL. I WILL ALLOW QUESTIONS.
BUT YOU MAY ASK ONLY *THREE.*
WHY ONLY *THREE?*
BECAUSE *THREE* IS THE MOST MAGICAL NUMBER.
PLEASE DON'T MAKE *THAT* THE FIRST QUESTION YOU ANSWERED!
I HAVEN'T STARTED COUNTING YET.
TO MAKE IT FAIR, EACH OF US TAKE ONE BLADE OF GRASS.
THE THREE WITH THE *LONG* BLADES EACH GET TO ASK A QUESTION.
SO, WILL *DEMETER* AND I EVER GET OUR *OWN* MAGICAL OBJECTS?
YES. IN TIME.
WHAT WILL MINE *BE?*
HEY! YOU ONLY GET *ONE* QUESTION!

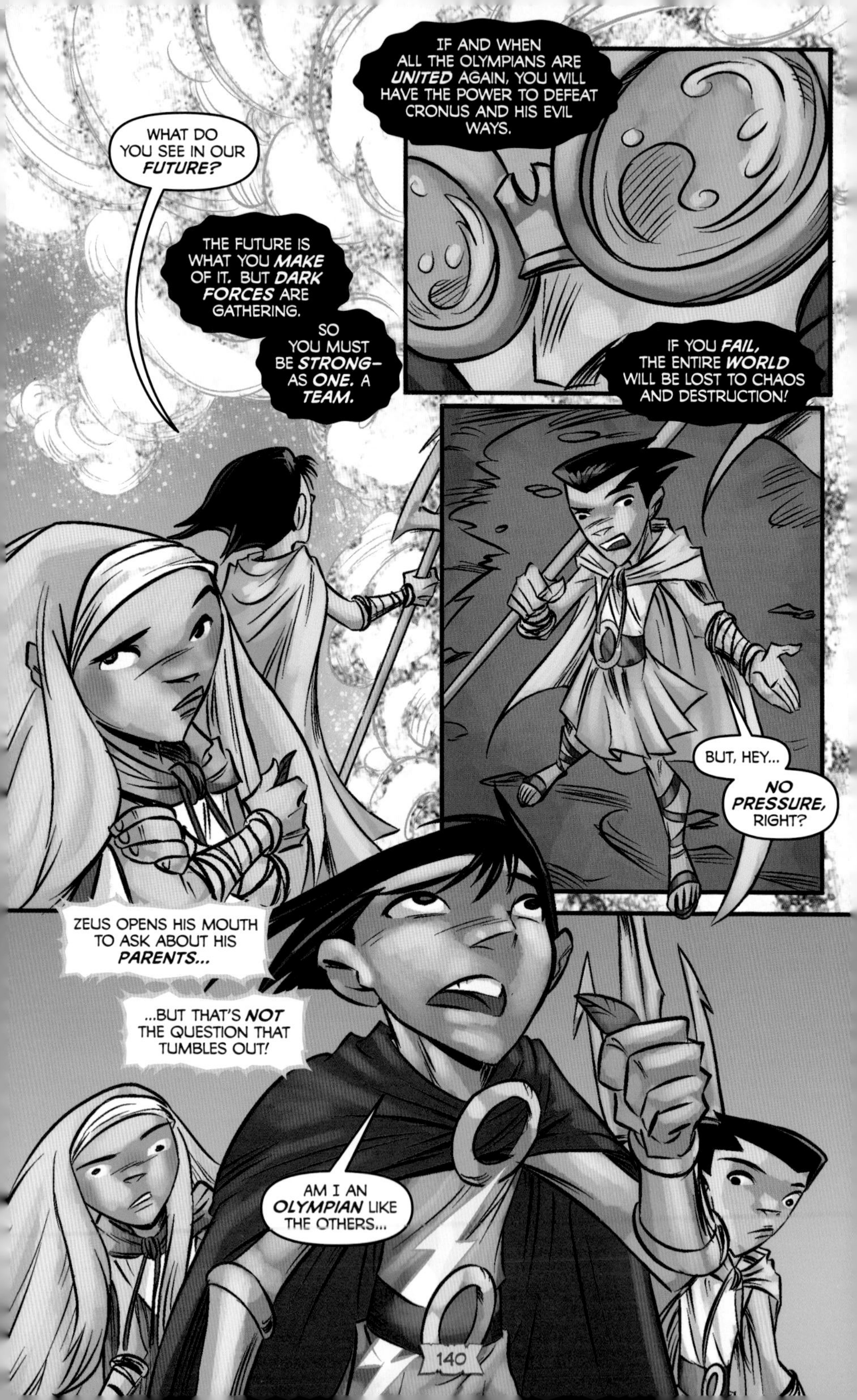
WHAT DO YOU SEE IN OUR *FUTURE?*
IF AND WHEN ALL THE OLYMPIANS ARE *UNITED* AGAIN, YOU WILL HAVE THE POWER TO DEFEAT CRONUS AND HIS EVIL WAYS.
THE FUTURE IS WHAT YOU *MAKE* OF IT. BUT *DARK FORCES* ARE GATHERING.
SO YOU MUST BE *STRONG*– AS *ONE.* A *TEAM.*
IF YOU *FAIL,* THE ENTIRE *WORLD* WILL BE LOST TO CHAOS AND DESTRUCTION!
BUT, HEY... *NO PRESSURE,* RIGHT?
ZEUS OPENS HIS MOUTH TO ASK ABOUT HIS *PARENTS...*
...BUT THAT'S *NOT* THE QUESTION THAT TUMBLES OUT!
AM I AN *OLYMPIAN* LIKE THE OTHERS...

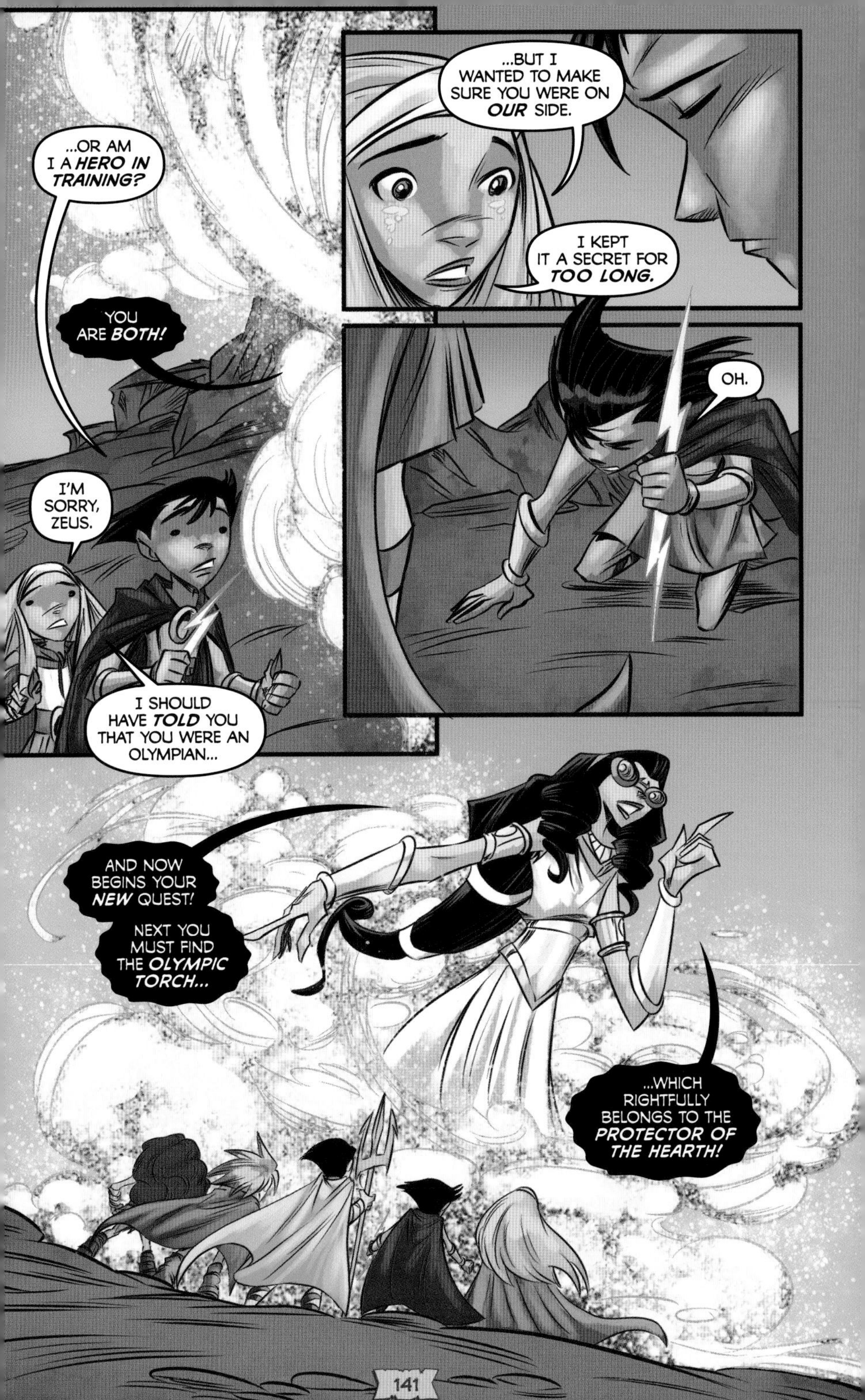

...OR AM I A HERO IN TRAINING?
...BUT I WANTED TO MAKE SURE YOU WERE ON OUR SIDE.
I KEPT IT A SECRET FOR TOO LONG.
YOU ARE BOTH!
OH.
I'M SORRY, ZEUS.
I SHOULD HAVE TOLD YOU THAT YOU WERE AN OLYMPIAN...
AND NOW BEGINS YOUR NEW QUEST!
NEXT YOU MUST FIND THE OLYMPIC TORCH...
...WHICH RIGHTFULLY BELONGS TO THE PROTECTOR OF THE HEARTH!

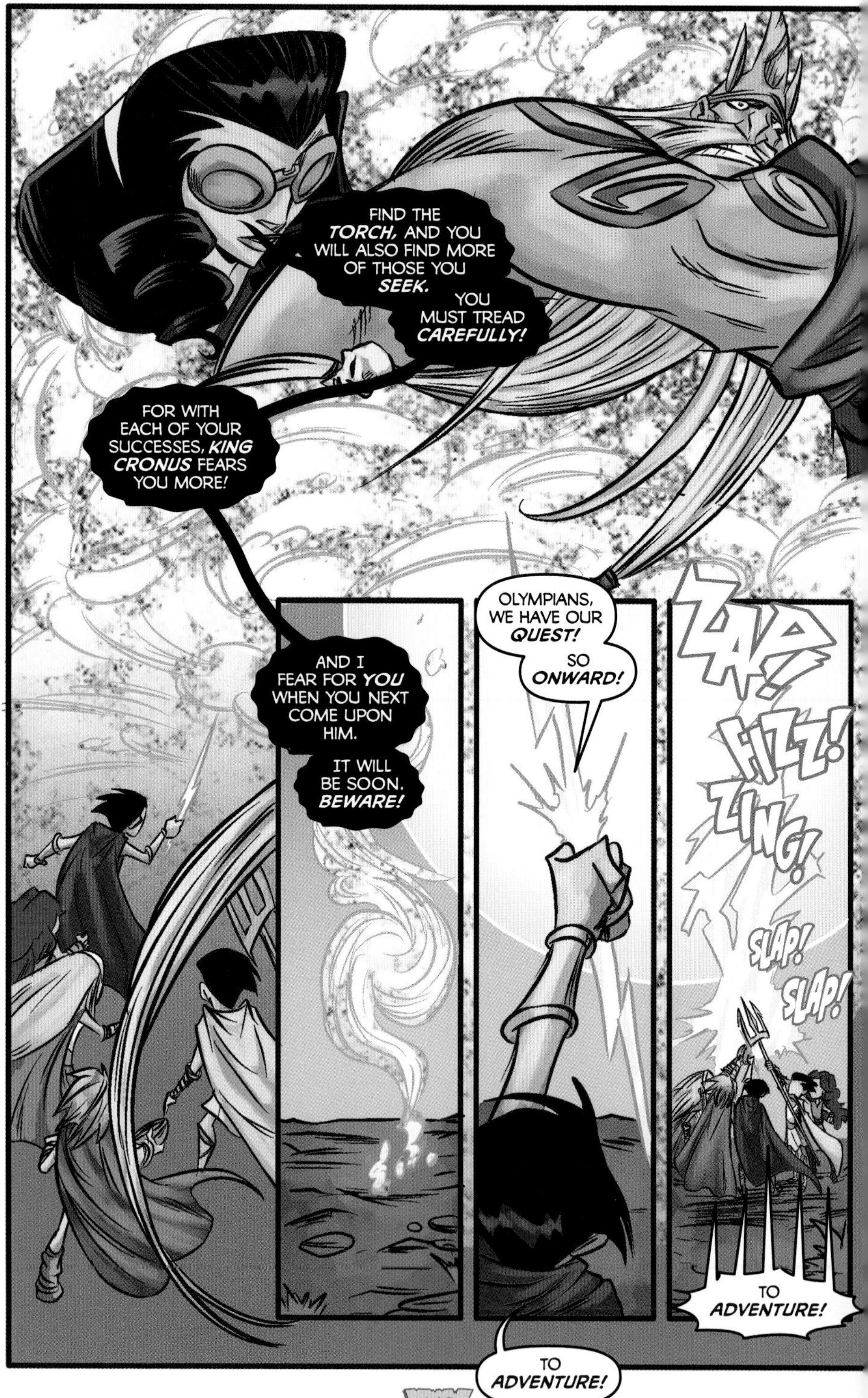
FIND THE TORCH, AND YOU WILL ALSO FIND MORE OF THOSE YOU SEEK.
YOU MUST TREAD CAREFULLY!
FOR WITH EACH OF YOUR SUCCESSES, KING CRONUS FEARS YOU MORE!
AND I FEAR FOR YOU WHEN YOU NEXT COME UPON HIM.
IT WILL BE SOON. BEWARE!
OLYMPIANS, WE HAVE OUR QUEST!
SO ONWARD!
ZAP!
FIZZ!
ZING!
SLAP!
SLAP!
TO ADVENTURE!
TO ADVENTURE!

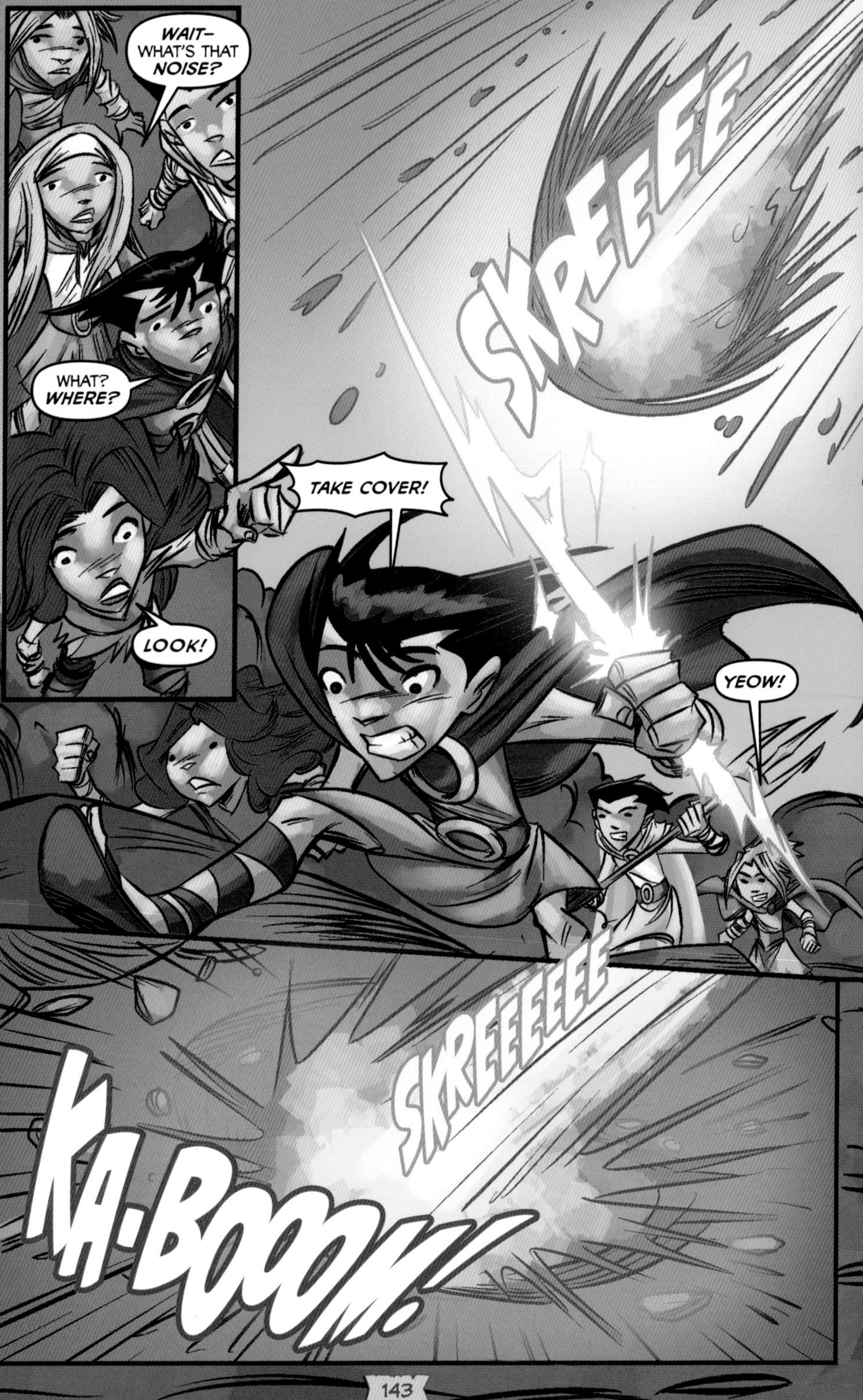
WAIT— WHAT'S THAT NOISE?
WHAT? WHERE?
LOOK!
SKREEEE
TAKE COVER!
YEOW!
SKREEEEEE
KA-BOOOM!

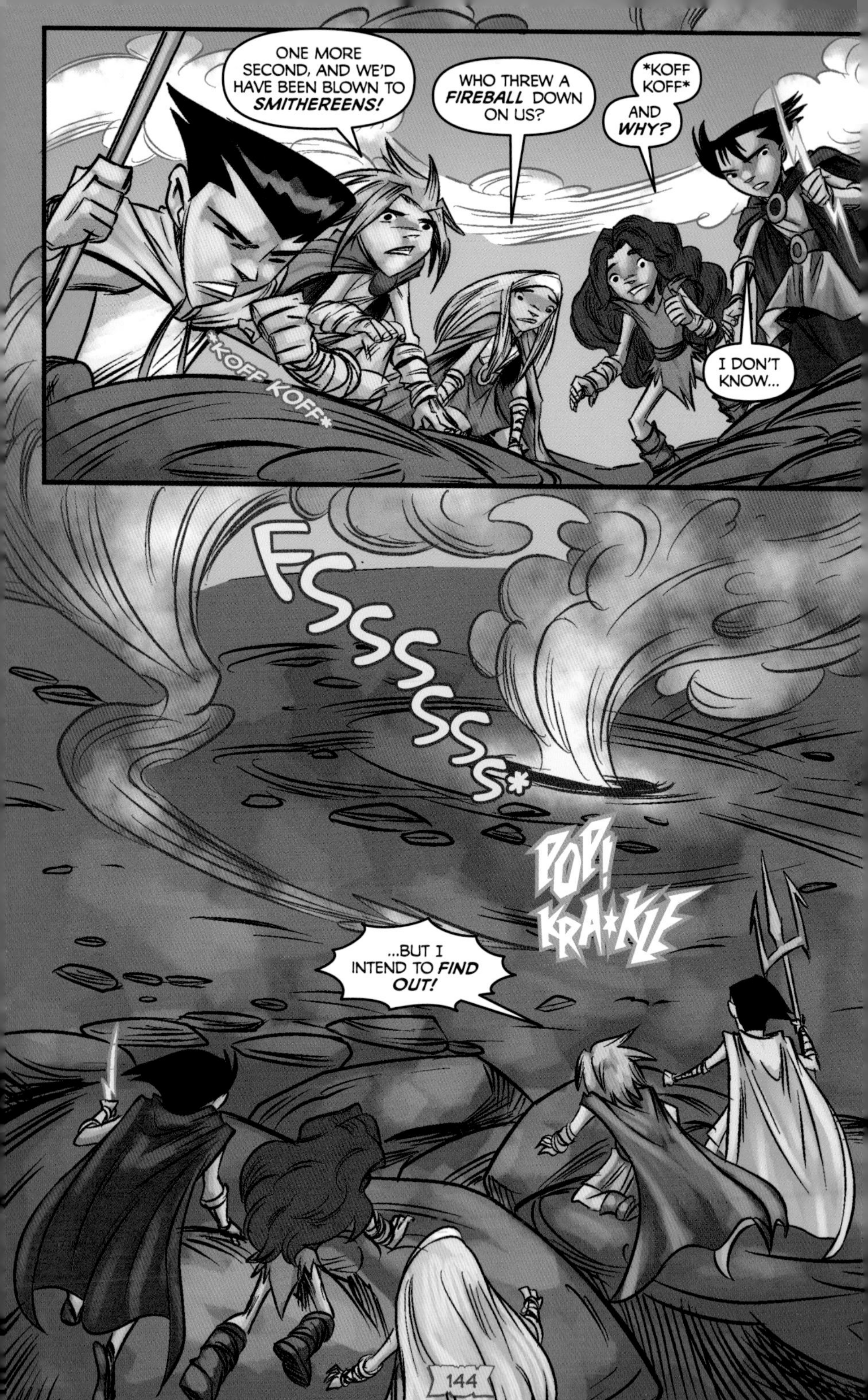
ONE MORE SECOND, AND WE'D HAVE BEEN BLOWN TO SMITHEREENS!
WHO THREW A FIREBALL DOWN ON US?
KOFF KOFF
AND WHY?
KOFF KOFF
I DON'T KNOW...
FSSSSSSS*
POP! KRA*KLE
...BUT I INTEND TO FIND OUT!